Raves for Joe McKinney

"A rising star on the horror scene!"
—FearNet.com

"Joe McKinney's first zombie novel, *Dead City,* is one of my all-time favorites of the genre. It hits the ground running and never lets up. *Apocalypse of the Dead* proves that Joe is far from being a one-hit wonder. This book is meatier, juicier, bloodier, and even more compelling . . . and it also NEVER LETS UP. From page one to the stunning climax this book is a rollercoaster ride of action, violence, and zombie horror. McKinney understands the genre and relies on its strongest conventions while at the same time adding new twists that make this book a thoroughly enjoyable read. That's a defining characteristic of Joe's work: the pace is so relentless that you feel like it's you, and not the character, who is running for his life from a horde of flesh-hungry monsters.

"And, even with that lightning-fast pace, McKinney manages to flesh the characters out so that they're real, and infuse the book with compassion and heartbreak over this vast, shared catastrophe.

"This book earns its place in any serious library of living-dead fiction."
—Jonathan Maberry, *New York Times* best-selling author of *The Wolfman*

"*Dead City* is much more than just another zombie novel. It's got heart and humanity—a merciless, fast-paced, and genuinely scary read that will leave you absolutely breathless. Highly recommended!"
—Brian Keene

"The pace never lets up as McKinney takes us through the zombie apocalypse in real time—every second of terror is explored in depth as the world goes to hell."
—David Wellington, author of *Monster Island*

"*Dead City* is an absolute must-read for zombie lovers, but McKinney's excellent storytelling makes it a great read for anyone who loves the thrill of a gruesomely delicious page-turner."
—Fran Friel, Bram Stoker Award–nominated author of *Mama's Boy and Other Dark Tales*

"*Dead City* is a zombie tour de force—the story moves along at breakneck speed and never lets up. Joe McKinney knows how to toy with readers' emotions, masterfully capturing the essence of humanity in the face of unspeakable horror."
—Amy Grech, author of *Apple of My Eye* and *Blanket of White*

"Joe McKinney's *Dead City* is a tense, thrill-a-page nightmare, written with great passion and authority. Surely one of the best zombie novels ever set down in blood."
—Lisa Morton, two-time Bram Stoker Award–winner

"*Dead City* wastes no time jumping straight into mile-a-minute thrills and gruesome action. This seminal zombie novel culminates in a heart-wrenching finale, and I found that as the undead hordes multiplied, so too did my respect and admiration for author Joe McKinney. If you like your thrillers served with an extra helping of intensity, you're going to love *Dead City*!"
—Joel A. Sutherland, Bram Stoker Award–nominated author of *Frozen Blood*

"*Dead City* is an action packed, pedal-to-the-metal zombie novel that never loses sight of its humanity. McKinney uses his background as a homicide detective to bring a level of realism to his vision of the apocalypse that is both urgent and frightening. A timely nightmare that you will not put down. I can't wait to see where this series leads."
—Gregory Lamberson, author of *Personal Demons* and *Johnny Gruesome*

"McKinney writes zombies like he's been gunning them down all of his life."
—Weston Ochse, Author of *Empire of Salt*

"*Dead City* is a full-throttle page burner that torques up the terror and does not let up. You'll want the shotgun seat for this wild ride. Bring a crash helmet."
—J. L. Comeau, Countgore.com

"Welcome to Joe McKinney's *Dead City* universe, a relentless thrill ride where real characters do bloody things on nightmare streets. Break out the popcorn, you're in for a real treat."
—Harry Shannon, author of *Dead and Gone*

"*Dead City* is a well-written and compelling first novel. A scary, fast-paced ride, full of hair-raising twists and turns that keep the reader spellbound. Do yourself a favor and snag a copy . . . thank me later."
—Gene O'Neill, author of *Taste of Tenderloin* and *Deathflash*

“Fast-paced, entertaining . . . five headshots out of five.”
—D. L. Snell, coauthor of *Demon Days*

“A fantastic tale of survival horror that starts with a bang and never lets up.”
—Zombiehub.com

“McKinney continues to lead the genre of zombie fiction.”
—Craig DiLouie, author of *The Infection*

“*Mutated* delivers pulse-pounding action with precision, intelligence, and most importantly, heart. McKinney proves once again that he understands the power of the zombie subgenre better than any other writer.”
—Peter Giglio, author of *Anon* and co-author of *The Dark*

MUTATED

JOE McKINNEY

PINNACLE BOOKS
Kensington Publishing Corp.
www.kensingtonbooks.com

PINNACLE BOOKS are published by

Kensington Publishing Corp.
119 West 40th Street
New York, NY 10018

ISBN-13: 978-0-7860-2929-7
ISBN-10: 0-7860-2929-3

First printing: September 2012

10 9 8 7 6 5 4 3 2 1

Printed in the United States of America

For Jon Michael Freiger
1978–2011

Miss you every day, my friend.

ACKNOWLEDGMENTS

A great many folks helped me get this book off the ground, far more than I can possibly thank here. But I do owe a special thanks to Sanford Allen, Beckie Ugolini, Thomas McAuley, and Brian Allen, of Drafthouse, and to Hank Schwaeble, Rhodi Hawk, David Liss, and Robert Jackson Bennett, of Candlelight. I couldn't have done this without you guys.

Hope bases vast premises on foolish accidents, and reads a word where in fact only a scribble exists.
—John Updike, *Pigeon Feathers*

What else could you expect from sending a man made of our common, tormented clay on a voyage of discovery? What else could he find? What else could you understand or care for, or feel the existence of even? There was comedy in it, and slaughter.
—Joseph Conrad, *An Outpost of Progress*

CHAPTER 1

Ben Richardson jammed himself all the way to the back of the oven and watched the zombies staggering around in the rubble that had once been the lobby of a Pizza Hut. He wanted to kick himself for being so careless. His head had been elsewhere, and they'd caught him completely off guard. If he hadn't turned around when he did and spied them through the busted-out windows at the front of the restaurant, they'd have made a meal of him. But chain restaurants like this usually had canned food in their prep areas, and the promise of something other than pork and beans had been too much to resist. Stupid, he told himself, risking his life for a gallon of tomato puree.

But he made the mistake and now he had to own it. All that was left was to wait. Be quiet, and wait. He silently let out a breath and relaxed his muscles, trying to get comfortable. No telling how long this would take.

There were three of them out there, two older men and a young girl who looked like she might have been about fourteen. It was hard to tell for sure, though. The disease and the malnutrition disfigured them so, and, truth be told, he wasn't such a good judge of how old children were anymore. He saw so few of them these days.

The zombies bumped into overturned tables and stopped as though confused when faced with padded booths and the overturned skeleton of the salad bar. The only sound came from the glass and fallen ceiling tiles crunching beneath their feet. But that could change at any minute. Richardson knew that from long experience. They always hunted in silence until they flushed something from the debris. Here, in the ruins of downtown St. Louis, that something would probably be a rat or, if they were lucky, a dog or a cat. Once they cornered it, the moaning would start. It would begin as a soft groaning sigh, but that would quickly swell to the breathy, almost desperate sobbing sound that Richardson had come to think of as their feeding call. It would carry for blocks, attracting more of their kind. Within moments the infected would swarm the streets.

Richardson had seen it happen too many times before.

And so he waited with a revolver in his left hand and a machete in his right, hoping these three would pass him by. Zombies were the ultimate opportunists, always on the lookout for an easy meal. But they lacked any sort of higher consciousness, and they certainly couldn't anticipate their prey's movements. As long as he stayed quiet, and stayed in the dark, he'd be okay.

You're a roving camera, he told himself. Just watch. Soak it all up.

One of the zombies stepped in front of the oven, stopped, and slowly swiveled its head in Richardson's direction. For a moment, the zombie was framed by a faint golden nimbus of morning light. But then Richardson's eyes adjusted to the glare and he saw the zombie clearly. The man had obviously fed recently. His shoulder-length hair was matted with deep arterial blood that had partially dried and looked like tar. Flies swarmed about his mouth and eyes, resting on his shaggy beard and on the soiled clothes that hung like strips of rags from his body. The smell of rotten meat brought bile to Richardson's throat.

He studied the man's eyes. They were a milky white and threaded with cloudy pink lines. The eyes told him everything he needed to know. This was a Stage I zombie, probably only infected within the last eight months or so with the necrosis filovirus, which caused the disease that had turned him into a zombie. He was slow and stupid, his brain charred to cinders by fever and his body crippled by malnutrition. If he survived long enough for the disease to enter its second stage—and that was highly unlikely from all that Richardson had seen—he would evolve into something far more dangerous, faster, even capable of rudimentary teamwork with other zombies. But for now, the man posed little threat.

As long as Richardson stayed quiet.

Just wait it out, he thought. Be a roving camera. He'll go away.

A sudden noise out in the street caught Richardson's attention. The sound of somebody running, breathing hard. A woman's voice, the words indistinct.

Slowly, the zombie turned toward the noise. The other two did the same. A moment later the moaning started. A chill crawled across Richardson's skin. Even after all these years and all the time he spent telling himself he was just an observer here, none of this affected him, the feeding call still made his bowels clench in fear.

He saw a flash of movement off to his left. The zombies were already moving to the exit, going after whatever it was, and so Richardson inched forward to the edge of the oven and craned his head as much as he dared around the corner.

The restaurant windows had been busted out long ago, so

that only shards of glass and dangling lengths of weather stripping hung in the frames. Through the window Richardson had a view of the street outside, weeds growing up through the cracks, and beyond that, the ruins of North St. Louis. He wasn't exactly sure of the name of the street and he supposed it didn't matter. All the streets of the world seemed to look the same now anyway: thick with wrecked cars and blown trash, bleak canyons between buildings that had long since been reduced to windowless hulks, their insides gutted by scavengers and rotting from the weather.

The zombies that had been inside the restaurant with him were moving off to his left, threading their way through a maze of cannibalized cars. Richardson could see a few more zombies emerging from an alley on the far side of the street.

"Hey, over here!"

It was a woman's voice, coming from his side of the street.

The three zombies stopped and slowly swiveled around to face the restaurant.

"Oh, no," Richardson muttered. *What are you doing you crazy fool?*

"Hey!" the woman yelled again.

He inched back into the oven. You're a roving camera, he told himself. Don't get involved. Choose the smart option, the one that lets you live.

But it had been days since he'd seen another person.

And it got lonely out here in the wastelands. God-awful lonely.

Well aware he was acting foolishly, he decided to chance it.

He poured himself out of the oven and, keeping low, moved to his backpack resting against the wall by the building's side door. Richardson kept binoculars in there, but he didn't need them. The woman had stopped where he could see her easily enough. She was about his age, late forties, early fifties maybe, slender, with frizzy gray hair pulled back in a loose ponytail that bounced between her shoulder blades like a tumbleweed on the wind. She carried a hunting rifle with a shoulder sling that she waved over her head like she was trying to flag the zombies down.

Richardson was stunned. I know her. Christ, where do I know her from? He studied her profile, leafing back through the Rolodex in his head, trying to place her face. Where had he seen her before? Montana, maybe? There had been several thousand people living in a commune there, years ago. Unbidden, thoughts of the two happy years he spent there rose up in his memory. Those two years, when Ed Moore and the others who had escaped Jasper Sewell's Grasslands cult were still alive, had been a sort of lull in the apocalypse. Ed had done everything right, and people had flocked from all over to enjoy the protection he offered. Straining his memory, Richardson went through the names of all the people he had known there in Montana, but he couldn't place the woman.

But he did know her. He was positive of that.

The zombies were getting closer to her now. Their feeding call was louder. Their sobbing had become urgent. The lead zombie raised his arms, his fingers clutching at the air, his addled brain unable to accurately perceive the distance to his intended prey.

Then the woman put the gun down on the hood of a wrecked pickup, pulled a wooden baseball bat from a holster she carried on her shoulder, and charged the zombie.

"What the hell . . . ?" Richardson said.

The woman sidestepped the zombie, ducked underneath its clutching hands, spun around, and came up behind the man. Then she dropped him with a practiced swing to the back of the head, grunting loudly as the bat cracked the man's skull. She put the other two zombies down with the same precise movements, and Richardson figured she had to have done that move before. It was too quick, too precise, too practiced.

Now she was looking around.

Richardson scanned the parts of the street he could see too. Don't get involved, he pleaded with himself. Stay out of sight. Be the roving camera that sees all but doesn't get involved.

But for once his curiosity overruled his common sense. This was crazy. What was she looking for? He couldn't figure it out. Richardson kept expecting her to run for it. She wasn't carrying any sort of gear except the bat and the rifle; and her clothes, though dirty, were in good repair. That meant she had to come from one of the compounds somewhere around here. There were five or six he had heard of. But she was definitely not a roadie, like him. She had friends somewhere close by, and maybe even transportation. A bicycle, probably.

The sounds of moaning in the near distance shifted his attention back to the other side of the street. It was just as he had feared. The frenzied feeding calls of the first three zombies had attracted more of their kind.

He reached into his backpack and quickly extracted his binoculars.

Scanning the rubble, he counted at least eighteen zombies, but it was hard to be sure through the morning haze and the dust clouds rising off the vacant lots.

Roving camera, he thought. Time to get the hell out of here.

He returned the binoculars to his backpack and zipped it up. He was sliding the straps over his shoulders when the woman let out an ear-piercing whistle.

"What?" Richardson blurted out, startled. "No."

He pressed his body up against the wall next to the door, his pulse quickening as he chanced a look outside.

She's gonna get herself killed, he thought.

An excited moan rose from the approaching zombies.

"Ah shit," Richardson said.

The woman whistled again, then turned to retrieve her gun, and in that instant, something in his memory clicked into place. He recognized her.

"I can't believe it," he said under his breath. "Sylvia Carnes."

Eight years ago, shortly after Hurricane Mardell ripped the face off the city of Houston, and the zombies rose up from the soup of oil and chemicals in the floodwaters, Sylvia Carnes had been an English professor at the University of Texas at Austin. Those were wild, uncertain times. Nobody knew what to make of the infected. They were alive, and infected with a deadly virus, that was true, but did they have to be summarily executed? Didn't America have an obligation to find a cure? Everyone, it seemed, had ideas. Nobody had answers.

The military was able to contain the outbreak behind a quarantine wall built up to shield the rest of the country from the Gulf Coast and the affected areas of South Texas, and for a while, America was able to take a step back and ponder what it was supposed to do next. Diseases could be cured, couldn't they? Shouldn't they? There were many Americans with family still inside the quarantine walls. They lobbied hard for the government to offer some kind of relief. They wanted a cure. At the very least a vaccine. But there were others who were disgusted and outraged by all the stories of cannibalism and senseless violence coming out of the Gulf Coast region. Why not hold the zombies criminally responsible for the things they did, they argued. You didn't waive charges simply because a murderer claimed to have the flu. Why would you do it here, for this disease? Better yet, why not simply exterminate them before the plague they carried had a chance to spread?

It had been a confusing time, a lot of people yelling.

And Sylvia Carnes was right in the middle of it. She was a member of a radical group called People for an Ethical Solution. They wanted to show that the infected were still people who wanted and needed our help. This was not some bumbling, half-baked attempt at universal health care. This was a national crisis, and we had a moral imperative, Carnes said, to do everything in our power to find a cure, and to do it now.

She filed a suit in a federal court allowing her to take forty of her graduate students into the ruins of San Antonio to prove her point, and it was a sign of just how crazy and uncertain those times were that a judge actually issued the okay for her to go inside the quarantine zone.

At the time Richardson was a reporter for the *Atlantic*, tasked to cover every aspect of the outbreak. He had walked the wall with guards from the newly formed Gulf Coast Quarantine Authority. He had interviewed hundreds of survivors from Houston and San Antonio. But he had never actually seen a zombie firsthand.

He got his chance when he accompanied Sylvia Carnes and her students into San Antonio. At the time he hadn't made up his mind about the infected. They weren't very well understood and the idea that they could be cured appealed to his modern American sensibilities that everybody deserved a second chance, that it was somehow our moral obligation to extend a helping hand—even if there was a very real chance that it would get bitten off in the process. But after seeing zombies attack and kill all but one of Sylvia Carnes's students, his doubts disappeared. Their deaths clarified everything. Put his views in focus. A concern for doing the right and honorable thing gave way to the realities of survival.

He hadn't thought of that trip into San Antonio in a long time. A lot had happened since then. The Ben Richardson who went on that trip wasn't the same Ben Richardson who now crouched in the doorway of a ruined Pizza Hut, watching the rubble like a hunted animal. The world had changed. He had changed. And he hated that about himself.

But she was looking at him.

He stared at her, not blinking. Did she recognize him? She didn't seem to. She just seemed surprised to see another living person there.

"Run," she mouthed silently. "Run!"

He didn't move.

She hesitated for a moment, then looked over her shoulder at the zombies coming into the parking lot. Their moaning was much louder now.

She looked back at him, no sign of recognition on her face, and said, "Run, damn it!" One of the zombies stepped on a large piece of glass and the crack made Sylvia whirl around. "Run," she said again, and then trotted off toward the back of the restaurant without giving Richardson another look.

The zombies were almost even with the door now. Richardson could hear their feet shuffling across the trash-strewn pavement, their moans forming a chorus of strained overlapping rhythms.

Richardson pulled back into the shadows and held his breath.

From where he stood he could see a small section of the lot behind the restaurant. There was a two-story red brick building there with all the windows gone. Tall grass and sunflowers had grown up around the edges of the building, giving it a long-abandoned look. He wondered why Sylvia had run off in that direction. He'd come from those parts on his way into downtown and he knew there was nothing of any value over there. Just more empty apartment buildings and quiet streets.

So where was she going? And why was she trying to get the zombies to follow her? He couldn't see her anymore. And he couldn't hear her over the mounting feeding call.

Zombies shambled into the grass at the edge of the lot, still moaning, arms dangling at their sides, heads canted to one side as though their necks weren't strong enough to hold up the weight. Out of habit, he counted them. Sixteen in all.

He'd counted eighteen before, so there were at least two more up near the front of the building. Richardson wanted to follow Sylvia Carnes, but he knew he had to think of his own survival first.

Be the camera, he pleaded with himself. Don't be stupid.

Ducking back inside the restaurant, he went to the front windows and scanned the street. There was nothing there but ruined buildings and more wrecked cars. He couldn't see the other two zombies he'd counted earlier, and that bothered him. He listened, and when it sounded as though the moaning had receded, he holstered his pistol and his machete, grabbed his rifle, and headed out the side door in a crouch.

He hugged the wall as he moved to the front of the building. There he stopped and scanned the street again.

All clear.

The air had a crisp early morning coolness to it, and he could smell the pungent earthiness of the Mississippi River less than a mile away. He glanced up at a large cloud bank overhead. He didn't think it would rain, but he had moved his poncho to the top of his pack before he set out that morning, just in case.

Looking out at the street once more he tried to get his

bearings. There was a street sign about fifty feet to his right, hanging by a single screw from an overhead traffic light. The sign was covered in grime, but it looked like it read FLORISSANT. He took the map from his back pocket and tried to figure out which way to go. He had heard of a trading market down near Herculaneum, and he figured he could get there by going south along the river. If he had his coordinates right that meant going south from his current location to Fourteenth Street, then east on Cole to Broadway, and from there he'd continue south to Herculaneum. It was going to be a long haul. Three or four days, maybe, depending on what he did or didn't encounter along the way.

He pocketed the map again and stood up just as a woman's voice sounded from the far side of the road. It wasn't Sylvia Carnes. This was the voice of a younger woman.

He'd been conditioned by years of living on his own, surviving by his wits, to drop down into a crouch and look for cover at the first sign of trouble.

He did that now.

Off to his right he could see the shell of an old supermarket, and across the street a Church's fried chicken stand and a bank parking lot. Tall, spindly weeds grew up through the cracks in the asphalt.

Richardson started looking for escape routes.

He wouldn't be able to make it across the street without being seen, and that meant his only option was to go back the way he'd come or go around the far corner, into the narrow gap between the Pizza Hut and the white concrete building next door. He'd been lucky once hiding inside the oven, but he knew he couldn't count on being lucky a second time, especially as all the noise was likely to make the place pretty popular here in a bit. He'd outlived everyone else he knew by playing it smart, and that meant not pushing his luck.

Roving camera, he thought. Just be the camera.

Staying low, he moved quickly along the front of the Pizza Hut and turned in to the narrow gap on the far side of the building. He knelt down in the shadows and turned to watch the street.

Four people, two big guys with AR-15s and two young women in their twenties, were walking through the bank parking lot. The women looked like they were carrying hunting rifles. The men—one walking point, the other, who wore a St. Louis Cardinals baseball cap, trailing behind—were obviously the lookouts.

They could be a scavenging party, he thought.

But that didn't look right. Like Sylvia Carnes, their clothes were in good repair. Their shoes were fairly new, and not held together with duct tape like his were. That meant they spent most of their time inside a compound. But a scavenging detail would have something to carry supplies in, like a horse-drawn truck, or a shopping cart, or a sled of corrugated tin with a rope or a chain to drag it by.

Maybe they were scouts for a larger party.

Somebody was running off to Richardson's right. The four people stopped and turned toward the sound. A moment later, Sylvia Carnes came trotting across the street. She went right up to the group. They obviously knew each other. The three women grouped together to talk. Sylvia Carnes was gesturing back in the direction she had come, and Richardson figured she had intentionally led the zombies away from the street in order to allow these four to move through in relative safety. That much made sense, at least. It was a risky strategy, but a proven one nonetheless.

But what were they up to?

He heard the sound of something hitting a hurricane fence off to his left. Four zombies had emerged from between a pair of red brick buildings. The zombies were trying to climb the hurricane fence, which meant they were in Stage II or maybe even Stage III of the infection. They would be trouble. It was hard to fool them with a simple diversion.

The guy walking point had already noticed them and was motioning the others to take cover. But he was too late. Four, then six, then nine more zombies entered the parking lot behind them, cutting off their retreat. Richardson spotted another five staggering toward them on a side street next to the Church's chicken stand.

He swallowed the lump in his throat as he scanned up and down the street. The infected were suddenly everywhere, coming from the alleys between the buildings and climbing over fences.

When the moaning started it was almost deafening.

Richardson felt confused and frightened. How did this happen? Where had they all come from so suddenly? In the early days of the outbreak, the zombies had been able to fill a street like this instantly. He'd read Eddie Hudson's book about San Antonio right at the beginning of the outbreak, and at first he'd thought Hudson was just embellishing to make himself sound more embattled than he'd really been. But then, in Houston, he'd witnessed seemingly empty streets suddenly become as crowded as the hallways of a sports arena right after the game gets out, and that convinced him Hudson had been telling the truth.

The zombies, especially Stage I zombies, tended to mass together. Slow as they were, it was easier for them to make kills that way. But most zombies didn't survive the first few weeks of being infected. Between the injuries that made them zombies and the things they ate after they became zombies, very few lived the eight or nine months it took the disease to progress to Stage II. That was the main reason he'd decided to chance a walk through St. Louis. It would have been suicide to walk through the city in the early days of the outbreak, but he figured after eight years, he'd be okay. He realized now the folly of that decision. There were more zombies out in the street in front of him than he had seen in the last month combined. But where had they all come from?

Sylvia Carnes and the others made a run for it. They crossed over to Richardson's side of the street and ran south, skirting behind the burned-out hulk of a car to block one of the zombies running their way.

They were close enough now that he could hear one of the younger girls tell the two men to cover for them. She was the one in charge. Even a quick glance was enough to tell Richardson that. She wore a formfitting gray sweatshirt, black BDU-style pants, and black combat boots. Her dusty brown hair was cut short. She gestured a command and the party broke into two groups, the men remaining in place to cover the retreating women.

A man whose arm had been chewed off above the elbow stepped into the street right in front of Richardson and started to moan. One of the men fired a three-round burst into the man's chest, spattering the wall next to him with blood and wet clumps of lung tissue.

"That one right there!" the woman in charge said.

Both men were firing now, the street echoing with loud pops.

"Fall back that way," the woman said.

"There's too many of them," Sylvia Carnes said.

"Just go. Move!"

Richardson lost sight of them in the commotion. The two armed men moved to either side of a wrecked car and fired into the approaching zombies with well-disciplined shots.

Richardson knew he had to get out of there. It was stupid to stay. There were way too many zombies out there now, and while these two guys were good, they weren't going to stop the flood.

But where did the women go?

Richardson scanned the front of the building to his right. He didn't see them. Richardson watched the zombies to see if any of them had changed direction to pursue the women, but none had. They were closing in on the two men, who were firing with everything they had now.

It was only a matter of time for them.

Richardson was left with a decision, he knew that. He could stay and play sniper and maybe help the two men, or he could turn and run.

His instincts told him to run. The two men were toast, surrounded, no chance of fighting their way through. But at the same time there was a part of him that refused to play into that logic. Richardson had traveled the country for the last few years, and he had seen survivors who thought they could eke out an existence by pretending to be one of the infected. Folks called them Fakers, and they were disgusting sights, often times looking every bit as much zombie as the crowds of infected in which they moved. Their survival strategy was to abandon all sense of self, existing without purpose, without a future. Richardson had watched one such Faker get mauled by a pack of the infected in a small town in Missouri and the experience had left him with mixed feelings. The man had evidently lived for many months as one of the infected, for he had so completely given up his sense of self that he refused to cry out, even as the zombies tore the plumbing from his belly. Richardson's empathy had nearly made him throw up. But another part of him felt an obscene sense of vindication. After all, what kind of life had the man really had? Was he giving up anything worth holding on to? Richardson didn't think so. After all, anyone who would give up their sense of self was already dead.

And running out on two people willing to fight to the bitter end seemed too much like giving up.

Knowing he was going to regret this, he raised his rifle to his shoulder and lined up the sights on a zombie across the street. But even as he released his breath and flexed his finger on the trigger, the noise of a truck downshifting made him lower the rifle.

He couldn't remember the last time he'd seen a working vehicle. What had it been, eight months? A year? Long enough, certainly. And yet, here he was, looking at not one, but four pickup trucks advancing down a side street toward the two men. The trucks were matte black and rode on large, off-road tires. They were caked with white streaks that looked like bird shit, like they'd been parked under a tree full of grackles, and from their throaty exhaust notes Richardson figured them for big block V8s, the kind of super duty gas hogs he hadn't seen since before Hurricane Mardell wiped out the nation's domestic oil and gas industry.

A few of the zombies turned toward the advancing caravan, but failed to get out of the way. The lead truck ran over one of the zombies and knocked several others to the side with its grille guard. At first Richardson thought they were the cavalry for the two men in the street, but he could see now that wasn't the case. The two men looked terrified. It was plain as day in their expressions, and for a moment he thought the men might try to push their way through the zombies that had surrounded them.

The lead truck swung a wide left into the street, the driver positioning the vehicle between the two men and the advancing zombies. The other three, each of which was loaded with a squad of armed men in black shirts, fell in to the right of the first truck. As the two men watched, the black-shirted soldiers jumped from the trucks and surrounded them, their backs to the zombies as though they weren't even there.

A man with a shaved, bullet-shaped head emerged from the passenger seat of the truck and walked behind the line of troops that had just climbed out of the trucks. Richardson stared at the man, mouth agape. He wore a ratty pair of jeans, no shirt, no shoes, and nearly every inch of his chest, arms, and face was painted a vibrant red. Thick black necklaces hung in skeins around his neck. From this distance, Richardson couldn't tell what was hanging from the necklaces, but whatever it was looked black and leathery. To Richardson, they looked like they might have even been dog turds. The Red Man moved slowly, limping slightly, his gaze on the zombies that were standing motionless only a dozen or so feet from him. His face had an odd punched-in look to it.

Richardson stared in disbelief. The zombies didn't attack. They didn't moan. They just stood there, swaying drunkenly, waiting, watching the Red Man like they were waiting for him to tell them what to do.

"No way," Richardson muttered, shaking his head. "Not possible."

The two men at the center of the Red Man's troops lowered their weapons, staring at the silenced zombies.

"Drop your weapons," one of the black shirts said.

The two men looked at each other, their expressions sick with fear, but obeyed. They dropped their rifles to the ground, then they slowly laced their fingers together behind their heads in surrender.

CHAPTER 2

From his hiding place in the narrow alley next to the Pizza Hut, Ben Richardson watched in stunned silence. Sugar ants crawled across the toe of his right boot, but he didn't bother to wipe them away. A strong smell of rotting flesh drifted over him from the zombies in the street, but not even that registered. All his attention was focused on the man painted red.

He was tall, and though he walked with a limp, he nonetheless moved with the unmistakable menace of a bird of prey hovering over a kill. The red paint that covered every visible inch of his body—it had to be paint, Richardson thought, not some weird form of rosacea—glistened on his bald head and on his back. And when he turned toward Richardson there was a self-amused smile on his face that betrayed a capacity for great cruelty and malevolence. Staring at him, Richardson felt a chill move over his skin.

The two captured men were on their knees in the middle of the street, heads down, the black-shirted soldiers forming a ring around them. Even from thirty feet away Richardson could see that the prisoners were trembling. The Red Man walked behind his soldiers, watching the two men, as though he were trying to make up his mind which one was the weaker.

The zombies followed the Red Man with their eyes, never looking away, and it was their single-minded fixation on him that fascinated Richardson the most. He had seen plenty of Stage III zombies in the past eight years. Some of them were even capable of limited cognition. They responded to their names. They were capable of delaying an attack, or working in teams with other zombies, if it meant making a bigger kill. Once, years ago, in the flood ruins of Houston, he'd been part of a small group of survivors flushed from a building by some Stage III zombies who were using a pack of Stage I zombies the way English fox hunters used to use their dogs. He respected the threat they represented. But he had never seen anything like this. The Red Man seemed to have them under his complete control.

He stepped through his line of soldiers and came up behind the man in the St. Louis Cardinals hat. He slapped the hat off the man's head, then grabbed his chin and turned his face toward him.

The man panicked and tried to scramble away on his hands and knees, but the Red Man grabbed the back of his shirt, lifted him bodily into the air, and threw him facedown onto the street. Richardson could see the man's eyes go wide. He could see the man's whole body shake.

The other man tried to get away, but the troops grabbed him by the shoulders and held him down on his knees.

"Turn him this way," the Red Man said. "I want him to watch this."

The Red Man knelt down next to the prisoner, lowering his face so that he looked like a question mark bent over the man, who was kicking and thrashing for all he was worth now. The Red Man's eyes were vividly white against the red of his skin. He still wore a hideous self-amused smile, though now he seemed to be smelling the man, drinking in his fear.

One of the soldiers, his combat gear rattling against the nylon rigging he wore over his chest, ran up to the Red Man and stopped. He shook his head. "We didn't find them," the man said. "There are some tracks through the mud over there, between those two buildings, but we lose them at the next street over."

The Red Man didn't seem to acknowledge him. Instead he made a sound that was part moan and part growl. The trooper glanced to his right and saw three zombies advancing into the inner circle. He stepped back quickly.

The zombies stopped right behind the Red Man and waited, their eyes fixed on the back of his head. The captured man continued to kick and punch the air beneath the Red Man, but as desperate as he was he couldn't break the grip that held him fast to the asphalt.

"Please," the man begged. "Get them away. Jesus Christ, please!"

Richardson was breathing hard, a cold worm of dread burrowing its way through his bowels.

"Where is Niki Booth?" the Red Man said. "You need to talk fast so you don't waste my time."

"I never heard of her," the man said. He was trying desperately to claw the Red Man's hands from the back of his neck. "We're on our way to the trading outpost at Herculaneum. Jesus Christ, get those things away from me."

The Red Man leaned in close to the prisoner's ear and whispered something that caused the man to stop fighting for a moment, then to start up again even harder.

The Red Man grunted at the three zombies behind him and they fell on the prisoner as though they hadn't fed in days. They tore at his back, at his ears, at his hands. The man's screams filled the street, echoing off the buildings. Richardson felt every single gut-wrenching sound, like somebody was jamming a needle deep into his ears.

Richardson closed his eyes.

He opened them when the screaming finally stopped. And he had to force himself to keep them open. The three zombies were feeding, the prisoner's body jerking as they bit into his back and arms and tore off strips of his flesh with their fingers.

Moans went up from the zombies all around them, but none moved.

The Red Man let go of the dead prisoner and stood up.

He backed away slowly, his hands and arms dripping with the prisoner's blood. He was opening and closing his fists, breathing hard, almost like he was aroused, his tongue dancing on his lips. He never blinked.

Richardson stared in confusion. He had long since resigned himself to the knowledge that men were capable of all manner of cruelty toward their fellow men. That wasn't what shocked him. It was the unmistakable control this man seemed to have over the zombies. How was that possible?

The Red Man motioned to his black shirts to bring the other prisoner forward. They threw him down in the street a few feet from his dead partner and pinioned his arms and legs so he looked like a scarecrow dropped on his face. He kicked and thrashed but couldn't move under the weight of three soldiers.

The Red Man knelt down next to the man and shoved his bloody hand in his face.

"Stop," he said. "Stop now. Stop fighting."

Richardson could see the veins standing out in the prisoner's neck. The man's face was taut with fear and rage. His lips were twisted into a grimace that showed his teeth.

"Stop it now."

The Red Man stroked the back of the man's head, smearing blood into his dark hair. The man turned his face away.

"I want you to tell me now where Niki Booth is. I know you know."

"Just kill me," the man said defiantly. "I don't know who the hell you're talking about and I'm never going to."

"Of course you know." The Red Man paused a beat, then said, "Look at me when I'm talking to you."

The man tried to pull away, his face still turned in the opposite direction.

The Red Man grabbed the hair on the back of the man's head and twisted his head around, forcing the man to stare him in the face. The man kept his lips shut tight. He refused to cry out.

"That's better," the Red Man said. He touched a bloody finger to the man's cheek and ran it from his earlobe down to the point of his chin, leaving a dark smear behind. "Now you're gonna tell me what I want to know, okay?"

"You're insane. He was telling the truth. We're turkey farmers. We were headed down to the trading market in Herculaneum."

"You're no turkey farmer. Not armed with brand-new AR-15s like these."

"We have to protect them from wild dogs and thieves."

"And where are these turkeys now."

"We found a hog farm, down by the river. North of town. We left them there."

"Why?"

"We wanted some vodka to celebrate for after we sold the birds. We were going to come back for them after we searched the liquor stores here in town."

The Red Man sat back on his haunches and sighed. The sunlight glistened off the thin layer of sweat that had formed across his back. There wasn't a hair on him, Richardson realized. Not a one. Just red paint slathered over every inch of skin.

"You try my patience," the Red Man said. "My people have been following you since you left Ken Stoler's camp. I know you are with Niki Booth. Now do not make me ask again."

Ken Stoler? Richardson wondered. Not *the* Ken Stoler? The same one Eddie Hudson had described in his book on San Antonio. The one who founded the People for an Ethical Solution foundation that Sylvia Carnes and her doomed expedition to San Antonio belonged to. It couldn't be.

"Fuck you," the man said. "Go ahead and kill me."

The Red Man wasn't smiling anymore. He slammed the prisoner's face down on the pavement and held him there, the heel of his palm grinding into the man's ear.

The Red Man turned slightly and motioned to one of the black shirts. A soldier came forward, pulled a hunting knife, and handed it handle-first to the Red Man. The Red Man took it, adjusted his weight on the prostrate prisoner, and then ran the tip of the blade around the back curve of the man's ear.

"There are a lot of ways to die, my friend. But you know what? You are not going to be given the luxury of any of them. You are going to have a long life ahead of you. And I fucking own it."

With a sudden, fierce effort he jammed the tip of the blade behind the man's ear and cut it off with a few rapid back-and-forth sawing motions.

The man screamed for a long time before fading off into a series of whimpers.

The Red Man rode the writhing prisoner's back like he was on a startled horse, waiting for the man to stop moving. When at last he did stop the Red Man let out a stuttering moan, and one of the zombies rose from the dead prisoner and approached, where he waited by his master's shoulder. Richardson could see the zombie was missing an ear. Richardson scanned the motionless zombies that surrounded the Red Man and saw that most of them were missing an ear. The skeins of leather necklaces around the Red Man's neck suddenly made hideous sense. He's branding them, Richardson thought as a shudder went through him—like cattle. The Red Man stood up and cupped a hand under the zombie's chin. He forced the zombie's mouth open and then stuck his fingers in there, like he was rooting around for something.

His fingers came away dripping ropes of blood and saliva.

"What in the hell?" Richardson muttered.

The Red Man knelt again next to the living prisoner and said, "Tell me where Niki Booth is. I won't ask again."

The prisoner's eyes were wide. He stared at the ooze dripping from the Red Man's fingers, shaking his head. His lips were clamped shut. Tears fell from his cheeks and the muscles in his neck twitched.

"No? Okay then. I want you to know you chose this," the Red Man said, and he jammed his fingers into the man's mouth, smearing the gore on his gums and on the inside of his lips.

When the Red Man took his hand away the prisoner dropped his face to the pavement and sobbed, defeated. Richardson thought he might vomit. He knew what the man's future held. Depending on his blood pressure and his overall health, he had anywhere from a few minutes to four hours of hell to look forward to. The necrosis filovirus would course through him, affecting his muscle coordination first. He would experience cramping and bloating. The muscles in his back and legs and neck would ache to the point that most men curled up in a fetal ball, unable to keep from crying. Next his breathing would turn ragged, phlegmy, and he would start to smell like rotting food. He would cough constantly, sometimes bringing up big black wads of phlegm. Depersonalization would follow, and the more he lost of his personality and his memories, the more aggressive he would become. By the time the change was complete, there'd be nothing but a hollow husk remaining.

Listening to the doomed man sobbing, Richardson could hardly breathe.

The Red Man stormed across the road unexpectedly. He was looking to the east, where red brick apartment buildings were crumbling into streets thick with weeds and blowing sand. He wheeled around, studying the faces of the black shirts nearest him. None of them dared look him in the face. Only the zombies failed to shrink from him.

"They are on foot," the Red Man said. "I know she hasn't gotten far. Search every street, every house, every shed, until you find her. And when you find her, bring her to me. I want her alive."

Soldiers and officers exchanged nervous looks.

"Now," the Red Man snapped.

His soldiers scrambled out of the street in their haste to leave. It was obvious to Richardson that they moved quickly not simply to obey his orders, but to get away from the violence gathering in his expression.

As the soldiers started their search, Richardson watched the Red Man. The zombies stood like terra-cotta soldiers all around him, following him with their dead stares. In eight years of wandering and collecting stories from survivors and studying every aspect of the outbreak, Richardson had never even imagined that something like this was possible. If someone had told him about it, he wouldn't have believed them. Whatever this was, whatever this man represented, it was completely unprecedented. This was either a new beginning, or the worst sort of ending.

He just didn't know which.

He heard voices and the sound of boots crunching through rotten wood coming from the other side of the building to his right, and he knew he had to leave soon. If he stayed here, they'd be on him in minutes.

Slowly, praying his knees wouldn't crack and give him away, he rolled over onto his butt and climbed to his feet. He slid his back up against the wall of the Pizza Hut and was making his way down the narrow gap between the buildings when a zombie stepped around the corner, blocking his path.

Richardson sucked in a breath.

Three more zombies rounded the corner behind the first, each of them missing an ear.

The lead zombie extended his hands out toward Richardson, opening and closing his fingers like he was begging Richardson for something. The man's neck was bent to one side, the muscles in his face slack, the skin a jaundiced yellow. Flies swarmed around his head, and his clothes were so soiled Richardson couldn't tell what color they had once been. For a moment, Richardson was lost in the pale white deadness of the man's eyes. He was still thinking of the downward slide the man out in the street was just beginning, and he wondered what, if anything, was left of the person this zombie in front of him had once been. Was there a part of him that still thought and felt and watched through those dead eyes, horrified by the murder and death that surely lay in its path?

"I'm sorry for you," Richardson said, and drew his machete as the man began to moan.

CHAPTER 3

Without warning the zombie broke into a sprint, running straight at Richardson, arms outstretched. Richardson let out a startled gasp and slashed at the man with the machete. The blade glanced off the zombie's left arm, cutting into the meat but doing nothing to slow him down. His momentum carried him headlong into Richardson's chest, and when they hit, they both went tumbling over backward, landing in a pile of bricks and rotten plywood and tall weeds.

The attack caught Richardson completely off guard. Watching the zombie's slow, staggering gait and jerky movements Richardson had thought he was dealing with one of the slow ones, the recently infected. But they were face-to-face now, rolling around in the weeds and the busted lumber, the man snarling and snapping his teeth just inches from Richardson's nose, and he could see the threads of red veins in the eyes. He could see the intelligence, too. Anger and insanity and intelligence. This was a Stage III zombie, and he had tricked him by pretending to be one of the slow movers. He never would have let the man get this close if he'd known he was dealing with one of the smart ones; and as the zombie managed to roll over on top of him, the stench of his fetid breath in his nostrils, Richardson had the terrible realization that the zombie must have known that, too.

The man had tricked him.

He grabbed the zombie under the chin and pushed his snapping teeth away with the heel of his palm. The man snarled like a fighting dog, a wet, snapping sound. His fingernails dug into Richardson's arms with unexpected strength.

"Get off, motherfucker," Richardson hissed.

Come on, he told himself. You gotta fight. You've got to.

Grunting, bicycling his knees up into the man's gut, Richardson broke the zombie's hold on his biceps. He turned his head, looking for the rifle, and saw it partially buried in some tall weeds. It was just out of reach. He rolled over to his right, creating distance from the zombie, and scrambled to his feet.

The zombie rolled off in the opposite direction, landing with his back against the wall of the Pizza Hut. He climbed to his feet easily and lunged for the machete in Richardson's hands. His fingers caught in the sleeves of Richardson's Windbreaker and for a moment they spun around an invisible pivot point as Richardson struggled to break loose from the man's grip.

The other zombies were halfway down the alley now. Too close. He had wasted too much time. Pushing the zombie's hands up and out of the way, he kicked the heel of his right boot into the man's gut, knocking him backward. When the zombie came at him again he swung the machete down on the man's outstretched hand and felt the blade whisper through bone. Two fingers and part of the zombie's hand hit the wall of the redbrick building with a dull thud and landed in the grass, the fingers curled toward the sky like the legs of an upturned crab. The zombie's arm dropped to his side but otherwise the man showed no reaction to the damage. He continued forward. Richardson swung the machete twice more, hacking at the zombie's outstretched arms. Then he stepped to his right and brought the machete down on the zombie's head with a two-handed overhead chop. The blade connected right above the man's missing ear and sank into the skull down to the top of the mouth.

The zombie fell to his knees, bringing the machete with him. Richardson yanked at the machete's handle frantically, causing the dead body to jerk and twitch like a poorly handled marionette, but the blade wouldn't come free.

The other zombies were too close. He felt one of them drop a hand on his shoulder and he twisted away, toward the front of the building. The zombies were grabbing on to his backpack, pulling him backward, but he was able to wrest free.

Barely.

He reached the rifle in the tall weeds and tried to swing it around like a club, but one of the zombies had closed the distance between them and was able to grab hold of the barrel and shake it back and forth so that Richardson couldn't gain control of it. The zombie managed to shift its grip forward and grabbed hold of Richardson's wrist. The gun and the zombie both fell to the ground as Richardson pulled himself loose, and he found himself standing over the zombie.

The zombie was on his knees, reaching for him, as Richardson backed away. The other zombies were still a few feet behind the one on its knees, but they were close enough to keep him from retrieving his gun and his machete. Still backing up, Richardson slipped on one of the bricks and nearly lost his footing. He reached down and scooped up a brick and smashed it down with both hands on the kneeling zombie's face, the brick connecting with a muffled clank and then crumbling.

He let the ruined bits fall from his fingers.

He was out on the sidewalk in front of the Pizza Hut now, stunned by what had just happened to him. In eight years of fighting the infected, he had never seen one use such a complicated ruse as pretending to be a slow mover. The implications of that were staggering.

Richardson turned away from the two remaining zombies, looking for a place to run, and froze when he saw the Red Man watching him. The Red Man had been kneeling at the body of the dead man in the St. Louis Cardinals hat, but when he saw Richardson he stood up and took a few steps forward. There was no self-assured smile on his face now. Just a steady, unyielding stare. He stepped forward again, eyes narrowed on Richardson.

Behind him, Richardson heard footsteps in the grass. He glanced quickly over his shoulder and saw the two zombies coming out of the alley. When Richardson looked back to the street, the Red Man was pointing in his direction. Then the Red Man threw back his head and began to moan. The zombies in the street all turned their heads in Richardson's direction. He made a quick scan of the street, all those dead eyes looking at him, and he swallowed.

One of the Red Man's soldiers fired at Richardson, hitting the wall behind him, peppering the back of his neck and scalp with bits of brick and mortar.

He ducked his head and ran.

Behind him, he heard the hacking cough of automatic weapons. The air around his head filled with high-pitched whines, like a swarm of invisible hornets. Bullets tore into the façade of the Pizza Hut, blasting off bits of wood and brick that sizzled against the sleeves of his Windbreaker. He rounded the corner where he had first seen Sylvia Carnes and veered to his left as the wrecked car ahead of him exploded beneath a hail of bullets.

Four zombies were staggering toward him from the overgrown alley behind the Pizza Hut. Richardson veered to the right of a pickup to avoid a zombie and kept on running, his heartbeat pounding in his ears. There was a ruined wooden fence to his right that ran the length of the property back to the alley, bright green weeds growing along the base. Without breaking stride he pulled his pistol and fired at the zombie that stepped around the back corner of the fence. The zombie sank to its knees but didn't fall.

A moment later he was in the alley, facing another crumbling wooden fence and a three-story apartment building beyond that. He looked to his left and saw two zombies coming at him through the grass. On the next street over he heard the sound of a truck engine revving loudly, coming closer. To his right the alley was thick with trash and weeds. A wooden light pole had fallen across the alley and it was covered with what looked like lilac. Beyond the pole was a zombie in the remnants of a red T-shirt and jeans staggering clumsily over a mounded pile of garbage.

Tires skidded on the pavement behind him. Men shouted. Again he heard the stuttering cough of automatic weapons, the bullets slapping into the brick wall to his right. He moved to the opposite side of the alley and ran toward the fallen light pole. His chest was heaving, his breath hitching in his throat, but he forced himself to stop, breathe, and focus on putting his pistol's front sight on the zombie's chest. Richardson fired twice, dropping the zombie, before ducking under the light pole and running through the trash-strewn alley.

He made it to the next corner and turned left. A long gray street stretched out ahead of him, the concrete cracked into oddly symmetrical squares and choked with weeds and rolls of carpet, insulation panels, soggy paper, plastic bags, and endless piles of concrete scree and lumber. To his left was a six-story brick building with nearly every window broken. To his right was the fossil of a parking garage, its gray concrete frame cracked and crumbling. Shrubs grew from the ledges. The bottom story had been walled up with a mismatched assortment of bricks, parts of the wall covered with the faded ghosts of graffiti from before the outbreak. One section of the wall had collapsed, creating a way in, and he ran for it.

"There he is!" came a man's voice from behind him.

Richardson turned and saw one of the black trucks turning the corner behind him. A soldier standing up in the bed was banging on the roof of the cab and pointing right at Richardson.

"Damn it," Richardson muttered.

He ran for the collapsed section of the wall and dove inside it as the truck roared to life and started down the alley.

Inside the parking garage he suddenly found himself in near total darkness. Here and there he could make out the silhouette of wrecked cars and he could smell the rancid odor of a dead body propped up against the wall to his right.

"He's in there," a man's voice said.

Richardson spun around and faced the patch of sunlight that led back out to the street. Two man-sized shapes appeared in the opening.

He pulled his pistol and fired.

One of the men let out a grunt, like he'd been punched in the gut. The other ducked back behind the corner.

"Choke on it, asshole," Richardson said.

He ran for the opposite side of the building, found a stairwell, and ran down it. He emerged onto another ruined street, a tall chain-link fence straight ahead of him. He ran for the fence and found a section that was peeled back from the post and he pushed his way through the hole into the overgrown alley beyond.

The alley was little more than an easement between two brick buildings. He had to turn his shoulders to fit through. On the far side of the easement he saw another building and he slipped inside one of its broken windows and stopped for a moment to listen to the silence and the shadows that had swallowed him.

Come on, he told himself. Breathe. Think. Come on, you have to think.

The room in which he found himself was large and empty, save for a few overturned chairs and ceiling tiles that had fallen to the floor and turned to powder. Electrical wires hung like vines from the exposed rafters in the ceiling. A gray haze hung in the air. The place smelled of rot and dust.

Richardson crossed to a window on the far side of the room and looked out. He could see a patchwork of vacant lots, the vegetation dead and brown. Gray streets led down blind alleys between endless red brick buildings. He couldn't remember ever seeing so much red brick in his life.

But he could breathe again. At least he had that much. He looked down at the pistol in his hand and opened the cylinder and ejected the spent shell casings onto the floor. He took a speed loader from his belt and was about to drop it into the cylinder when he suddenly smelled the odor of rotting meat.

He glanced over his shoulder and saw a child, no more than ten years old, staggering toward him, dragging a useless leg behind him.

Richardson groaned.

The boy dragged himself forward, one arm coming up, the fingers too mangled to work. The other arm hung uselessly at his side. It too had been partially eaten. The boy's face was crusted over with dark splashes of dried blood, his eyes milky white with cataracts. He was obscenely thin. He began a long, low growl that ended with a snarling, snapping cough. Then he fell forward.

Richardson stepped to one side, coming up behind the boy and pushing him face-first into the wall next to the window. Electrical wires hung down around them and Richardson balled up a section of them and looped the ends around the boy's throat. The boy's arm flailed against the wall, smearing blood on the bricks. Richardson kept pulling the wires down and down until he heard the long, low growl cut off abruptly. Then he stepped back from the wall and staggered back toward the center of the room.

The boy turned clumsily and came after him, his head snapping back as the wires went taut. He kept reaching for Richardson with his one working arm until there was no more air left in his lungs.

He jerked against the wire and a choking gurgling noise came from him. Then his legs bent and his body sagged, though his knees never quite reached the floor.

The head lolled to one side, the dead, white eyes still open, watching Richardson.

Richardson stood there, unable to look away from the dead boy. This was too much. This was just too much. There was no sound, save for the creaking of the wooden rafters as the boy's body swayed back and forth, and all Richardson could do was stand there, shaking his head.

He could hear voices outside the window, but they were not close. A truck raced by, shifted gears, and the sound faded away into the distance until it was indistinct.

He'd lost them, at least for now.

He went to the window and put a hand on the brick frame

and watched the vacant lots outside. A few zombies roamed between the apartment buildings; but for the time being, Richardson felt safe enough to relax a little. God knows he needed it.

He glanced back at the dead boy, then lowered himself to the dust-covered floor and slid the straps of his backpack off his shoulders and removed a plastic bottle of water and leaned against the wall while he drank. Sweat dripped into his eyes and he pinched it away. He was so tired. He wanted so badly to rest. But he couldn't. He could never stop, never rest. He hated living this way.

A large black bird—a crow, judging by the size of it—landed on the window ledge.

Richardson regarded it without moving. The bird squawked at him, a harsh, rude sound. Another landed beside it, and another.

He stared at them; they back at him.

Another flew inside and lit near the dead zombie boy's feet. It squawked at Richardson, then jumped onto the dead boy's shoulder and pecked at one of his eyes until it pried the thing loose.

The bird held the boy's eyeball by its trailed bundle of severed optic nerves, then tossed it up in the air and gulped it down. Another crow was already prying the second eye-ball loose.

Richardson turned to the window. The first three crows had become dozens. Beyond them were hundreds more. Thousands. They sat on the telephone poles and wires and in the street and on the roofs of the ruined apartment buildings. All of them stared back at him with dull black eyes, empty as a void, empty as forever.

A crow squawked.

Another answered.

The sound grew large, bird answering unto bird. It became a din, became a living, breathing thing trying to cover him, beat him down, snuff him out. It was a painful thing, that noise, huge, godlike in its aspect.

He clapped his hands over his ears but it did no good. The noise was all around him. It was *inside* him.

He closed his eyes and pulled his knees up to his chest. He hugged them. He pressed his face into his thighs and thought: No! Stop it. No!

Richardson sat there, whimpering, for a long time.

When at last he opened his eyes, the birds were gone. The dead boy was still hanging from the electrical cords, still creaking with his slow pendulum movements in the torpid heat of the darkened building.

Richardson mopped a hand over his face. He was sweating badly. He finished off the last of his water and sat watching the beads run down the inside of the bottle. He was numb. Mentally drained and numb.

He tried to clear his mind so he could figure out what to do next. Over the last eight years he had seen so many messed-up things, so many lives wasted. But he had never seen anything like the Red Man. Sitting there, his head between his knees, Richardson asked himself again how it was possible for a man to control the infected the way the Red Man had, and he didn't have any answers.

You have to think about this, he told himself. You have to. This is important.

But he couldn't. His eyes burned. The muscles in his lower back ached. He was unable to concentrate on anything but the stiffness in his body.

From outside he heard the familiar sound of a wooden door getting smashed open. That wasn't good. The zombies were searching the surrounding buildings—maybe looking for him, maybe looking for Sylvia Carnes and the two younger women she had with her. But it didn't matter who they were looking for. Whoever they found was as good as dead.

He pulled himself up to one knee and looked out the window. From where he stood he could see row upon row of red brick apartment buildings, with vacant lots between them. So many broken windows. Here and there was a fire-damaged roof. The brown weed-filled yards were starting to encroach through the ground-floor windows.

He was scanning the buildings for the broken wooden door he'd heard when he saw a zombie falling from a second-story window off to his right.

A small crowd of the infected was fighting to get through the front door.

Framed in the window above them was the young, dark-haired woman he'd seen back at the Pizza Hut, the one who had seemed to be in charge of Sylvia Carnes's group.

Get out of there, he thought.

But she seemed to know already that the zombies were coming for her. She turned from the window and he thought he heard the sounds of a struggle. A moment later she burst out of the front door with a wooden baseball bat in her hands. Sylvia Carnes and the other young woman emerged behind her. The dark-haired woman sidestepped one of the zombies, came up behind it, and swung the bat at the back of the zombie's head, dropping it with one blow. It was the same practiced move he'd seen Sylvia Carnes do in front of the Pizza Hut, but this woman did it with an athleticism that Sylvia Carnes could only try to mimic.

And I bet this is the one who taught it to you, Sylvia, he said to himself. Not bad.

There weren't many zombies around them now, maybe twenty, and the women worked quickly to put them down. When the last zombie fell, the women formed up back-to-back-to-back and surveyed the field. They had an easy escape route to the south, lots of wide open ground. The nearest zombies were still a good 150 feet away.

But just as it looked like they were going to make it, Richardson heard the sound of a truck engine racing, tires skidding. He turned to his left, following the noise, and saw one of the Red Man's trucks coming up the street toward them.

"No," he said. He looked at the women. "Run. You have to run."

The women heard the truck, too. The dark-haired woman lowered her bat and turned. She watched the truck approach.

"Come on," Richardson muttered, "what are you waiting for?"

Then she tossed the bat to the ground.

"No," Richardson said. "What are you doing? Run!"

Niki Booth counted the black shirts on the truck racing toward her. Four men in the back, probably two more in the cab. Nothing she couldn't handle.

"Niki?"

She turned. Sylvia Carnes was looking at the bat on the ground. Beside her, Avery Harper was scared. It was a bad idea bringing her. She looked like she was holding on to her self-control with both hands.

But of course she'd no choice in that. She couldn't leave Avery behind. Not the way things were back home.

This has gone far enough, Niki realized. She had to do something now or they were all going to be murdered by the black shirts. And that just wasn't going to happen.

"You two need to run. Go, hurry."

Sylvia looked at her. "Niki, what are you going to do?"

"Don't ask me any questions, Sylvia. You and Avery, you need to run. Please. I won't let you get caught."

"Niki," Avery said, "you can't."

Niki nearly barked at her, but she caught the words in her throat. This wasn't a patrol, and Avery and Sylvia sure as hell weren't soldiers. She breathed out slowly, getting herself back under control.

To Avery, very gently, she said, "Baby, I mean it. Run. If I don't catch up with you on the road, I'll meet you in the trade market down in Herculaneum. Now go."

"They'll kill you," Sylvia said.

"These idiots won't even get to first base. Now look, whatever happens to me, you get to a little town called Chester, you understand?"

"Chester? Is that where we're going?"

"You need to be there by Wednesday of next week, understand?"

Sylvia shrugged helplessly. "I . . . but, what about you?"

"I'll be fine." Niki glanced over at Avery and made sure that Sylvia saw the look in her eyes. "You take care of her, okay?"

"Niki . . ."

"Promise me. That's all I ask."

Sylvia nodded.

"Good enough."

"But Niki . . ." Avery said.

Niki took her younger cousin by the hand. "Listen to me, Avery. It's like when you were a kid, remember? I'd tell you to lay low while I took care of the bad guys? Remember that?"

Avery nodded.

"It's like that now. I got bad guys that need takin' care of. You go with Sylvia. You stay close to her. Understand?"

Avery nodded.

"I need to hear it, Avery."

"I understand."

"Alright." She turned back toward the black truck and pulled both her pistols. Then she looked back over her shoulder at them. "Go," she said, "both of you."

Richardson's pulse raced. He could feel it pounding at his temples. From where he stood he could see the truck barreling down on the women. He could see the young dark-haired woman with a pistol in each hand, running at the truck. Sylvia Carnes was yelling something. He couldn't catch all of it, but he heard her call the dark-haired girl Niki, and he figured this was Niki Booth, the name he'd heard the Red Man mention while he was interrogating the two men that had been with them.

Niki fired at the truck, and as soon as she did the driver jumped on the brake and the men bailed out, running for cover behind wrecked cars. The black shirts were armed with shotguns. They got behind cover quickly, moving in a crouch, the muzzles of their weapons pointed down at a low ready, the stocks up against their shoulders.

Richardson had seen pros before, and he knew these men were trained for combat. Not just a couple of thugs from the local gangs.

But for pros, they sure were taking a foolish chance. The truck had been their biggest tactical advantage. If they wanted Niki and her group, why not just run them down? A truck against pistols was no fair match at all.

Niki ran to her right, where three zombies had just come around the far side of a small apartment building, their focus on Sylvia Carnes and the other woman, who had yet to run. Niki fired again—but not, Richardson realized, at the soldiers. She shot at the zombies, and her shots caused the zombies to change direction. They came for her, and as they did, they crossed behind two of the black shirts who had taken up position behind a wrecked car. The black shirts were forced to turn and fire at the zombies, and when they did, Niki Booth charged them.

She ran around the car and fired at the man closest to her, hitting him twice that Richardson could see.

The soldier fell onto his back and didn't move.

The second soldier managed to squeeze off a shot before Niki shot him, and the deep *whumpf* of the shotgun drowned out Niki's shots.

A moment later, Niki Booth staggered around the wrecked car and into the street. The blast had knocked her backward a good five feet, but she hadn't fallen. And there was no visible wound on her either. Her T-shirt was as gray as it had been in front of the Pizza Hut, no blood at all.

But she did look punch-drunk. She weaved noticeably, and it looked like she was having trouble aiming her pistols at the other soldiers, who were coming out from behind their cover.

She turned toward Sylvia Carnes and the other woman, both of whom had only fallen back perhaps twenty yards, and that only because a few of the infected had managed to close on them, and she mouthed the word, "Run!"

The soldiers were closing on her. She fired at one of them and missed.

The man already had his shotgun up. He lined his sights up on her chest and fired, and once again the weapon made an odd, deep *whumpf* that didn't sound anything like a normal shotgun blast. Richardson wasn't sure, but he thought he saw a flash of something red leave the weapon and bounce off Niki Booth's chest.

She staggered backward. Her arms dropped to her sides and her chin sagged forward. One of the pistols fell from her fingers and clattered on the pavement.

The soldier racked another shell into the chamber of his

shotgun and fired. The same sound. The same flash of something red. And this time the shot laid Niki Booth out flat on her back. Richardson could see her writhing sluggishly on the ground, on her back, a weak moan coming from her; and only then did it occur to him that the black shirts were using rubber donut rounds, the kind of nonlethal ammunition riot police had used on crowds before the outbreak. They were taking her alive. But why?

The black shirts swarmed over her then and handcuffed her hands behind her back. Two of the soldiers scooped her up off the ground and carried her between them to the waiting truck, while the remaining two turned back to the south and looked around for Sylvia Carnes and the other woman.

They weren't there, Richardson realized.

Quietly, he stepped back from the window and crossed to the opposite side of the room. There he stepped out of the back window and hugged the wall of the building, moving south.

When he got to the corner he stopped and looked around. More windowless red brick apartment buildings. More brown, vacant lots. Gray paved streets with scraggly weeds coming up through the cracks. Sylvia Carnes and the other woman were there, standing out in the open, just waiting to be captured. Or worse.

Roving camera, he thought. You're safe here. You can just watch. Record. You can keep yourself safe, detached, uninvolved.

"Move," Richardson said aloud. "Come on, Sylvia. Move."

He heard the truck start up at the far side of the building. He heard the black shirts yelling, one of them directing the others to the south. They'd be on Sylvia Carnes and the other woman in less than a minute.

Decision time, he told himself. You can walk away. You don't need to be a part of this.

Richardson leaned forward and cursed himself. He was mad at his own stupidity. And at Sylvia. Why couldn't he ever take the easy option? Why couldn't he just turn his back and walk away?

He ran for them.

They were watching the lots to the north—still hoping against hope, he knew, that Niki Booth would come running around the corner—and they didn't even realize he was there until he grabbed them both by the arm.

Both women looked like they were going to scream. The younger one actually tried, but the sound caught in her throat and all she could manage was a weak, choking gasp. She sucked in a breath and he knew she was going to try again.

"Don't make a sound," he said. His voice was barely more than a whisper. "If they hear you you're dead."

We're all dead, he thought.

He pulled them back toward the building where he had been hiding.

"Come with me," he said. "There isn't much time."

CHAPTER 4

When Niki Booth awoke, she was on her stomach in the bed of the truck, a tan-colored boot right in front of her face. Her hands were cuffed behind her back. The truck bounced on the bad roads, telegraphing every bump through its worn springs to her aching ribs. Every breath was an effort. Every bump brought tears to her eyes.

"She's awake," one of the black shirts said from above her.

She turned her head to the side and looked up at the man. He was a lot older than she, forty maybe. He had a long, stringy red beard and freckles on his neck and face, and a tattoo of a raven on the inside of his left wrist.

She tried to roll over, but the pain in her side made her wince and then she started coughing up blood. Big phlegmy wads of it darkened the dirty bed of the truck. She groaned.

And then she caught herself. These bastards weren't going to see her hurt. She steeled herself against the pain and looked up at her captors, scanning their faces, their clothes, the way they handled their weapons.

The black shirt with the raven tattoo followed her gaze to his hand and adjusted his grip on the shotgun, perhaps thinking that she was debating her chances of getting the weapon from him.

"It'd be a mistake," he said, and the faintest hint of a smile touched his mouth. It suggested that he wouldn't mind if she tried, though.

Another bump in the road caused her to roll to her left, and when she did she got a view of the second guard. He was sitting on the edge of the bed, smoking a cigarette and looking across the deserted city. The shotgun rested across his thighs. He was even older than the first guard. He didn't even bother looking at her. The expression on his face, Niki realized, was boredom laced with sadness at the way the world was now.

Niki rocked back in the other direction, toward the first man.

"Keep still," he told her.

"My ribs hurt. I think you broke something."

"Yeah? I hope it fucking hurts."

She rolled over onto her right side so she could get her legs free.

"What are you doing?"

"I can't breathe. How about loosening these cuffs?"

"Yeah, right. Just sit still. We're almost there."

The truck hit a pothole, bouncing her off the bed. She winced. Every bump sent a pulse of pain through her ribs, sharp as a knife in her side. Niki closed her eyes and focused on her breathing, forcing the pain down, down, down. A moment later she was still breathing hard, but she had the pain mastered. If she was going to get out of this she needed to act quickly, and that meant playing dirty.

She rolled over onto her shoulder and arched her back, turning her breasts up toward the black shirt.

"Please," she said, a bit of the helpless female creeping into her voice. "Loosen them up just a little. They hurt real bad."

He didn't react, at least at first.

He was looking right into her eyes, still tough, still the pro. But she could see the sweat on his forehead, his Adam's apple pumping up and down in his throat. Finally, he broke. He glanced at her breasts and swallowed, and Niki knew that she had won a little ground. Men and boobs, she thought. God, they're idiots.

The redheaded soldier looked at the older man across the bed from him, hesitated for a moment, as though about to ask permission, then seemed to think better of it.

He stood up. Took the keys from his belt.

"Turn over," he said. "Put your ass up here where I can get at those cuffs."

She could see him waiting for it. She could see his grip loosening on the shotgun. And when she saw the barrel of the gun swing up and away from her, she kicked, planting her heel squarely into his balls. He doubled over with a grunt, the air rushing from his lungs. She twisted over onto her back and kicked again, this time catching him under the chin and sending him sprawling over the side of the truck.

"What the . . ." the older guard said.

He jumped to his feet. Niki was watching his knees. As soon as she saw his weight come down on his left knee she kicked it, and a momentary thrill shot through her to hear the crack of his bones.

Spinning over onto her shoulder blades she jammed a heel up into his teeth. He fell backward, the shotgun falling overboard onto the road when he grabbed the side of the truck to try to keep from falling.

She didn't lose any time. Niki rolled over onto her knees

just as the driver hit the brakes. When the vehicle stopped she was ready.

She jumped over the tailgate and hit the road running.

To her left was nothing but vacant lots. She turned right and ran for a series of mismatched concrete buildings, the colors faded from years of neglect and exposure. Where there were buildings, there were places to hide.

She heard the familiar *whumpf* of their shotguns and felt something hit her in the back, but it wasn't hard enough to knock her down. They were still using the rubber rounds, and those things only had a range of twenty yards or so. Beyond that, they were just a nuisance. She'd been hit harder during sparring practice.

It didn't slow her down. She ran toward the buildings and veered to her right, looking for a way to create distance and conceal her position. The more buildings, the better, just like in training; and the building at the far end of the row was a storefront, mostly windows, the glass all busted out. She glanced through it, saw the way was clear around the corner, and ran for it.

Three black shirts were waiting for her near the back of the row of buildings, advancing abreast in a skirmish line.

She stopped and turned.

The ones from the truck were already sprinting around the front of the store.

The older guard she'd kicked in the teeth drew a bead on her with his shotgun, and the last thing she saw before the world went black was the orange-white blast of fire from the end of his muzzle.

She was back in the bed of the truck when she came to.

The guards pulled her roughly to her feet and handed her

down from the truck. Only then did she see she was back in the bank parking lot, the Pizza Hut across the street. The infected were all around her, watching her with their dead white eyes. Many of them appeared to have fed recently, for their faces and their hands were wet with blood.

A zombie crossed in front of her path, dragging a severed arm. From the shred of fabric still clinging to the wrist she realized the arm belonged to either Steve Lewis or Tommy Bishop, the men who'd volunteered to come with her.

"Oh no," she groaned.

But there was no time for her to mourn. The guards were leading her toward a smoky fire in the middle of the road. She felt a cloud of menace envelop her. Squatting in front of the fire, a bloodstained St. Louis Cardinals hat next to his left foot, was Loren Skaggs. He wore only a loose-fitting pair of blue jeans. The rest of him was covered head to toe in red paint. Even from ten feet away she could smell the waves of rot and corrupted flesh rising from his skin. Her stomach heaved, but she pushed it down.

He looked nothing like the stoner kid she'd known back in high school. The infection had ruined his face. Old abscess scars, barely hidden by the red paint, pitted his face. One ear had been nearly torn from the side of his head, but had since healed. It was an imperfect fit now, the earlobe pointed forward much more than was natural. The rest of his face looked like it might slide from his head at any moment.

He was stoking the coals with an iron rod, watching the brand at the end turn orange hot. He turned toward her, still stoking the fire, and his eyes were very white against the red paint on his face. His lips parted to show his yellowed teeth.

It wasn't really a smile. There was too much gloating in it, like a predator savoring the prey beneath its claws.

She flashed back ten years, to Gooding, Illinois. Niki had just graduated from the University of Nebraska with a degree in Child Development. She wanted to teach elementary school. And then Hurricane Mardell hit, and the nation's economy just sort of dried up and moved on down the road. The Midwest was already hurting before the storm. But after, it died on its feet. When she returned to Gooding, she found no jobs, no schools in need of teachers. The town was dying. Most of the shops up and down Main were for sale. Some had their windows boarded over. The scourge of meth was everywhere. The only good-looking, non-druggie guys she'd known growing up were shipping off for the military.

And then, while shopping for some canned beans and tomatoes at the Family Pantry, she'd turned the corner and saw her town's death personified in the form of Loren Skaggs, son of Gooding's police chief. He'd been one of the metalheads smoking in his truck between classes back in school, Queensrÿche concert shirt on his bony frame, haunted look in his eyes. He played around with meth in high school, but now he was its poster boy. Rail skinny. Losing his hair. Cheeks sunken. Dark circles under his eyes. Bad teeth. He'd been trying to read the labels on a wall of antihistamines and turned to look at her. He smelled like something that had died on the side of the road three days earlier.

"Hey," he said, "I know you."

She'd recoiled from his breath. Looking away, in equal parts horror and dismay, she'd turned down the first aisle she saw and walked straight to the registers.

"See you around, Niki," he'd called after her, and coughed.

She paid and left in a hurry. The memory of that hideously vacant smile shook her, but she would have swum the Mississippi to trade it for the smile he was giving her now.

Niki bit down on her lip, fighting to master her fear. She tried to tell herself that the red paint he wore was just crazy, but the truth was he sent an icy shiver down her skin.

This must be how the people of the Calimar compound

felt when he and his army of black shirts and zombies came for them, she thought. Nearly three thousand people. People she knew. He hadn't wanted more black shirt converts, or even more zombie slaves. His army came with torches lit, their minds bent on murder and sending a message to the other compounds.

The Red Man never even gave them a chance to surrender. He and his black shirts burned the perimeter fence and put the school and barracks and medical center to the torch. Those who were able tried to flee, only to get swallowed up by the Red Man's zombie army waiting in reserve. But most were cornered in the dining hall.

Niki had led a contingent of her soldiers into Calimar two days later, all of them wearing biohazard masks as protection against an endless plague of flies. Blood had stained everything. There were huge coagulated pools of it on the floor of the dining hall and spattered on the walls. Swirls of it on the ceiling. There were broken teeth embedded in the tables. Bodies lay mangled and tangled in piles. Niki had given the order to burn the rest of the complex and then gone back to Ken Stoler at Union Field. She and Stoler had been at odds for a while before then, but that day marked the beginning of the end of their friendship. And when she considered how she had come to be a traitor to the people of Union Field, and turned her back on the man who had taken her in and turned her from a feral hunter into a leader of men, she thought of that day at Calimar.

And now, here she was, about to die at the Red Man's hand. Ken Stoler would probably appreciate the irony.

The guards had let go of her shoulders. She hadn't even realized it. She'd been standing there, light-headed, her mind still drifting over the events of the last two years, when suddenly she became aware that she was supporting her own weight. She was swaying like one of those zombies waiting on the edge of the road. Niki squeezed her eyes shut and willed herself not to fall. She would not let herself do that. She didn't dare. And when she spoke, there wasn't the slightest tremor in her voice.

"Hello, Loren."

He hesitated for just a moment, then went back to stoking the fire.

"What do you think you're doing, Loren? This is suicide for you. You know that, don't you? My people are going to tear you to shreds."

He shrugged. "That's the price of doing business where we play, isn't it?" His eyes never left the fire.

"What's this about, Loren?"

The muscles along his back tensed. He jabbed the poker into the fire, no longer stoking it, but attacking it.

"No one is coming for you, Niki. Let's not pretend."

"What happened to you, Loren?"

"I would have thought that was obvious."

"No, I can see the change you've been through, all that ridiculous paint you wear. That's not what I mean. What happened to your mind? The last time we spoke you sounded like the meth had charred your mind to cinders. Now, you actually sound like you can string a sentence together. So what happened, 'cause from I'm standing, you may be the only person who ever got better by becoming a zombie."

"Ah," he said, "you're trying to tease me."

"Would that do any good?"

"Sexually, you mean?" He looked back at her and chuckled at the stricken look on her face. "Ah, no, I see that's not what you meant."

He went back to the fire. "A pity."

She looked at him coldly, but inside she was aghast and dismayed by the double entendre he'd made. Another chill spread over her skin.

He rose from the fire, the poker in his right hand. Niki watched the smoking orange raven at the end of the iron shaft and a muscle in her cheek twitched, but she showed no other reaction. The truth was, she was terrified. But she had no intention of giving him that satisfaction.

"Can I tell you something, Niki?"

Her eyes flicked from the orange tip of the smoking poker to his face.

"Back in high school," he said, "I used to dream of fucking you. Seriously, that was the only reason I ever showed up to Algebra. Oh man, the sick shit I wanted to do to you. Tell me, Niki, you ever take it in the ass?"

She swallowed, trying hard to breathe in the stench of his breath without gagging.

He shrugged.

"Who knows?" he said. "Maybe here in the next few days we'll get a chance to find out. You and me, we're gonna be spending some quality time together."

"You'll never get the chance," she managed to say. "Ken Stoler's gonna—"

"Ken Stoler has been betrayed by his little favorite." He brought the poker closer, passing it within inches of Niki's face. She could see the glowing tip reflecting in his eyes like a sadistic joy. "He may come looking for you, Niki, but he'll be hunting, not rescuing. You're a traitor. How does that feel, knowing you turned your back on the one man who believed in you?"

"You don't know what you're talking about," Niki said. "I'm on a scavenging mission. I'm looking for antibiotics."

"You're looking for Dr. Don Fisher," he said. "Don't lie to me."

He dipped his face close to hers, and the stink of rot that emanated from him made her eyes water. But even worse than the smell, worse even than the bloodstains between his teeth, was the bright glow of insanity that filled his expression. The necrosis filovirus had eaten honeycomb chambers through his psyche, and what remained of his mind was like a window straight into hell.

"You're not on any scavenging mission," he went on. His voice was barely more than a whisper now, but still full of hate. "I have my spies in Union Field. I know the trouble you've had with Ken Stoler. And I know what you're planning on doing. You've sent messages to Fisher. Where are you planning on meeting him?"

His words sent a chill through her. How could he know that? Was it true, did he really have spies in Union Field?

She forced the questions down.

"I don't know what you're talking about," she said. "Loren, please. Just let me go. You don't have to do this."

He leaned in and whispered in her ear. "That name died when I did, Niki. Just like your name will die."

"Loren," she said. "Please . . ."

He took several steps back and nodded to his soldiers. They grabbed her by her arms and threw her facedown on the pavement.

"Pull down her pants," the Red Man said.

Niki felt the guards groping at her belt buckle, then at her waistband as her pants and panties came down over her hips.

She kicked and tried to bite the hands that held her down, but there were just too many of them. And when her pants were down around her ankles, the guards pressed their knees into her back and shoulders. She might as well have been nailed to the street with railroad spikes. No matter how hard she fought, she couldn't move.

The Red Man put the iron on the pavement in front of her face and she could hear the metal hissing. "Hey," he said, "I've got a confession to make. I don't really care if you tell me or not where Fisher is. You know why?"

She shook her head, unable to take her eyes off the smoking tip of the poker.

"I used to dream about fucking you. I did. I thought about it all the time. But pretty soon, I won't have to wonder what it would have been like, because I'm gonna have as much of you as I want. Here in just a bit, I'm gonna be knee-deep inside of you."

"Stop it!" she said. She hated the fear she heard in her voice, but she couldn't hold it back now, not with her pants down around her ankles.

"Tell me where Fisher is."

She shook her head. "No, I won't."

"Where are the others you were with?"

"There aren't any others. You killed the two men who came with me." She struggled against the hands that held her to the pavement.

The Red Man turned his head slightly and one of the soldiers ran forward.

"Find the others she had with her. Bring them back here alive, if you can. If not—just bring them back here."

"Yes, sir," the soldier said. He cast one last longing look at Niki Booth's bare ass and then climbed into one of the trucks.

"If you tell me where they are, I won't turn them. They'll die quickly. I promise."

Niki didn't speak.

"No? I think that's too bad, Niki. And a bit hypocritical. I remember you from school. Little Miss Homecoming Queen. Gooding County Corn Princess. You made me sick with your Meals on Wheels and your church choir. Someone who puts such a premium on life shouldn't give it away so casually."

He reached out a diseased hand and stroked her ass longingly.

"You know what I'm gonna do?" He grabbed himself by

the crotch. "I'm going to take away everything you love, Niki. And when it's all gone, I'll be there waiting for you."

The Red Man stood and walked around Niki until he was behind her. He forced her thighs apart. He got down on his hands and knees and crawled over top of her. She could feel his bare chest pressing down on her back and feel the heat of his breath at her ear.

"Remember back in the old days?" he said. "I think they used to call this a tramp stamp."

A moment later, the orange-hot poker tip was frying the skin at the small of her back, and Niki Booth's screams echoed down the lonely street as the windowless buildings and the swaying zombies silently watched.

CHAPTER 5

There was a storm coming. Richardson could smell it in the air as he and the two women watched the Red Man's soldiers moving south through the abandoned buildings. He figured they had two, maybe three hours before the rain started and he wanted to be out of this place and tucked in someplace warm and dry when the weather hit.

But there was Sylvia and this other woman here with him, and that was a problem he hadn't counted on.

"You guys know someplace we can hunker down before the rain gets here?"

Sylvia Carnes gave him a quick look, then went back to studying the street. Richardson had the feeling he'd just been dismissed. Evidently she had decided he wasn't much of a threat. Or perhaps the least of her worries. Either way, she wasn't saying anything. And as the soldiers and the zombies moved off to other lots and searched other buildings, the younger woman calmed down as well. Richardson was glad for that. He'd never had much patience for sobbing, and even less since he started wandering the roads.

Maybe too much of the old roving camera, he thought. Not enough empathy.

He smiled.

No, screw that. Empathy had led Marshal Ed Moore and the rest of the Grasslands survivors to their deaths. It wasn't going to get him too.

"Hey, you hear me?"

It was Sylvia. She was looking at him, expecting an answer.

"I . . ." he said, shaking his head.

"I said we can't stay here." She motioned for him to head toward a large section of tar paper that was hanging from the side of the roof behind him. "Over there."

"Sylvia," the younger woman said, "what are we gonna do about Niki?"

Sylvia's expression softened. If Richardson was reading her right, the tenderness in her face almost looked motherly. "Avery, listen to me," she said. "I know we have to get her back, but we have to get ourselves out of sight first, okay? We can't help her if we're dead."

"But they shot her." Even in the low light, the girl's plump face looked stricken.

Sylvia took the woman's hands in her own. "They were using riot guns, sweetie. They were trying to take her alive."

"So they could torture her."

Sylvia frowned. "We'll find her," she said. "I don't know how, but we'll find her."

She glanced at Richardson. "You ready to move out?"

Richardson nodded. He couldn't hear the trucks anymore, but there were still eight of the zombies out there, searching the apartment buildings on the east side of the street.

Sylvia pointed at two of the zombies trying to pry the plywood off an apartment window across the street. "Those are the smart ones. They'll search those buildings systematically. We need to leave here as soon as we can."

"But what about Niki?" the younger woman said.

"We'll find her, Avery. Please, just work with us here, okay? Niki let you come along because she knew you could handle the risk. I need you to be tough now. Can you do that for me?"

The girl started crying again.

Richardson looked away.

It was humid and sticky. Richardson could feel a thick, oily sweat coating the back of his neck, seeping down under his shirt. He watched Sylvia Carnes run her hands through her frizzy gray hair, trying, unsuccessfully, to press it down on the back of her head. She had tied it back into a ponytail with a black piece of cloth, but the band didn't seem up to the task. It occurred to him that she was actually quite pretty. Prettier than he remembered.

"What are you looking at?" she said to him.

"Do you remember me?" he asked. "It was a long time ago, in San Antonio."

Her expression didn't change.

"Eight years ago? You were leading a group of kids from—"

"I remember you, Mr. Richardson. I recognized you when I saw you back at the Pizza Hut."

He waited for her to say more, but she didn't.

"So, what brings you to—"

"It's a long story, Mr. Richardson. If you don't mind, I've kind of got a lot on my plate at the moment—*Oh shit!*"

Sylvia Carnes was on her feet and running from beneath the awning before Richardson could react. One of the zombies from across the street had spotted them and he was advancing on their hiding spot with a crooked, hobbling gait. But he was moving fast, grunting rather than moaning, his eyes locked on them with the keenness of a cat stalking a bug.

A rusty ventilator fan had fallen from the wall above them and was resting against a pile of bricks a short distance away. Sylvia reached the fan and scooped it up just as the zombie stepped into the brown patches of weeds on their side of the street. As the zombie closed on her, she swung the fan and caught him on the cheek with one of the blades. The man dropped to his hands and knees, but didn't cry out. He glanced back up at Sylvia. The shiny red gash on his cheek spread open as he reached for her, revealing a row of busted, bloodstained teeth. Sylvia brought the fan down on the zombie's face right as he lunged for her, sinking one of the fan blades deep into his forehead. He fell back into the weeds, dead.

Sylvia whirled on Richardson and the girl. "Run." She pointed at an eight-foot-high brick wall on the other side of the collapsed awning. "That way. Hurry it up."

Responding to the commotion, four other zombies were already crossing the street.

"Come on," Richardson said. He grabbed the girl by her upper arm and pulled her to her feet. They ran for the wall, jumped onto a pile of debris that had collected in one corner, and grabbed for the top of the wall.

Richardson heard the girl grunting as she tried to pull herself up onto the top of the wall. *She's not gonna make it*, he thought.

A moment later, she dropped. She was still holding on to the top of the wall, but just barely. She looked at him, the ligaments standing out in her neck, her expression a mixture of pain and abject fear.

"I can't," she said.

Richardson turned back to the street and saw Sylvia Carnes sprinting toward him.

"Hurry up," she yelled.

"It's okay," Richardson said to the girl. "Pull yourself up. I'll help you."

He grabbed her by the knees and pushed her up until he felt her crest the top of the wall on her own. Then he pulled himself to the top of the wall and sat facing the street just as Sylvia Carnes reached the debris pile below him.

"Let me have your hand," he said, reaching for her.

"Get out of the way," Sylvia said, and a moment later was scrambling past him and dropping down on the other side of the wall.

She landed next to the younger girl and looked up at him.

Wow, he thought. Not bad.

"You coming?" Sylvia Carnes asked.

They landed in a small, weed-choked alley. Sylvia led them to the head of the alley where they stopped and looked around. There was nothing to see but a tattered plastic bag floating down the empty street on a sluggish breeze.

"Come on," Sylvia said. She stepped into the street, turned south, and moved out at a trot.

Richardson, walking briskly alongside her, started to tell her how surprised he was to see her again after so many years, but she frowned, shook her head, and went back to scanning the surrounding buildings.

"Later," was all she said.

Richardson quieted down, focusing on his breathing. Though he was accustomed to living on his own, and doing just about anything he had to do to survive, he wasn't exactly in the best physical condition. Over the last few years he'd had to do little by way of real work. Nothing beyond a light sprint now and then. Sometimes a few whacks with the old machete. Occasionally, he had to chop wood with a hatchet, but nothing strenuous. He was about to ask Sylvia Carnes if they could stop when she turned and looked at the younger girl running along behind Richardson. The girl was not doing well. Her weight, he guessed. Her arms were jerking by her side, rather than swinging back and forth naturally, and Richardson could hear the rattling wheeze in her chest.

Sylvia stopped and waited for the girl to catch up. When she finally did, Sylvia put a hand on the girl's shoulder and asked her if she was doing okay.

The girl nodded unconvincingly.

"We should rest for a second," Richardson said.

"No," Sylvia said flatly. "We need to put some distance between us and the Red Man's people."

"That man back there in front of the Pizza Hut? Is that who you mean?"

"You see anybody else around here who paints themselves red?"

"No," Richardson said, a little stunned. "I just . . . who is he?"

"The enemy."

"Whose enemy?" Richardson asked.

Sylvia didn't answer, but she did slow her pace to accommodate the younger woman. What had she called her, Avery?

"He killed those two men you were with," Richardson said.

Sylvia Carnes had started to lead the younger woman away, but when she heard that she stopped and stared at Richardson. "You saw them die?"

Richardson nodded, remembering how he'd wanted to help and had almost stepped into the street to do it. "He killed one of them. The one in the St. Louis Cardinals hat. The other he turned, I think."

The girl let out a sharp, nasally gasp.

"Tommy," the girl groaned. "No, not Tommy."

Sylvia put an arm around the girl's shoulders and squeezed, still looking at Richardson.

"Why did he kill them?" Richardson said, when what he was really wondering was why the man would paint himself all red. "Who is he? Why is he after you?"

"Because he's one of them," Sylvia Carnes answered. "He's a zombie."

Her comment stopped him cold, but she wouldn't say more. The younger woman was still sobbing over Tommy—a boyfriend or a relative of some sort, Richardson guessed—and Sylvia was more interested in comforting her than she was in filling in the backstory for Richardson.

"He's going to kill Niki," the girl said. "Just like Tommy, and Steve. What are we going to do?"

"I don't think he's going to kill her, Avery. He knows how important she is. She's worth a lot more to him alive than she is dead. Or as one of his zombies."

"So what are we going to do?"

"Niki told me what to do. She said no matter what for us to go to Chester. She said she would catch up with us there."

"But how is she gonna do that?" Avery said.

Sylvia drew in a breath, measuring her response. "I . . . I don't know, Avery."

"Shouldn't we go after her?"

"I don't know," Sylvia said.

"Can't we get somebody to help us?"

"I don't know, baby."

She pulled the girl close to her and smoothed the hair on the back of her head. The girl sank into Sylvia's chest, her wide, rounded shoulders hitching now and then with a sob.

Sobbing women made him feel helpless and oafish, so he

did the only thing he knew how to do. Richardson took off his backpack and unzipped the main flap. Digging past his poncho he found a plastic water bottle and removed it.

"Sylvia," he said, and motioned toward the girl with the bottle. "Does she want some of this?"

Sylvia Carnes looked at the bottle, and then to him, and the hard edge in her features softened a bit.

"Thank you," she said, and took the bottle and offered some to the girl.

Avery drank it eagerly.

When she was done, she wiped the moisture from her lips and handed the bottle back to Richardson. He took the bottle from her without comment, then offered some to Sylvia.

They definitely didn't come prepared for this, Richardson thought as he watched Sylvia drink. She had her eyes closed, savoring the taste of the water. He was about to ask her what they were doing out here when she opened her eyes and extended the bottle to him.

"We need to get going," Sylvia said.

"Uh, okay," Richardson said.

He took the bottle and screwed on the cap. Sylvia and Avery started walking while he slid the bottle back into his pack and zipped it up.

And then he stopped, and listened. A faint rustling, like rubble shifting underfoot. He scanned the surrounding buildings, looking for signs of movement, and saw only a vast, empty city.

"Hey," Sylvia called back to him. "You coming?"

"Yeah," he said. He took one last look at the empty street. "Yeah, on my way."

They walked south, and soon fell into a marching order, with Sylvia and Richardson out front, and the younger woman trailing along about ten feet behind them. Richardson tried to make room for the girl next to them, but she seemed to prefer to be by herself. Richardson let her be.

They stayed on Florissant Street wherever they could. Occasionally, they'd hear one of the infected chasing after a rat or a dog and they would hide, but the infected down here didn't seem to move as packs, and so they were easy to avoid. Gradually, the feeling they were being followed began to fade.

"I think if we keep at this pace we can reach some of the open farmland south of town by nightfall," Sylvia said. "The Red Man's troops will be searching the area north of here for us for the rest of the day. When they don't find us, they'll head back to their home base."

Richardson was suddenly interested. "Where is that?"

"About a hundred and fifty miles south of Herculaneum. The Kirkman Hyatt Hotel and Convention Center."

"And you're sure he'll go there? He won't stay around here and try to hunt us?"

"We're not his priority. Niki Booth is."

"That's the woman you were with?"

Sylvia nodded. "We're not out of the woods yet. We need to stay off his radar for the next day or so. After that, we'll be able to move around a little easier."

Richardson shook his head. There were a thousand questions he wanted to ask her, but he kept coming back to what she said about the Red Man. "You said he was a zombie. What does that mean?"

"What do you think it means? He's a zombie. He's infected."

"I know what a zombie is, Sylvia," Richardson said.

"So then what's your question?"

He bristled at her tone. Eight years had passed but Sylvia

Carnes was still the same old bitch. Everything out of her mouth was just plain wrong.

Richardson forced himself to smile. "How is it possible?" he said. "That's what I want to know. I watched him walking around. He limped, but he was as coordinated as any of us. And he talked. Zombies don't talk. They don't think. That guy—he may be crazy, but he was capable of carrying on a conversation. I heard him."

"That's true."

"So how is it possible? It's not."

"You saw him control those other zombies."

"I don't know what I saw," he said. "But it couldn't have been him controlling those zombies."

"They didn't attack him, did they? They didn't attack his black shirts. If not him controlling them, what exactly do you think you saw?"

"No," he said, shaking his head. He huffed, but it came out a laugh. "No, Sylvia, we're not gonna go over this again."

"Go over what, exactly?"

"We're not gonna do San Antonio all over again. I've seen Stage III zombies, Sylvia. I know they can use Stage I zombies as tools. But that's not what I saw back there. You keep wanting to ascribe abilities to zombies that they just don't possess. Their brains are gone, Sylvia. For all intents and purposes, they're dead. And they aren't coming back."

"You're an idiot," she said.

"Calling me names doesn't prove your point, Sylvia. Tell me how he controls the zombies. You can't, can you?"

"He controls them because he's a zombie, just like they are."

"But what's the mechanism? There has to be a mechanism. You see that, right? If he's controlling them, how does he do it?"

She looked mad. Her eyes were drilling holes in him, but he didn't look away. Damn it, he'd forgotten how much fun it was to fight. He was actually enjoying himself.

"I don't know," she finally said. "I don't."

They had arrived at an intersection. Sylvia stopped beneath a faded yellow traffic light and looked left, then right. There was a park to their right that stretched south several blocks. It was overgrown with weeds, the tall grass swaying in the wind. Richardson breathed deep and could smell the approaching rain and the musty vegetable rot of river scent.

And something else, too. Something unpleasant. The sour-sweet stench of decayed flesh.

Once again that feeling that they were being followed sent a sweaty chill down his back. But there was nothing moving out there amid the wrecked buildings and abandoned cars.

Sylvia wiped the sweat from her forehead, then retied the black ribbon that held her ponytail in place. Her hair was wiry as a bird's nest.

A part of Richardson wanted to engage again. He had her on the ropes and it wasn't his nature to stop when he got under an opponent's defenses. But the feeling that they were being followed had sapped some of the flavor out of the fight. He held his peace.

"I don't like the looks of that," she said, pointing toward the park. "Better veer left, toward the river. We'll be going through more buildings, but that'll also give us more places to hide if we need it."

"Okay," Richardson said, though he got the distinct impression that she wasn't asking for his advice. "Where are you planning on going?"

"The free trade market down in Herculaneum," she said.

"That's where I was planning on going, too."

She looked at him, but said nothing. She turned to Avery. "You okay?"

"I'm fine," Avery said, though it wasn't a convincing act. Her face was flush. There were sweat stains all down the front of her baggy shirt.

They moved out again, this time at a walk, and entered a wider section of the street. Richardson had the distinct impression that they had crossed some kind of cultural or economic dividing line in the old city's demographics. The red brick buildings were fewer and farther between. He saw more and more banks, modern two-story houses that had originally been painted white but were now peeling and faded, and here and there a dry cleaners and a grocery store and a theater. There were also lots of wrecked cars, most of which had been cannibalized for parts or destroyed by fire. But luckily, no zombies.

"I remember what you told me when you asked permission to come along with my group in San Antonio," Sylvia said. "You said you were trying to write the definitive history on the zombie outbreak."

Richardson remembered the conversation well. It had taken place in her office at the University of Texas in Austin. Her office was a small room in Parlin Hall with a window overlooking a wooded courtyard, and beyond that, Guadalupe Street, known affectionately on campus as "the Drag." The walls were one continuous bookshelf, each shelf sagging beneath dusty rows of novels. She had been a moderately attractive middle-aged woman then, maybe a little plump, a little pale for his taste, but smart.

He'd sat in the one chair in the room that wasn't mounded with books. On the desk between them was the court order signed by Justice Allen Woods. The order allowed her to take forty college kids who didn't know the first thing about the risks involved inside the quarantine wall around San Antonio.

Back then, before anybody really had any idea at all about what was going on with the infected, there were strong feelings on both sides about the proper way to handle the problem. Most of America wanted to eliminate the infected by any means necessary. Dr. Carnes, and a few very vocal people like her, disagreed. The infected were victims of a plague, she said. We wouldn't be talking about wholesale murder if this was a flu outbreak, or rabies, or anything else.

"But you're leading them into a meat grinder," he said to her.

"I disagree. All my students are dedicated members of the People for an Ethical Solution. They have made informed choices. They believe, as I do, that the infected are still human, and therefore have the same rights and expectations that any human being has in an enlightened society. This trip will show that we don't need to be afraid of them. This trip will show the U.S. government that the time has come to send in researchers to try to combat this outbreak."

"Sounds like you rehearsed that."

She simply stared at him.

"Your students are just kids," Richardson went on. "How can they make informed choices?"

"Each member of my group is over twenty-one. They're legally adults, capable of making their own choices."

Richardson choked down his objection. He'd never met a twenty-one-year-old kid responsible enough to shop for groceries by himself, much less make an informed choice on an issue where the stakes involved life and death. But he knew it wouldn't do any good to tell Dr. Sylvia Carnes that. She was a zealot, and arguing with a zealot did about as much good as pounding your head against a wall.

"You think this is a mistake, don't you, Mr. Richardson?"

He shrugged. "I thought I'd been pretty clear on that point, yes. I think you're going to get those kids killed. I think we'll probably all get killed."

"And yet you're still going?"

Richardson smiled. "I wouldn't miss it."

"Why? You know why I'm doing it. Why are you doing it?"

He just went on smiling. "Because Simon & Schuster asked me to write the definitive history of the zombie outbreak. And because they backed a dump truck full of money up to my door."

But it wasn't the real answer, and both of them knew it.

Now here he was, eight years later, and the world was a completely different place. Everything had changed. Off in the rubble to his left he saw a zombie trying to wade its way through the debris, but it was no threat. Its injuries were too severe for it to do anything but fall over. It couldn't even moan. It was, in many ways, a lot like the world it haunted.

"Did you ever write your book?" Sylvia asked.

The question surprised him, and he wasn't really sure how to answer her. "I never really stopped," he finally said. "These last few years, I've been wandering the country, talking to survivors, building up a library of stories. That's what has kept me alive." He laughed, an unpleasant sound with a note of bitterness beneath it. "It's given me a reason to get up each morning."

She was quiet for a moment.

"That zombie you were just looking at," she said, gesturing with her chin toward the building on Richardson's left.

"Yeah?"

"That's a Stage I. If I had to guess I'd say he got turned sometime this summer, maybe even a few weeks ago. You know the difference between a Stage I, II, and III zombie, right?"

He nodded.

She started walking, and Richardson and the girl fell in with her. "Then you know how they are nearly back to where they were before they were infected. Mentally, I mean. They are capable of extremely complex actions, such as—"

Richardson frowned. "Now hold on for a second. I don't think I buy that at all. Perhaps they regain some limited cognitive faculties, but to say they—"

"Such as manipulate other zombies," Sylvia interrupted. "Use strategy to hunt prey. You even mentioned that one yourself. If you ask me, it sounds an awful lot like near-full use of cognitive faculties. But have you ever wondered what comes next?"

"After what? You mean, after Stage III?"

She nodded.

Richardson's mind didn't want to take in the possibility. "Are saying the Red Man is . . . what, a Stage IV zombie?"

She touched the tip of her nose.

"That's . . ."

Richardson wanted to say that it was impossible, but it did make a weird kind of sense. Was that really the next step?

"Oh my God," he said.

Sylvia nodded. "Yeah, well, the zombies sure seem to think so."

Chapter 6

By late afternoon the rich, muddy smell of the river was thick in the air. The sky above them was churning with storm clouds and Richardson could see lightning off to the east. He hadn't eaten since before daybreak and he was about to recommend they stop when Sylvia did it for him.

"What do you think?" she said to Avery.

Sylvia was pointing at a small, two-story office building with an upstairs balcony that looked like it might afford a pretty good view of the street. Her hair had once again worked itself loose from her ponytail so that now it resembled the ball moss that hung from the pecan trees down by the river, but otherwise she looked as solid as ever. Richardson imagined she could walk all night if she had to.

By contrast, Avery looked even worse than Richardson felt. Why in the world did they bring her along, he wondered, and not for the first time. Niki Booth, the other woman they'd had with them, had handled herself pretty well against the Red Man's troops. And Sylvia was no slouch herself. But this girl was about to fall apart.

And then she surprised him.

"There's no outside staircase," she said. "That's good. And it's small enough that there's probably only one on the inside. It shouldn't be too difficult to secure."

"I agree," Sylvia said. She scanned the sky. The wind was out of the east and carried the smell of mud and humus and wood smoke over them. "Rain's coming this way. If we set up a water trap on the balcony we should be able to get as much drinking water as we need."

But Richardson wasn't watching the building. He had turned to the old fire station across the street. Its red brick front, with its dark, empty windows, was absolutely still. And yet he was certain he had heard something.

"Something wrong?" Sylvia asked.

"Huh?" He turned toward her. "Did you hear something?"

Both women stopped and listened. The street was absolutely silent for a few moments, and Sylvia slowly shook her head.

"Nothing," she said. She looked to Avery, who also shook her head.

"Let's just hurry up," he said.

They went inside and looked around. Like every other building they'd seen, most of the windows were busted out. Rainwater had entered the building, and in places had mixed with fallen ceiling tiles to form a muddy gray sludge on the floor. The wallpaper had blistered, and in a few places it sagged to the floor in loose scrolls. But overall the building looked to be in pretty good shape. It would certainly do for an overnight shelter.

Avery Harper was right about there only being one interior staircase. They used furniture from the offices to block it off, making it all but impassable to any zombie that might happen to find his way in during the night. That done, they retreated upstairs and Richardson cleared out spaces for them to sleep while the women went out on the balcony and set up the water trap in case it rained.

When they came back inside Richardson was unloading his backpack. He removed two cans of pork and beans, a small wire rack he'd made from a coat hanger, and a can of Sterno.

"You guys hungry?" he asked, lighting the Sterno.

"God, yes," Avery said.

Sylvia nodded, her eyes on the open can of pork and beans.

"Have a seat," Richardson said, as he arranged the wire rack over the can of Sterno. "This thing's only big enough for one can at a time. Takes about five minutes."

"Five minutes is just fine," Sylvia said. "I thought it was going to be beef jerky again tonight."

"You have beef jerky?"

She reached under her shirt and removed a belly band. Inside the band were several sheets of dried beef wrapped in cellophane. "Road food," Sylvia said.

"I've got a can of green beans. If you want to save it, we can have the beans and the jerky for breakfast."

"Deal," she said.

"Mr. Richardson?" Avery said. She was looking over the things he'd removed from his backpack. "What is all this stuff?"

"Just supplies. Things I've picked up over the years."

But it was quite an assortment, honed from years of living on the road: extra socks; canteen; water purification tablets; matches; compass; small LED flashlight; waterproof poncho; a large tarp he'd made from an Army surplus Gilley suit; signaling mirror; bedroll and blanket; a fifty-foot length of nylon rope; a slim collection of Wordsworth's poems he'd found in a small-town library in Nebraska; first-aid kit; Swiss

Army knife; binoculars; ammo and cleaning kit for the rifle he'd lost earlier that morning; jacket; BDU pants; a T-shirt; long underwear.

"Living on the road," he said, "you never know what you're going to need."

She examined the gear with obvious fascination, and it occurred to him that she had never spent more than a few nights away from her compound, wherever that was.

Then she picked up his iPad and said, "What's this?"

"It's an iPad," he said. "It was state of the art back before the outbreak. I found it in a computer store in Seattle, Washington, about five years ago."

"What do you use it for?"

"I store my interviews on it."

"Interviews? Of who?"

"Anybody. People I meet."

"What do you interview them for?"

"To get their stories," he said. "It's what I do."

"Mr. Richardson was a reporter before the outbreak, Avery," Sylvia said. "That's how we met. He was writing a book about it."

"That's right," Richardson said. "But call me Ben, please. I mean, if that's not too weird for you."

Sylvia took a long time to consider it. "I guess that'd be okay," she said finally. "You did kind of get us out of a bad spot today. Yeah, I guess that'd be okay."

Richardson wrapped a rag around the beans and took them off the heat. Then he got a spoon from his pack and handed it to Avery. "You too," he said to her. "Call me Ben, okay?"

Avery took the can and spoon from him and ate a spoonful with her eyes closed. She savored it for a long time. When she opened her eyes she smiled apologetically. "That's really good," she said.

"There's more," Richardson said. "Help yourself."

Avery looked at Sylvia, who nodded. Then she helped herself to two more spoonfuls and passed the can to Richardson.

"How many interviews have you collected?" she asked him.

"I don't know," he said. "Six or seven hundred maybe."

"Really?"

"Yeah. Here, I'll show you."

He took a battered trash can from the corner and upended it and set the iPad on it like a picture frame. "This should pick up all three of us," he said.

"You want to interview me?" Avery asked.

"Sure. If that's okay."

She looked uncertain, and nervous. She kept touching her hair. "What do I do?"

"Just talk," Richardson said. "Tell me about yourself. Who you are? What you guys are doing? What you plan on doing in the future? Anything, really."

"Is it running now?"

Richardson nodded. Avery's cheeks colored slightly. She ducked her head and fiddled with her blond hair. She swallowed a few times, then looked at Sylvia Carnes. From the expression on her face it looked like she was asking for permission.

"Go ahead," Sylvia said. "I think it's alright. We can trust him."

"Okay," Avery said. She fingered her hair back from her ears and looked at the iPad. "How do I start?"

"Tell me your name," Richardson said.

"Avery Harper."

"How old are you, Avery?"

"Twenty."

"So you would have been how old when the outbreak happened?"

"I was twelve when Hurricane Mardell hit. I was living with my dad in Houston at the time."

Richardson handed the can of pork and beans to Sylvia. "You were in Houston during the storm?"

"No, we evacuated to Dallas before the storm. We were with some of his friends when all the fighting started. After that, Dad said we couldn't go back."

"Where did you go?"

"To live with my cousin, Niki Booth."

"That's the young woman we saw earlier today? The one with the short brown hair?"

Avery's smile faded. "That's right. Her dad was a doctor in Gooding, Illinois. It's this tiny little town on the other side of the river, about a hundred miles from here."

"So you were twelve, and making this big change. What was it like there?"

"Well, at first it was scary, you know? I didn't have any friends. I was in a new school. I had Niki, but she was just back from college and I was just a kid, so it wasn't like we hung out or anything. But then, after a while, I got used to it. Living in a small town is actually kind of boring, you know?"

"I know," Richardson said, and laughed. "I grew up in Port Arthur, Texas, birthplace of Janis Joplin."

"Who's Janis Joplin?"

"It's not important," he said, trading a sly smile with Sylvia. "So you and Niki eventually left Gooding, right? How did that happen?"

"Like I said, Gooding was kind of boring. There were a lot of drugs and stuff like that. Niki used to tell me all the cute guys had gone off to the military and the ones who didn't were too busy doing meth. The town was pretty much dying when the quarantine wall fell. People had been moving away for a while, but after the wall came down, things pretty much went to hell, you know? We both lost our parents during that second wave. I was lucky I had Niki. Without her, I would have died too. Probably a bunch of times."

"I'm sorry about your parents," Richardson said. He scanned the girl's face, but the memory didn't seem to cause her any obvious pain, so he pressed on. "What did you guys do after you lost them?"

"We lived on the road."

"What did you do?"

"Nothing. Just sort of wandered, you know?"

Richardson smiled. "Yes," he said. "I know wandering very well indeed."

Avery didn't look like she knew how to respond to that. "Before the outbreak, Niki was just a normal girl, you know? But afterwards . . ."

She shivered.

"What, Avery? What happened while you guys were on the road?"

"Niki changed. I mean, she loved me. I think she loved me more after her dad died than she ever did while he was alive, but after he died she turned . . . I don't know, dangerous. I've seen her do things to people that . . ." She trailed off, shaking her head, as though to push unpleasant memories down.

"Survival is a rough business," Richardson said. "And if she was looking out for a twelve-year-old girl . . ." He shrugged.

Avery said nothing.

"But you're not still living on the road, are you? You found Sylvia here, right?"

She nodded.

"Mr. Stoler was forming his compound just north of St.

Louis about that time. We used to see patrols from Union Field scavenging around the river."

"Union Field? That's the name of the compound where you guys have been living?"

Avery nodded. "Mr. Stoler was just starting to get control over the area. His patrols were all over the place, but they were sloppy. Most of them were just regular people playing at being soldiers. I remember when Niki would come back after a day of scavenging to wherever we were hiding out at the time. She would make fun of them. Sometimes she'd steal their supplies. She fought them a couple of times, but it was never a big deal to her. To her, it was just a game. At least at first."

"So what changed?" Richardson asked.

"I got real sick. My appendix. It hurt real bad. Niki didn't know what else to do, so she brought me to Ken Stoler's compound. That's where we met Sylvia."

"Wait a minute," he said. "You said Ken Stoler. You don't mean the same Ken Stoler from San Antonio, do you? The one Eddie Hudson mentions in his book?"

Sylvia laughed. "If you ever meet him, Ben, do yourself a favor and don't mention Eddie Hudson. Not a good subject with him."

"Yeah, I bet," Richardson said. "God, I'd love to meet him."

During the interview, Avery seemed to grow comfortable. She looked at ease. The flame from the Sterno gave her plump face a pleasant glow. And when she smiled, her teeth were white and straight and healthy. But the smile drained away from her face as soon as Richardson mentioned meeting Ken Stoler. He could see her body stiffen beneath her baggy clothes.

"Did I say something wrong?" he asked.

Avery swallowed several times, very fast, but wouldn't

meet Richardson's gaze. He looked from the girl to Sylvia. Sylvia looked back at him, and she seemed to be taking his measure, as though she was wondering just how far she could trust him.

Finally, she looked at Avery. "Go ahead. It's okay."

Avery said nothing.

"Avery, honey, it's okay. We're going to have to trust somebody. We can't help Niki on our own." Sylvia studied Richardson for a long moment. Then she said, "It didn't take very long for Niki to completely redo the way Union Field sent out patrols. Niki organized our defenses, trained our people. She turned a bunch of clueless survivors into a fairly professional fighting force. She and Ken Stoler were very close."

"Were?" Richardson asked.

Avery nodded. "Before the Red Man came."

"Tell me about that," Richardson said. "What's his story?"

"There used to be five other compounds just south of Union Field," Avery said. "We used to trade with them fairly regular. We knew each other. Then the Red Man came with his zombies and his black shirts and one by one they took over the compounds."

"When did this happen?"

"The first one was Wagner-Green. It fell about a year and a half ago. After that it was Las Cruces, then the Wilhelm-Crowder compound, then Mud Flats. Niki and some of the men from the Calimar compound managed to push the Red Man back into St. Louis. For a while, we all thought he'd given up, but then he went after Calimar. Niki was there right afterwards. She told me it was . . . awful."

"And Calimar, that was . . . when?"

"About two months ago."

Sylvia put a hand on Avery's arm. To Richardson, she said, "Niki and Stoler got into a really bad fight after that."

"About what?"

"Ben, you don't understand. When the Red Man takes over a compound, he's usually after people. If they'll join him voluntarily they can become one of his black shirts. If not . . ."

"They get turned?"

"Most of the time." She frowned. "But he didn't do that at Calimar. He was furious about losing to them at St. Louis. I saw the pictures Niki and his patrols took of what they found at Calimar. Ben, he didn't even try to take prisoners. He slaughtered them all."

Richardson was quiet, waiting for her to go on. Lightning flashed outside, followed by a deep, bellowing roll of thunder.

"After Calimar, Ken wanted Niki to take the fight to the Red Man. He thought if they beat the Red Man once, they could do it again."

"But Niki didn't agree?"

Sylvia shook her head. "She said that would be suicide. She said the Red Man would just keep her busy in the field while the rest of his troops did to Union Field what they did to Calimar."

"So she wanted to fight a defensive war?"

Sylvia and Avery smiled at each other. "No," Sylvia said. "Niki wouldn't even consider fighting a defensive war."

"So . . . what then?"

"Niki was looking for a cure."

Richardson stared at them, a half smile on his face. "You're joking?"

"No, Ben, I'm not. She was pretty sure she found one, too. That's why we left Union Field. That's what we're doing out here."

Richardson shook his head in dismay. "Sylvia, that's absolutely ridiculous. I have been all over this country. I've even been into Mexico a few times. People everywhere talk about finding a cure. It's like some kind of fairy tale."

"That's what Stoler said."

Richardson laughed. "Huh, what do you know? I never thought I'd agree with that idiot on anything."

"It's real, Ben. Niki believed in it."

"Yeah, so much that she turned her back on however many people you've got back at Union Field. She's your best fighter, and she went off hunting red herrings when her people needed her most. No wonder Ken Stoler is pissed."

Sylvia's eyes narrowed. "Don't talk about things you don't understand, Ben."

"I understand things just fine, Sylvia. I understand that there's no such thing as a cure to the necrosis filovirus. The only cure for a zombie is a bullet in the brain."

"Now you really sound like Stoler."

"Yeah? Well, it sounds like he finally came to his senses, if you ask me."

"That's the difference between us, Ben. You never did believe."

"And you were always a dreamer, Sylvia."

She slapped her palm down on the floor, kicking up a thin cloud of dust. "You don't mean to tell me, after everything you've seen today, that you still believe these people can't be saved. I would think this, finally, would convince you."

"What do you mean, after what I saw today? Were we watching the same thing? Because what I saw was some guy who fed a living person to a huddle of zombies, and then deliberately infected another man. That doesn't sound like somebody in need of saving. What I saw was a man in need of being cut up into little bits and buried beneath a ton of lime."

"He's insane, Ben. I'll give you that. But he is regaining his sense of self. He is living proof that the disease isn't permanent. That's there hope."

"Hope? Sense of self? Sylvia, I didn't think it was possible, but you might actually have gotten crazier since San Antonio."

"Crazier?" She pulled her hair and made a noise that, to Richardson at least, sounded a lot like a growl. "What do you think is going on out there, Ben? The Red Man is proof that this disease can be dealt with. You've seen him with his troops. Surely even you can see that he's capable of working with uninfected people to achieve a common goal. That's all we want. We want to coexist until a cure can be found."

"That's not gonna happen, Sylvia. Look around you. There's nothing left. We have one chance to survive, and it doesn't involve subjugating ourselves to some freak of evolution."

"Freak of evolution?" Sylvia scoffed at him. "That's nice, Ben. Is that really what you think this is? How can you study so much about this disease and still be so ignorant? I have tried to—"

"Don't call me ignorant. I'm not the—"

"Stop it, both of you!" It was Avery. She had her hands cupped over her ears, a gesture that reminded Richardson of a child cowering in a closet, trying to shut out the noise of the screaming his parents made while they fought. Looking at her, he saw himself a long, long time ago, frightened, alone, feeling small in the face of a very large and very unfriendly world. "Please," she said again. "Don't yell anymore."

Sylvia crawled across the floor on her knees to the girl and hugged her. Richardson watched her go. His blood was up and he still wanted to hash it out with Sylvia. It was just like San Antonio all over again. The only difference was that it had taken them a whole day together before they were at each other's throats. He wondered if that was a good sign.

He also found himself wondering about the curious dynamic between the two women. The girl clearly looked up to Sylvia like some kind of mother figure. But why would she lean on her the way she does, he wondered. She's twenty years old. Living in the world she lives in, she should be stronger than that, more independent.

Sylvia stroked the girl's blond hair. She looked at Richardson and motioned to the iPad with her chin. "Can you turn that thing off?"

"Sure." Richardson tapped the STOP button at the bottom of the screen.

"Avery," Sylvia said, "Do you want to rest?"

The girl nodded without speaking. Richardson handed her the coat from his pack and Sylvia rolled it up as a pillow for Avery.

Within moments she was asleep.

"Let's step outside," Sylvia whispered.

They went out to the balcony and watched the advance winds of the storm blow trash and dust down the street below. The river was a thick dark line in the near distance, and they could smell it on the wind. Somewhere behind them they could hear a dog barking, very faintly, but otherwise it was quiet. That was one thing about this world that Richardson liked. It was always quiet.

Sylvia turned to face him, her frizzled hair rustling against her cheek. He didn't like the strange look on her face, as though she were about to gloat.

"What is it?" he asked.

"The cure is real, Ben."

"Oh come on, Sylvia. You've already tried this one on me. There isn't going to be any cure because there isn't anyone to—"

"Ben, there *is* a cure. It's already been found."

The smirk on his face remained for a few moments before he blinked at her. Then it faded. "You're serious, aren't you?"

"Absolutely."

She wasn't smiling anymore. Her light blue eyes flashed in the darkness, and he could tell how excited she was.

"But . . . how? Where is it?"

"That's what we're doing here, Ben. We're going to see the man who's working on the cure. His name is Dr. Don Fisher. He's immune, Ben. Or, at least mostly. Niki heard about him through her foraging parties. He was bitten more than four years ago, and he hasn't turned. It crippled him, but it didn't turn him. He's been working on a cure ever since. This is it. We think he's finally found it."

Richardson was shaking his head. "But you haven't spoken to him? I mean, how do you know this is the real deal?"

"It is, Ben. We just have to find him. Niki's foraging parties made the arrangements. We were supposed to go to Herculaneum tomorrow and meet a man from Union Field who's agreed to help us. He's got AR-15s like the ones we have. Niki told me to trade those weapons for passage on a trawler down to Chester. We're supposed to meet Fisher there on Tuesday of next week."

"That's . . ." He trailed off. He had no idea what to say. To him, the whole thing sounded insane, but, at the same time, if it was real . . . the possibilities were endless.

He shook his head. Crazy.

"But the Red Man has Niki now. Don't you think that changes your plans?"

She shrugged. "I trust in Niki Booth, Ben. I trust in her like nobody I've ever met. If you knew her like I do, you would too. The Red Man won't get anything out of her."

A few light raindrops splattered on his hands and face.

The next instant the rain swept over them, and they moved inside the building. Sylvia looked down at Avery, who had curled up in the fetal position and was cradling Richardson's jacket like it was a child's teddy bear. She was sleeping soundly.

Sylvia turned to face him. And when she spoke again, she was whispering. "I know you don't believe in this, but we're going to do it. We're going to bring back a cure. This is too important to fail."

CHAPTER 7

The next morning Richardson woke before dawn and dressed by candlelight. The floor creaked as he walked toward the patio door. Sylvia rolled over, murmuring thickly, but didn't wake. Avery was curled in a ball next to her, sleeping soundly. Richardson waited for a moment, letting Sylvia settle, then went outside.

The storm had passed during the night, leaving a clean, earthy smell on the air. There was a light breeze and the early morning chill felt good against his skin. During the night the rain trap they'd set out had collected almost a gallon of fresh water. It wouldn't be enough to bathe with, which a quick sniff had told him he sorely needed, but at least they wouldn't be leaving here with dry throats. It wasn't all bad, he guessed.

But a rude squawk made him freeze. He'd been kneeling next to the rain trap, but when he heard the bird sounds, he closed his eyes and steeled himself against the horror he knew was waiting for him.

He opened his eyes.

The crows were back, staring at him. There were hundreds of them. They sat on the patio railing, on the light poles and wires, on the edges of roofs, on derelict cars and in trees and on signs, hundreds, thousands of eyes turned on him in silent judgment.

He stared back at them, trembling. He remembered what it was like when he came back to the Paradise compound six years earlier to find everyone he cared about getting fed upon by crows. Remembered the sight of all those people, twelve hundred in all, getting picked clean to the bone by birds that squawked and fought over the scraps.

You won't get me, you carrion birds, he thought. You missed me when you came for my friends in Montana, and you won't get me now. You ate the people I loved most in this world, but you didn't eat my heart. That you won't ever have.

Though even now the memory of all those carrion birds, black as soot, glassy-eyed and squawking furiously at each other, made him cower in fear. Richardson and a few others had gone down to California to get seeds for the coming spring. They were gone four months. When he left, Ed Moore and the blind girl Kyra Talbot and Billy Kline and Jeff Stavers and all the others were alive and well, arguing about whether or not to open the compound to the hundreds of refugees coming north because they had heard of the wonderful things Ed Moore was doing in Paradise Valley. Billy had warned refugees would bring diseases, but Ed had overruled him. Fate had proven Billy right. Richardson never figured out what had done the killing. Bubonic plague? Cholera? Yellow fever? Anything was possible. But when he was standing there in the middle of the compound, snow swirling around his feet, he remembered thinking that causes didn't matter, not when everyone you loved was dead. How he had loved those people. He and Robin Tharp and a few others from the original Grasslands group had walked from body to body, shooing away angry birds and trying to figure out who was who, but all Richardson could think about was how much love had just gone out of the world.

"Ben?" Sylvia said from behind him. "You okay?"

Richardson stiffened, wiped his eyes with the back of his hand.

"Fine," he said, without turning around. "You guys about ready to leave?"

"Just about. How much water did we get last night?"

He turned, sniffled, and handed her the trap. "Looks like about a gallon."

She took it from him. She looked at him curiously, watching his eyes. "Thanks," she said. "You want to have that breakfast now? Green beans and beef jerky?"

He nodded, grateful she had the good grace to leave his grief alone.

Later, when they were packed and ready, Richardson dangled his rope over the balcony. They scaled down to ground level and he pulled the rope down after them and stowed it in his backpack. Then they set out, walking through the darkened ruins without speaking, their feet sloshing in the muddy puddles left by the rain.

The ruins seemed deserted, as Richardson expected them to be. Most of the infected, he knew from long experience, preferred to hunt in the daytime. Walking under cover of early morning darkness, they hoped to get out of the city proper by dawn.

They got on Interstate Highway 55 and followed it all the way to the southern edge of town without seeing anything. There weren't even any rats scurrying around. Even still, Richardson couldn't shake the feeling that something was watching them. He kept stopping, and turning, scanning the road behind them.

Once, it took him so long to start back up that Sylvia and Avery had to double back to him.

"What is it?" Sylvia asked.

Richardson strained his senses against the darkness. He heard the dull drone of cicadas in the overgrown fields on either side of the highway. The chatter of birds. The wind whistling through the holes in buildings. And something else. A wet, rattling sound. Like a man struggling to breathe through lungs nearly flooded with phlegm.

"We're being followed," he said.

She scanned the road behind them, and then the buildings off to the west. "Yeah, I think you may be right."

Richardson glanced east. Daylight was overtaking them. Already he could see reds and oranges spilling over the horizon. Up and down the highway, the ghostly shapes of long-abandoned cars waited silently for nothing.

"I don't like this," Sylvia said. "We're too easy to spot out here."

"It can't be the Red Man, can it? Following us, I mean. If he had us in sight, wouldn't he just overtake us with his trucks?"

"I would think so," Sylvia said.

"Could it be Ken Stoler?"

She grimaced. "God, I hope not."

They passed a ruined movie theater on their left and Richardson slowed to look at it without even realizing what he was doing. Abandoned buildings like this fascinated him. Pulled him in. Even before the outbreak places like this had held a special fascination for him. Now, they were everywhere. Like this theater. Grass had grown up in the parking lot. There were a few cars abandoned there, but they had been stripped and a few had been burned. He could see skeins of metal wire encircling the wheels where the tires had melted. Beyond, the building was a mess. Gone were the windows and the glass front doors, all of them smashed. The lobby was a black maw that resembled the entrance to a cave. They had been showing *Duma Key* when the outbreak swept through here, but the D was missing now.

"What is it?" Sylvia asked. "You hear something?"

"No, just looking."

"At what? The movie theater?"

He nodded.

"Do you miss it?"

"Hmm? Miss what?"

"You know, the world. Going to the movies? Tater tots from Sonic. A McRib at McDonald's? Concerts, picnics in the park, going to the bookstore, catching a favorite song on the radio?"

"And paying bills and traffic jams and politicians?" he said, smirking at her.

She had seemed playful when she brought up the topic, but her smile slowly dried up. "I guess not."

"No," he said, suddenly turning serious. "I'm not being fair, Sylvia. I do miss it. Sometimes. Every once in a while, I dream about how good things used to be. Do you do that?"

She didn't answer, but he could tell by her expression that he'd touched a nerve.

He went back to looking at the movie theater, and for a second, he almost told her about a piece he'd written comparing zombies to abandoned buildings. Thinking about it now, there was actually something to it. Both, after all, were crippled wrecks somehow still on their feet. But beyond that, both were single serving–sized doses of the apocalypse. Both existed in a sort of temporal neverland, so that you could see their present reality, that of the wreck, but also hints of what they once were and the potential of what they could be in the future, all three realities existing at the same time, overlapping each other.

But he knew where the conversation would lead. Where Richardson saw the zombie as a dead end, a being whose only future was a long, slow trek into the grave, Sylvia saw a cause, a soul to be reborn. She was a dreamer; he was a realist. What could possibly come of that but another fight? Yesterday, he'd have been up for it, but today, he was too tired. And from her expression, so was she.

"You still looking at that thing?" Sylvia asked.

"It's hard to look away," he admitted.

"I thought you were collecting stories of people, not buildings."

"I am."

Sylvia considered the movie theater for a long moment. Then she said, "But there's no passion in it, Ben. Last night, when you were telling us about what you've been doing, all the interviews you gathered, you sounded tired. You sounded like you were on autopilot. But I look at you now, the way you're looking at that thing, and I see your eyes on fire. There's passion there."

He started to answer, and then realized he couldn't figure out if she'd actually asked a question.

"You know what I think?" Sylvia asked.

"What?"

"I think you've been reading too much Wordsworth."

He hadn't expected that, and the smile that came to his face was cracked.

And, as though she possessed some kind of rudimentary mind-reading skills, she said, "I saw that copy of the *Lyrical Ballads* in your backpack last night. Let me guess, 'Tintern Abbey.' "

He shrugged. "Guilty as charged."

Sylvia turned away from the building to where Avery Harper was sitting on the tailgate of a rusting pickup truck, her feet dangling in the air like a little kid sitting in a big chair. The girl looked very hot and very tired. Her chin was resting on her chest and she looked like she was having trouble catching her breath.

"Avery, honey, you okay?" Sylvia called.

The girl looked up. "Don't mind me," she said. "Just resting."

"Okay, go ahead and get ready to move out, okay? We'll be leaving in a few."

The girl waved a halfhearted acknowledgment.

Then Sylvia lowered her voice so that only Richardson could hear. "Ben, you want some advice?"

His cracked smile grew wider. "You're offering me advice? I can't wait to hear this."

"I'm serious, Ben."

He waited.

"Put away the Wordsworth. Read some Whitman instead."

He let out a disappointed huff of air. "That's your advice? Sylvia, you should know this about me. I despise Whitman. He was great at first lines, but piss-poor in the follow-through."

"You're not being fair to yourself, Ben. Don't you see? You've lost touch with your real purpose. You know what I think?"

"What?"

"I think you love the rubble more than the people."

"Sylvia, the people you're talking about, the ones I'm supposed to love more than the rubble, they're eating each other. In a way, I guess that's an improvement over the way things used to be. At least now there's no duplicity. I mean, what you see is what you get, right? A zombie, all it wants to do is eat you. It's not going to try and wine and dine you first, you know?"

But he couldn't put her off track with sarcasm. He realized that as soon as the words left his mouth.

She leaned in closer to him. "Ben, I told you to read Whitman. I wasn't kidding about that. You need to see that the zombie and the abandoned building are exactly the same. They are both in need of restoration. They are both in need of us to make the connection with them. Have you read 'Crossing Brooklyn Ferry'?"

He was startled at hearing his thoughts spoken aloud. But at last he shook himself and answered. "Uh, yeah, I guess. A long time ago."

"Remember how he addresses his future readers. 'It is not upon you alone the dark patches fall / The dark threw its patches down upon me also / The best I had done seemed to me blank and suspicious / My great thoughts as I supposed them, were they not in reality meager?' Ben, he's talking about the same kind of personal negativity you're experiencing. He's talking about making connections between generations. He's talking about the kind of continuity you're craving, whether it's with the person living a hundred years ago, or a thousand years from now. What he's saying is that people are the only kind of continuity that truly matter. It's what you're doing with your stories, but I think maybe you don't believe it anymore."

She stopped there, as though she was waiting for him to argue, but he didn't. Instead, he smiled.

And then a thought came to him. Shortly after the quarantine fell, he and a small group of refugees from Houston had made a cross-country trek to the Cedar River National Grasslands, to live in the compound built by a mad Mississippi preacher named Jasper Sewell. That had ended in a nightmare, with the senseless suicide of over a thousand people.

But for all of Jasper's madness, he did have the gift of leadership. He had taken a weary collection of suffering survivors, and made them into a thriving community, a John Winthrop–style City on the Hill. And he had done it by identifying that glowing spark of talent within all of them, that one thing they were meant to do. He had made a porn star into an elementary school teacher, a Harvard-educated millionaire playboy into a manure-shoveling cabbage farmer, and a retired U.S. Deputy Marshal into an outlaw. What would he have made of Sylvia Carnes, Richardson wondered. The way she so doggedly held to her faith in the cure that might one day turn all these shambling hordes back into the humans they had once been humbled him. She was a teacher at heart. With her unbridled confidence in the potential of the human spirit, could she be anything but?

"What are you thinking?" she asked him.

"I was wondering if Ken Stoler put you to work teaching poetry in his compound."

"Not quite," she said, chuckling to herself. "I do a little carpentry. Some gardening. I can also make a fairly good bottle of beer, believe it or not."

"Well, you did spend an awful lot of time on a college campus."

"True."

"But no teaching?"

Sylvia pulled the black band from her pocket and used it to tie back her frizzled mass of gray hair into a ponytail. "I'm afraid not," she said. She looked at Avery Harper, who was finally starting to look ready for the road again, and said, "Besides, you have any idea how hard it is to make Wordsworth relevant to twenty-year-olds? It was hard even *before* the world ended."

* * *

A little farther up the road they saw sunlight glinting off something in the trees lining the left side of the highway.

"Could be broken glass," Avery said.

Richardson wasn't so sure.

They were kneeling behind a heap of wrecked cars, watching the trees for signs of movement. The plan had been to follow IH 55 all the way down to Herculaneum if they could, but now Richardson didn't think that was going to be possible.

"Should we chance it?" Avery said.

"Hold on," Richardson said.

He retrieved the binoculars from his backpack and scanned the trees. He saw a group of six men in BDU-style pants and dark T-shirts sitting around a campsite. They were drinking coffee, laughing. At least two of them had hunting rifles. The others had AR-15s.

"Damn it," Richardson said.

Sylvia looked over at him. "What is it?"

He handed her the binoculars. "Look for yourself. Over there, by that patch of sycamores."

Sylvia took the binoculars and pointed it at the camp. Then she lowered the binoculars. "That's Jude McHenry's squad," she said to Avery.

The younger woman groaned.

"Friends of yours?" Richardson asked.

"That's one of the squads from the Union Field. Niki trained him. McHenry's about as dumb as the day is long, but he's focused. Once he gets on our trail, he won't lose it easily."

"They don't exactly look like they're ready for an ambush."

"That's not their job," Sylvia said. "Remember, they're used to hunting zombies. The way Niki trained them, they'll wait for us to get on the bridge over the river. Most of the force will be on the other side. Once we get on the bridge,

McHenry's squad will come up behind us and we'll be trapped."

"So Niki taught them that, and now they're trying to use it on her? I guess they assume she's still with us."

"I said he was focused, not smart." Sylvia turned to Avery and said, "Honey, we need a way out of here. Where do we go?"

The question surprised Richardson. "I've got a map, Sylvia."

"And I bet it's nowhere near as good as the one I've got. Avery?"

The girl looked behind them, then to the west. "That's Meramec Bottom Road up there. We can follow that to Highway 21, which will take us to State Highway M. From there, we head east and cross back to 55."

"Where does that come out?" Sylvia asked.

"Just north of Barnhart. That'll put us about a day's walk from Herculaneum. Assuming, you know, we don't run into any other problems."

Richardson was staring at her. Avery noticed it and looked away bashfully.

"You have a map of this whole area in your head?" he said, amazed.

She nodded.

"What are you, Rain Man?"

The girl cocked her head to the side. "Who's Rain Man?"

"A joke," Richardson said. It was suddenly clear to him why Niki Booth and Sylvia Carnes brought the younger woman along. "How much of this area do you have memorized?"

"All of it," Avery said. "I like maps. If I see one, I can usually memorize it in a few minutes. City maps take a little longer, because of all the streets. But maps for areas like this, out in the country, they're easy."

"Impressive," he said. And then, to Sylvia, "Sound good to you?"

"If Avery says that's the way, I trust her."

"Fair enough," Richardson said. "After you."

Meramec Bottom Road was a gently curving two-lane blacktop that had faded to gray from exposure and the constant scouring action of the dust that blew in from the open fields on either side of it. Here and there it passed through some thickly wooded areas, and occasionally they saw the remnants of big houses behind screens of trees in the hills above the road, but nothing moved. In the early morning sunlight, the air hazy and golden, it seemed perfectly peaceful.

As they walked, Avery began to open up. She made small talk to Sylvia, and sometimes to Richardson, telling him about the country they were passing through.

But she didn't have his full attention. Ever since they'd left the highway, the feeling that they were being followed had intensified. At the limits of his hearing he could almost make out a faint doubling of their footsteps on the road, and while it might have been an echo from the tree line, he doubted it.

An image of the Red Man rose up in his mind and his guts rolled over queasily. It didn't seem possible, the things Sylvia had told him. But after seeing the Red Man control the zombies around him, he found it difficult to deny. And not for the first time he found himself wondering how such a thing was possible. Was it really a sign, as Sylvia Carnes believed, that the disease was curable? Was the person that a zombie had once been still inside that damaged husk, waiting to be freed of the infection?

That really seemed to be the big question. He supposed it was possible. After all, people sometimes got sick and got delirious with fever. Then they got better. Might this be a far more serious version of the same thing? And, if so, if it was possible to restore the person within the zombie to their former selves, would they remember what happened to them during their infection? Would they remember the cannibalistic horrors they committed?

He wasn't sure. And he wasn't sure if he wanted to know.

Ahead of him, Sylvia was still wrestling with her ponytail. The heat and the humidity were working on her, he could tell. A wide sweat stain spread from her shoulders down her spine.

"Sylvia," he said, "you wanna stop for some water?"

She turned back to him and nodded. "Over there," she said, "in the shade."

She was pointing to a ruined gas station up ahead and to their right. Most of it was still white, though the paint was curling off the walls and the metal poles holding up the awning over its pumps were brown with rust. Its driveway and the sides of the service bays were thick with brown weeds. With a glance behind him, Richardson realized it was about as good as any point they could have chosen. From the building, it afforded a pretty good view of the road in both directions.

"Yeah," he said, "that looks good."

They walked up the driveway and were nearly under the awning when Avery pointed into the shadows and said, "What's that?"

"A hammock," Richardson said. It was strung between the gas pumps. He followed the ties at either end and saw where they had rubbed some of the rust off the pumps. Someone had strung it up recently.

"Hello?" he called out.

"Ben!" Sylvia hissed. "What are you doing?"

A glass bottle skittered across the pavement from somewhere behind them. The three of them turned as one, their expressions full of surprise and panic.

A child was standing in the road. A girl, maybe ten years old. She stood perfectly still, watching them. Her greasy hair lifted in the breeze. Richardson immediately thought, *zombie*: but something was wrong. The girl's clothes were hardly new, but they were clean. There were no bloodstains, no abscesses on her skin. And he didn't see any signs of injury. Still, his internal alarms were ringing at top volume.

"Ben," Sylvia said, "what do you think? Oh God! *Avery, no!*"

But it was too late. Avery was trotting down the driveway, toward the girl.

Richardson ran after her, and he was nearly close enough to grab Avery and pull her back when two women stumbled out of the woods to his left.

Both were obviously infected. No doubt there. Their bodies were stiff, their movements clumsy. One woman's mouth and cheeks and hair were black with dried blood. Her clothes had been reduced to rags. The other woman raised her hands and began the familiar clutching that Richardson had seen so many times. Both began to moan at the same time.

Richardson grabbed Avery by the back of her collar and pulled her behind him. Then he pulled his pistol and fired at the female zombie closest to him. The bullet caught her in the left eye and blasted off black, ropey bits of her face onto the ground behind her. She dropped to the ground without a sound.

He pivoted to his right and fired at the second female zombie. The bullet smacked into her shoulder and spun her around in a weirdly graceful pirouette as she staggered down the slope of the driveway. Then she turned back around, raised one arm, and slowly staggered back up the driveway toward Richardson.

Behind him, he could see Sylvia pulling Avery out of the way. "Get back, both of you," he shouted.

He raised his pistol again and was about to fire at the female zombie when the little girl ran at him. She moved with incredible speed. He tried to point the pistol at her, but she was moving too quickly. She was on him before he knew it. She knocked the pistol from his hand, then lunged for his throat.

He staggered backward, but didn't fall. Now he could smell the rot coming from her breath. He could see two rows of small, busted teeth behind her slowly spreading grin. She was snapping her teeth at him like a dog, a wet, stuttering growl rising from her chest.

He turned and ran toward the building. There was an old sedan there with the passenger door hanging partially open. Richardson ran around the back side of the car and dove into the front seat. Then he sat up and pulled the door closed just as the little girl reached it, her hands beating against the window, yanking on the door handle.

For a horrible instant her face was framed by the passenger window, her diseased mouth pressed up against the glass. Her teeth scratched against the window, her tongue darting out and touching it, testing it like a finger. He saw a smear of dark blood forming across the glass. And a terrible thought occurred to him: They used this one as a decoy. Someone had actually cleaned her up enough that she could pass for one of the uninfected, and was using her as a decoy.

But there was no time to follow the thought through to its implications, for at that moment the little girl jumped onto the hood of the car and started kicking the windshield with her heel.

Richardson heard a pop, and then the soft, almost liquid

splash of glass breaking. Bright white spiderweb cracks formed along its surface. The windshield separated from the top of the roof and sagged inward, held together now only by the protective plastic film on the inside of the glass.

Through the shattered windshield he saw the little girl's ruined face. The glass gave way with a series of loud pops and the next instant it was draped over him like a sheet with the girl on top of it, shredding her hands to bloody ribbons as she tried to claw her way through to Richardson.

"Help! Goddamn it, get me out of here!"

His arms were pinned between the seat and the steering wheel and he couldn't get the leverage he needed to push the girl off him.

"Sylvia. Help me!"

The little girl's snarls got louder. Bits of broken glass were flying all around her face. Her blood was spattering across the dashboard, running down into the puddles of water that had collected on the floorboards. Richardson was kicking madly at the passenger door, trying to get leverage against the girl's weight, when suddenly there was a shot. Her face seemed to swell above him, actually growing larger, until it slopped down on the remnants of the windshield and oozed off onto the floorboards. Her headless corpse sagged down on top of him.

"Ben?" It was Sylvia's voice. "Ben, are you okay?"

He looked to his left and saw part of the little girl's face on the floorboard, empty, bloody eye sockets staring up at him.

"Ben?"

"Get her off me, Sylvia. Jesus, hurry."

The passenger door opened and they pulled the little girl's body off him. "Careful of all the glass," Sylvia said, as she helped him sit up and then climb out of the wrecked car.

He stood and checked himself for wounds, any possible sign of infection.

"You okay?" Sylvia asked.

"Yeah, I think so."

"Come here," she said. "There's something you need to see."

She turned and walked down the driveway. The two adult female zombies were there. Both, he realized, had an ear missing.

"Look at that," Sylvia said, pointing to one of the zombies.

The woman had been wearing jeans and an Ohio Buckeyes sweatshirt. She looked like a scarecrow inside the baggy clothes. Not sure what he was supposed to be seeing he let his gaze wander down to her ankles. One of her pant legs had been pulled up to her knee, revealing a small, black box about the size of a pack of cigarettes strapped to her ankle. It was beeping quietly.

"What is that?" he asked.

"It's an ankle monitor," Sylvia said. "The kind they used to put on people who were on house arrest."

He was still feeling a little sick from all the adrenaline going through his system, and it was hard to focus. A lot of half-formed questions rose up in his mind, but he wasn't able to articulate them.

"Why?" was all he managed.

"They were tracking her. They were tracking her while she was tracking us."

"Who?"

"Isn't that obvious?"

He looked at her, still confused.

"The Red Man," she said. "Remember last night, when we told you his father used to be chief of police in Gatling.

Where else do you think they would have gotten this kind of equipment?"

"I don't . . ." he said, and then trailed off with a shrug. "Why not just capture us?"

"I think that's obvious. The Red Man is hoping we'll lead him to Don Fisher."

"Why us? Doesn't he have Niki?"

"That's exactly my point," Sylvia said. She looked almost triumphant. "If he's tracking us, that means he hasn't gotten anything from Niki. Best case scenario, that means she's still alive, still holding out."

He almost said, "But the worst case . . ." Fortunately, he stopped himself. Avery was hanging on their every word. He looked at her and nodded. Then he turned back to Sylvia. His head was beginning to clear now. He examined the car where he had nearly died. There was blood all over it, running down the hood and the fenders. Richardson let out a long breath, and then turned his attention back to the blinking ankle monitor.

"Do you think they have any way of knowing we killed their trackers?"

Sylvia shrugged, but before she could answer, they heard the sound of trucks in the distance.

"It's him," Avery said. "What do we do? We got to hide."

"Not in the building," Richardson said. "That's the first place they'll look."

"Where?" Sylvia said.

Richardson reached into his pack and removed the tarp he'd made from the old Gilley suit. "Under here," he said. He looked around and his gaze fell on a section of an overgrown ditch thick with tall brown weeds. "Over there. That ditch across the street. Come on."

CHAPTER 8

Nate Royal woke with a fire burning in his head. He blinked his eyes open and the daylight stabbing in on his eyes only made the pain worse. Groaning, he fell back into the hammock he'd suspended between the service station's rusting gas pumps and closed his eyes.

He was not doing well.

He skin was filmed over with a cold sweat. Sometimes he felt like he was burning up; other times there didn't seem to be enough blankets in the world to keep him warm. The clouds in his head never seemed to clear, and even when he tried to work through it, really concentrate, his heart would start to race and he'd grow short of breath. Not for the first time that week he wondered if he was going to die.

He suspected that what he had right now was the flu. A really bad case of it. There'd been that old man he'd shared a campfire with the week before, the one who kept him up all night with his hacking cough and sneezing and his moaning in his sleep. Maybe he got it from him.

But did it really matter? Hadn't he been going downhill

for a while now anyway? Even if he hadn't gotten sick from that miserable old man, he would still be in a bad way. He was hungry all the time. His face was so badly sunburned that he could barely touch it. He kept losing his supplies. They were stolen, or misplaced, or forgotten, whatever. They just disappeared on him. A lot like the rest of the world.

He'd seen a farmhouse a few miles down the road, but had decided to pass it by because there might have been people sleeping inside and he didn't want to be around them while he was sick. He felt weak and defenseless, and all he wanted to do was curl up like a dog behind some bushes somewhere and hide, to be by himself. Now he realized how stupid that had been. What he needed was someplace warm to rest. Some clean water to drink. What he needed—

The thought broke off cleanly.

He heard the muffled cracking sound of glass breaking underfoot, and suddenly he knew he was being watched.

Very slowly, he opened his eyes and turned his aching head toward the sound.

There were three of them, standing there, watching him. A little girl of about ten, just a few feet from him, and two older women behind her. They stood absolutely still, draped in the shadows of the gas station's awning like something materializing out of a nightmare. They didn't make a sound.

Even through the fever clouds in his head he knew they were infected. He could see it in their yellowed, bloodshot eyes, and the way the flesh slacked off the bones of their face, and the deep black hollows under their eyes. The two women had dried blood all over them. It was matted in their hair and crusted around their mouths and down the front of their clothes.

But not the little girl. She was a zombie, too. He knew that. But she was wearing clean clothes, and her hair, though oily and dirty, was free of blood.

He was hallucinating, he decided. A trick of the shadows.

Nate raised a hand, his index finger outstretched as though he was about to lecture them, and then he let it fall. He didn't have the energy.

Not even to defend himself.

"Go ahead and kill me," he muttered. "You got me netted in this thing like a country ham. You ain't gonna get a better chance."

A country ham.

He'd seen a bunch of them hanging in fishnet bags from a ceiling in a ruined deli in Atlanta a few years earlier. In the dark, he'd seen spiders moving all over them.

Now he was the country ham, and the zombies were the spiders.

But the thought didn't frighten him. Nate wasn't afraid of the infection that the zombies carried. For reasons that had been explained to him many times, and yet he still didn't understand, he was immune to the necrosis filovirus. He had been bitten at least fourteen times in the last eight years, with the attendant scars to prove it, but the disease was unable to gain purchase in his body.

When the quarantine wall fell, Nate had been living in Martindale, Pennsylvania, with his dad and his dad's girlfriend Mindy. Up through his mid-twenties, he'd led a thoroughly disappointing life, one spent drinking beer and smoking dope and watching lots of porn and pretty much avoiding anything remotely close to responsibility. But that all changed when the outbreak spread through the East Coast like a wildfire. Bitten by a zombie during the evacuation, he'd retreated, scared and all alone, into a neighbor's lawn mower shed. Shortly afterwards, a roving military squad discovered him and put him in a holding cell with hundreds of other infected victims. But while the others became zombies, he did not, and for several hours he clung to the top of a chain-link fence, with hundreds of the infected snarling below him, reaching for him, while soldiers in biohazard suits watched him from the other side of the fence. Finally, he was taken down by a team of military doctors and turned into a lab rat.

But they did derive a cure from his blood. And if only the doctors who worked on him had lived, he thought, maybe that would have counted for something.

He blinked at the zombies. They were still standing there, watching him. "Come on. Do it."

But they didn't move.

Their eyes shone in the dark. The weight of their stares was oppressive. He could smell the faint charnel-house odor of them in the still morning air, but he couldn't hear them breathing. They were enveloped by stillness so perfect, so absolute, that they seemed to have been transmuted into granite, like statues in a graveyard. A chill crept over Nate's skin, and he shivered involuntarily.

Run, he thought. He was immune to their sickness, but that didn't matter. Their stillness was something completely new. It terrified him, and that little voice inside his head began to scream: Run! Get away as fast as you can.

Then, without warning, all three zombies turned their heads as one and stared down the road. And that simple gesture, like their heads were all mounted on the same pivot, turned by the same dial, scared him more even than their stillness had.

He leaned his head forward and tried to see what they were looking at, but there was nothing there.

Nate turned back to the zombies. "What are you . . ." But he trailed off, the question left unasked. The zombies were leaving. They turned and walked into the daylight, staggering along a crooked path to the woods at the edge of the pavement.

One by one, they slipped into the woods.

"What the . . . ?"

With effort, he climbed out of the hammock and stumbled to the edge of the awning's shadow line, one hand on a rusted pole to support his weight. He watched the zombies disappear into the thicket, and he realized with a sense of horror and shame that he had been ready to die. Had they attacked him, he would have welcomed the death that followed. He rubbed the computer flash drive that hung from a lanyard around his neck and coughed. Had it really come to this? Was he really giving up?

There used to be writing on the flash drive, but it was worn down and faded now from all the long nights he spent rubbing it with his thumb, thinking about Dr. Mark Kellogg, the man who had encoded the cure onto the drive and then slipped it into Nate's hand as he lay dying.

He tucked the flash drive back inside his shirt.

"We are put into this hostile, alien world as isolated individuals," Kellogg had told him, shortly before he died of suicide by pistol to keep from turning into a zombie. "We can learn to like other people, even love them, but we can't ever truly know them, and so we remain isolated. We're not allowed to know why life has meaning, not for sure anyway, and yet we feel compelled to create some sort of answer. It's an absurd downward spiral of impossible things, and yet it is our lives."

Nate leaned on the support pole and stared miserably into the thicket where the zombies had disappeared. He'd never felt so lonely as he did now. More than fast cars, more even than pretty girls, he missed Kellogg. In the short time he'd known him, Kellogg had become like the father Nate never had. His own father—his real father—was a small, stupid man, who saw in Nate a reflection of his own limitations and failure. They had hated one another, and as far as Nate was concerned, the outbreak was about the best thing that had ever happened to them.

But Kellogg was different. He had taken the time to talk with Nate, really talk with him. He explained how sometimes the world didn't make sense. He explained how the only thing that really mattered was looking for a way to make life make sense. The answer itself didn't matter, because there probably wasn't one. Not a perfect one, anyway. Only the looking for an answer made any difference, because when you stopped looking, you started dying.

Sometimes, Kellogg spoke to him. Nate, from time to time, saw him standing next to him, heard him talking with him. He had met a Thai man around Phoenix several years back who told him that holy people sometimes communed with the ghosts of those who had been important in their lives and still had lessons to teach, and sometimes Nate liked to think that the vision he saw was really the ghost of Kellogg trying to keep him alive. It was a pleasant thing to believe.

But of course Kellogg hadn't appeared to him lately.

Nate closed his eyes, and he could almost hear the man saying, "Even a world defined by bad reasons can give you cause to live. You must find those reasons, whatever they may be."

"But I tried," Nate said. He opened his eyes and scanned the crumbling gas station around him. "I tried really hard."

Kellogg was standing there, smiling calmly.

Nate smiled back. "Hey, Doc."

"The cure, Nate. That's your reason. You have to get it to somebody who knows how to use it."

"But what else am I supposed to do? I can't go much farther."

But Kellogg was gone.

Nate waved a fly away from his face. He heard the noise

of a young woman's voice coming from the road, and instinctively, he stepped back into the shadows. Stop, watch, and listen before you meet new people. Be careful what you tell them. Know who they are before they know you. That had been some of Kellogg's best advice to him. It saved him numerous times over the years, and he followed it now without hesitation.

Turning toward the gas station, he happened to catch his reflection in a grimy, jagged triangle of glass still clinging to the edge of the window, and he sucked in a shocked breath. It was a world without mirrors, and it had been a long time since he'd seen his reflection. He hadn't been a bad-looking guy back in the day. He'd had a few girlfriends. But he looked bad now. He'd lost so much weight. His hair was down past his shoulders, ratty with oil and dirt, as was his beard. Flies swarmed around his face, dipping now and then toward the raw sunburn cracks in his skin.

No wonder they didn't attack you, he thought; then waved the flies away from his face and disappeared into the shadows of the station's service bays, where it was hot and smelled dusty and stale.

There were three of them, a man and woman who looked to be in their fifties, and a younger girl, who looked to be about twenty. The girl looked nice. A little thick around the middle, maybe, but nice. She had pretty blond hair, and Nate hadn't seen that in a long while.

The man and the woman were out front as they approached the service station, and only then did Nate realize he'd left all his gear strung up out there.

They'd steal it all, he realized; and then, Christ, not again. Why couldn't he hold on to his gear?

He thought maybe he had time to dart out and grab it before they saw him, but then the pretty blond girl stepped around the man and the women and pointed at the hammock and said, "What's that?"

Dammit, Nate thought.

"A hammock," the man said.

Nate studied the three, and it took him a long moment to realize that the man was dressed differently from the two women. The women wore baggy sweatshirts and BDU-style pants over Magnum Hi-Tec boots that looked practically brand new. But the man wore jeans and a long-sleeve T-shirt and tennis shoes that were held together near the toe with duct tape. He carried a heavy-looking backpack and a pistol at his belt, and he looked to be the only one who was armed.

Maybe they were okay. They looked okay.

The man came forward and examined the place where the hammock's ropes were tied on to the gas pumps. "Hello?" he called out.

"Ben!" the older woman hissed. "What are you doing?"

Kellogg appeared at Nate's shoulder. "Wait a moment," he said. "Just wait and watch. Know who they are before they know who you are."

"Okay," Nate whispered.

He watched them. They were looking around, studying his meager possessions on the ground when a glass bottle scraped along the asphalt down at the road. All three of them turned at the same time. It was weirdly similar to the way the zombies had turned. But where the zombies had stared in eerie silence, these three newcomers gasped.

Nate followed their gaze down to the road and saw the little girl zombie standing there, waiting for them. She's trying to lure them out in the open, Nate thought: and answered that thought with the same mental breath, It'll never work. They can tell she's infected.

"Ben," the older woman said, "what do you think?"

Then the younger woman muttered, "Poor thing," and broke into a trot down the length of the driveway.

No, Nate thought. What are you doing?

"Avery, no!" the older woman yelled.

The man—the one called Ben, Nate remembered—took off running after the girl. Nate leaned forward, watching them, his hand reaching involuntarily into the empty air in front of him, pantomiming the man's actions as he tried to stop the girl before she ran right into the zombie's waiting arms.

Just as he reached her, the girl stopped, turned toward the thicket next to the driveway, and let out a little scream as she staggered away from the two zombie women who had just emerged there. The man pulled the blond girl behind him and drew his pistol and shot one of the zombie women with his pistol.

The zombie crumpled to the ground.

He turned and shot the other zombie, but his aim was bad and he managed to hit the woman in the shoulder, spinning her around without dropping her. The older woman with the wild gray hair yelled, "Get back, both of you." She grabbed the blond girl and pulled her toward the building.

The child was attacking the man by then. She lunged for his arm and knocked the pistol loose. It went skittering across the driveway, out of reach. The man backed away, then turned and ran for the old rusty car that was just beyond the awning. Nate watched, horrified, as the man barricaded himself inside the wreck. The little girl zombie climbed up onto the hood and started beating on the windshield. Then it caved in with a crash of breaking glass and the little girl fell in with it and landed on top of the man inside the car. She was trying to claw her way through the busted windshield when the woman with the wild gray hair shot her in the back of the head.

And then, everything went still.

The sound of the pistol shot faded away, and seemed to take all the sound in the world with it. The two women pulled the man out of the wrecked car and led him down the driveway, where they studied something on one of the female zombie's legs.

"What do I do, Doc?" he muttered.

"Wait, Nate," Kellogg said. "Just wait. And watch."

He heard a rumbling coming from a long ways off, and it took him a moment to realize that it was the sound of a truck coming toward the service station. Nate thought maybe he was imagining it, but then he saw the man and the two women looking at the road too, and they seemed frightened.

The three of them started talking as one. He couldn't make out what they were saying, but the pretty blond girl was gesturing toward the service bay where Nate was hiding. "No," he said. "Not here. Not here."

The man was motioning toward the road. He pulled something that looked like a shaggy carpet from his backpack and the three of them took off running.

"Yeah, that's it," he said. "Get going. Don't send their attention my way."

With a great deal of difficulty he pulled himself to his feet and stumbled to the edge of the service bay, watching them go. Now that the sound was very close, he could tell that it was coming from several trucks. A caravan, he thought. Jesus.

"You think it's a foraging party, Doc?"

"No way to tell, Nate. Stay out of sight for now."

"Right—Oh shit! My stuff."

He ran over to his hammock and started wrestling with the ropes that secured it to the pumps. "Come on, come on," he said, tugging at the knots. "Please."

Nate heard the sound of tires moving across the blacktop

and he looked to see a line of four trucks trundling into sight. They were Fords and Chevys, big black work trucks with oversize tires and loud exhausts. Black-clad soldiers with rifles rode in the first and last vehicle, while the middle two, with slatted wooden rails around the beds, seemed to be packed with zombies. The trucks rolled to a stop in the street in front of the station and the soldiers jumped down from the beds of the trucks and set up a perimeter.

"What in the . . . ?" Nate said, ducking quickly back into the service bay.

Two of the soldiers ran over to the dead zombies in the driveway while another pair checked out the car where the little girl zombie had died. Nate pressed himself all the way back into the corner, murmuring a prayer that they wouldn't come inside the bay and find him.

But as he did he saw something odd. A man, painted head to toe in red, stepped from the second truck and walked part of the way up the driveway. He was bald, and his face looked bad, like maybe it'd been scarred by acne when he was a teenager. He walked with a slight limp, and he didn't carry a weapon, but every black-clad soldier hurried to get out of his way. There was something menacing about the man that chilled Nate to the core, and it didn't help that the zombies in the trucks watched every move he made with unblinking attention.

One of the soldiers removed the black thing from around the dead zombie's ankle and brought it to the Red Man. The Red Man took it without a word, turned it over in his hands as he examined it, and then handed it back to the soldier.

Nate was so busy watching the exchange that he failed to notice the two soldiers up near the wrecked car where the little girl's headless body still protruded from the busted windshield. They had spotted the hammock and the gear on the ground and were silently peering into the service station's lobby. Nate finally noticed them when they looked around the corner and into the service bay.

"Let me see your hands," the soldier shouted, swinging his gun up and pointing it directly at Nate's face.

A flashlight mounted below the gun's barrel came on, blinding Nate.

He put up his hands and said, "No, wait, dude. I didn't do—" But the words were cut off mid-sentence as the soldier came forward and planted the butt of the gun's stock squarely into Nate's teeth. An explosion of pain went through him, and his legs turned to sand. He sagged forward into the soldier's arms and a moment later he was being dragged into the daylight and dropped at the Red Man's feet.

"What the hell is this?" the Red Man said.

Nate looked up at the Red Man. Sunlight glistened off his bare chest and off the dome of his bald head.

"We found him hiding in the service bay," the soldier said. "Looks like he killed these other three."

"You idiot," the Red Man said. "Look at him. He can't keep his balance. He's not even wearing a weapon." The Red Man yelled up toward the station. "Did you find a gun?"

"No, sir," another soldier answered. "Just a bunch of trash up here. His clothes and stuff."

"What's your name?"

"Nate Royal."

"And the others?" the Red Man said. "Where are they?"

Blood was oozing out of the corner of Nate's mouth and into his scraggly beard. He blinked a few times, trying to clear his head. Things were getting hazy again.

"Dude, why are you all red?"

"Where are the others?"

Nate blinked at him. "I dunno."

The Red Man grabbed him by the throat and hauled him

to his feet. "I won't ask you again. A man and two women came this way. Where are they?"

"Ask me all you want," Nate said. "I didn't see shit."

The Red Man glared at him. His nostrils flared with every breath he took. And as Nate struggled to breathe through the Red Man's iron grip around his throat, the Red Man bit the index finger of his own right hand. When he took it away, it was dripping blood.

"I will own you," the Red Man said, and jammed the bleeding finger into Nate's mouth.

At first Nate resisted. He tried to turn his head away, but the Red Man had too tight a grip around his throat. Desperate for air, he spread his clenched teeth apart and bit down on the Red Man's finger with everything he had—and he went on biting until he heard the sickening crunch of bone and a gout of blood jetted over his tongue as his teeth ripped the finger off at the knuckle.

The Red Man's howls filled the air. It was an unearthly sound, part rage, part lowing moan, but all of it echoing with pain.

He dropped Nate to the ground and staggered backward, holding his bleeding hand in shock. Nate, for his part, didn't lose any time. There was a soldier advancing on him from behind. Nate leaped to his feet and spun around, throwing an elbow into the soldier's face and catching him cleanly on the jaw. The soldier dropped his weapon in surprise and Nate was off, running toward the thicket as fast as he could run.

He heard the Red Man screaming at his back, and a moment later, the soldiers yelling commands.

They started firing as he slipped into the thicket. The next instant, the air around his head filled with the high-pitched whistles of ricocheting bullets.

Nate didn't stop. He ducked his head and ran with everything he had.

CHAPTER 9

Bullets chewed up the branches around his head. A wall of sound, like a wave, tore at his heels. Nate, breathless and sick, was panting in terror; his vision tunneled; eyes went wide with terror; spittle flecked on his lips; every muscle strained to carry him faster, faster from the Red Man's soldiers as they bore down upon him with their guns roaring and their screams swelling up behind him like some huge beast, gaining on him with every step.

He found a pig trail. Running blind with his hands in front of him, swatting at the endless tangle of branches in his face, he twisted through the underbrush. The soldiers were on either side of him, closing on him, and above it all he could hear the Red Man roaring in his pain and rage. "Get him back here! I want him now!" And the soldiers, their voices like an echo, yelling, "Get him!" "He's over there." "I see him over here."

The steady roll of the guns slacked off to a series of scattered pops and he turned quickly to look behind him.

The Red Man's soldiers were entering the woods right behind him. He could see their hunched-over black silhouettes moving through the thicket with terrific speed.

Panting, sticks and leaves caught in his scraggly beard, Nate Royal ran with no idea where he was going. The will to live that had been lacking earlier, when he was caught in his hammock by the zombies, came back to him as a full-blown blind panic adrenaline surge, and though his skin was laced with cuts, he felt none of it. The world was a wolf pack snapping at his heels, driving him deeper into the woods.

He crossed a muddy creek bed and when he came up on the other side, the pig trail had vanished. The air was full of leaves and thick with the smell of rotting vegetation. Ahead of him, the ground rose abruptly to a small ridge, the slope a slick carpet of wet, brown leaves.

Chancing a look behind him, he saw one of the Red Man's soldiers closing fast. Nate let out a startled yelp and ran up the slope. He lost his footing and had to scramble up to the top of the ridge with his fingertips digging into the damp earth.

The soldier clamped a hand down on Nate's shoulder as they crested the ridge and Nate screamed. Their momentum carried them over the top and then they were falling down the slope on the other side.

Nate landed in a thick layer of dark mud. The soldier came down next to him, his forehead striking a jagged corner of a large rock with the sickening crunch of broken bone.

Breathing hard, Nate looked at the soldier. The man's eyes were wide open and frozen in sightless surprise. Part of his skull, thick and jagged and honeycombed inside, jutted up from the wound amid a thick black spreading ooze of blood. He could see the brain inside, grayish-yellow, like old cheese.

Nate drew back in horror, his breath hitching in his throat.

More soldiers were coming. He could hear them just on the other side of the ridge, and Nate was scrambling to his feet when he saw the dead soldier's AR-15 poking out from under his body.

"Hot damn," he muttered.

He pulled on the weapon and managed to free it from the soldier's weight. But it was caught on something. He yanked on the gun again and again until he saw the black nylon strap still securing the gun to the soldier's shoulder.

"No," he said, still tugging on the gun. "Come on, please."

Three more soldiers crested the ridge above him. Without aiming, Nate raised the rifle and emptied the entire magazine into their guts.

All three doubled over and slid face-first into the thick carpet of leaves. The whole thing took less than two seconds, and though Nate saw every detail, it was as though he was outside of himself, looking down. The guns made no sound. All he could hear was the rush of blood in his ears, his heart pounding in his chest. The moment seemed to stretch on forever.

And then, suddenly, the spell was broken. His senses opened up and it was like a wave breaking all around him. Time accelerated to normal speed. More soldiers were yelling, coming closer. And meanwhile Nate, stunned and light-headed, was looking down at two dead soldiers and a third who was groaning like an animal struggling to give birth. He'll be dead in less than three minutes, Nate thought, surprised by his detachment.

The shouting was growing very loud. "Ah, shit," he said, and dropped the rifle and turned and ran through the woods.

He ran parallel to the streambed for about a hundred yards, then dropped behind a tree and sank to his knees in a thick blanket of rotten leaves. Nate could hear voices coming toward him. "You see him?" "Clear over here." "You two cross back over the streambed, see if he doubled back on us."

They've lost me, he thought. But he couldn't run anymore. Years earlier, long before the outbreak, he'd shattered his ankle running from the police, and now the ankle was starting to pulse. Any more movement and that pulsing would turn to unbearable waves of pain.

The leaves beneath him felt deep. He tested it by jamming a hand down until he touched bottom, maybe six inches.

Good enough, he thought, and hurriedly buried himself.

Two of the soldiers passed inches from his left shoulder and then stopped near his feet.

"He couldn't walk through that stuff down there without leaving tracks," one of the men said.

"Yeah," agreed the other. "Back up that way."

Please oh please, I need a break.

Flat on his stomach, peering out at a little patch of thicket from the cover of the leaves, Nate listened as the soldiers moved away. He let out a long breath and waited, straining his ears for the sound of voices and breaking twigs.

"What do I do, Doc?" he muttered.

Kellogg knelt beside him. "Shhh. Don't move. Don't speak. They're moving away."

And from the sounds of their voices, Nate knew it was true. They were a good ways off, and moving farther away with every passing second.

He closed his eyes and laughed, then winced at the sharp pain in his ribs. But it felt good to know he had saved himself. The pain aside, it felt good to know that he was still alive, and he laughed again.

* * *

But it was a considerably more subdued Nate Royal who, later that evening, found himself within sight of the Mississippi River without any food or fresh water or blankets under which to sleep. His headache, his aches, his fever chills—they were all returning now in spades, repaying him for the exertions of the morning and the all-day walking. With his vision turning soupy at the edges, he stumbled toward the water, figuring he would drink and take his chances. Rivers that ran through cities had bad water, he had learned, but he was desperate.

Ahead of him, the water was plum-colored in the pale light of the setting sun. It seemed as flat and calm as a sheet of cooled lead. He saw a pair of white birds gliding over the water, and it seemed very peaceful until the quiet was broken by the giggling of a pair of young girls.

He stopped dead in his tracks.

They crossed the trail in front of him, maybe ten feet away, completely unaware of his presence. He only caught a glimpse of them; a young girl of about eight, and an older one, a teenager, about thirteen or fourteen. They were both dressed in simple white dresses, and they were carrying baskets filled with blackberries and wild corn.

"Wait," he said, stumbling after them, though his mouth and throat were so dry only a gasp of air escaped.

"Nate, no," Kellogg pleaded with him. "Don't. Watch them first."

But Nate wasn't listening. He hurt everywhere. The ringing in his ears had grown painful beyond the point that he could stand. He just wanted to fall over and drink some water before he passed out.

He turned down a thin side trail and caught a second glimpse of the girls as they entered a clearing. Nate smelled the faint tinge of wood smoke and heard other voices talking, laughing. Crashing down the side trail, he staggered into a clearing and found himself standing in the midst of a camp, half a dozen people staring at him.

It took a moment before anybody could react.

Two young men in their twenties grabbed shotguns and pointed them at Nate. He looked from one barrel to the other, swaying on his feet, and blinked.

"Don't shoot me," he muttered, but wasn't sure if the sound came out or not.

The others just stared at him. Everyone was on their feet now. He saw an older woman in her late fifties put her arms around the two little girls and pull them back. A younger boy, who looked about five and was holding a thick stick blackened at one end, stared at Nate with wide, terrified eyes. There was a pile of fresh tinder smoking and popping in the fire pit in front of him.

Nate looked at one of the men holding a shotgun. The man adjusted his grip on the weapon.

"I'm not infected," Nate said, and coughed. "Please. Help me."

"Turn around," the man said. He raised the shotgun to his shoulder and squinted one eye down the length of the barrel. "Do it now."

With effort, Nate raised both hands and showed the men his palms. He could barely keep his head up. He turned slowly, clumsily, and stopped with his back to the men.

"Run, Nate," Kellogg said. "Run while you've still got the chance."

"I can't," he said.

"You can't what?" one of the men said.

Nate lowered his hands slightly. "I can't run," he said.

"You just stay right there," the man said. Then, to the other man, he said, "You see anything?"

"No. Hey, man, you bit anyplace?"

"No," Nate said.

"What's that?"

"No," he said again, straining to be heard. "I'm thirsty."

The older woman said, "He's sick, Jason. It looks like he's got the flu."

"It looks like he came out of the back end of a goat is what it looks like. Eddie, what do you think?"

"Hell, I don't know. I can't see any bite marks on him."

"I'm not bit," Nate said.

"I know what you said," a voice said. It sounded like Eddie's voice, but Nate was still turned around and couldn't see them. "Just stay there." Then Eddie lowered his voice a little and said, "Go down there and tell Dad we got a sick man up here. Ask him what he wants us to do."

Nate turned slightly and saw the little boy throw down the stick and run off toward the river. He also saw the one named Eddie bring up his shotgun again.

"Just stay there, mister."

"Can I sit down?" Nate said.

"Nope. Just stay where you're at."

A moment later the little boy ran back into the camp. "Daddy said to bring him on down. He wants to look at him."

"Alright," Eddie said. "Come on, mister. Turn around real slow."

Nate did as the man asked and Eddie motioned him down toward the river with the barrel of the shotgun. The path led him down to the bank and around a stand of willows. There was a man there, lying on his side, a fishing pole in his hands. He was a thin man, his high, oddly square-shaped head going bald on top, and the little hair he had left was as soft and white as powder snow. He was smiling when he turned around, but the smile slipped a little as he took in the sight of Nate standing before him.

"Good lord," he muttered.

The man planted his hands palm down in the witchgrass and struggled up from the bank like an animal that has had its back legs run over by a car and is now pulling itself out of the road. It was an ungainly motion, one that Nate found disgusting. Only then did Nate notice that the man's legs were tied together with loose, yellowed bandages that seemed to have soaked through from underneath.

"This is wrong, Nate," Kellogg said. "This is all wrong. Get up and run."

"What happened to you, son?"

"I was running," Nate said, "through the woods."

"What from?"

Kellogg leaned into his ear. "Don't say a word, Nate. Not a word."

But the man was waiting, looking him in the eye. Nate found it hard to look at him. The injuries to his legs had an unnatural look that turned Nate's stomach.

"What were you running from, son? Was it zombies?"

"I dunno," Nate said. "Could have been. Could have been wild hogs, I dunno. I hid in some leaves."

"Well, hopefully you didn't pick up any ticks. Last thing you want is to get sick with Lyme disease. You probably wouldn't survive it."

Nate said nothing.

"What other symptoms do you have?" the man said.

"Huh?"

"You running a fever? I heard you coughing just a bit ago. You feel congested—sneezing at all—achy?"

"Yeah, all that."

"How long you been sick?"

"Couple of days. I'm real thirty, mister."

"I bet. It's alright, son. My name's Don Fisher. I'm a doctor. You already met the rest of my family, I guess."

Nate just looked at him. His head was swimming so badly

he wasn't catching but every other word. "Could I have some water?" he said.

The man nodded. "Eddie, can you do that for me, please? Get him some water—and bring me a package of Tamiflu." Eddie nodded and started to walk off, but Fisher called out to him. "And Eddie, better bring me a package of Zithromax, too. Just in case." Nate was feeling like he needed to throw up. It was getting harder and harder to stand. Fisher, recognizing the look, said, "Go ahead and sit down, son. Sit down before you fall down."

"You're not gonna hurt me, are you?"

Fisher gave him a curious look. "No, son. I'm a doctor. Sit down. Nobody's going to hurt you."

Nate tried to sit, but what he actually did was closer to falling. He looked over at Fisher, and the man nodded. Then he planted his palms in the grass again and pulled himself over to where Nate sat.

Nate, for his part, tried unsuccessfully not to flinch. It was like watching a poisonous snake inch closer and closer.

Fisher pulled himself up alongside Nate and felt his forehead. "Yeah, you're burning up. We need to get that fever down. Ah, good—here's Eddie."

Eddie handed Nate a Mason jar full of water. The water looked clear and clean, but Nate would have drunk it all down even if it had come straight up from the river. Nate took a sip of the water. His cracked lips hurt on the rim of the jar, and his throat felt like it had broken glass stuffed down it, but he went on drinking.

"When was the last time you ate, son?"

"I dunno."

The man nodded to himself. "Well, this won't hurt your stomach even without food." He had two shiny tinfoil cards with blister packs of pills on them. "These white and yellow pills—these are Tamiflu—take one in the morning and one at night. These pink ones are Zithromax—an antibiotic—you take this once a day. You understand?"

Nate didn't, but he nodded like he did.

"Let's get you started right away." Fisher popped the pills from the blister pack and handed them to Nate. Nate swallowed both with the remainder of the water in the jar. "You want some more water?" Fisher said, watching him closely.

Nate nodded, his eyes closed. His throat was killing him.

Eddie brought another jar of water, and Nate took it gratefully, but he passed out before he had a chance to finish it.

When he woke it was dark. The river was an immense sheet of black stretching far off into the distance. Nate could hear a soft murmur of mosquitoes in the tall weeds at the water's edge, and somewhere, out on the water, the muffled plunk of a fish breaking the surface.

He rolled over and saw the campfire had worked itself down to a flickering bed of embers, glowing softly in the darkness, its orange light casting a faint glow over the sleeping faces of Fisher's wife and her two youngest children.

He couldn't see the two younger men or the teenage girl.

"Are you awake?"

Fisher's voice, coming from behind him, startled Nate. He rolled over and looked at the man.

"How you feeling?"

Nate coughed. "Still hurting."

"It'll take you a while to get better—a few days at least. You're gonna need to get yourself cleaned up before you head off again—it'll do your morale some good to cut your hair and get rid of that beard. You could stand a new set of clothes while you're at it."

Nate closed his eyes and tried to make the world stop spinning. "How am I gonna do all that?" he said.

"You're about Eddie's size—we'll give you what you need."

Nate opened his eyes, then narrowed them at Fisher, trying to see the man's motives in his face. "Why?"

Fisher just smiled. "Why not?"

"You don't know me. Why are you doing this?"

"That's true—I don't know you—what's your name?"

Warning lights flashed in Nate's brain. This was exactly the thing Kellogg had warned him about. We can learn to like other people, Kellogg had said, even love them, but we can't ever truly know them, and so we remain isolated. The words played through his head like they'd been spoken only yesterday, though in reality it had been, what, six years ago? Seven?

"Don't want to tell me, huh?"

Nate shook his head slightly.

"That's okay. But listen, son, there is going to come a day when you will have to trust somebody. You can't survive in this world without trust. Look at how hard it is—look at all the things you have to do for yourself if you're the only one you trust. You'll probably be dead before you're forty if you don't learn to spread some of the labor around. It's the helping each other that gives the world meaning, son—gives us a sense that we belong to something."

But that's a lie, Nate thought, once again remembering the words Kellogg had spoken to him all those years ago. We're not allowed to know why life has meaning, not for sure anyway, and yet we feel compelled to create some sort of answer. It's an absurd downward spiral of impossible things, and yet it is our lives.

"I'm okay for now," Nate said.

Fisher looked him over with a doubtful expression on his face. "Well, at least one of us is. Excuse me for a second."

"Huh?" Nate turned at a sound behind him. One of Fisher's sons—not Eddie, but the other one, whose name

Nate had forgotten—was coming down the path with a large syringe in his hand. He walked right past Nate and handed the syringe over to his father.

"Thanks, Jason."

The young man leaned down and kissed Fisher on the top of his bald head. "Susan's on the way. She's getting the water."

Fisher nodded. Nate sat there, watching the syringe closely.

"Don't worry," Fisher said, smiling warmly. "It's not for you."

Nate didn't reply. Fisher's oldest daughter was coming down the path carrying a white tray. On the tray Nate saw a glass measuring cup with a little bit of water in the bottom, some kind of stove burner, a couple of red and white packets of Fleischmann's yeast, and a single slice of bread.

The girl put the tray down next to her father. "Good night, Daddy. I'm going to turn in."

"Okay, sweetheart. I'll come check on you later."

She bent down and kissed Fisher, just as her brother had done, and then went back up to the campsite.

"Do you see what I mean?" Fisher said. He was setting up the stove, turning on the gas and lighting it with a match he struck on the side of his shoe. "Being with other people—Sartre was wrong—it's anything but hell. It's our connection to them that makes us strong. That's what gives our lives meaning."

Nate kept his silence. Perhaps Fisher hadn't intended for him to respond, because he went immediately to work setting the glass measuring cup on a small metal rack over the burner's low flame. Both men watched it work in silence, and after a few minutes Fisher reached into his pocket and removed a thermometer from his shirt pocket. "The yeast needs the water at a hundred and five degrees." He dunked the thermometer into the measuring cup and watched the mercury rise. "Takes a few minutes," he said.

He looked at Nate and smiled.

Nate listened to the mosquitoes buzzing a short distance off. Somewhere out in the woods an owl hooted.

"There it is," Fisher said. He removed the thermometer and poured in the yeast and swirled the measuring cup around to distribute the mixture. Then he took the syringe and squirted the thick, reddish liquid inside into the yeast mixture. "Stuff tastes horrible without the yeast," he said. Then he poured the liquid onto the slice of bread and ate it, wincing at the taste. "Of course, it tastes horrible with it, too—but it won't work without it."

Then Fisher pushed the plate away and rolled over on his back, staring up at the stars. Nate did the same. There were no clouds, and very little breeze; a pleasant night. It had been a long time since Nate had looked at the stars, really looked at them, and he was amazed at how many there were. They filled the sky, and for the first time in his life he realized how people could see patterns up there.

"You don't talk much, do you, Nate?"

Nate turned his head. Fisher was still looking at the stars, his hands laced together behind his head.

"Not really, no," Nate said.

"How about a family? Mom? Dad?"

"My mom died when I was little. My dad was going with his girlfriend to pick up her parents when the outbreak hit Martindale. I don't know what happened to him. I guess he's dead."

"So it's just you?"

Nate rubbed the flash drive through his shirt. "Yeah, just me."

There was a flash of movement as Fisher flipped over

onto his belly and pushed himself up with his hands. He dragged himself toward the path that led up to the rest of the campsite, then stopped and turned around.

"I hope you find what you're looking for, son—and I hope you find it soon. It's a big lonely world out there without other people."

Nate watched him go in silence; and when he was out of sight, Nate rolled over onto his back again and watched the stars until he fell asleep.

He woke the next morning with sunlight on his face. Nate listened for the sound of voices, and heard nothing but birds squawking at each other. Slowly, he rose to his feet. He was still stiff in his shoulders and in his lower back, but his head was clearer. He touched his forehead and it was cool. And, he realized, last night had been the first time in two or three days where he hadn't woken in the middle of the night trembling from head to foot. Had the fever broken?

"Hello?" he called out.

No answer came back to him. He turned up the path and climbed to the campsite, but no one was there. There wasn't a single piece of trash anywhere. The stones that had ringed the fire were still in place, but the embers had been buried in dirt. Here and there he saw faint footprints and the impressions of bedrolls where the individual members of the family had slept. The only thing they'd left behind was a cardboard box, tucked just out of sight of the side path that led back to the main path between the road and the river.

Nate pulled the box out and looked inside. He found a bar of soap sitting on top of a change of clothes, a blue backpack, a bedroll, a pair of scissors, some razors, a Mason jar, a small cast-iron pan, a can of Wolf Chili, and the rest of the medicine Fisher had given him the night before. The blister packs were stashed inside a plastic zip-top Baggie with a handwritten note under the baggie.

It read:

Hope this helps. Cut your hair and beard and take a long bath in the river with the soap. You'll feel better, I promise. Also, don't forget to take one of the yellow and white pills in the morning and at night, and one of the pink in the morning. Take them all, even when you start to feel better. Good luck to you, son, and remember: the sooner you learn to trust others, the sooner you'll find what you're looking for.

Best,
Don Fisher

Nate took a long time working his way through the note. Even back in high school, when they were putting him through those special classes and working with him every day, he had a lot of trouble deciphering something that was more than four or five words long. But eventually he got the sense pulled out of it and put the note aside.

Then he picked up the scissors and the soap and headed down to the river.

CHAPTER 10

Richardson awoke to the muffled *pop pop pop* of automatic weapons fire.

At first he didn't recognize it for what it was. He lay still, his eyes open wide, listening, trying to zero in on the sound and identify it. His eyes were itchy, watery, his sinuses congested. The hay and dust in the barn's loft were playing havoc with his allergies, and his senses seemed wrapped in a fog that wouldn't dispel.

Pop pop. Pop pop pop pop.

The second time there was no mistaking the sound. Guns, lots of them. And he could hear men yelling, too. Richardson sat up and looked around.

"What was that?" Sylvia said. Like him, she was sitting up, a startled expression on her face. There was hay on her clothes and in her shaggy mass of gray hair.

Avery Harper had slept next to her, curled up like a child. All the walking they'd done the day before had left her exhausted, and she'd been the first to fall asleep. But now even

Avery was coming around. "What's going on?" she said groggily, rubbing the side of her head.

"Gunfire," he said.

Richardson scrambled to the wall on his hands and knees and peered through the slats. He could see a corner of a farmhouse and a large, overgrown field on the other side of the house. Before the outbreak, the field had been used for corn, and he could still see remnants of that crop out there, though now the ordered rows were rangy and crowded with spindly shrubs and weeds. Looking closely, he saw a dozen or so men crouched in the field, using the tall weeds for cover. They were firing in every direction, pinned down by a squad of black shirts.

"That's Jude McHenry," Sylvia said. "Damn it. How did they find us?"

Richardson let out a sigh. Looking back on it, it wasn't much of a mystery. The scraggly looking man the soldiers pulled from the gas station's service bay had saved their lives. He'd led the Red Man's soldiers away on a wild chase, and when the soldiers returned empty handed, the Red Man and his caravan moved out, leaving Richardson, Sylvia, and Avery a little confused by what had just happened, but still conscious of the fact that they had dodged a mighty big bullet. Foolishly, he realized now, Richardson had let himself think they were in the clear. They'd walked the remainder of the day, eating fruit they found growing along the road and chatting happily, eventually coming to this farmhouse, where Richardson managed to shoot a small turkey hen with his pistol while the women gathered wild corn and oranges. They roasted the turkey over an open fire on the driveway that led up to the farmhouse. The oranges were small and full of seeds and almost as tart as a lemon, but they were very good, and very juicy. They ate until they were bloated and tired, then they crawled up here to this hayloft to sleep.

But it was the smoke from the fire that had given them away. That's where they had screwed up, he realized. The evening had been a clear one, and the white column of smoke from their campfire must have been visible for miles. They might as well have put up a neon sign. Stupid, he thought. He knew better.

"We've got bigger problems than that," Richardson said. "Look over there." He nodded toward the road. The Red Man's caravan of trucks was parked there, and a few of his soldiers were offloading the zombies.

"What are they doing?" Avery asked.

The answer seemed obvious to Richardson. If the Red Man could control zombies, he'd obviously use them to fill the front lines of an attack on McHenry's squad. He was more worried about how they were going to escape.

Richardson crawled over to the far side of the hayloft and peered out of the west side of the barn. The cornfield stretched into the distance some four or five hundred yards, terminating at a line of trees, the edge of which was thick with early morning fog. He saw the zombies right away, forty or fifty of them at least, stumbling their way through the rows.

"Damn," he muttered.

"What is it?" Sylvia asked.

"No go," he said. "They've got us surrounded."

He moved back to his previous position next to Sylvia and squeezed the hay and dust from his eyes.

"You okay?" Sylvia asked.

"Allergies," he said.

"Yeah, well, do us all a favor and don't sneeze, okay?"

He gave her a halfhearted smile and then went back to watching the battle develop down below. Roving camera, he thought. Don't get involved. The mantra that had carried him through so many dangerous situations over the last few years seemed ridiculous now. He was in this up to his eyeballs.

He leaned forward through shafts of sunlight and put his face up against one of the gaps in the barn's wall. They were in a unique position to see the battle develop, like a high school marching band director up on a ladder stand. A group of black shirts ran forward, firing their guns into the weeds, sending up a spray of exploded corn in the process. McHenry's squad just hunkered down on their bellies, letting the shots tear up the corn over their heads. They didn't return fire until the black shirts broke through the corn rows right in front of them, and then they started shooting back.

It was, Richardson saw, a deliberate feint on the part of the black shirts. As soon as McHenry's squad started shooting, the black shirts fell back. One of them popped a canister of orange smoke and threw it at McHenry's location. Immediately, a column of smoke rose into the air. A moan went up from the west side of the barn, and the zombies moved forward, converging on the smoke.

Beside him, Avery groaned. "They'll be slaughtered," she said.

Richardson was thinking the same thing. This wasn't going to be pretty. There were even more zombies in the corn than Richardson had at first thought. They were everywhere. The corn rows were writhing.

McHenry's men had already spotted the first few zombies coming at them and were forming themselves into a defensive circle. The men were keeping their cool, firing in controlled bursts at the zombies as they appeared, perhaps because they didn't know exactly how outnumbered they were. But from his position in the hayloft, Richardson could see that the end was a foregone conclusion. It was just a matter of time.

"Where did all those zombies come from?" Richardson

asked. "There's way more down there than what he brought in those trucks of his."

"He collects them as he goes," Sylvia said. "That's why he's so strong. No matter where he goes, his army comes to him."

Her voice seemed strangely flat, and Richardson turned to look at her. Sunshine was slanting down into the shadows of the loft through the gaps in the slats. Dust and bits of hay floated around her hair. Her beauty surprised him for the second time, and it was all the more striking for the somber expression on her face.

From the cornfield down below, a man let out a sudden, terrible scream, and Sylvia flinched. And in that moment, the tone of her voice and the sadness in her eyes made sense to him.

"You know those men down there, don't you?"

She nodded. Then she closed her eyes and ducked her chin to her chest as she tried to shut out the noise of the screams and the constant roll of the gunfire.

"I'm sorry," he said.

"They came here because of us." She rubbed her knuckles into her forehead, as though trying to scrub away a mounting headache. "Why do so many people have to die because of what I believe, Ben?"

Her question was spoken so faintly he had trouble hearing it. He started to tell her it was going to be okay, that what was going on down there was not her fault, but the end result of a course of action those men had chosen themselves, but then he realized that she wasn't talking about those men down there.

He had driven the bus out of San Antonio eight years ago, when she lost all the students that came with her as part of the People for an Ethical Solution expedition, and he had stolen a few glances at her as they trundled through the ruins. She hadn't spoken a word, and that had bothered Richardson at the time. It more than bothered him. He'd been offended to the core by what he perceived as her icy indifference to the deaths she had just caused. Forty college kids were dead because they had placed blind faith in her. Richardson knew she hadn't planned on their dying. If anything, their deaths would be a mortal blow to her cause. So no, he didn't believe she had intentionally caused their deaths. But she had used her position as a professor, as an intellectual authority in their lives, to lead them into a meat grinder, and wasn't that just as bad?

At the time he thought so. And a part of him hated her because she sat there on that bus refusing to utter a word. She simply sat there, her chin in her hand, watching the ruins of San Antonio slip away outside the bus.

At the quarantine wall, they'd been stopped by the military. Soldiers had led them off the bus and checked their papers and stripped them and checked them for injuries and then sprayed them down with antivirals and disinfectant. Right before they were separated, he had asked her, "What are you going to tell them?"

She wouldn't look at him, even then. "Tell them whatever you want," she said. "I don't care what you say."

And then the soldiers led her away for her debriefing, and he watched her go, feeling angry and, for some reason that he couldn't quite fathom, betrayed. He had no idea what he had expected her to say, but it hadn't been that.

Sylvia turned from the slats in the wall and looked at him. She looked ill, and it occurred to him that he had forced the old wound open by coming back into her life like this.

Good, he thought, surprised at how fresh the anger still seemed, *I hope it hurts*.

She said, "I told myself I would go to the parents of each of those kids on that bus, Ben. That was the promise I made myself. I figured those kids deserved it for believing the way they did. I knew none of those parents would understand but I told myself I would do it anyway."

"But you never went," he said. He intended the words to have more heat than they did. She was tearing herself up inside, he realized. She was doing more damage to herself with her memories than he ever could with his harsh words.

"No," she said. "I never went. I had all their names, all their addresses. The university fired me, of course, so I had nothing but time. But then the weeks slipped by, and I hadn't visited a single one. All I did was stay in bed and cry. I told myself I'd at least write a letter, but . . ."

She trailed off there, shaking her head at the memory of her failure.

A bullet struck the slats down at the other end of the loft and a laser of light lanced into the darkness. The yelling was getting louder now, the fight spilling into the driveway in front of the farmhouse. Just a quick glance was enough for Richardson to see that McHenry's squad had completely broken ranks. They were fighting hand to hand now, totally unorganized.

"Sylvia," he said, "you two come over here with me. We need to stay—"

There was a crack and something sliced the air in front of his face. He felt a tingling spread across his cheek that suddenly turned into a burn. His first thought was, I've been shot: and then, as shock gave way to denial, he touched his fingers to his face and felt small bits of wood splinters stuck in his skin. Only splinters, he thought. Oh thank God.

He turned to the wood slats and saw the jagged hole left by the bullet that had narrowly missed his head. Looking through it, he could see one of the last of McHenry's squad down there on the road, swinging his rifle like a club at a zombie.

The zombie went down, but there were more pouring out of the corn every second.

Richardson heard men yelling orders off to his right and turned to see several of the Red Man's soldiers running toward the farmhouse. One of the black shirts raised his rifle as he ran and fired at the last of McHenry's squad.

The man who had been using his rifle as a club was struck in the chest and was flung backward, with bloody bits of flesh and fabric spraying up from the wound. One of the zombies behind him twisted suddenly and stumbled to his knees. The zombie's hands were swatting at the air like he was being attacked by bees, bright gouts of blood oozing down his chest from the wound where his face had been.

When the zombie fell over dead, Richardson turned back to Sylvia. She and Avery were still holding each other.

"Get down," he hissed. "Both of you get down."

Avery looked at him from beneath Sylvia's mass of hair. Her eyes were shining with tears.

He motioned to her to lie down in the hay, and after a moment, she and Sylvia both lowered themselves down on their bellies.

A pair of trucks pulled up to the driveway below them and Richardson crawled back to the wall and looked through the bullet hole. The Red Man was standing next to one of the trucks, surveying the destruction. There were bodies all around him. Most were zombies, but here and there Richardson could see a few of McHenry's squad and even one or two of the black shirts. He could also see a lot of wounded zombies, some of them so badly shot up they couldn't even crawl, while others, dragging dead legs or waving armless stumps, staggered toward the trucks.

The Red Man let out a low, rattling moan, and all the zombies stopped. None of them blinked. They just stared at him, swaying on their feet as though drunk. Then he motioned toward the truck and two of his soldiers pulled Niki Booth from the cab.

"Oh my God," Avery said. "Niki."

"Shhh," Richardson cautioned her. "Not too loud."

The Red Man held out a hand and one of his soldiers handed him a knife. Then he crossed the driveway to where one of McHenry's squad was dying. The man was on his back, twitching and moaning, trying to point a finger at Niki Booth.

Two of the black shirts grabbed Niki and pulled her over to the Red Man, who knelt down next to the dying man and began carving one of the ears from his head. Screams echoed over the corn.

Niki tried to turn her head, but the soldiers wouldn't let her.

"This was Ken Stoler's mighty rescue party," he said, holding up the bloody ear. Black blood dripped off the Red Man's fingers. "Nobody's coming for you, Niki. You realize that now, don't you? Do the right thing and tell me where I can find Don Fisher right now."

Niki said nothing.

"No?" The Red Man held up the ear he'd just cut from the dying soldier's head. "You know that man, don't you? I bet you trained him yourself, didn't you? Well Niki, you have the power now to decide how he's gonna die." Then the Red Man turned and flung the man's ear between two zombies, who immediately fell on the morsel like snarling dogs in a pit. "He can die like that. Or you can tell me where I can find Don Fisher, and I'll have my soldiers shoot him in the head. It'll be over in one shot."

Even from the hayloft, Richardson could see Niki Booth steeling herself against the decision she was forced to make.

She shook her head.

"You sadden me, Niki," the Red Man said. "You truly do."

He let out another low, rattling moan, and the zombies who had been waiting at the edge of the corn moved forward like a wave and descended on the dying soldier, whose panicked whimpering had turned to screams once more. They ripped him open in seconds, pulling him apart, leaving nothing but a bloody puddle in the dirt. Richardson nearly threw up watching one of the zombies drag an arm across the driveway and into the ditch, where it started feeding.

Roving camera, he thought. Roving camera. I'm a roving camera. He repeated it in his head again and again, as though in the repetition of it he could force the images of the man's death out of his head.

A moment later the black shirts were stuffing Niki Booth back in the truck and the whole caravan was driving away, leaving a driveway full of bodies and zombies too wounded to climb into the trucks.

Richardson fell back on his butt in shocked disbelief. Had life become so cheap that it could be tossed aside like that? He turned to look at Sylvia and Avery, but they were as horrified as he was.

They sat that way for a long time, none of them speaking, until they heard a man's voice say, "Dude, just stay down."

Richardson glanced at the women.

"Who is that?" he whispered.

Sylvia shrugged.

Richardson leaned forward and peered through the slats. He saw a scraggly looking younger man on the driveway. He was holding an AR-15, but it was obvious from his stance and the way he gripped the weapon that he didn't know how to use it. Ten yards ahead of him was a zombie, struggling to stand on the one leg he had left. The other was a burned and bleeding stump severed just above the knee. Both the zombie's arms looked broken as well. Every time it tried to stand, it collapsed in a heap. It was breathing hard, and when at last it couldn't muster the strength to stand, it tried to pull itself along with its mangled fingers.

"Dude, come on," the scraggly looking man said. He pointed the rifle at the zombie and pulled the trigger. It jumped in his hands as a three-round burst left the gun, killing the zombie. Then he lowered the weapon and looked around. A dozen more zombies were pulling themselves along with their fingers, inching closer to him.

"That's the man from the gas station," Richardson said.

"No," Sylvia said. "Impossible. He'd have changed by now."

"It is. Look at him."

All three of them did. Then Sylvia sat back and shook her head. "That's impossible . . . Ben, wait! Where are you going?"

CHAPTER 11

The morning had greeted Nate Royal with a kick in the ribs and something heavy dropping down on top of him.

Nate groaned with the pain.

He tried to roll over, but the body on top of him wouldn't budge.

"Get off," he said, pushing the body away. His arms felt limp as wet pasta. There was no strength in them; and even the slight effort of rolling over left him exhausted. With his head spinning and his stomach threatening to rise up his throat, he blinked at the man who had tripped over him and was now rising to his feet.

"Oh shit," Nate said.

The man was a zombie. He was dressed in soiled rags, his face covered with abscesses and oozing sores. One ear was missing, and that side of his head and the shoulder beneath it was dark and crusty with dried blood. The zombie bared his teeth at Nate, and a stuttering moan escaped his lips.

The moan was answered by other zombies all around them, just out of sight in the corn. Backing away from the zombie, Nate looked around. He couldn't see through the head-high cornstalks, but even through his fevered disorientation, he could sense movement all around him.

"Christ, not again."

Nate tripped over a backpack on the ground, and for a moment couldn't place it. The fever still gripped him. His body felt achy and weak, his head in a fog. But he remembered walking up by the river and finding the family that had taken care of him gone, their campsite cleaned of everything but the backpack at his feet. He remembered picking up the backpack and walking most of the day. The smoke and the smell of roasting meat had brought him to this place. He'd hoped that it was the family who had gone off and left him. But he hadn't been able to make it all the way. He got lost in this cornfield in the dark, and when he tripped and fell, he just stayed there, unable to get back up.

But he had to move now. The zombie brought its hands up and started clutching for him. Its moans were becoming louder, more insistent. And other zombies were answering it. Nate looked over his shoulder and saw movement in the corn.

The zombie put its hand on Nate's arm. He felt pressure from the thing's fingernails.

"Get off," he said, and yanked his arm away.

The zombie stumbled forward and fell face-first at Nate's feet. Nate backed away quickly. The zombie was on top of the backpack and Nate reached down and pulled it out from under the zombie. And as the bag came away, a can of green beans fell into the dirt between them.

The zombie was trying to get to its feet. Nate tossed the backpack aside and scooped up the can of beans just as the zombie turned to face him. Gripping the can with both hands he swung it down on the zombie's forehead. The edge of the can struck the thing's forehead and bounced off, and

Nate, who with his fever could hardly keep his balance, went tumbling after it.

He landed painfully, his hands bunched up underneath him. Nate heard a moan and rolled over. The zombie's head was haloed by morning sunlight, but Nate could still see the enormous gash across its forehead where the edge of the can had cut it. Fresh blood was streaming down the thing's face, getting in its eyes. It was reaching for him frantically, its moaning coming in a quick, animal-like snarl as its fingers tore at the stalks of corn all around it.

Nate clambered away on his hands and knees. The zombie was right behind him, stepping on his feet, its fingers at the small of Nate's back.

Nate gave the zombie a kick in the knee and rolled to one side, and when he did he saw a stick about as long as his arm in the dirt. He picked it up and climbed to his feet. The zombie was turning toward him, its face covered with blood. Nate took the stick in both hands and stabbed the zombie in the face, catching it in the eye and causing it to fall to the ground, where it rolled over onto its side, twitching as if it had been electrocuted.

Watching it, Nate let out a long sigh. He felt like he had to throw up, but as soon as he bent over, he saw more of the infected crashing through the corn, coming his way.

"Damn it," he said. He didn't have the energy for this.

There was a farmhouse behind him. He turned and staggered off in that direction.

Nate was aware of noise, but his fever-addled mind couldn't pick it apart. He couldn't identify it.

But he could hear the zombies moaning behind him. There was no confusion there. A bite from one of the zombies wouldn't hurt him—not a small bite anyway—but if they caught him there would be no way in hell he'd be able to wrestle with them. Two or three of them would be able to pull him apart, and his immunity couldn't help him with that.

The noise was growing louder. He could hear men screaming. And was that gunfire he heard? It sounded sporadic. Panicked.

Something invisible whistled past his face. The next moment, the air seemed to come alive around his head. A high-pitched sizzle, like the sound of an angry swarm of bees, enveloped him. Stalks of corn and leaves were exploding, filing the air with floating bits of plant matter.

Bees? he thought. *Oh shit, bees.*

Nate swatted at the air, trying to wave away the dark specks floating all around him. Between the noise and the fever and the floating bits whirling around him, he felt disoriented. He stumbled as he turned, trying to find the farmhouse but suddenly unable to do so.

Someone ran in front of him—a man in a gray shirt and black military style pants. He was carrying a black rifle. Nate caught a flash of him before the darkness of the corn swallowed him up.

"What the . . . ?"

Nate turned around again, and this time he could see another man, dressed just like the first soldier who had sprinted by him, firing at a pair of zombies. Both zombies went down, but not before a third stepped out of the corn next to the man and tackled him to the ground. The zombie ripped into the man's throat, spattering blood all over the corn as the soldier's body twitched and convulsed under the attack.

Nate could only stand there and stare at the ferocity of the attack.

Thankfully, the man's screams were cut short by gunfire.

He had wandered into a full-fledged battle, Nate realized.

Looking around, he could see men in gray shirts and black pants fighting the zombies pouring out of the corn. Bullets continued to fly, but the soldiers had lost control of the situation. Even Nate could see that. The zombies had broken through their lines and now the soldiers were on their own, firing at random into the corn, swinging their guns like clubs when their ammunition ran out, dropping to the ground beneath a hail of hands and teeth, their shrieks rising into the air unheeded.

Nate was nearing the edge of the corn. Beyond it, he could see a dirt driveway that led between the farmhouse and its barn. A few of the soldiers had managed to make it there already, but they were dying just like the others still stuck in the corn.

One of the zombies moaned behind him and Nate turned. It was the same zombie he'd gouged with the stick, and he could still see its blood and dirt–stained end protruding from the eye.

A sickened groan escaped Nate's lips.

"No," he said. "Dude, stay down."

He was about to rush forward and push the zombie down when one of the soldiers stumbled out of the corn next to him and opened fire. The bullets whizzed past Nate's head and thudded into the zombie with the stick in its eye. The zombie convulsed and fell to its knees.

Nate, for his part, turned to watch the soldier run out of the corn and into the driveway, and right into the path of two big black trucks. The soldier turned his rifle onto the men in black pouring out of the trucks, but he wasn't fast enough. One of the men got off a burst of fire first and hit the soldier in the gut. The man collapsed into the dirt of the driveway and rolled over, groaning, unable to get back up.

Nate recognized the men in the black shirts right away. They were the same men who had chased him from the gas station. Recognition went through him like an electrical surge. He backed up from the edge of the corn and knelt down.

As he watched he realized that the sounds of the fighting were gone. There was no more shooting, no more screaming. The only noise came from a warm breeze whistling quietly through the corn and the faint murmur of groans from the wounded.

How did they find me? Nate thought. *Jesus. It's me. They're here for me.*

"What do I do, Doc?" Nate said. "Come on, Doc. I need some help."

Kellogg stepped through the corn, bits of floating leaves drifting through his form. He knelt down next to Nate, studying the events playing out in the driveway.

"Looks like you got yourself into a mess," he said.

"Just tell me what to do, Doc."

"Stay down. Keep quiet. If they see you, run back into the corn."

"I can't run, Doc. I'm hurting really bad."

"Then keep your head down and hope they don't see you."

A flash of red caught Nate's eye and he looked up. The Red Man, the same one who had tried to infect Nate by sticking his finger in Nate's mouth, was getting out of the truck and walking over to the gut-shot soldier.

"What in the hell . . . ?"

"That right there," Kellogg said, "is trouble. Bad trouble."

The Red Man looked down at the wounded man, then turned back to his truck, where two men in black were leading a pretty girl in handcuffs to the middle of the driveway.

Despite his fear and his fever, Nate tilted his head to one side in appreciation. The girl had a nice shape, even in those military-style pants.

One of the black shirts handed the Red Man a hunting knife. Without flourish or hesitation, the Red Man knelt down next to the wounded man and sliced his ear off. "This was Ken Stoler's mighty rescue party," the Red Man said to the handcuffed girl. He showed her the ear, the blood dripping from his hand. "Nobody's coming for you, Niki. You realize that now, don't you? Do the right thing and tell me where I can find Don Fisher right now."

Don Fisher, Nate thought. Holy crap.

"Doc, what's going on?"

"Quiet, Nate."

"No?" The Red Man held up the ear he'd just cut from the dying man's head. His eyes were locked on the pretty girl's face. "You know that man, don't you? I bet you trained him yourself, didn't you? Well Niki, you have the power now to decide how he's gonna die." Then the Red Man tossed the ear to a couple of waiting zombies, who tore into it like they hadn't fed in days. "He can die like that," the Red Man went on. "Or you can tell me where I can find Don Fisher, and I'll have my soldiers shoot him in the head. It'll be over in one shot."

Nate had no idea what was going on, why the Red Man was trying to bargain with this girl, but he could tell the girl was tough. She clearly knew the dying man. The way she looked at him, it was obvious she had known him for a long time. But when she straightened her back and shook her head at the Red Man, there was no hesitation.

"That one's got some grit," Nate muttered.

"Quiet, Nate," Kellogg said. "Just watch. Don't get involved. Whatever that is, it isn't your fight."

The Red Man said something to her after that, but it was drowned out by the dying man's screams as the zombies swarmed over him.

The next instant, the Red Man's soldiers were pushing the

handcuffed girl back into the truck. Then the trucks lurched forward, gravel popping beneath their tires, and they were gone, leaving only a slowly settling cloud of white dust and the muffled groans of the dying.

"Doc, what just happened?"

No answer.

"Doc?"

But Kellogg was gone.

Something rustled in the corn behind him and Nate turned. It was the zombie with the stick in its eye, crawling now, its bloody hands almost close enough to tighten around his ankle.

"Goddamn it," Nate said. "Dude."

He walked crookedly out onto the driveway. The Red Man's trucks were a long way off, almost out of sight.

Nate breathed a sigh of relief.

Turning, Nate saw the bloody mess on the driveway where the gut-shot soldier had died. There was little left but a hand here, and a foot with part of a leg still attached over there.

But his rifle was still there.

Nate walked over to the gun and picked it up. It felt light in his hands. He wasn't quite sure how to hold it, but he could see the selector switch on the side of the gun was set to BURST, and he knew that meant it would fire a bunch of rounds at a time when he pulled the trigger.

He sensed movement behind him. It was the zombie with the stick in its eye again. It had managed to crawl out of the corn and onto the driveway, its fingernails tearing off its fingertips as it pulled itself toward him.

"Dude, come on," Nate said.

Nate was exhausted. His head was swimming from the fever, but he forced himself to focus. He leveled the rifle at the zombie and pulled the trigger.

The bullets tore into its head and shoulders and broke open its skull like an egg that was dropped on the floor, its blood and brains oozing into the dirt.

"Fucking right," Nate said, swaying on his feet. "Now leave me the fuck alone."

Richardson had thrown himself over the side of the loft and was going down the ladder. Sylvia appeared above him and said, "Ben, wait. What are you doing?"

"I'm going out there, Sylvia."

"You can't. Ben, don't."

He was at the bottom of the ladder, looking up at her. "Sylvia, this is important. That guy should have turned by now. He hasn't. We have to find out what's going on with him."

She tried to argue, but Richardson didn't bother listening. He walked out of the barn and into the driveway.

And there he stopped.

He'd thought he had a good view of the fighting from the hayloft, and he had. He'd been able to see the big picture, the ebb and flow of the battle. He'd been the roving camera. But down here, on the ground, the view was something else, more visceral, more immediate. Being the camera was fine, but not like this. He saw body parts everywhere—hands, a part of a leg, a shirt with just a hunk of shoulder left in it. A few zombies were still pulling themselves along as best they could toward the wounded soldiers who blinked at the morning sunlight and reached for Richardson with bloody, trembling fingers, groaning for help. A few zombies had already latched onto the dying men, their diseased faces tearing into the soft parts of the soldiers' necks with eager, slurping sounds.

"Ben, don't go out there."

He looked over his shoulder. Sylvia was standing there, at the entrance to the barn. Her expression was desperate, terrified.

"I'll be right back," he said.

But when he walked to the middle of the driveway and got a close look at the man from the gas station, he thought that maybe he had made a bad mistake. The man's eyes shone with fever. It gave him an almost feral intensity. His face was flushed, covered in sweat and grime. There were twigs and leaves and bits of corn silk stuck in his long, shaggy hair and beard. He looked like a man who has reverted to a wild state.

"You're not infected, are you?" Richardson said.

The man raised the rifle and tried to point it at Richardson, but he was swaying badly, and he looked clumsy with the gun in his hands, like maybe it weighed too much for him.

"I don't want to hurt you," Richardson said.

The man just stared at him, like the simple act of standing up was almost too much for him.

The barrel of the gun was pointed off at the barn. Every few seconds the scraggly man's swaying would cause it to drift back toward Richardson, and then it would just as quickly slip off again. Richardson figured he could probably bum-rush the guy and get the gun away before he had a chance to fire off a shot, but an instinct told Richardson that would be the wrong way to play it.

"There are two women with me," Richardson said, "back over there at the barn. We saw what happened at the gas station yesterday, how the Red Man tried to infect you. Why haven't you turned yet?"

At the mention of the Red Man, the barrel locked on Richardson and stayed there.

"Stay away," the scraggly man said.

"Easy," Richardson answered. "I'm a friend."

"Bullshit. I ain't got no friends."

The gun barrel dipped to the ground. Richardson watched it sink, suddenly alarmed at how badly the other man was swaying. *He's gonna fall over any second*, Richardson thought.

"Doc, what do I do?"

Richardson looked around. A few zombies were slowly inching their way onto the road, pulling themselves along with ruined fingers at garden slug speed. Behind him, Sylvia and Avery were watching apprehensively. But there was no one else around.

"Who are you talking to?" Richardson asked. "Who's Doc?"

No answer.

"Hey, can you hear me? Who's Doc?"

"Zombies can't hurt me," the man said. "Nobody can hurt me. Doc said so. I'm immune."

Richardson wasn't sure he'd heard him correctly. "You're what? Hey, can you hear me?"

The man's head lolled on his shoulders and his face blanched. The gun fell from his hand. Richardson rushed forward to grab the man before he too fell to the ground, but he didn't make it in time.

The man hit the ground like a bag of rocks.

Later that afternoon, Richardson was back in the driveway, this time with a wooden baseball bat in his hands. They had hoped most of the zombies wounded during the fighting that morning would die off within a few minutes, but that hadn't happened. More than a few had gone on moaning throughout the day, and those moans had attracted other zombies who were not injured. One of those zombies had come crashing through the front door and Richardson had been forced to put it down before it got a chance to take a bite out of Avery.

After that, he'd gone outside with the bat to finish what they should have done as soon as the Red Man and his soldiers left.

"Ben." It was Sylvia, calling to him from the front porch of the abandoned farmhouse. He looked away from the zombie skull he'd just turned into mush and saw her waving at him. "He's starting to come out of it a little," she said.

He nodded, then looked back to the dead zombie at his feet, and his continued existence suddenly seemed so pointless. The wandering, the stories, the fight to survive—why was he bothering with it? Wasn't he just going to end up like this poor bastard? They all would, in the end; and everything he'd done, all the interviews, all the thinking, all the friends he'd lost since the first zombie rose up from the flooded ruins of Houston eight years ago, all of it would be for nothing. Just wasted effort.

"Ben?"

"Coming," he said, and with a sigh he turned away from the dead zombie and trotted to the farmhouse porch.

Sylvia was waiting there, leaning against a doorway that had no door. "Are you okay?" she asked. She nodded toward the driveway and the dead zombie he'd just pounded into a bloody puddle. "Did something happen?"

"No," he said. He was aware of what she was asking, but he didn't feel like getting into it with her. Not now. "We're good, I think. I checked to the edge of the corn all the way around. I didn't see any movement."

She took a long time to answer. "Okay. Well, that man is starting to come around. He's still burning up, but I think the fever will break soon. Especially once that Tamiflu kicks in." She glanced at the sky, the air already turning hazy and golden beyond the farmhouse. "Ben, I think we ought to head out as soon as we can. I'd like to be away from here before it starts getting dark."

Richardson stepped over to the doorway and glanced inside. Looters had taken most everything that wasn't nailed down. They'd left trash scattered in with the bits of the ceiling plaster that had fallen to the floor over the years. Avery had cleared away a clean area on the floor. The man was lying in the middle of that clear spot, groaning miserably, with Avery on her knees next to him. But his groaning was an improvement over the tossing and turning and constant fevered babbling he'd been doing most of the day.

"And what about him?" Richardson asked.

"What about him?"

"You're not seriously suggesting we leave him here, are you?"

"What would you have us do with him, Ben? We need to go. Avery and I, we have to get to Herculaneum and charter a boat to Chester. We don't have time for strays."

"But he's important, Sylvia. You've heard him calling out for Doc. He's got all that Tamiflu, and those antibiotics. He got those from somewhere, from somebody who knew what they were doing."

"Well, why didn't those people take care of him?"

"I don't know."

"But you think we should take care of him? Ben, how are we going to do that? We can't even defend ourselves. And somehow we have to find a way to rescue Niki."

"If we leave him here, he'll die."

"You don't know that. He's survived since the outbreak. Obviously he can take care of himself."

He grunted. Shook his head. "You were the one who tried to tell me that the infected were worth all this effort to save. Well, he's not infected. He's a human being, a living, disease-free human being. Shouldn't he be more important than those zombies out there?"

"You're being overly dramatic, Ben."

"And you're being a coldhearted bitch."

She chewed on her lip while she considered him. "I'd slap your mouth if I thought you meant that," she said.

Let it go, he thought. Make a bubble. Count to ten.

"Look," he said, "that guy is immune to the necrosis filovirus. That means something huge. In all the wandering I've done, I've never met anybody like that. Hell, I've never met anybody who even thought that was possible. And then, I meet you and Avery, and you guys tell me you're looking for somebody who's immune. Well there he is, Sylvia. He's right there. All we have to do is take him with us."

"All you've got is his word that he's immune," she said.

"And the fact that he's right there. Sylvia, you saw the Red Man try to turn him into a zombie. He should have changed by now. But he hasn't. Can you think of any other way to explain that?"

Richardson stopped there, waiting for her to reply. But when she didn't, he threw up his hands in exasperation.

"Unbelievable," he said. "You're as obstinate and bull-headed as you ever were." He shook his head, turned, and went inside.

"What are you doing?" she said to his back.

"What does it look like? I'm going to talk to him."

"You can't talk to him. You heard him raving in there. He's out of his head."

Yeah, Richardson thought. He'd heard him raving. He'd heard him talking to Doc, whoever that was. He'd heard him talking to himself, saying not to ever tell anybody anything unless you know more about them than they do about you.

"I've got an idea," Richardson said.

Avery rose from the scraggly man's side and gave

Richardson a wide berth as she made her way back to Sylvia. Richardson, meanwhile, knelt by the man's side and shook him gently.

"Hey, can you hear me?"

The man's eyes fluttered open. He took a look at Richardson, and then he crab crawled away from him.

"Easy, easy," Richardson said. "I don't want to hurt you. My name's Ben Richardson. That's Sylvia Carnes over there, and Avery Harper there."

The man's eyes went from Richardson to the women and then back to Richardson, but he said nothing.

"What's your name?"

The man seemed to consider it, then, with effort, he said, "Nate."

His voice was soft, barely a whisper. Avery had been giving him water from a plastic bottle, and there were little bubbles of water trapped in his beard.

"Nate," Richardson said. "Okay. It's good to meet you, Nate." Richardson sat down on the floor, grimacing at the stiffness in his joints. "It sucks getting old, Nate," he said, laughing.

Nate's expression didn't change.

"You've been feeling sick lately, haven't you?" Richardson said. "I saw that Tamiflu in your backpack, and those antibiotics. And you were talking to somebody named Doc while you were sleeping."

Richardson was watching Nate carefully, expecting him to glance over at his backpack. When you lived on the road, as Nate surely did, you guarded your stuff like your life depended on it . . . because it did. But to Richardson's surprise, Nate never even glanced at it. Instead, he reached to his chest and clutched something under his shirt, like he was checking to make sure it was still there.

"You don't talk much, do you?"

"No," Nate said.

"Well, that's okay. Sometimes, it's best not to say anything until you know a little bit about who you're talking to, you know what I'm saying?"

"Yeah."

"Yeah, of course you do. So I'll make it easy for you. You know my name, Ben Richardson. Before the outbreak, I was a staff writer for the *Atlantic*. That was a magazine. Ever heard of it?"

"I'm not much of a reader," Nate said.

"Ah," Richardson said. "Well, that's okay. It was a magazine, and I was a reporter. My job was to write a book about the zombie outbreak. As part of my research I went into San Antonio with Sylvia Carnes there. That's her there." Sylvia raised her hand and smiled. "San Antonio didn't work out so well. After that, I went to Houston to interview members of the Quarantine Authority. I was in a helicopter that crashed into the ruins of Houston. I met a couple of survivors and together we slogged our way to the wall. We didn't know it, but we were right in the middle of the second wave of the outbreak. We got to the wall right as it was coming down."

Richardson studied Nate's face for some sort of reaction, but there was none.

"Well," he said, pushing on, "after we reached the wall we just decided to keep going. I mean, we couldn't stay there, you know? So we wandered north until we saw signs for a community this preacher named Jasper Sewell was forming."

"The Cedar River Grasslands."

The words stopped Richardson cold. "That's right," he said. "You heard what happened at the Grasslands?"

Nate didn't answer right away. He looked around the bare, dilapidated farmhouse. He wouldn't meet their eyes.

Finally, he said, "I was there."

"You were there?" Richardson said. "At the Grasslands?"

Nate nodded.

"Uh, look," Richardson said, "it was kind of a small community. And I was there for about three months. I got to know pretty much everybody. I don't remember you."

"I was there," Nate said. A slow struggle seemed to be going on behind his scraggly beard and dirty face, like he was arguing with himself about how much to say. But at last he said, "I was at Minot Air Force Base. The doctors there were working on me because I'm immune to the disease that makes people into zombies." He ducked his head slightly and reached under the collar of his shirt and pulled out a flash drive hanging from a lanyard around his neck. "They were using me as a guinea pig to find a cure. There was a doctor there named Mark Kellogg. He managed to find the cure, and he put it on this right before the base was overrun. They all died. All of them except for a few of the officers. They put me on a helicopter and flew me to the Grasslands, hoping to keep me safe."

"Oh my God," Richardson said. "Now I remember you." His past was rushing up to meet him, and it was coming faster than he could process. First Sylvia Carnes, and then this guy, another survivor of the Grasslands. He didn't know what to say.

But Sylvia didn't give him a chance to say anything. She knelt down beside him and said, "Nate, you said there was a cure. You have it? You have the cure there?"

Nate made a fist over the flash drive.

"This doctor," she said, her voice almost trembling with excitement, "is he the one who gave you the Tamiflu and the antibiotics?"

Nate shook his head. "No, some guy gave me those."

"Who?" Sylvia said.

"I forget. Some guy. I met him down by the river. He was camping there with his family."

"What was his name, Nate? Did he tell you his name?"

"Yeah, uh, something Fisher. Weird dude. Looked like he was crippled or something. His legs didn't work. He had to pull himself around, like a snake, you know? It was kind of creepy."

Sylvia made a sound that was part laugh, and part disbelief. "Don Fisher," she said. "Was that his name, Don Fisher?"

"Yeah, I think so," Nate said. "Sounds right."

"Did you tell him about the cure? You told him that you were immune?"

"Uh, no," Nate said.

"You didn't. Nate, please tell me you're kidding. You met the man who could have interpreted that flash drive, who could have produced a cure, and you didn't say anything."

Nate didn't speak, which Richardson figured was probably for the best, for the next moment Sylvia grabbed two big handfuls of her own hair in fists clenched so tightly the knuckles cracked. Her body was shaking with anger. Then she stood up and stormed out the front door, giving the wall a good solid kick as she left.

"I'm sorry," Nate said, turning to Richardson. "I didn't know. Doc Kellogg, he told me to never tell anybody about the cure unless I was sure they were on my side. And after the Grasslands, everything's been so confusing."

"It's okay, Nate," Richardson said. "It's nothing we can't fix. I hope."

CHAPTER 12

Two days later, after Nate was well enough to travel, they entered the outskirts of Herculaneum. It was late morning and already hot. There wasn't much of a breeze, just the muddy earthy smell of the river nearby, and the sun was beating down on the back of Richardson's neck. He felt like he was being punished.

Richardson and Sylvia were out in front, while Nate Royal and Avery Harper followed about twenty steps behind. Richardson, breathing hard, wiped the sweat from his face with a rag and then folded the rag into a small square and stuffed it back into the pocket of his jeans. He was carrying his own pack, plus all the rifles they'd collected from the dead soldiers at the farmhouse battle, and the weight was starting to drag him down.

"You mind if we stop for a sec?" he said.

Sylvia looked at him. She was frowning with frustration.

Richardson was certain he saw fear there as well. With good reason, too. The night before she'd told him it had been years since she'd been this far from the compound, so this was all new to her. And the carefully constructed plan Niki Booth had set up for them was falling apart. For the first time in a long while, Sylvia Carnes was working without a safety net.

It probably didn't help matters that he'd been with her the last time she did that, back in San Antonio.

Sylvia looked over her shoulder at Avery and said, "How much farther?"

They were standing in the middle of a long, straight street, ruined buildings on either side of them. Most of the wooden telephone poles that ran the length of the street were still standing, but here and there a few had fallen and were blocking the street. Weeds and spindly shrubs grew out of cracks in the sidewalk and along the base of the buildings. In the distance, they could see the shadowy outline of a big industrial wreck, the remnants of a lead smelting plant.

Avery Harper pointed at the smelting plant and said, "We're almost there. We just keep going toward that. The free trading market is just around the right side of it."

"Okay," Sylvia said, irritably. "I guess we can rest for a second. But just for a moment."

She shook the hair off her shoulders and then pulled it back into a tight ponytail. Richardson watched her as she tied it off with her black ribbon, wondering why she bothered. The way her hair frizzed up on her, she'd be retying it before they made ten blocks.

He tried to remember her the way she'd been back in San Antonio. A little heavier maybe, softer looking, her hair still black. The years since then had made her lean and given her face an almost birdlike angularity. A funny thought occurred to him: at times, she looked an awful lot like the lawyers in the pen-and-ink drawings in the Charles Dickens books he'd had in his apartment before the outbreak. He smiled inwardly at the thought. She would be offended by the comparison, even though he didn't intend it that way. Far from it. She was actually quite pretty, knobby elbows and hooked nose and frizzy gray hair notwithstanding.

"What are you looking at?" she said, not even trying to disguise the petulance in her voice.

"I was trying to remember if you wore glasses."

"What?"

"Did you? Wear glasses, I mean? I've been thinking back to San Antonio and I can't remember if you wore glasses back then."

"No."

"You didn't? I could have sworn you did."

"I said no. Besides, you just said you couldn't remember."

"I was just asking."

"No, you weren't. You weren't making any sense. First you say you've been trying to remember but you can't. The next minute you're swearing that I did. You don't make any sense, Ben."

He didn't know what to make of that.

"I was just asking," he said.

She let out a frustrated sigh and rolled her eyes. She was carrying their water and she slid off her pack and took out a bottle of water and drank from it.

"You want some?" she asked.

He took the water and drank from the bottle and handed it back to her.

"Thanks."

She handed the bottle to Avery.

Sylvia scanned the buildings and the side streets for signs of movement. They had already seen a few turkey farmers driving their flocks to market and vegetable dealers with their carts and several people hauling wheelbarrows full of pecans and walnuts, and the increased activity had them all on edge.

"Just out of curiosity," he said, "what did you guys do for people who needed glasses? Did you have an optometrist in the compound or something?"

"What?"

"It must have come up, right? I mean, Ken Stoler wears glasses. I remember that from Eddie Hudson's book. I'm sure you had other people there who wore glasses, right? Prescriptions change over time. Glasses break, get scratched. People need new ones all the time. How'd you guys handle that?"

She stared at him, her mouth agape. "What are you asking me for? I told you I don't wear glasses. How the hell should I know what people do to get new glasses?"

He adjusted the packs on his shoulders.

"I was just asking."

"Jesus, Ben, drop it, would you? You always do that. You don't know when to leave well enough alone. You just keep picking at me."

"Me?" he said. "I can't leave well enough alone?" He knew the argument wasn't going anywhere, and by speaking all he was doing was fueling her fire, but he couldn't help himself. He said, "Hello? Pot, you're black."

"I'm what?"

"It's an expression," he said. "The kettle calling—"

"I know the expression. But you've got it backward, you moron. It's the pot calling the kettle black. The hypocrisy is on the pot's side, not the kettle's. You're calling me the pot while you're ignorant of your own hypocrisy."

"Hypocrisy? Sylvia, Jesus, I was just asking you what you guys did for glasses."

She threw up her hands and made an angry huff. "Idiot," she muttered. Then she turned away and stormed off.

He watched her go. He'd made her mad, and he didn't understand how the whole thing had gotten so out of control. It was just an honest question. And a not very important one, in the great scheme of things. He should have just let it go.

But it wasn't all his fault, he reminded himself. She'd been like this since the battle at the farmhouse, since meeting Nate and hearing that he could have saved them all a whole lot of trouble if he'd simply introduced himself to Don Fisher. It wasn't hard to figure out she was disgusted by that missed opportunity. He was, too. But that didn't account for her being angry with him.

Or maybe it did. Hell, he didn't know. It'd been six years since he'd spent any time at all with a woman. More than twenty since he'd lived with one. Most of what he remembered of women was like trying to picture a diamond through a pawnbroker's grimy yellow display case. But now that he thought about it he did remember that they saw the world differently from men. They weren't pragmatists. Yes, they had reason. But it wasn't the same kind of reason that men had. When they thought about a problem, they didn't think in a straight line, from problem to solution. Their way of thinking made countless loops and diversions on its way to a conclusion. They seemed to thrive on subtext and implied meaning, the kind of things that men just didn't have the time or patience for. Richardson found the whole thing really aggravating.

"Are you two married?"

"Huh?"

It was Nate Royal talking to him. Avery had paused for a second, then hurried on after Sylvia, leaving Richardson and Nate standing there.

"You sure act like you're married."

"We're not married," Richardson said. He adjusted the packs on his back and started walking after the women.

"Is she still angry with me?" Nate asked. His expression was wide-eyed and innocent.

"Yeah, I think so," Richardson said.

"Oh." Nate walked on sullenly beside him for a few moments before adding, "So, why is she taking it out on you?"

Richardson stopped and looked at him. Nate's fever had broken that first night after the battle at the farmhouse, and the next morning Richardson had gotten a pair of scissors and a razor and some soap and helped Nate get himself clean. They'd shaved his beard and his head and now all that remained of the shaggy mess that had once hidden his face was a light brown shadow of stubble on his cheeks and the top of his head. He had looked like a refugee from an Iron Maiden concert. Now he reminded Richardson of the wraithlike extras Hollywood movies used to show in Victorian era mental hospitals.

But he didn't look so bad that Avery Harper hadn't taken an interest in him. Shortly after his big cleanup, Nate and Avery had actually hit it off quite well. So much so that when Richardson and Sylvia had returned from gathering water and walked into the farmhouse's entranceway they'd seen Nate on his back on the floor, Avery sitting next to him, his hand on her leg while she laughed at something he was telling her.

"I don't like that," Sylvia had said.

"They're just kids," Richardson had responded.

"I don't like it," she said.

"Sylvia, you taught college. You know how this goes. Kids'll be kids. You can't keep 'em apart."

Sylvia had let out a noise somewhere between a groan and a growl, and with that one gesture she'd made it clear what she thought of Nate and Avery hooking up.

And he'd said a silent prayer for Nate.

"Mr. Richardson?"

"Huh?"

"I said why is she taking it out on you?"

Richardson laughed to himself. "You ever been married, Nate? Lived with a woman, maybe?"

"No. I lived with my dad and his girlfriend before the outbreak. Since then I haven't had too much time with a woman, if you know what I mean."

"Yeah, well, I knew Sylvia years back. There's a history there."

"You guys—" Nate made a lewd, two-handed pushing gesture, accompanied by a clicking of his tongue "—you know?"

"No. Not that it's any of your business."

Nate raised an eyebrow, then shrugged good-naturedly and let it drop.

A few minutes later they reached a slight rise at the edge of town that gave them a good view of the free trading market below. The primitive collection of tents and carts were bordered to the north by the ruins of a large lead smelting plant, to the west by a spaghetti-like tangle of railroad tracks, and to the east by the great expanse of the Mississippi River.

The free trading market was actually a lot larger than it appeared. Many of the more permanent vendors had reclaimed the abandoned boxcars on the railroad tracks and set up shop there. The main hive of shops and vendors were knotted together into lanes on the vast concrete slab that had once served as a loading area for trains and ships, but other vendors—mostly turkey and sheep herders—were spread far to the south, where their animals could drink from a large tributary that curled around the southern edge of old Herculaneum.

"Well," said Richardson, pointing down at the bustle of humanity, "there it is. The Herculaneum free trading market."

"Looks like fun," Nate said. He caught Avery's eye and gave her a wink. She giggled back at him.

Sylvia's expression was hard. "There's not going to be anything fun about it," she said. "We all need to keep our heads. There's a pretty good chance Ken Stoler has operatives down there. If so, they'll be looking for us. We need to be on the lookout for them."

They headed down a narrow business road, toward the market. There were others on the road with them, women mostly, standing in the doorways of the abandoned buildings. One of the women, a girl actually, no more than sixteen or seventeen, who looked like one of those sad-eyed waifs in the old Feed the World posters, leered at them with a crooked, black-toothed smile. She was skinny as a junkie, but her blouse was open far enough to expose most of her small breasts.

"Hey there," she called after them. "You lonely?"

Nate veered toward her. "Hey there, yourself," he said.

"Whatchu want, sweetheart?" the girl said.

Before Nate could answer Richardson grabbed him by the arm and pulled him back toward the middle of the road.

"What are you doing?" Richardson snapped.

"What?" Nate said. He flashed that wide-eyed innocent smile. "What did I do wrong?"

"Just cool it, okay? We can't afford to draw attention to ourselves."

Sylvia made another angry huff and walked off. Avery was watching the hooker, who was backing away into the shadows but still smiling at Nate, and her face was a rapidly shifting pattern of emotions, confusion and indignation and jealousy.

She ran after Sylvia. "What was that woman doing?" Richardson heard her ask.

He gave Nate a slap on the shoulder. "Come on."

The crowds got thicker as they entered the market. It had been a long while since he'd been around so many people, and Richardson felt his anxiety rising with every passing moment. They brushed against him in a constant shuffle. Vendors bartered with customers, their voices loud, abrasive. A sense of claustrophobia welled up in his chest. He was sweating, breathing fast. He couldn't stop swallowing.

And then he saw the soldiers from Ken Stoler's compound. It was a squad of five. They were dressed in the familiar gray T-shirts and black BDU pants, each of them armed with rifles. Richardson watched the man in charge of the squad, saw his head swiveling as he scanned the crowd.

"Sylvia," he said.

The soldier's eyes swept over Ben, then came back to him. He squinted at Ben, his mouth turning down at the corners. Three women carrying chickens in birdcages crossed the path between them, and the soldier craned his neck to look over the women.

"I see them," Sylvia said. "Ben, we have to get out of here."

"Over there," Richardson said, and pushed Sylvia and Avery between a pair of tents. Nate was right behind him. They pushed their way to the back of the tents, where they butted up against a brick wall. There was nowhere to go. "Damn it," he said.

He heard a commotion behind them, people being pushed out of the way.

"Hey," said the soldier. He and his squad were working their way back between the tents. "Get out here. Now."

"Ben," Sylvia said, "what we do?"

Richardson could hear the soldiers coming. Damn, there

wasn't time. "Here," he said, lifting the skirt of a tent. "Get under here."

"What are you gonna do, Ben?"

He took a water bottle and splashed some against the brick wall, then he handed the bottle and his backpack full of weapons to Sylvia. "Just get under there, both of you."

"Hey," the soldier barked again.

"Hurry, Sylvia."

She and Avery got down on their bellies and worked their way under the tent flap.

Nate tapped him on the shoulder and said, "Dude, here they come."

"Got it. Come on, whip out your dick."

"What?"

"Hurry." And before Nate could protest further, Richardson unzipped his fly and pulled out his penis and pointed it at the wall. "Do it," he said to Nate. "Come on, hurry."

Nodding slowly, Nate did the same right as the soldiers came around the corner of the tent.

"You two," the soldier said, "turn around. Slowly."

"Oh man," Richardson said, feigning surprise. He turned toward the soldier, still holding his penis in his fingers. "You scared me, man."

The soldier—his rifle was leveled at Richardson—glanced down at Richardson's penis, then to the wet spot on the wall. His face wrinkled in disgust.

"Ah," he groaned. "Put that away."

Richardson did as he was told.

"How come you didn't answer me?" the soldier said.

"Were you calling me?" Richardson said. "Wow, I'm sorry. I really had to go." He rubbed the hand he'd been holding his dick with on his pants and stuck it out to the soldier. "I'm Ben Richardson," he said. "If you were calling me, I'm sorry. I couldn't hear you."

The man lowered his rifle. "I'm not shaking your hand," he said. He pushed his way past Richardson and glanced up and down the alley behind the tents. The rest of his squad was waiting in the gap between the tents. "You guys double back," he said to his squad. "Search in between the tents." He turned back to Richardson. "Where you from?"

"Well, gosh. All over," Richardson said, scratching his head. "This is my first time here in Herculaneum, but I've been all over. Mostly, I've been up in the northwest. That's where I met Nate here. We've been going around together about two years now."

"You talk?" the soldier said to Nate.

"He can talk fine," Richardson said. "But most of what he says just tends to get us in trouble where there was no trouble before. You know what I mean? He's got a little problem understanding social cues. It ain't his fault. He fell off a two-story balcony one night when we almost got cornered by some infected and he ain't been the same since. We go around together. I watch out for him."

The soldier studied them, nodding slowly. And then, much to Richardson's relief, he turned and went back to the crowd at the front of the tents.

Watching him go, Richardson let out the breath he was holding.

"That was close," he muttered.

"What was that about me falling from a balcony?" Nate said.

"You ever read Steinbeck's *Of Mice and Men*, Nate?"

"Huh?"

Richardson smiled. "Well, that guy hasn't, either, apparently. Good thing."

"They gone?"

Richardson glanced down at the tent flap. Sylvia was looking up at him. She looked frightened.

"Yeah, they're gone." He knelt down next to her and spoke in a whisper. "Sylvia, this isn't going to work. We're gonna have to split up."

"I know. What do you want to do?"

"Nate and I will find us a boat. Can you and Avery make it down to the docks on your own?"

"Yeah, I think so."

"Okay. We'll find somebody. You guys should probably take most of the weapons, too. We need to keep those out of sight. Meet us up at Ferry Street Point."

"Good luck," she said.

"Yeah, thanks."

Nate gawked at all the stuff. He saw vendors with carts full of vegetables and tools and canned goods and jerry cans of gasoline. There were carts loaded down with pornography and dried beef and sacks of flour and nuts and sugar and even one guy selling marijuana. The smell of it caught Nate like a fishhook in his nose and he stopped to stare at the buds hanging from the roof of the vendor's cart, mouth agape. The buds were so dark in color they almost looked brown, and they were practically dripping with resin. Some of them were as fat as a leg of mutton. The old hippie behind the cart sat puffing on a small brass pipe, his face wreathed in smoke. He gave Nate a knowing smile and a nod.

"Come on," Richardson said, pulling him away by the arm.

"Dude," Nate said, "did you see the size of those buds? I ain't seen weed like that since before the outbreak."

"And what are you gonna trade for it?" Richardson said.

Nate's smile slid off his face.

"Yeah, that's what I thought. Come on."

Richardson led him toward the river and into a maze of

tents packed together as densely as a hive. They were interconnected, giving total coverage to the patrons inside, shrouding them in shadows. Right away Nate could see they were in some kind of bar. A still was cooking off to his right and the air was thick with the smell of tobacco and wood smoke and stale liquor.

"I don't see any soldiers," Nate said.

"Shhh," Richardson said. "We've been lucky so far. But keep your head on straight, okay? These are rough people. Don't say anything about yourself or what we're doing here. Just try to be invisible."

"You sound like Doc Kellogg."

Richardson gave him a sidelong glance. "Yeah," he said. "Well, it's good advice most of the time. Just watch yourself, okay?"

Nate sniffed at the tobacco smoke in the air, his mouth watering. Everywhere he looked people were smoking and drinking, whispering to each other. They glanced up at him as he and Richardson walked into the tents.

"I'm going over there," Richardson said, and pointed to a pair of old, heavyset women off at one corner of the tents. "Just try to stay out of trouble, okay?"

"Sure," Nate said. He watched Richardson approach the women. Their expressions grew hard as soon as he started speaking, and a moment later one of the women picked up her drink and walked away. The other stayed, though, frowning while she listened.

Richardson's advice to try to be invisible felt like a joke to him now that he was on his own. He felt like every eye in the place was watching him, but he tried to look like he belonged as he quietly scanned the crowd. Most had gone back to their conversations, though a few weren't even trying to hide the fact that they were staring at him.

"You're not from around here, are you?"

Startled, Nate turned and saw a girl of about seventeen leaning against a counter to his right. She was smiling at him, her dark eyes sparkling with reflected candlelight. Her dress was open at the neck, and he could see right down the front of it.

"Hi," he said, his voice cracking as he spoke.

Jesus, he thought, she's not wearing a bra.

She didn't say anything. She leaned forward a little more and put her chin in her hand, her elbow on the bar. In the shadows just beyond her face Nate could see her hips swishing back and forth.

"What's your name, sweetie?"

"Nate," he said, and swallowed nervously.

Her gaze drifted down his frame, then back up to his face. Her expression seemed to suggest that she liked what she saw.

"Where you from, Nate?"

"Up north," he said. His throat suddenly felt dry. The girl was giving off vibes that he felt down in his groin.

"They have girls up north, Nate?"

"Girls?" he repeated. Then, regaining some of his self-control, "Yeah, sure, they got girls."

"You got a girlfriend?"

"A girl—no," he said, laughing. "I'm a lone wolf, you know?" He glanced behind him and saw Richardson sitting on what looked like a roll of carpet, talking in confidential whispers with the older, heavyset woman. She was smoking a cigar now, not speaking, staring at Richardson through the smoke.

When he looked back the girl had come out from around the counter. She was very close to his right shoulder now, close enough to whisper in his ear.

"A girl gets awful lonely around here, Nate. All these old men. Wanna go out back with me and smoke a joint?"

"You bet," he said, wincing at the desperate note of enthusiasm in his voice.

She winked at him. "Follow me, Nate."

She took him by the hand and led him to the back of the maze of tents, where she slipped through the seam.

"Come on, Nate." Her voice was smooth as ice cream.

He glanced back at Richardson for just a moment, then at the girl, her breasts rising and falling slightly with each breath, her dress clinging to her erect nipples. He swallowed the lump in his throat and followed her.

But no sooner had he made it through the flap when something heavy hit him at the bundle of nerves at the base of his neck. His legs turned to water beneath him and he slumped to the ground, looking up in shock at the two men who had materialized out of nowhere. He tried to raise a feeble hand to stop the second blow, but it did no good. His vision turned purple, then black.

When he came to there were hands all over him, jerking his body from side to side as they dug into his pockets.

"Hey," he groaned. But he was unable to move. Somebody's knee was in his back.

The girl stuck a knife in his face. It was old and rusty, a double-edged stiletto with the handle wrapped up in duct tape. Nate had seen a lot of knives in a lot of hands while living on the road these last six years or so, and he doubted she knew how to use it. But of course that didn't matter. The blade was only inches from his eyes and he couldn't move his arms. He was a Thanksgiving turkey about to be carved.

"Please," he said, hoarsely.

"Fuck you, sweetie," she said. Her teeth were grinding together, her lips flecked with spit. The come-on he had seen in the bar was replaced by viciousness now. She looked like a hungry dog, ready to fight for its dinner.

He felt the knife dig into the soft flesh of his cheek and a scream welled up in his chest. He was about to let it loose when the tent flap behind him snapped open. The two men grunted as they stumbled over Nate. In the confusion, Nate scrambled away from the blade and sat against a tentpole a few feet away. Richardson was standing at the tent flap. One of the men who had jumped Nate climbed to his feet just as Richardson reached into the waistband of his jeans and pulled out a black leather blackjack.

The man let out a honking noise like an angry goose as he charged Richardson. But he never finished his attack. Richardson cuffed a backhanded swing across the man's face, catching him in the chin with a noise halfway between a slap and the clink of heavy beer mugs knocking together.

The man sank into unconsciousness.

The other man watched his partner fall. When he looked back at Richardson, the blackjack was already connecting with his groin. He doubled over with a rush of air, falling to his knees. Richardson followed the blow with a downward slap to the back of the man's head that put him flat on his face.

"Fucking asshole!" the girl shouted.

She charged Richardson, the knife waving wildly in front of her.

It did her no good. Richardson punched her in the face with his blackjack and she sank to her knees, her hands cupped over the bloody bloom that had been her nose just a moment before.

"Youth fucking bathtard," she said.

The blood was pouring out between her fingers, her face ruined.

"Shut up, bitch," he hissed, bringing the blackjack down on the side of her ear.

Nate watched the girl sink into a heap on top of the tent skirts. He stared at her, then slowly became aware of Richardson standing above him, watching him. And behind Richardson was a heavyset woman, the same one he'd been speaking to on the opposite side of the bar. She was looking at Nate like he was a dog that had just rolled in something nasty.

"Are you okay?" Richardson said.

"Huh?" Nate said.

Richardson pointed to the side of his head. "Your cheek . . . you're bleeding there."

Nate touched his own face. His fingers came away bloody.

"Yeah," he said. "I think."

Richardson nodded. "This is Gabi Hinton," he said, pointing to the old woman next to him. "She and her husband own a trawler. I think they might be able to help us."

"That remains to be seen," the woman said. She turned to leave, spreading the tent flap open. "You and Odie there want to follow me?"

The Mississippi River moved sluggishly by. Sylvia Carnes and Avery Harper knelt in a stand of tall weeds next to the water, watching the commotion up on the docks. Soldiers from Ken Stoler's compound, men Sylvia had known for years, were patrolling the docks with AR-15s at the ready. She knew they were looking for her, and she knew what would happen if they were found.

She pulled Avery close.

"What are we going to do, Sylvia?"

"Shhh. Just keep quiet."

A man named Justin Roth stopped a few feet from the weeds where the two women were hiding and pulled the walkie talkie from his belt. "Yeah, this is Squad Nine, go ahead."

The voice on the other end was broken, but Sylvia did hear it say something about trouble over at the bar.

"Squad Nine, copy," said Roth. "We're on the way."

Roth motioned to his men and then to one of the other squad leaders. Stoler's soldiers, most of whom looked bored and itching for a fight, perked up at Roth's command. From the weeds, Sylvia and Avery watched as the men huddled together, and then moved into the middle of the trading center.

"What's going on?" Avery asked.

"I don't know," Sylvia said. "But I don't like it."

Nate followed along behind Richardson and the old woman, feeling a little numb from his close encounter with death. The way that girl had looked at him, he had no doubt she'd wanted to drive that knife into his eye socket. Even now that the danger was behind him he could still feel his stomach churning with a charge of adrenaline. He scanned the faces that had just a few minutes earlier looked at him with the unabashed contempt one reserves for the stupid and was surprised to see that none of them would meet his gaze now.

Nate shifted his gaze to the old woman. She wasn't *that* old, Nate realized, just seemed that way at first glance. He guessed she was probably over sixty or thereabouts. She had large, deeply tanned arms and a bushy mess of hair that reminded Nate of smoke rising from her head. Her bottom wriggled and shifted beneath her brown linen skirt. But despite her weight and her age, she moved with confidence through the crowd, and as he watched it zipper apart for her he was reminded of a mama bear herding her cubs.

That's it, he thought, smiling. She's Mama Bear.

She led them out of the main section of the bar and into a dark, back corner. Nate followed with an odd sense of déjà vu. They saw a man sitting in a cloud of smoke, his white-bearded face illuminated momentarily by the orange glow of a lit joint. Right away, Nate caught the earthy, sweet smell of marijuana. Inhaling deeply, he sat down next to Richardson.

Gabi leaned down and gave the old man a kiss. He was older than her, and even more rugged. His beard was bushy and unkempt, his dark eyes lit with the severe confidence of a lifelong sailor. He had both of his huge arms on the table, and to Nate his fists looked like bricks.

"Hello, Sugar," he said. He winked at his wife as he gave her a pat on her prodigious butt.

She giggled as she slid in next to him. "Get your mind out of the gutter, you dirty old man. These guys want to talk business."

Right away the smile faded from his face. He put his joint down and examined Nate and Richardson. "I saw what you did to Mary and her brothers over there," he said to Richardson. "That was good work." Then his gaze shifted to Nate. "You, on the other hand. Boy, you ain't got the sense God gave cow shit if you fell for that come-on-in-the-back-with-me routine. It's a wonder you're still alive, you know that?"

"I, uh—" Nate said, fumbling over his words.

Richardson came to his rescue. "You have a boat," he said.

"That's right," the man said. "I'm Jimmy Hinton. My wife and I are the co-owners of the *Sugar Jane*. Gabi here tells me you guys want to go downriver."

"We do."

"How far downriver?"

"To a little town called Chester. You know it?"

"Chester?" Hinton glanced at his wife. "Gabi, I thought you said these guys were serious. Mr. Richardson, you have any idea what's going on that far downriver? You two ever heard of the Red Man?"

"We know about the Red Man," Richardson said. He appeared amused. "Naturally we want to avoid any contact with him. But we would like you to take us to Chester, and we'd like to leave this afternoon."

"Yeah, well, what you need to understand here, Mr. Richardson, is that an emergency on your part doesn't guarantee a sense of urgency on my part. And it occurs to me that your big challenge right now is to convince me why I need to drop everything I've got going on just to accommodate you."

Nate laughed at the man. "Everything you've got going on? Who are you kidding, guy? From where I'm sitting it looks like you ain't doing much beyond sitting on your butt getting high."

"Say that again," Hinton said, both fists on the table.

"You heard me," Nate said, rising to his feet.

"Gentlemen," Richardson said. He grabbed Nate by the elbow and pulled him back down to his seat. "Nate, please." He turned to Hinton and said, "We understand your situation, Mr. Hinton. And you're right. It is a seller's market." He reached down to his packs on the floor and put a long burlap sack on the table in front of Hinton and his wife. The rifles inside the bag clanked heavily.

"What's this?" Hinton said.

"Payment," Richardson answered. "Look inside." Richardson waited for Hinton to open the bag. When the man let out an impressed whistle, Richardson said, "You can have those two now. You can have another nine when we board your boat."

"You have eleven of these things?" Hinton said. His voice dropped uncertainly.

"That's right. All of them that good. These aren't refit jobs held together with duct tape. They're all military grade."

"Military grade," Hinton repeatedly, dreamily.

"We have ammunition, too."

Hinton let out a laugh. He glanced at his wife and an entire conversation seemed to pass between them without a single word being spoken.

"Okay," Hinton said. "We can leave first—uh oh." He nodded toward the opposite side of the bar.

Nate and Richardson shifted in their seats. Across the bar, one of Ken Stoler's squads was coming through the crowd. Hinton knocked on the table in front of Nate. "Looks like your little run-in with Mary and her brothers has brought down the law."

"Me?" Nate protested. But Hinton and his wife weren't listening. They were already rising from their chairs and stepping through a hidden flap behind the table.

"Where are you going?" Richardson said.

"To the docks," Hinton said. "Let's just say we have our own reasons for not wanting to talk to Ken Stoler's people. We'll meet you at the *Sugar Jane* in one hour. Don't be late."

"We'll be there," Richardson said. "You can count on us."

Hinton cocked an eyebrow at him, and a moment later he was gone.

CHAPTER 13

Jimmy Hinton and his wife ducked behind a vendor's cart draped with tattered winter coats and watched one of Ken Stoler's squads run into the bar. There was no mistaking the soldiers' intent. They were looking for somebody, and it didn't look like they were in the mood to do much talking.

Stoler's people were no strangers to Herculaneum's free trading market. In the five years or so that Hinton and Gabi had been doing business here, he'd come to know Stoler's people all too well. He'd done business with them many times; and, on one occasion fairly recently, lost a large shipment of beef bound for their compound to pirates up near the Iowa border.

"Jimmy," Gabi said, "we need to go."

"I know. I wonder what they're doing there, though."

"They're looking for somebody."

"Jesus, woman, I can see that." He rubbed his chin thoughtfully. Stoler had always been unpredictable, even when he got his money's worth. But he'd been especially high-strung lately. Same with his troops. Jimmy supposed it was because the Red Man's black shirts had finally broken and defeated the other compounds in the area. That would certainly account for Stoler and his people feeling on the defensive. Everybody was feeling a little bit afraid of the Red Man's growing power in the area. But even still, Stoler's people were behaving more like Nazi storm troopers than an embattled private security detail. Jimmy sensed restlessness in them. Uncertainty, maybe. Was there some kind of internal trouble in the compound, perhaps? Maybe in light of the Red Man's recent successes, and Stoler's seeming inability to stop him, his popularity with his people was waning.

Jimmy suspected that was probably the case. And it was bad for business too. Everybody along the river was starting to notice that. Regardless of what he thought of Stoler and his people, he did have to admit that at least they always demonstrated a pragmatic streak when it came to commerce. They knew to leave this bar alone. It was where all the river business got done. If your cargo needed to go anywhere on the Mississippi, from Memphis to Minneapolis, you arranged for its transport in the bar at Herculaneum. Now the bar too seemed to be a victim of Stoler's increasingly questionable leadership. Raiding the place would upset the delicate economy of trust that had grown up among the river pilots who made the place their home base. For Stoler, the effect was like pissing in his own pantry. Nobody would trust him after this.

"I want to go, Jimmy."

"Yeah," he said. "I think that's a real good idea."

They slipped through the maze of carts and the crowds of dazed people, all of them moving slowly in the heat of midday. In his mind, Hinton ran through the list of supplies they were going to need. It would take three, possibly four days to make the trip, and they still needed canned goods, toilet paper, and an auger to fix the crapper on board the *Sugar Jane*, which had been stopped up for over a month now. They had less than an hour to get it all done, but they could do it. At least he'd had the forethought to gas up last night. That was going to make things a lot easier.

"This is a good deal for us, right?"

"Huh?" Hinton turned to his wife, the fragility in her expression taking him by surprise. After forty-six years of marriage, after having a child together, after losing a child together, losing a grandchild together, after walking hand in hand through the apocalypse together, he had come to look upon her as his rudder. She nursed him when he was sick. She satisfied him when he was drunk and horny. She had once pulled his unconscious body from a burning warehouse down in Bartlett. And after all that, he had almost forgotten that she could, at times, look so fragile.

"Yeah, I think so," he said. "You did good setting this up. Eleven military-grade rifles." He shook his head in wonder, a smile spreading across his face. "This could be our ticket, Gabi."

"You mean it? We could really leave all this, head down to Mexico? Finally?"

"You bet," he said, still smiling.

"Tell me again how it'll be, Jimmy."

"I already told you," he said.

"Tell it again. I like to hear you tell it. Tell me about the island with the sand so white it looks like salt. And the fruit hanging off the trees. And the—"

"And the fish so big and dumb they jump right in the boat. You don't even need to put your hook in the water."

"Yes," she said, breathlessly. She took his hand in hers and squeezed it. "Tell it to me again, please."

"Okay," he said. "Jesus, woman, the things you put me through." It had been six years since they'd lost their only daughter, Eileen, and her daughter, Sarah, to a zombie attack in Sarasota, Florida. After that, Jimmy and Gabi had taken their trawler, the *Sugar Jane*, and gone cruising, always staying one step ahead of the zombie hordes, and finally settling here on the Mississippi. For five years, they'd lived as river Bedouins, hauling pick-me-up cargo up and down the river in a never-ending loop.

In many ways, their marriage had taken on the same kind of circularity. They were both running from their memories of the past, never staying in one place long enough for the images of what they'd lost to catch up with them. They floated up and down the Mississippi, Jimmy telling Gabi about the island to which they would one day run. They would settle there, eating fruit from the trees, drinking booze with their toes buried in the white sand, eating pan-seared red snapper by a campfire at night. He'd told the story so many times that he could picture that dream island down off the Mexican coast as clearly as he could remember the way his granddaughter had squeezed his finger when she took her first steps. But like that memory, the island had always seemed like it belonged to another time, one that he and Gabi would never live to see.

The eleven military-grade weapons would change that. They could trade those guns for everything they'd need to make the trip down to the wild zones of old Mexico. It might actually be happening for them; finally, after all these years, after all they'd been through together. And it was then, as they walked through the market toward the docks, and as Jimmy began reciting, yet again, his description of the island, that he suddenly realized the fragility he had seen on Gabi's face just moments before was actually the fragility of a cherished dream birthing itself into reality. She was scared to let it see the light of day, for it was all that sustained her in this ruined world. If it died, so would she. And so would he.

"Hello there, Jimmy Hinton. Where are you guys going?"

A tall, bowlegged soldier stood in front of him. His name was Justin Roth, livestock manager for Ken Stoler's compound, and now, apparently, a squad leader. Three other men, all dressed in the Union Field gray and black uniforms, stood by looking smug.

"Hello, Justin."

Justin Roth raised a rifle at Jimmy's midsection. Behind him, his squad did the same.

"You have a lot of nerve showing yourself around here, Hinton."

"It's a free trade market, isn't it?" Jimmy replied, trying to sound unconcerned and not totally succeeding. His gaze darted across the surrounding maze of carts and the crowd of people milling about. He saw several other squads of soldiers searching the area. They could run for it, Jimmy thought, but they wouldn't get far.

"You owe Union Field six thousand pounds of beef, Hinton. It won't be a free market for you until you've paid that back. Now get your hands up."

Jimmy did as he was told. He raised his hands up around his shoulders, at the same time taking a barely perceptible half step in front of Gabi.

"What are you planning on doing, Justin?"

Jimmy could feel Gabi's hand inching down his back, then pulling the tiny metal canister from the waistband of his slacks.

"I'm gonna drag your sorry pot-smoking ass to Ken Stoler. What he's gonna do with you I can't say. But I can promise you that it is going to be a rough ride for you getting there. You might just fall down a few times, if you know what I mean."

A hard-edged smile played at the corner of the cowboy's mouth, exposing his tobacco-stained teeth.

"Yeah, I think I get you loud and clear," said Jimmy. "Gabi, what do you think?"

"Loud and clear," she said, stepping around from behind Jimmy with the metal canister raised high. She pulled the trigger on the head of the canister and it let out a liquid spray of oleoresin capsicum. Justin Roth and his squad flinched as the pepper spray hit their faces, and for a moment, nothing seemed to happen. But then, suddenly, the air seemed to catch fire. Roth and his soldiers dug their fists into their eyes. They were screaming. A few of them doubled over, coughing.

Gabi pulled Jimmy back into the startled crowd. He too could feel the pepper spray burning the back of his throat. "We gotta move," she said, and before they turned and ran she sprayed the remainder of the canister into the crowd.

Angry yells rose up all around them. People elbowed each other, trampled one another, in a mad dash to vacate the area. The scene was complete confusion. Carts were up-ended, people were yelling, fighting, scrambling to scoop up their belongings amid the rush of bodies.

Through the panic, Jimmy could see other squads of soldiers turning their heads toward the outburst. A few were already running.

"This way," Gabi said, pulling him through the crowd.

He tightened his grip on her hand and let her lead him. They ran with the crowd, slowing to a walk only when they encountered people who were facing the direction from which the couple had just come.

Jimmy glanced left, then right. Stoler's soldiers were everywhere.

"Jimmy, there," said Gabi, pulling at his sleeve. "You see it?"

She was pointing at a man who was trying to guide a flock of sheep away from the turmoil. The big dumb animals were bleating irritably, but reluctantly obeying their shepherd's pushing and prodding.

Gabi ran for the flock, and before Jimmy had a solid idea of what she had in mind, she was ducking down onto all fours and crawling into the middle of the flock.

He shook his head, laughing.

"God, I love that woman."

And then he jumped down onto all fours and crawled after her.

Watching Nate gawk at the vendors and the hookers and the crowds of people, Richardson had to laugh. The man was acting like they'd landed on Sunset Strip back in its heyday, instead of some run-down flea market at the edge of a dead world. Nate's reaction was humorous to watch, but also a little sad once Richardson really thought about it. This is what they had been reduced to. Places like Herculaneum had become their Mecca, their temples. Good God, he thought, have we really fallen so far as all that, where even our dreams are small?

"Keep an eye out for the girls," Richardson said, adjusting the pair of packs on his shoulders. The rifles and the ammunition were surprisingly heavy when you had to carry them all day.

Nate chuckled. "Dude, I see a couple of them right now."

They were almost to the docks, where ten battered trawlers rocked gently in the river's current. Richardson looked back at Nate and saw him waving to a pair of rough-looking women whose occupation was obvious at a glance.

"Seriously?" Richardson said. "After what just happened, you haven't learned your lesson?"

"What?" Nate said. His smile was huge. He was really

enjoying this. "You know how long it's been since I got laid?"

"No idea," Richardson muttered, and thought: And I don't care so please don't tell me, even though I know you're about to.

"Yeah, well, I don't know, either. And brother, that's too long."

Richardson smiled perfunctorily at him, then went back to scanning the riverbank, hoping to catch some sight of Sylvia Carnes and Avery Harper. The market thinned out quite a bit this close to the docks. He saw a few vegetable stands and the occasional flock of turkeys or sheep or goats, but no sign of the women. He was worried about the squad of soldiers from Ken Stoler's compound who were standing on the dock, but he and Nate had bought the women a change of clothes that he hoped would make it easier for them to sneak onboard the *Sugar Jane*. They'd play it by ear, adjust as needed.

"How long's it been for you?" Nate said.

"Huh?"

"How long's it been since you, you know?" Nate clicked his tongue suggestively.

Richardson rolled his eyes. He had no desire to fill Nate in on the details of his sex life, just as he had no desire to think of how little there was of it to tell about. The last sexual encounter he'd had was in the winter, three years earlier. He'd been sleeping in a tent next to a road outside of Laramie, Nebraska, a foot of snow on the ground outside. A woman had come along. She was too skinny, too hungry-looking to be attractive, but she needed shelter, and food, and Richardson had enough of both to spare. He let her stay, and they slept side by side in his sleeping bag, cuddling each other, not for the thrill of it, but for warmth. Richardson had gone straight to sleep, not expecting the woman to give up anything in exchange for his kindness; but he woke with her stroking his cock with her hand, tugging on him until he came. It had been an empty, pathetic scene, devoid of passion. He hadn't made a sound. They hadn't even kissed. He never knew her name.

"That long, huh?" Nate said.

"What?" Ben said.

Nate smiled and shook his head. "Say, what do you think about Avery Harper? She's got a little meat on her, I know, but she seems pretty cool. I wonder if she's got a boyfriend back at that compound she's from."

"I doubt it," Richardson said.

"She told you that?"

"No, Nate. She didn't say a word to me about it. But seeing as all these soldiers around here are trying to kill her, I doubt she has anyone back at the compound anymore. Know what I mean?"

Nate nodded, the smile leaving his face. "Yeah," he said. "I think I got you."

They found Sylvia and Avery hiding behind a row of wrecked cars that had been there so long that weeds were growing up around the wheels and through the empty engine compartments. Richardson gave them the clothes he'd found for them and he and Nate waited while the women crawled inside one of the wrecked cars and changed. When they came out, Richardson told them about the boat he'd chartered.

"Hinton and his wife," Sylvia said, "you think we can trust them?"

"I think so. The wife seemed to have a pretty good head on her shoulders, and I got the feeling they weren't any more eager to meet up with Ken Stoler's soldiers than we are.

That's their boat right over there, the white one at slip six. It's called the *Sugar Jane*."

She nodded. The ponytail between her shoulders looked as lively as a squirrel back there, and he frowned, looking at it.

"What is it?" she asked.

"Your hair." The clothes he'd obtained for them managed to change their appearance somewhat, but that head of frizzy gray hair of hers was going to give them away for sure if any of Stoler's soldiers got close. And they still had to get past the squad stationed at the entrance to the docks. "Have you ever thought of cutting it? I mean really short?"

"Cut my hair?" she said. She looked momentarily horrified.

But she didn't get to finish the rest of it. Before she could say anything else, they heard a lot of yelling coming from the edge of the market. The soldiers who had been lounging around the entry to the docks sprinted toward the disturbance.

"That doesn't look good," Nate said.

They heard two shotgun blasts and more screaming.

Avery put a hand on Sylvia's shoulder. "There's no one guarding the docks," she said. "We should get going."

Sylvia took the young woman's hand and squeezed it. "She's right, Ben. Let's move while we have a chance."

Another shotgun blast from the edge of the market made them turn. Jimmy Hinton and his wife, who was wielding the shotgun, were running into the clearing. Though it wasn't really a run. Both husband and wife were in their late sixties and overweight, and they advanced with an awkward loping gait that looked terrifyingly slow compared to the soldiers chasing after them. Richardson saw one of the soldiers bring his rifle up to his shoulder and fire at the couple. Little umbrellas of dirt exploded around Hinton's feet, and he raised his arms and wobbled like a man trying to stay balanced on a high wire. Gabi Hinton turned and jammed the stock of her shotgun into her belly and fired twice at the advancing soldiers. One of the soldiers dropped to his knees, holding his side. Then she turned and ran after her husband, who was still gesturing to Richardson to get onto the dock.

Richardson ran up the short flight of stairs that led to the dock. Twenty feet ahead of him, Sylvia, Avery, and Nate were face-to-face with a soldier—the man was barely Avery's age; just a kid, really—who had his rifle leveled at them. The soldier looked frightened, almost like he was seasick, but when he saw Richardson charging up the stairs he turned and fired at Richardson. The bullet whined through the air, narrowly missing his face. Richardson ducked behind a thick wooden pylon and drew his pistol.

He gave a quick glance over his shoulder and saw that Jimmy and his wife had almost reached the dock. Then he looked back at Sylvia, Avery, and Nate, who had backed up to the edge of the dock, their hands in the air. The soldier was still standing in the middle of the gangway, the rifle down around his hips. His mouth was hanging open and his eyes were darting back and forth between his prisoners and the pylon where Richardson was hiding. It looked like he couldn't make up his mind what to do. Richardson made it up for him. He stepped out from behind the pylon with his pistol in both hands, leveled it at the soldier's chest, and fired twice before the man could register what was happening. The soldier kept his feet, even after getting hit. He staggered back to the opposite edge of the dock, his hands hanging limply at his side, the rifle dropped and forgotten on the wooden planks. His face had an elastic, slack-jawed expression as he stared about him. He never cried out. He saw a wooden pylon and fell against it. There was a look of utter disbelief on his face as he sank down onto his butt. His eyes never closed.

"David," Avery shouted. The girl ran over to him and stopped, wanting to touch him, but unable to do so.

Sylvia gave him a sad, pained look before grabbing Avery by the shoulders and pulling her toward the *Sugar Jane*.

"Good shot," Jimmy Hinton said from the top of the stairs. "You seen the boat yet?"

"Huh?" Richardson said.

"No time like right now." He turned to his wife. "Gabi, you got this rifle?"

"Got it," she said, as she too crested the top of the stairs. "Get the boat started."

"Yes, ma'am."

Gabi Hinton ran over to where the dead soldier's rifle lay on the dock and scooped it up. More soldiers were coming up the stairs. She turned the rifle on them and started firing in short, controlled bursts, aiming every shot, making them count.

"You got those rifles you promised me?" Hinton said to Richardson. "Now's the time to prove they work."

The world seemed to be swirling around Richardson, going too fast. Feeling dizzy, he took one of the AR-15s from his pack and started firing at the soldiers who were running toward them from the market. From where they were firing, he and Gabi had both cover and concealment behind the heavy dock timbers, while the soldiers had to cross nearly thirty yards of open concrete slab. They were sitting ducks down there.

"I'm out," Gabi said to him.

"Go to the boat. I can cover us."

"We'll need at least two minutes to get the boat loose from the dock."

"I got it," he said. "Go."

Gabi slung the rifle over her shoulder and waddled down the length of the dock. Richardson watched her go, then turned back to the concrete slab between the dock and the market. Nearly all the vendors had fled. Here and there he saw carts overturned, their contents spilled on the ground. Dead soldiers were everywhere. Here and there he saw a few dead vendors, and their animals.

The soldiers had taken up cover and concealment at the edges of the market. He could see their gray shirts and black pants moving in the shadows. He fired whenever he had a chance, then stopped to reload.

He ejected the empty magazine, slapped in another one, and brought the rifle back up. It had taken him less than five seconds, but in that time, two of the soldiers had sprinted from their hiding places to an overturned vegetable cart off to his left. *They're trying to flank me,* he realized. *Draw me out.*

He could see their feet under the cart, and that was enough. What he knew of fighting he'd learned from Ed Moore, the retired U.S. deputy marshal who had helped Richardson and a handful of others escape Jasper Sewell's compound years before, and he could almost hear the old marshal's voice in his ears, reminding him that, when it came to gunfights, there was no such thing as cover. You could conceal yourself, but you couldn't ever cover yourself. That was a myth.

"Damn right," he muttered, as he centered the rifle's sights on the vegetable cart and started to fire.

The bullets cut through the cart like a chainsaw, filling the air with splinters of wood and bits of vegetables, and when the dust settled, the cart was in four large pieces, dripping with the remains of pureed vegetables.

The two soldiers lay dead on the concrete behind it.

From behind him, he heard the *Sugar Jane*'s engines coughing and spluttering to life. Sylvia was calling his name. He fired at the few gray shirts he could see moving in the shadows, then turned and ran for the boat.

It was already pulling away as he reached the end of the dock. Sylvia and Gabi Hinton were motioning to him to hurry up.

"Hurry, Ben!" Sylvia shouted.

He heard more yelling behind him, and the sound of running footsteps on the wooden pier. Richardson glanced over his shoulder and saw a handful of soldiers coming up the stairs.

Jimmy was right beside him. "Let's go!" he said.

Suddenly Gabi popped up behind Sylvia. She had something in her hand. "Get your head down!" Gabi yelled, and lobbed what looked like a green baseball over Richardson's head.

A second later, there was an explosion that knocked him off his feet. He looked behind him, toward the market. The dock was in a shambles. Men were dead or dying. Burnt pieces of wood floated on the water. Smoke drifted on the breeze. There was a giant hole where the stairs had been.

She threw a grenade, Richardson realized. Holy shit. That woman's nuts.

But the shooting hadn't stopped. More of Stoler's men were emerging from the edge of the market, firing toward the *Sugar Jane*.

"Hurry!" Gabi said. "Come on."

He ducked his head and jumped into Sylvia's open arms, the two of them crashing into a padded seat on the far side of the deck. A sharp pain went through his right shoulder, and he groaned.

"Are you okay? Ben?"

He opened his eyes. He was face-to-face with Sylvia, their noses only inches apart.

Richardson nodded.

"You did good back there. Thanks."

He smiled and let out an exhausted sigh. "Yeah, you're welcome."

They were powering away from the dock now, the diesels making a huge noise, but it still seemed to Richardson like they were creeping along. He licked his lips, all at once aware of just how close he was to Sylvia. She didn't look away. He could hear her breathing and see the sparkling drops of river water in her hair.

"You still want me to cut it?" she asked.

He was about to laugh when he heard sobbing behind him. Frowning, he rolled over and saw Avery Harper with her face pressed into Nate Royal's chest. Nate seemed at a complete loss as to what to do with the crying girl, and as he put his hands on her back and slowly patted her shoulders, he looked like he'd just been handed more responsibility than he wanted to deal with.

"Is she okay?" Richardson asked Sylvia.

Sylvia shook her head. "That boy you shot on the dock—that was a friend of hers."

"Ah, Christ," Richardson said. He gave the sobbing girl another glance. "Ah, Christ."

He pulled himself up to a seated position on the gunwale and watched the Missouri coastline slip slowly away.

CHAPTER 14

The truck lumbered to a stop. Rough hands pulled Niki Booth from her seat and threw her to the ground. Even before she rose to her feet she could smell the sour-sweet stink of putrescence in the air. She was wearing a burlap hood, and the stench of rotting bodies mingled with the heat of her breath and her own suffused terror. But her isolation under the hood was also a small blessing, for it gave her a chance to steady herself before she had to face the place she had only heard of in whispered rumors from the river Bedouins in Herculaneum.

She felt a hand grip the top of the hood and yank it off. Niki wheeled around on the soldier, but he had already stepped back out of range of her feet. Apparently, he had learned his lesson after the incident the night before, when they agreed to uncuff her so she could go to the bathroom. Two of the guards, she saw, still had nasty bruises on their faces where she had kicked them.

But her anger evaporated when she saw what lay before her. And despite her best efforts to look like she could handle herself come hell or high water, she couldn't help but gasp.

She was standing on a gravel road that led down to the dock at the riverside. A forest of heavy stakes—there were two hundred, maybe more—rose up on either side of the road. Most were topped with the naked bodies of dead men who had been impaled through the rectum and allowed to slide down the spikes. Each body had its hands and feet bound together, their mouths hanging open in eternal screams. Some had been burned from the feet up, the ground around them blackened by the fire. Others had been partially eaten by the infected. The air swarmed with black crows and flies. There were more of the loathsome birds roosting on the impaled bodies, while still others fought over scraps of rotten flesh on the ground. The smell was enough to make the bile rise to the back of her mouth, but she managed to keep it down; and somehow she was able to maintain that control right up to the point where she saw the mouth of one of the men on a stake near her start to move. One look at the man's eyes and she knew he was still conscious, aware of every bit of the hell he was experiencing. At that point Niki doubled over and vomited.

When she looked up again she saw one of the guards watching her, smiling, like he was enjoying her suffering.

"What's wrong with you?" she said. "These are men. You're a man. How could you do this?"

The smile left his face.

Behind her, she heard a chorus of moans. She turned and saw Loren Skaggs leading an enormous troop of zombies toward them. Niki began to back away, but one of the guards stepped close to her and grabbed her arm tightly.

"It'd be a mistake," he said. "Stand still. Don't move."

She looked at the man as she struggled to break his grip. He wouldn't let go. Loren and his zombies were almost on them now, and she could smell them. Their moaning had blotted out everything, even the squawking of the crows.

"Hold her still," Loren said, and the sound of his voice sent a chill through her.

She stopped struggling and watched him as he passed, the red flesh on his bald head glistening like a puddle of oil.

"Bring her over with us on the ferry," Loren said to the guard.

"Yes, sir."

And with that Loren walked on down to the river and the waiting ferry, his zombies following behind like a congregation headed for baptism. They passed on either side of Niki, so close she could have reached out and touched them had her hands not been cuffed behind her back.

"Let me go," she pleaded to the guard.

"Stand still, girl. Don't you move or we'll both die."

"Please," she said. She heard the whining in her voice but she didn't care. She felt utterly defenseless and more terrified than she had been since her father died, leaving her to fend for herself and for Avery in the wilds of a blasted landscape. Her skin was crawling, the gooseflesh rising on her arms and neck. She was holding her breath, trying not to scream.

"Easy," the guard holding her arm said. "Almost through them."

A zombie—a woman in her late fifties—passed just inches from her. The zombie turned to look at Niki as she staggered by. Her face was covered with boils and abscesses and swarming with flies that probed her sores and the oozing fluid at the corners of her milky white eyes.

Unable to stand it anymore, Niki squeezed her eyes shut. She couldn't stop trembling.

* * *

When the zombies were loaded onto the ferry, two guards led Niki aboard. The guards put her in a chair in the back of the boat and she didn't resist. In front of her the zombies swayed with the motion of the boat. Loren Skaggs stood at the head of the ferry, looking off toward the crumbling ruins of the Kirkman Hyatt and Convention Center on the opposite bank. The two guards pulled on the guide rope that connected the two sides of the river, and slowly, the ferry inched its way across, the only sounds the creaking of the ropes and the squawking birds behind them.

Before her, silhouetted by the setting sun, was the hotel that Loren had turned into his own private hell on earth. Niki watched as it grew closer, and a feeling of deep despair washed over her.

Into the land of the dead, she thought.

Flanked by guards, with zombies in front of and behind her, Niki Booth was led up a concrete ramp to the ruins of what had once been the loading dock for the Convention Center portion of the hotel. The building was falling apart now. Everywhere she looked she saw broken windows. The floors were covered with mud and leaves and trash, the walls spray-painted with fading graffiti.

But there was no furniture, no equipment, no signs that an army was using this place as its headquarters. It took her a moment to notice that. All she felt walking in to the facility was a distinct sense that something was off about it. And then a soldier ordered her to stop and his voice echoed inside the two-story-high emptiness of the loading dock and it hit her. *There's nothing here, no signs of occupation.*

"What is this place?" she said.

No one answered her, and she knew she'd made a mistake. Don't show them you're afraid, kiddo. Keep 'em guessing about you.

She sensed the guards behind her had stopped and she tried to turn around.

Somebody hit her in the shoulder. "Don't turn around," one of the guards said.

"Come a little closer and say that."

A different man spoke, this one older, and a smoker, Niki guessed. His voice sounded like gravel. "You heard the lady. Uncuff her."

Niki tensed. So they wanted to have some fun with her, eh? Well, bring it, assholes.

One of the guards grabbed her handcuffs and worked the key into the hole. He was a bundle of nerves. She could feel it in the way his hands fumbled with the key and hear it in his breathing.

Niki curled her fingertips up into the man's palm and smiled when he jumped. But she didn't move. She just waited for him to come back, and when he did she curled her fingertips into his palm again and gently stroked the length of his index finger, purring under her breath as the muscles in his finger relaxed.

She heard him swallow, and then one of the cuffs fell away.

It was the break she was waiting for. She slammed her elbow back into the guard's face and felt the satisfying crunch of the bridge of his nose. Blood gushed from the man's face. He bent forward, screaming, his hands over his nose. Niki raised her boot and brought it down hard on the side of the man's knee, breaking it. He sank to one knee, the other leg bent the wrong way, eyes rolling wildly in his head. His mouth was hanging open in a scream that he couldn't quite get out. Niki still had one cuff around her right wrist, the swing arm on the left cuff dangling free. She swung the open cuff down on the man's face and the exposed swing arm caught inside his cheek like a fishhook snagging a river trout. She yanked back on the cuff and it tore through his cheek, widening his mouth by a good two inches. The man fell to the floor, writhing in pain.

Two other guards were charging her from the left. She swung the dangling handcuff at the closer of the two, catching him across the side of his face, dropping him to his knees.

The other guard had his hands up like a boxer, ready to block her next swing. Niki feinted with a backhand, then stopped midway through the arc and mule-kicked him in the balls. He doubled over with a gasp, and when the back of his head was exposed, she slammed the handcuff down, catching the swing arm around his ear and yanking back as hard as she could. The man barrel rolled in midair, landed on his face, and didn't move.

Niki didn't know if he was dead or just passed out and she didn't care. One of the guards yelled, "Beanbag her!"

She spun around to face the rest of the guards and got a glimpse of a shotgun's muzzle blast. The round hit her in the stomach and doubled her over, the pain blindingly intense. Every muscle in her gut and her chest had constricted and she couldn't breathe. She fought with her body to pull in the air she needed, but couldn't make it happen. All she managed was a thin, croaking groan.

She coughed up blood on the floor and a wave of dizzying nausea overtook her. She nearly fell over on her side.

Come on, kiddo, she told herself. *You gotta fight. Get up.*

She lifted her gaze to the narrowing circle of guards around her and tried to stand up straight. One of the guards racked a shotgun and Niki had just enough time to mentally brace herself when the second beanbag round hit her in the chest and dropped her to the ground, unconscious.

When she awoke, one of the guards had her by the ankle and was dragging her across faded red carpet. "What are . . . stop," she said, still feeling groggy. Her vision was a blur. She tried to grab hold of something, anything, but the floor beneath her had been worn smooth and all she managed to do was rake her fingernails across Berber.

The guard glanced back when he felt her start to squirm and jerked her leg even harder. "Fucking little bitch," he said.

The side of his head was dark with a livid bruise and dried blood where the handcuff swing arm had caught him. Beyond him was a large room. He was dragging her straight for it.

"No," she said. "No, stop."

"Stop my ass," he muttered.

He reached the middle of the room and grabbed her ankle with both hands and flung her across the wooden floor.

"Stay down, you little bitch," the guard said.

She looked up at him in time to see his heel come crashing down on her face, and then her world went black again.

Niki hurt everywhere. She curled into a fetal ball and cried. She had never been hurt like this before. Every muscle ached, and her mouth was thick with the coppery taste of blood.

The room was dark. Dark, and heavy with the smell of rot. The floor beneath her was cold. She blinked the purple spots from her eyes and tried to peer into the darkness. She could see dim shapes, people, but couldn't make out details.

"Hello?" she said, her voice coming out like a groan.

Her call was met with a chorus of moans. The moans rose and fell in an uneven, but urgent, ululation that she had come to know all too well over the years.

"No," she said, shaking her head.

She pulled herself to her feet, forcing her way through the pain, pivoting around in a circle, waiting for the attack she knew was sure to come.

The moaning grew louder and louder. The zombies in the dark were in a frenzy now. She heard the musical clinking of a chain-link fence, and in her mind she remembered visiting the St. Louis Zoo as a child, holding her father's hand as the two of them stared at a chimpanzee shaking furiously at the bars of his cage with both hands. She was hearing the same kind of noise now and knew there was a terrifying, frustrated, insatiable rage fueling it. But the question that mattered—indeed, the only question that really mattered—was which side of the cage was she on?

Turning in a circle, she bumped into something heavy hanging from the ceiling. Her shoulder hit the bottom edge of the object and it rocked away from her. It felt like a huge birdcage. And as soon as she moved it, the zombie inside it turned wild. Its moans rose to a fevered panting as the ghostly shape of its diseased arm shot out at her from between the bars.

Niki jumped back, her heart in her throat, her hand over her aching chest.

"Oh Jesus," she said. "Oh Jesus, oh Jesus."

She staggered backward and fell, landing on her butt. She was surrounded, and for the first time in her life she found that she couldn't make herself get back up. This was the end of the line. Her train stopped here. She was down in the bowels of the zombie king's lair and she was going to die here. The realization made her feel like she'd been run over by a truck. It flattened her, numbed her to the point that she was prepared to just let it happen. It wasn't scary anymore. All she had to do was sit still and wait for death to clamp its filthy jaws on her.

She was crying, sobbing, when a series of bright lights came on. Black shirts, she realized, standing on the edge of the room holding hand-cranked spotlights.

Niki lifted her head and saw at once that she was in a large room, lined on either side by improvised cells constructed of chain-link fencing strung over recessed chambers in the walls. Leering from behind the fencing were hundreds of zombies. They pressed against each other, clawed at each other's ruined faces, trying to squeeze through the diamond-shaped holes in the fence to get to her.

And hanging from the ceiling were three large bell cages, each one containing a zombie. It was the middle cage she had run into. The zombie inside was on his knees, his face wedged between the bars, his hands reaching for her, clutching at the empty air between them. Its milky white eyes never blinked, never looked away from the vein throbbing in her neck.

Horrified, she crawled away from it.

A door at the far end of the room opened a moment later and Loren Skaggs, the Red Man, strode into the room.

Instantly, the moaning stopped. A calm spread over the zombies as each one focused on Loren.

He walked straight for her, stopping at her feet and looking down at her with a murderous hunger in his eyes. For a terrifying moment, Niki wasn't sure if he intended to eat her or not. He just stood there, breathing heavily, watching her.

"You're bleeding," he said at last.

She didn't respond.

"What? No nasty comeback? Where's the fire, Niki? What happened to Niki Booth, the ferocious zombie fighter?"

"Your soldiers hurt me, Loren," she said. It was suddenly very difficult to keep her eyes open. She wanted to pass out.

"My soldiers haven't even started to hurt you, Niki. The worst is yet to come. There's so much more." He knelt down so that he could look her in the eyes. "But you could stop that from happening. You know that, don't you? You could tell me where Don Fisher is. Tell me where he is, Niki."

"Or what?" Niki said. Being threatened woke something primal in her, something that refused to be cowed by Loren Skaggs. Zombie king or not, he was still the same old methhead loser she'd known back in Gatling. "Or what, Loren?" she repeated, her voice stronger this time. "What do you think you can do to me that will make me betray everything I've worked for?"

He smiled.

"Niki, don't fool yourself. You're brave now. You're full of anger and meanness. You even dare to look me in the eye. But I can take away everything." He motioned toward the wall of faces watching them from between the bars. "Do you see them, Niki? There's nothing behind those eyes but what I put there. They have no will but the purpose I put in their heads, and they will obey it, even if it means their own death. I can make you like that, Niki. I can take away your very soul. And when I do, there will be nothing left inside but what I put there. I will own every inch of you. I will do everything I ever dreamed of back in school."

"Go to hell, Loren," she whispered.

He laughed as he stood up straight.

"Niki, I heard you say earlier that I have gone insane. I don't think you've judged the situation right. You see, I can be reasonable."

"What are you talking about?"

"I want Don Fisher. You know that. I know you can give him to me. And so, I propose to make a trade."

"You've got nothing I want," Niki said.

"Oh, I think I do." He walked over to the hanging cage and stuck his hand through the bars. He waved away the flies that swarmed around the zombie's sores. Then he turned back to Niki. "I remember you back in high school, Niki. You were everybody's darling, weren't you? A cheerleader, class valedictorian, volunteer at the Special Olympics. You were all kinds of hot shit."

"The past is what it is, Loren. We can't do anything about who we used to be."

"That's true," he said. "But the past can tell us about who we are now. It can tell us the kind of things we're likely to hold dear."

"You're not making sense, Loren."

"Aren't I? No? Then let me put it to you this way. Tell me where Don Fisher is right now, or I will pull every zombie for a thousand miles and use them to overrun Ken Stoler's compound. Is that plain enough for you? Every person you have come to care about, every man, woman, and child, will be gnawed to the bone. There will be nothing left of your home. What happened to Calimar, that will be a mercy killing compared to what I do to Union Field."

His face was lit with madness, and it rattled her. But it wasn't the looming threat of his red body that frightened her. No, it was more than that. She had been a member of Union Field since she was twenty-two. Ken Stoler had taken a nearly wild young woman in charge of a twelve-year-old little girl and turned her into a leader among men. She had made friends there. No, don't mince words, she thought. They're your family. The people there in Stoler's compound had become her family. Her recent fights and falling-out with Stoler were beside the point. They didn't change anything, at least not where it counted. When she left Union Field, she left a lot more than a safe haven. She left her family. And the idea of Loren's zombies killing them, improbable as it was, rattled her to her core.

"Do whatever you're gonna do," she said, praying that he would believe her. "I've got nothing there anymore."

A sneer played at the corner of his mouth. "You fight better than you lie, Niki. I know what you're really thinking. You're scared, but not scared enough. You don't think I can make good on my promise, and that's why you think you can lie to me. You've seen what, a hundred, two hundred zombies? You think that is all I control. You're wrong. Niki, I control them all. Have you ever watched an enormous flock of birds in flight? Seen the way they wheel and turn, like one mind is working them all? It's morphic fields. I don't know how, but I can see those fields. It's like a fog that I can move and push. I can control it." He gestured to the zombies behind the chain-link fencing. "I can control all of them without making a sound."

"You believe that? Loren, you really are insane."

"Niki," he said, shaking his head. "You haven't been paying attention. I know you've seen a quiet street suddenly fill with zombies. You've seen that, right? You've seen one zombie turn into a stadium full of them in the blink of an eye. Haven't you ever wondered how that happened, how they converge on a victim so suddenly, so completely?"

She didn't answer.

"Yes, you have, haven't you? I can see it in your face. You're wondering how it happens. But I know the answer, Niki. I know because I can see what connects them. I can make them do anything, go anywhere. And I can do it without ever leaving this room."

"I don't believe you."

"Like calls to like, Niki. A virus will invade a host, but it won't make its presence known until it has sufficient numbers to control the host. We've known that for a long time, even though we've never understood how it works. I still don't. But I can use it, Niki. If I concentrate, I can make a zombie in Los Angeles walk into the Pacific Ocean. I can make a crowd of them in Mexico City come north. Viruses are like that. No matter where they are in the host, they can communicate. It's not telepathy, or pheromones, or any of that shit. But it happens just the same."

He stopped there, watching her.

"You know what I think you need," he said. "You need a demonstration."

He didn't take his eyes off her. He didn't do anything but stand there. And yet, somehow, he delivered a message to the zombie behind her. It suddenly slammed itself against the bars of its cage, snarling, pounding on the metal.

She staggered to her feet and turned to watch it.

The zombie tried to tear a strip of iron with its teeth. It clamped down on the metal and tore at it, even after shattering its teeth. And when that didn't work it jammed a shoulder into the gap and pressed hard.

An uninfected person would have given up, but the zombie pushed and pushed until it bent the bars, stripping the flesh from its shoulder as it forced itself out of its cage.

"Oh my God," Niki said, backing up.

"He left here a long time ago, Niki."

She turned to look at the Red Man. He smiled back, then gestured toward the cage. One of the strips of iron snapped from its rivet and clattered to the floor. The zombie, a huge flap of bloody skin hanging loose from its shoulder, slid through the newly opened gap and dropped face-first to the floor, its right arm snapping beneath it.

With its skin hanging down around its waist like a skirt the zombie rose to its feet.

"No," Niki said. "No." That's a man, she thought. How can he still be alive?

It took a few faltering steps toward her, smearing the ground with blood. The zombie was less than five feet from her when it stopped and turned its diseased face toward the Red Man. It was swaying in a circular motion, barely able to keep its feet.

"He will walk a thousand miles more, if I want him to," the Red Man said.

"Loren, stop it, please."

"Then tell me where I can find Don Fisher?"

"Herculaneum," she said, her voice barely more than a whisper. She couldn't bring herself to look at anything but her own boots. All the fight had bled out of her. "I was supposed to meet him in Herculaneum this morning. He's probably still there."

The Red Man smiled. "Better and better, Niki. My zombies will move through Union Field, and then we will go looking for Dr. Fisher."

"What?" she said, aware of the fear in her voice but unable to stop it. "You can't. You said you just wanted Fisher."

"I do want Fisher, Niki. And when you're ready to give him to me, I'll take him. But you're still lying to me. You have three days to give me what I want. It will take at least that long for my zombies to gather at Union Field. If I have not heard the truth by then, it won't matter—not for you, or for Fisher."

With that, he turned and strode out of the room. And when the black shirts turned out the lights, the only sound she heard was the exhausted breathing of the dying zombie on the floor just a few feet away.

CHAPTER 15

It was shortly after daybreak and the light was struggling to break through the mists and white vapors that clung to the marshlands on the Illinois side of the river. Though he had been in good spirits as they powered away from Herculaneum, a night of rain that had never really been more than a thick, cold mist had left Jimmy Hinton feeling sober and uneasily alert. As soon as possible, for fuel was worth almost as much as blood these days, he'd cut the motor and let them drift downriver along the Illinois side, where they were less likely to encounter any patrols from Ken Stoler's compound. He knew it was unlikely Stoler's goons would come this far, for they were rapidly approaching the Red Man's domain, but one could never tell what Stoler might do. The man was an enigma. So they went on through the drizzly, miserable night, and for a while they traveled parallel to a dirt road that ran along the riverbank. They hid whenever possible in the thick overhanging cottonwoods because the banks were crawling with the infected moving south through the streams of mist, as though they were responding to some kind of migratory impulse, a Pied Piper call that only they could hear. Several times they'd turned as a body to regard the *Sugar Jane* as it drifted past, and on one such occasion the sight of all those eyes glinting in the darkness had been enough to drive a half-drunk Richardson down into the cabin, muttering something about apex predators. Now Jimmy Hinton was alone once more, regarding the feeble morning light and the white, cloudlike puffs of mist and fog that drifted like wraiths through the stands of rushes and out over the wetlands. The place was utterly desolate and darkly sinister with the threat of the infected lurking somewhere out there, their hungry moans echoing through the night.

He had pulled the *Sugar Jane* into the dead water under a towhead and broke up the outline of her hull with cottonwoods and young willow branches, like a latter-day Huck Finn. The process took a lot of work, especially for a man his age, but the unusually large amount of northbound river traffic they'd seen, and his jangled nerves, in his mind, justified the added caution. On a normal night, with the darkness so complete that you couldn't see the water when you looked over the railing, it wasn't unusual to hear the Bedouins on other boats beating on pots and pans or calling out to each other in friendly salutations. They'd touch off a candle and raise a light to each other as they passed. It was the custom of the river. It was good etiquette. But there had been none of that on this trip. In fact, a day before, just hours after they'd hustled away from Ken Stoler's people up in Herculaneum, they'd seen a trawler much like their own steadily chugging upriver. Jimmy had hailed the pilot, a thin, bald black man, with a friendly wave. But one look at the stark and strangely haunted emptiness in the man's eyes had caused the smile to shrink from Jimmy's face and his hand to fall to his side, his fingers curled into his palm as though to pull the hail back from whence it had come. Jimmy had stared after the man as they passed, his face a pale yellow in the guttering candlelight, and the man had stared back at him, never saying a word. The man's haunted expression never wavered, and it had unnerved Jimmy in a way that he couldn't quite identify.

Since that disturbing moment he'd seen a steady stream of traffic moving upriver. There had been other encounters that were equally unsettling, and those encounters, coupled with the crowds of infected moving south through the desolate Illinois swamps, had prompted him to take to hiding in the daylight, as they were doing now, moving only when they had the cover of darkness to conceal them. He wasn't sure exactly what was going on, but he had survived a long time by listening to the warning bells in his head, and they had been ringing loudly since that first encounter with the black man with the haunted eyes.

Pausing to look over the screen of tree branches he'd made, his mind wandered as it sometimes did back to the time before the outbreak, and for one glorious moment he could once again sense the intoxicating smell of his infant granddaughter, and hear the infectious burbling of her laughter. Warmth spread through his chest. His world was perfect, inviolate, his spirit soaring on a thermal uplift of a memory so complete it eclipsed everything else around him.

And then the sound of a motor somewhere out on the expanse of the river knifed through the happy shell of his daydream, and his eyes opened to the misery of the present.

"I love you, baby," he said, fetching a deep sigh. "I miss you."

And then he went below.

Jimmy Hinton stopped at the bottom of the stairs and surveyed the cabin.

Gabi was sitting on the couch. The fat girl, Avery Harper, was seated on the floor between Gabi's knees. Gabi was combing the girl's hair and laughing at something the older woman, the college professor, had just said. He almost asked Gabi to come topside and help square away the deck just in case the mist actually turned into rain, but seeing her with the other women, talking, laughing, he realized it had been too long since she'd shared a little friendly conversation with another woman. Poor thing didn't have anybody else but him to talk to most of the time, and Jimmy knew he wasn't that entertaining.

Off to his left, Richardson and Nate Royal were huddled together, talking about something on Richardson's iPad. The two of them had been thick as thieves since they'd left Herculaneum, Richardson teaching the kid how to use the device.

"I got us hid pretty good," Jimmy announced to the room. "There's still a bunch of northbound traffic on the river, but they ain't gonna be able to see us. Same with the zombies. They'll probably stick to the road, and it cuts east of here to miss the wetlands."

Gabi favored him with a smile, but her attention never really left the other two women.

Richardson and Nate didn't even look up.

"Good to know you people appreciate my efforts," Jimmy said. He surveyed the room again, waiting for somebody to acknowledge him, but nobody did.

Finally Gabi looked over at him.

"Quit hovering, Jimmy. Why don't you take a nap? Take your Hush Puppies off and sleep a little. I bet your feet are hurting." She turned to Sylvia and said, "It's the gout, you know. We keep looking for Epsom salt for him to soak his feet, but nobody seems to have it."

"Can't you improvise something?" Sylvia asked. "Baking soda, maybe?"

"Well, I don't know. You think that'd work?"

Jimmy opened his mouth to argue, but shut it without saying a word. They had already tuned him out, anyway. And besides, Gabi was right as always. He was exhausted. His feet were killing him, especially his ankles, and the bunk did look inviting.

He slipped off his Hush Puppies, the gentle vibration of the deck soothing the soles of his feet, and walked over to the sink for a cup of water. Richardson and Nate were still murmuring over the iPad. Jimmy caught a flash of a home movie on it, a pretty girl in a simple white cotton dress teaching a group of children.

"I bet you recognize her, don't you?" Richardson said to Nate. There was a touch of mischief in his expression.

Nate squinted at the dim, grimed-over screen, frowning in concentration.

But then his lips spread open, revealing badly yellowed teeth. "Hey, is that . . . ?"

"Uh huh. Bellamy Blaze."

"No shit." Nate let out a whistle. "You're not shittin' me, are you? You met her?"

"I thought you'd like that." For a moment, there was genuine mirth in Richardson's voice, but it faded quickly. He looked at the screen and his smile turned sad. "Her real name was Robin Tharp. She was one of the ones who escaped the Grasslands with me. Smart lady. A natural when it came to teaching kids."

Nate laughed. "That girl could swallow a nine-inch cock and smile while she did it. Before the outbreak, I think I had all her movies. Me and her and a case of beer spent a lot of quality time together on my couch, if you get my drift."

Richardson nodded. He seemed to be looking inwardly now, staring back across years. "She was a good friend," he said. "A good leader, too."

"Did you ever—" Nate made that hitching noise again "—you know? Tell me you hit that."

"No, Nate. Nothing like that. She was devoted to this guy named Jeff Stavers. Jeff was a Harvard grad, but he was working as a video store manager right before the outbreak. You would have liked him, I think." Richardson turned back to the iPad. "You know what I remember about her?"

Nate shook his head.

"Do you remember me telling you about Ed Moore and how he led us all out of the Grasslands? Well, when Ed died, it was Robin here who took up the reins. Not only was she the schoolteacher for our compound, but she was also our leader. She did a hell of job, too."

Richardson shook his head. Absently, he ran a finger down the side of the iPad.

"I miss her, Nate. She tried so hard. What happened wasn't her fault. I remember when we came back and found everybody dead. Those of us who were still alive really leaned on her after that. She was . . . she was just a well of energy. Up before everyone else. Didn't get to bed until way after everyone else was already in bed, exhausted. But you know what she told me that really impressed me?"

"No. What?"

"She said that the outbreak was the best thing that ever happened to her because it let her start her life all over again. That's what I wanted to show you, Nate. I think you can probably identify with that, can't you?"

Jimmy didn't hear the kid's reply. He was watching the woman on the iPad's screen. She was making a dozen little kids laugh over something they'd just read. Jimmy cocked his head to one side, studying the image. He could see it now. She really was Bellamy Blaze, the porn star. A little older, maybe, a little worn down by the weight of leadership . . . but it really was her. He remembered watching her videos on the Internet, the girl bent over the arm of a couch while three guys with huge dicks took turns going at her ass like it was a punching bag.

He felt uncomfortable, sad somehow. It wasn't her sexual exploits that held his attention. It was the children giggling. The sound filled him with sadness.

"You're wasting your time with that shit," Jimmy said.

Both Nate and Richardson looked up at him.

"You said that before," Nate said. "You don't like hearing stories about how people came through the outbreak. Why not?"

Jimmy regarded him, amazed once again at the people who managed to live through the apocalypse, and mourning those who didn't. This guy, he was bland and uninteresting, dumb as the day was long, and yet he was still alive.

There didn't seem to be any justice in it.

"Ain't nothing good about what's gone, kid," Jimmy said. "It ain't coming back, so what's the point?"

"But that is the point," Richardson said. "So much of everything is gone . . . both the good and the bad."

"That doesn't answer my question," Jimmy said. "Look at us. Look at what we got here. Ain't none of us what we used to be. Ain't none of us got what we used to have. There's no point in reminding us of how bad things are."

"You think that's what I'm doing by saving these stories?"

"Isn't it? Tell me. You ever brought back one moment of happiness by saving up all these stories? Have you? Seems to me all you're doing is dredging up a lot of pointless heartache."

Richardson put his iPad down on the deck. Nate started to

speak, but Richardson put a hand on his shoulder and quieted him with a gentle smile. "It's okay," he said to Nate. Then he looked up at Jimmy and said, "Storytelling isn't about bringing back the past, though you're right about everything else you said. There's nothing in these files that will undo what's been done. The world's not what it was. There's no changing that."

"So what's the point? Why bother? You're old enough you should know better than to add cruelty to a world that's already got too much of it."

"Yeah—and you're old enough not to believe that."

Jimmy let out a huff, unimpressed.

"Do yourself a favor, kid," he said to Nate, "and get yourself a new teacher. This one ain't got enough sense to pour piss out of a boot if the directions were written on the heel."

Richardson laughed.

"What's so funny?" Jimmy challenged him.

"That was one of my dad's favorites," he said. "That, and you're running off the reservation. I used to love all the shit my dad used to say."

Jimmy stared at him for a long moment. "Yeah, well, we old folks are great for that."

"And yet you've totally missed my point," Richardson said. "You're wrong when you said all I was doing was adding cruelty to the world." He held up the iPad. "That's not what this is. This right here, this is how we rebuild. These stories . . . this is how we make the world anew. Storytelling is our therapy. It's where we go for healing."

"Spare me the lit lecture, professor."

"That's her job," Richardson said with a grin as he hooked his thumb in Sylvia Carnes's direction. "I'm a reporter by trade. My job is to find the thread that connects us. And stories do that."

Jimmy was unimpressed. He loosened his belt and untucked his shirt and dropped down onto his bunk. Suddenly he didn't feel at all tired. He felt angry, but not at Ben Richardson, not at any of them. He was angry at himself, angry at his life, angry at everything that had turned out so god-awful wrong.

"I'll tell you what's obvious," he said. His comment was directed at Richardson, but he was staring up at the ceiling. "Humanity was made to suffer. There is no saving us. You're preaching a fairy tale. The world was made with more cruelty than kindness, and the scales won't ever balance."

"Do you really believe that," Nate asked.

In the morning light that was quickly spreading through the cabin his face looked far younger than it had when Jimmy first met him.

"Yeah, I do," said Jimmy. "Now lemme alone. I'm going to bed."

And with that he turned his face to the wall and pulled the covers up to his ears.

Nate woke to the sound of splashing. He blinked his eyes and listened. The cabin was in darkness. From the couch where he had fallen asleep he could see a light rain falling on the windows. It was dark beyond the windows. The splashing was muffled, but constant, and it sounded like it was getting closer.

Rubbing the sleep from his eyes he climbed the stairs up to the deck and saw Jimmy Hinton, his wife, and Avery Harper near the front of the boat, looking toward the Illinois side of the river. Ben Richardson and Sylvia Carnes were in the back of the boat. Nate couldn't see them back there, but he could hear them, rummaging through their packs.

The splashing continued. Nate rose to his tiptoes and tried to peer over the edge. All he could see was darkness, and here and there, overlapping rings in the water from the rain.

"What's going on?" he said.

"Shut up," Jimmy hissed at him.

The old man gave him a hard look that Nate didn't feel like challenging. Only then did he notice the long, hooked pole that Jimmy Hinton was holding. The hooked end looked dark and wet.

Slowly, quietly, moving in a crouch, Nate crossed the deck and knelt down next to Avery Harper.

"Hey," he whispered.

"Hi," she said. "Be quiet, okay?" She pointed toward the Illinois shore with a chubby finger.

Nate followed the line of her finger but couldn't see anything in the darkness. He shrugged and turned back to her, but before he could speak he saw a shape, a man's back, bobbing in the dark water below them. The man's arms were at his side, his face turned down into the depths. As Nate watched, the dead man's shoulder hit the prow of the boat and turned in a slow pirouette before slipping into the weeds along the bank.

"Zombie?" he asked.

Avery nodded, her lower lip between her teeth. In the darkness, her eyes had a glassy shine. She was actually kind of pretty, Nate thought. There was a softness to her, an innocence, that made him feel strong, like he could be something meaningful for her, and he liked that. He liked the way she looked at him.

"It was close," she said, still whispering. "That one there climbed up the side of the boat. If Jimmy hadn't been here, there's no telling what would have happened."

"There's more out there," Jimmy said. The way he held that long boat hook reminded Nate of the Indians he'd seen in the old Westerns, the way they'd kneel on a ridgeline and watch the cowboys riding through the valley down below. "You can hear 'em splashing."

"You sure it's zombies?" Nate asked.

"Course I'm sure, you jackass. Who the fuck you think it is?"

Jimmy stroked his chin with a free hand, his eyes focused on something Nate couldn't see out there in the dark.

He turned to Nate. "Make yourself useful, kid. Run back there and find out how they're doing with those rifles. I want two of them back there and two up here. You got that?"

"Yeah," Nate said. "Yeah, sure."

"Move. But be quiet about it."

Nate scrambled aft. He found Ben Richardson and Sylvia Carnes each with a rifle slung over their shoulder. They were digging through their backpacks.

"Jimmy says he needs two rifles up front," Nate said.

"They're right there behind you," Sylvia said. "We're trying to find magazines."

Nate turned, but he couldn't see very well in the dark. He was standing on a large coil of rope and some kind of bag. The boat was rocking with the current. It wasn't much, but between the darkness and the uneven footing it was enough to make it hard to move, and when he saw the rifles and reached for them, he pitched forward and slipped.

Instinctively he tried to grasp at the wall. His hand hit something solid—it felt like a lamp of some kind—and knocked it to the deck. It hit with a muffled clank, a noise that reminded him of an aluminum bat hitting a baseball, and then shattered.

"Oh shit," Nate said.

For a long moment, there was no sound. The air around him seemed to go preternaturally quiet. A light breeze touched his face, cool and scented with the heavy, but still pleasant, scent of the river and the overhanging cottonwoods. Nate looked down at the shattered glass and blunt piece of brass at his feet. His mind felt hazy and numb, like he was experiencing déjà vu, though he knew that wasn't what this was. This was the way he had felt in the time before the outbreak, the way he felt when he fucked up bad when someone else was counting on him. There had been a lot of times like that in the time before, but none recently. Not while he was living and traveling on his own, when he had no one else to blame for his mistakes but himself.

He turned his gaze on Richardson, who was staring at him with rheumy, soul sick eyes. Something was haunting Ben Richardson, a fatigue so complete it seemed to invade his body like a cancer, and it scared the crap out of Nate Royal.

"I . . . I'm sorry," he said.

Richardson never had the chance to reply. From somewhere out on the water there came a moan, a deep, ululating sound that was full of hunger and pain and blind rage.

Suddenly the water was alive with splashing.

"What the hell?" Jimmy Hinton called out. "We need those rifles. Now!"

"Go," Richardson said. "Take 'em and go."

Nate didn't waste any more time. He grabbed a rifle in each hand and scrambled forward. Jimmy Hinton was already on his feet, the boat hook discarded, and grabbed the rifles from him as soon as he rounded the cabin.

"Gimme those," he said.

He snatched the rifles from Nate's hands and tossed one to Gabi. She caught it and spun around toward the water, the rifle already seated in the crotch of her shoulder and cheek.

There was a rustling in the cottonwoods in front of them.

"Right there," Avery said, pointing.

"I got it," Gabi said.

And no sooner had she spoken when a zombie stepped

into sight, his hands slapping at the screen of branches in front of his face. The zombie was covered in swamp mud. The yellow glow of his eyes stood out against the mud, as did his bloodstained teeth. Raindrops spattered against his face, and Nate had just enough time to realize that the zombie was freshly turned before Gabi opened fire.

The man's head exploded like a punctured water balloon, clotted chunks of gore splashing into the water behind it. The body dropped a moment later.

"I got movement back here," Richardson shouted, and the call was followed a second later by the rattle of his AR-15.

"There!" Avery shouted, pointing over the side.

Jimmy Hinton pushed Nate to one side with a hard shoulder shuck. Nate started to protest, but closed his mouth before he spoke. Jimmy and Gabi Hinton knelt down next to each other and started firing at the infected that were coming through the cottonwoods. There were dozens of them, and Jimmy and Gabi laid into them with a steady stream of fire, churning the river to a froth as the bullets tore into the zombies and sent them convulsing into the water.

Watching the husband and wife work, Nate was reminded of the Air Force guards back at Minot when the infected broke into the hospital where he was held captive during the six months or so following the outbreak. For a kid who got his military education watching Arnold Schwarzenegger fight the Predator, the kind of teamwork he'd seen from real soldiers had seemed anticlimactic, like there was almost no drama in it. It was just simple and businesslike and to the point. It was tactics over snappy one-liners, a group effort instead of a one-man show. Jimmy and his wife did it the same way. They covered each other during reloads. They conserved their shots. It was more than just turning the rifle loose and spraying and praying. They were always under absolute control. And when the last shell casing clinked against the fiberglass deck of the boat, and Gabi's call of "Clear this side," was answered the same way from Jimmy, the water around the prow of the boat was choked with the dead, the bodies leaking blood into the black water.

Gabi lowered her weapon, then turned to Avery. "Are you okay, sweetie?"

Avery nodded.

"How about you?"

Nate was still looking at the bodies floating in the water. They had killed at least twenty, and it had taken them less than a minute to do it.

"Nate?"

"What?" he said, turning back to Gabi.

"Are you okay?"

"Uh-huh."

Jimmy rose to his feet. He surveyed the dead bodies down in the water, and when he was satisfied that none of them were still moving, he called aft to Richardson.

"You guys okay back there?"

"We're clear back here," Richardson said.

"Okay. One of you stay back there as watch. The other come forward."

A moment later, Sylvia Carnes appeared. She still had the rifle in her hands. She pushed her way past Nate and went straight to Avery and hugged the girl.

"We're gonna have to hustle out of here," Jimmy said.

"But we can't," Gabi said. "The river traffic . . ."

"We can't stay here. What would you have me do?"

"I don't know, find a place somewhere. Maybe cross to the Missouri side. There's less cover over there, but . . ."

"But what?"

"We've got to stay hidden," Gabi said. Her voice had taken on a high-pitched, plaintive note that to Nate sounded an awful lot like panic. It was the first time since he woke up that he felt like somebody else was as confused and frightened as he was, and it didn't make him feel any better.

"I don't get it," he blurted out. "What's going on? Why can't we just take off? I mean, there's gonna be more of those things, right?"

"Maybe," Jimmy said. "Probably, actually. You saw those ones we just dealt with. Those were all Stage I zombies, freshly turned. They wouldn't get this far into the wetlands unless they were down here already."

"I don't get it," Nate said. "What does that mean?"

"You're saying there are Stage II or Stage III zombies out there somewhere?" Sylvia said. "What are you thinking, that maybe those zombies got ahold of a boat nearby and turned the crew?"

"That'd be my guess," Jimmy answered, nodding to himself.

"Well, that's bad," Nate said. "What are we waiting for? Let's shove off."

"Haven't you been listening?" Gabi said. "We've had northbound traffic all over this river since we left Herculaneum. That's not normal. All those people, they're fleeing from something. If we head out onto the river we're likely to run across that northbound traffic."

"So?" Nate said.

"Nate," Sylvia said, and pulled Avery Harper to her chest, "where do you think those people are going? They're running from something. Who do you think they'll turn to for protection?"

Not really knowing what to say, Nate shrugged, his gaze wandering over the faces around him and finally settling on Avery.

"Ken Stoler's troops are that way," Avery said. "Nate, we can't let them see us. If they find us, do you have any idea what they'll do to us? They think we're traitors. They'll kill us. If we don't find Niki, then all of this'll be for nothing. I can't let that happen. I just can't. Do you understand that?"

Nate's mouth twitched in a gesture that looked something like a smile, but was really the awkwardness and discomfort inside him trying to work its way to the surface. But Avery didn't look away.

He nodded.

The next instant Jimmy Hinton pushed Nate to one side and charged up to the flybridge. He feed the throttle enough to turn the boat out of the cottonwoods and get them chugging out toward mid river.

In the darkness, the river seemed strange, ominous. In the daylight it was wide open, the far bank, when it was visible at all, a lush tropical green. Staring at it, Nate had the feeling he was part of something vast and slow and ageless. Its power was suggestive, as though he could tap into it if only he could discover the right mystical combination of peace and concentration. But it was a far more sinister and constricting world at night. The darkness had a way of enveloping him, like a large snake slowly tightening its coils around his chest, choking off his air. It frightened him.

"Keep your ears open," Gabi said. "Anybody hears anything, say something."

Nate turned to the darkness and listened. He couldn't hear anything but the low gurgling rumble of the *Sugar Jane*'s engine. Two minutes slipped away with him leaning over the railing, listening intently, before Jimmy Hinton cut the engine. A sudden silence dropped over all of them as the boat began to drift downstream.

"There," Avery said. "Do you hear that?"

They all listened.

"I don't hear anything," Nate said.

Gabi silenced him with a look. Chastened, Nate turned back to the darkness, and that's when he heard it. It was another boat, the engines off, the waves lapping against its hull.

"You kids get down," Gabi said.

She lowered herself down behind the *Sugar Jane*'s gunwale and adjusted the rifle against her cheek. The sound was getting closer. Nate could hear it clearly now, the rhythmic slapping of water against a drifting hull. Staring up at Gabi, he held his breath as he waited for her to shoot.

But she didn't fire. Instead, Nate saw the weapon sag in her hands. She rose part of the way to her feet, murmuring "Oh my God. Oh my sweet God."

The boat, a lot smaller than the *Sugar Jane*, was resolving out of the darkness as Nate stood up, and right away he saw what was wrong. The boat was drifting backward with the river current. There were five or six bodies on the deck, all of them dead. Blood dripped off the side of the boat and down its hull toward the water. Scanning the deck, Nate saw a hand with no arm attached, palm up, the fingers curled in on itself. It reminded Nate of a bug on its back.

It took him a moment longer to realize that the body next to the hand was still moving. The zombie was on its knees, its back to them. It was feeding out of the belly of one of the corpses.

Nate groaned. It was a sight he had witnessed hundreds of times since the outbreak, but the sight of it, the smell of a dead man's bowels opened, was something he never got used to.

At the sound of Nate's groan the zombie rose to its feet, turned, and stared at them. It let out a stuttering moan as its hands came up, the fingers clutching for them, completely ignorant of the gap between them. It was a freshly turned zombie, like the ones they'd encountered in the cottonwood grove on the Illinois bank, and its glazed-over eyes showed only an empty pit leading straight into nothingness.

Before any of them could react, answering moans rose up

from the bank behind them. Nate turned to the sound. Out of the corner of his eye he saw Jimmy doing the same thing.

"Shoot him," Jimmy said. "Stop him before he attracts more."

"I got him," Gabi said, and raised her rifle and fired a single round, cutting off the moan in the zombie's throat.

The next few hours were tense ones for Nate. Though Jimmy Hinton did his best to avoid Nate, it was a small boat, and they did bump into each other. It couldn't be helped. And when they did, Nate could see the simmering anger in Jimmy's eyes. He would squeeze up against the wall of the cabin to let Jimmy pass and mutter, "Sorry, I . . ." and Jimmy would grunt something inaudible in reply and move on. Nothing was said, but the incident with the broken lantern was still very much between them.

And so it was with more than a little trepidation that Nate climbed the stairs to the deck to see how far off the morning was. The mist that had been threatening to turn into rain over the last day and a half had finally succeeded, and the darkness swirled with silvery curtains of rain. Jimmy and Gabi had stretched a blue tarp over the forward section of the deck and the rain sizzled and popped against it.

Nate could see Jimmy and Gabi sitting in lawn chairs next to the railing up near the prow, Gabi with a rifle across her ample thighs. Avery Harper was sitting off to his left watching a coffeepot steam on a camper stove.

"That smells good," he said. "You got any left?"

She smiled at him, and it was such an innocent, sweet gesture that he couldn't help but smile back. At least *she* didn't want to throw him overboard.

"I think maybe I made it a little strong," she said.

"Don't apologize. I like my coffee strong."

She poured him a cup and watched him as he blew the steam from the cup and sipped it. She looked on the verge of wincing at some expected criticism.

"Well?"

He tried to keep on smiling, but the coffee was the worst thing he had ever tasted, and he had put away some pretty nasty attempts at coffee in his time. This was even worse than the shoe leather and chicory root combination he'd had outside of Memphis a few years back. It was thick as sludge and tasted like burned cooking grease. He couldn't stop his mouth from puckering.

"You don't like it, do you?"

"No," he said, coughing, "it's okay."

"It's too strong, isn't it? I've never made it before. Usually, Sylvia or Niki does it. When we can get it, that is."

Nate set his cup down on the deck.

"You go way back with them, don't you?"

"With Niki and Sylvia?"

"Yeah."

"They're my family, Nate. Niki raised me since I was ten. My own mom died before the outbreak. Niki and Sylvia have been like mothers to me."

Nodding, Nate picked up his coffee. "Look, um, would you mind if I, uh, poured this out?"

She smiled. "Go ahead. I saw Jimmy pour his over the side when he thought I wasn't looking."

"Okay," he said, chuckling at the image that popped into his head of Jimmy trying to sneak the stuff away without being seen. She was looking at him again with that mixture of innocence and trust and obvious attraction that quickened something inside him. The more time he spent with her, the more he liked her. "You mind if I ask you a question?"

"No," she said. "Anything."

"Why are you here, Avery? I get why Sylvia's here. I even

get why I'm here, sort of. But you're a mystery to me. What are you doing here?"

She didn't even hesitate. "Because I believe in Niki, Nate. Haven't you been listening? She is everything to me. Without her, I'd be dead. Oh I might have gone on living, but inside . . . I'd be dead. She did more than take me in." She smiled, and for a moment, her eyes shone with the light of admiration. "You should hear her talk. How passionate she is about saving what's left of this world. Every time I hear her speak, I feel this chill. She's like a battery. Do you know what I mean? When you stand next to her, you can feel the energy coming out of her. It's impossible to be around her and not feel like the world is worth saving."

Nate didn't answer her back. He nodded, but inside he was doubtful that Niki had done Avery any favors. Most of the people who had survived this long had developed a hard inner grain of resiliency. But Avery seemed soft. He liked that about her, but it worried him, too. Was she too much in Niki's service? Anybody who relied so heavily on another to define them couldn't be entirely healthy, could they?

"Avery, honey."

It was Gabi. Both Nate and Avery stared up at her. The woman had a wonderfully comfortable smile when she wanted to, like a friendly grandmother.

At least Nate imagined it as a grandmotherly smile. He had never known his.

"I'm gonna go down to the galley and cook up some eggs. You wanna join me?"

Avery looked at Nate and he smiled and shrugged.

"Okay," Avery said. "Yeah, sure."

When the woman went downstairs, Nate turned toward the prow and saw Jimmy Hinton still sitting there, staring off into the darkness.

"Jimmy?"

Jimmy looked up over his shoulder at Nate and grunted.

"You mind if I sit down?"

"I don't care. Do whatever you're gonna do."

Nate sat down in the chair Gabi had just vacated and tried to see what Jimmy saw when he looked out into the predawn darkness that covered the river and its environs, but whatever the man saw there was a mystery to him.

"You don't like me much, do you?" Nate said.

Jimmy slowly turned to him, his mouth pinched together like a man who keeps getting interrupted every time he sits down to read the morning paper, and said. "Nate, I'll be honest with you. I've flushed turds smarter than you. I think an awful lot of good, intelligent folks have died since the outbreak, and it breaks my heart sometimes looking at the folks God decided was good enough to go on living."

Nate cleared his throat. He wasn't mad. He'd never had any illusions about the brains he'd been given, and he actually found it refreshing to hear people talk about his lack of smarts. There was something honest in it.

"I guess that's fair," he said. "I'm sorry if I'm not the man that whoever you lost was."

Jimmy turned to him. He was frowning, at first, but then the frown turned into a slow smile. "It was a woman, actually. My daughter. And my granddaughter."

"I'm sorry."

"Me too." Jimmy didn't look away. He looked Nate over, then hooked a thumb toward the cabin. "You're kind of sweet on that girl, aren't you?"

"A little," Nate said. "What do you think? You think I got a chance there?"

"A chance? Hmm, I don't know. Maybe. Women are idiots, you know."

That made Nate laugh. "I haven't found that to be true."

"No, I reckon not. I imagine you've met dead dogs with more brains than you got. It's true, though. Women are idiots. Nate, you ever looked at a man? I mean really looked at him? You ever put yourself in a woman's mind and wondered why she'd ever wanna fuck something that looked like an anemic pink gorilla? Look at a woman. She's got all those curves, all those beautiful curves. She's got breasts. She's got hips that feel like the steering wheel of a brand-new Buick. She looks like a fucking piece of art in blue jeans. Hell, she even smells nice. Then look at a man. He's all angles and dangling parts. He looks ridiculous. He farts. He scratches his ass. He'll live like a billy goat if you let him. I tell you the only real mystery in life is why every woman on this planet isn't a lesbian."

Jimmy laughed. He picked at a piece of skin at the corner of his thumbnail and flicked it over the side.

"And don't even get me started on the actual act of sex," he said suddenly. "Have you thought about that? For a man, it's hurry up, hurry up, unh uh, I'm done. But think about what a woman's got to look forward to. She's got this big clumsy oaf climbing up on top of her, sticking his pork in her, and then banging away like it's a sprint to the finish. For a man, an orgasm is kind of like a moment of freefall. But I've heard women describe an orgasm like every part of her body is sending up fireworks. I hope that's true. I hope they get at least that much from us. God knows they need something special to make up for the shit we put 'em through. Don't seem like nearly enough to me, though."

From downstairs in the galley they heard a sudden staccato of laughter. In the darkness, Nate could just barely see Gabi and Avery laughing over something.

"I don't know," Jimmy said. "Maybe motherhood's got something to do with it. I loved being a dad. I really loved being a granddad. But I don't think I got near as much from it as Gabi got from being a mother and a grandmother. Being a dad can sometimes feel like a spectator sport. You're working most of the time. You get to spend a few hours here and there in the evening, a little more on weekends. You crack jokes and if you're lucky your kids think you're cool. At least some of the time. But it's the mother who does all the real kid raising. When they're hurt, it's Mama they're crying for. When they crawl into bed in the middle of the night, they cling to Mama like barnacles. A man can feel like a man for keeping a roof over his kids' head, but there ain't nothing a man can do that can top what Mama does."

"My dad was an asshole," Nate said. But there wasn't any bitterness to it. All of the screaming and the hitting and the bullshit that was life in the Royal household was a long time ago, and if Nate hadn't yet forgiven the bad times, he had mostly forgotten them. It was just like what that porn star, Bellamy Blaze, had said to Ben Richardson. The end of the world had pretty much given her a new life. It had done the same for him.

"Dads have a way of seeming like assholes," Jimmy said. "It is their special skill. I know I sure fit that description some of the time. Hell, maybe most of the time." He shook his head, his gaze still locked on Gabi. "But you know, when I think of all the shit she has to take being married to me, I figure she must be an idiot. There ain't no other reason why she'd stay with me. My thinking is, if you're truly sweet on that girl in there, she's probably dumb enough to find something she likes about you."

Nate nodded. "You're an encouraging guy, Jimmy. Thanks."

"Don't mention it."

When the morning finally came, Nate was sitting next to Ben Richardson down in the cabin. After each of them had finished a plate of eggs, Richardson took out his iPad and handed it to Nate.

"Go ahead," Richardson said, "fire it up."

Nate turned the device on. Slowly, aware that Richardson was watching him carefully, Nate ran his fingers over the grimy screen, tapping files until he had all the hundreds of interviews that Richardson had collected over the years displayed on the screen. He had seen Avery's down at the bottom, but he hadn't looked at it yet. He wanted to, but at the same time he felt kind of creepy because of that want. Somehow, the idea of watching her interview felt improper, sort of like watching her change her clothes when she didn't know she was being watched.

It was an odd feeling for him.

"I've been thinking about these interviews a lot lately," Richardson said, and there was a solemn tone in his voice that immediately made the hairs on the back of Nate's neck stand up. "I've been thinking about what they mean, what they're worth."

Nate didn't speak. Though he'd never been a particularly sensitive man, he was aware that the conversations he'd been having with Richardson over the past few days had been leading up to something, and whatever that something was, this was it. Richardson was struggling to get something out, and nothing Nate could say would hasten that.

"I want you to have that, Nate. The iPad."

"You what? But what about your book? All your notes are on here."

"That's true. I still want you to have it, Nate."

"But why?" Nate looked at him, honestly and completely confused. But then it donned on him. "You're not gonna finish it. You never had any intention of finishing it, did you?"

Richardson smiled. "Maybe in the beginning I did. Certainly not lately. Lately, it's just been a thing I do, like a condemned man putting hash marks for the passing days on the walls of his cell. Does that make sense? It's something that you do because your mind won't let you rest. You do it because your mind has more stamina than your body."

"What are you saying? Are you . . . you're not gonna . . . do anything stupid, are you?"

"No, Nate. No, you don't need to worry about that. But I am being a realist." He pointed to the iPad. "This is what's been keeping me afloat for the last few years. I think that's why I've made it a point not to finish it. But you, I think you're finally coming into your own. I've listened to your story about where you came from, all the troubles you had growing up. You're not that guy anymore, Nate. You may not feel like it, but you've grown up. This world, for all its faults, has made you a man. You're the pony to bet on. That's why I'm giving this to you. Do what you want with it. Do what you think is right. I have a feeling it'll be the right thing to do."

Nate stared at the iPad in his hands. He couldn't, he wouldn't, look Richardson in the face. He looked back over the last few days, over all the things he had told Richardson while the two of them followed along behind Sylvia Carnes and Avery Harper. He had told him all about his life, from a high school dropout living in the shack behind his father's clapboard house, to Air Force medical experiment, to transient searcher for the meaning of life, and finally to nitwit messiah with the fate of mankind coursing through his veins. It had been, like that old Grateful Dead song said, a long, strange trip. And though he hardly grasped the full scope of it, he felt that, somehow, Richardson had. Perhaps he saw in Nate that which he couldn't himself become. Perhaps he was simply tired. But whatever the reason, he had given Nate the iPad that contained so much, and it felt right that he should have it.

But still, for all the rightness of it, Nate didn't like the way Richardson was talking. In the short time he'd known him, Nate had come to think of Richardson as a survivor. He was simply too well put together in the brainpan to short circuit. But what he was hearing now sounded like a man teetering on the verge of emotional collapse. Nate was hardly an expert on such things, but he had lived in the wastelands of America for six years. He had done his share of wandering. He had come to learn that, when it came to men and the minds of men, there was broken, and there was broke. He'd met some who were flat-out crazy. He'd met others who'd gone wild, feral. Still others who seemed to be in love with self-destruction. But the really scary ones, the ones you didn't dare trust, were the ones backsliding into a cocoon of depression and exhaustion. Those were the ones you could never predict. They were truly dangerous.

And Richardson . . . he seemed to be going down that road.

"Hey, you guys need to come up here."

It was Avery, staring down at them from the top of the stairs. She had a funny way of holding her mouth when something was wrong that Nate had come to like, like she had just taken a big bite of a lemon. He saw the look on her face now.

"What is it?" Richardson said.

She seemed like she was searching for the right words, but they just weren't coming. All she could manage was a quick shake of her head.

Then she turned and went back up on deck.

"That doesn't sound good," Richardson said.

"No, it doesn't."

Nate got up to go topside, but Richardson put a hand on his arm.

"Hey Nate . . ."

Richardson had the iPad on his thigh, holding it as

though he was about to thrust it into Nate's hand but wasn't sure if the younger man would accept it.

"I'll take it," Nate said. "If that's really what you want?"

Richardson nodded.

A moment later, they were both topside, and what they saw made them both stiffen. A thick morning fog drifted over the water, white fingerlike clouds inching over the swampland that made up the country in this part of Southern Illinois. On the shore they saw a winding dirt road leading down to a ferry house, and beyond the ferry house, rising like horrid scarecrows over dead fields, were hundreds of rotting corpses impaled on spikes. Circling above the bodies were thousands of shrieking birds, and when the wind shifted, the assembled crew and passengers of the *Sugar Jane* got the stench of all that death full in the face.

Jimmy Hinton turned from the scene. "No way," he said. "Out of the question. You people hired me to take you to Chester, but this ain't part of our deal."

"Jimmy," Gabi said.

"One second," he said. He turned on Richardson. "You lied to me. You said Chester. This wasn't part of our deal."

"Jimmy." It was Gabi again, her voice more insistent this time. She was trying to grab his shirt, but couldn't seem to make her fingers work like they were supposed to.

"What is—" The rest of the question broke off in his throat. He was staring straight ahead, into the fog, his mouth hanging open.

Nate followed Jimmy's gaze, and he too stood speechless.

There were shapes emerging from the fog, hundreds of zombies wading into the shallow water.

And the *Sugar Jane* was drifting into their midst.

CHAPTER 16

One by one the zombies separated from the fog and shadows, their tattered bodies curdling the river water and sending up the deep, fetid odor of mud and dead things as they surrounded the *Sugar Jane*.

"Get down!" Jimmy shouted.

Nate didn't move. He couldn't. He was frozen by the sight of all those zombies wading through the dark water, black silhouettes stirring in the shadows of the overhanging willow trees, their eyes glinting, teeth bared, full of the promise and the emptiness of death. Their moaning was deafening.

They never blinked, never showed any sense of urgency, or fear, or hunger. There was nothing in their expressions but a bottomless, soul-sucking emptiness. For Nate, it was like looking into the mirror during his darkest moments while he was still Dr. Kellogg's lab rat back at Minot. He was transfixed, not by fear, but by the reptilian emptiness of all those eyes turned up toward him.

"I said, get down!"

Jimmy was pulling on his shoulder, trying to get him

away from the railing. Nate turned toward Jimmy. The younger man was confused, and for a moment none of this made sense. It was as though the fog that rolled over the river was creeping into his mind as well. He didn't understand. Seconds before, everything had been so quiet. But now, it was like he was standing still and the whole world was swirling around him, too fast for him to make any sense of it. Jimmy was yelling at him again. Really yelling. The old hippie had a wild look in his eyes. His hair was standing on end, and with the morning sun behind his head he looked like his head was on fire.

"What the hell, boy? You wanna get shot? Get your head down."

Shot? What was he talking about?

Only then did Nate see the AR-15 that Jimmy was trying to point over the bow.

"Move!"

Nate took a few steps out of the way and the next few moments went by, not like a smooth, movie-scripted action sequence, but in flashes of horrible violence, disjointed images rushing at him without context.

He saw Jimmy Hinton, the rifle held over his head, flecks of spit flying from his lips, a scream frozen in his throat as he kicked one of the lawn chairs out of the way and leaned over the side, firing as fast as he possibly could.

Zombies were scrambling up the railing, their mangled hands and faces visible in the searing orange light of Jimmy Hinton's muzzle flashes, mud and sludge oozing from their hair and tattered clothes.

Gabi screamed something at him. Nate was looking right at her, only a few feet away, though he heard nothing but the indistinguishable roar of noise.

From somewhere off to his left, he heard the crash of broken glass.

Nate looked that way and saw Avery Harper and Sylvia Carnes on their knees, Avery's face buried in Sylvia's chest. Behind them, a zombie had fallen from the railing into one of the port windows, shattering the glass. It pulled itself loose from the broken window, its right arm a bleeding mass of deep cuts, and staggered forward, reaching for the two women.

But they couldn't back away from it.

They were trapped by two more zombies climbing over the railing right in front of Nate.

At that moment Avery looked up at him, and the confusion that had clouded his mind was swept violently away. Anger supplanted confusion and he surged forward, his fingers curling into fists. None of these rotting bastards were going to touch her, not while he was around to do something about it.

The two men closest to him were bone skinny, both of them stinking of rotting meat and river mud, their heads lolling on their shoulders. Nate rushed forward, determined to shove them back over the railing and pull the women to safety, but he hadn't taken more than two steps before somebody threw him sideways into the cabin wall.

"Get your head down!" Gabi Hinton said. She pinned him against the wall with one massive arm. "Stay there."

She let go of him long enough to bring her rifle to bear on the two zombies, dropping both of them with a single shot to the forehead.

"Don't move," she said.

The intensity in her stare held him against the wall as surely as her arm had.

He nodded.

Gabi fired again, this time at the bloody zombie staggering toward Avery and Sylvia.

"Get over there with Nate," she said to Sylvia. "All of you, inside. Now!"

Nate helped them toward the door. Through the fog he caught a glimpse of Richardson in the back of the boat, burning his way through a magazine as he shot over the sides at anything that moved.

Zombies were pouring over the railing now, all down the length of the boat, rising out of the fog like demons. Gabi kept firing, her brown dress swishing with every move of her vast bulk, but to Nate it seemed like she was fighting against an inexhaustible force. There were just too many of them.

A woman was staggering toward Jimmy, her hands outstretched, the ruins of her dress hanging in strips from her waist. There were leaves and sticks caught in her hair. Her breasts swayed with every step, leaking mud. Her face was a patchwork of oozing sores and her back was covered with leeches. One ankle was almost certainly broken, the foot twisted under so that she hobbled forward on the blade of her foot.

Nate took a step forward, ready to push the woman out of the way, but his foot slipped on the blood and mud and viscera that had pooled on the deck and he went down hard on his butt.

"Jimmy, behind you!" he yelled, but the words were lost beneath the rattling guns.

The woman was almost on him. Her mouth was opening and closing, her fingers clutching instinctively, as though already pulling the meat from Jimmy's corpse.

Nate looked around and saw Jimmy's lawn chair folded up on the deck. He scooped it up, pulled himself to his feet like a man struggling to stand on wet ice, and swung it at the woman's head. The flimsy chair bounced off the zombie's head with the crunch of cheap metal, but it was enough to send them both sprawling toward the railing.

The next instant Nate found himself leaning over the side, staring down into water that was churning with zombies, all of them reaching for his face, the smell of death and rotting vegetation assaulting him like a slap in the face.

When he pulled himself back from the edge Jimmy was standing over the woman, slamming the butt of his rifle down on her face again and again, caving it in until it was unrecognizable.

Gabi looked back over her shoulder and found her husband. "Get us out of here!" she said. "We can't do this much longer."

Another zombie, this one a one-armed woman with half of her face bashed in, rolled over the railing, flopped awkwardly onto the deck, and then slowly climbed to its feet. Gabi shot her right through the damaged part of her face and flipped her backward over the railing.

"Jimmy, get movin'!"

"You got this?" he answered.

"Yeah. Go!"

She didn't wait for a reply. She spun around to face the surge of hands and faces rising over the gunwale, rifle at the ready. Nate watched in awe and rapt fascination as she calmly flipped the weapon's selector switch to BURST and went back to firing at a zombie less than an arm's length away. Her bullets nearly sliced the man in half, causing him to slide back into the water that was rapidly turning to a bloody sludge.

Suddenly, and for no reason that Nate could see, an appalling collective moan rose up from the zombies still in the water, like someone had just turned on a switch. The sound made everyone pause, even Gabi, and in the momentary lull of the guns, Nate could hear countless hands slapping against the hull, searching for purchase to climb over.

"I'm out!" Richardson shouted from the back.

Gabi kicked a loaded magazine toward Nate. "Take that back there."

Without saying more she brought her weapon up and emptied her magazine into three of the infected who had managed to hook their arms over the side. But there was a fourth behind her that she hadn't seen, and that one was already over the railing and trying to climb to its feet on the blood-soaked deck. Nate yelled for her to watch out, but Gabi couldn't hear him over the screams and barking of the guns.

The zombie, a fat man wearing nothing but shorts and the remnants of a tennis shoe on one foot, managed to get to its knees. Its gut swung out in front of it, its hands out of control, flopping around like wounded things on the side of the road. But it didn't lose any of its momentum. The man's right hand came down on the back of Gabi's leg and she jumped.

She pointed the rifle at the thing's head. It tried to twist toward her calf, but she batted the zombie's hand away with the barrel and lined up her sights on the back of its head. But before she could pull the trigger the man grabbed the muzzle and pulled it down, using the counterleverage to climb to his feet.

Without thinking Nate rushed forward and kicked the zombie in the ear. It rolled over, emitting a noise that was somewhere between a growl and a feeding moan. It clutched at Nate's foot, snagging the hem of his jeans. Nate tumbled down to the deck, landing face-first on top of the zombie. It raked its fingernails across his cheeks, cutting his skin deeply, though in the adrenaline rush that came with the fight he didn't notice the pain. He jammed the heel of his left hand into the zombie's mouth and pushed its head to one side. There was a brick next to his head, one of the ones Jimmy had used to anchor the lawn chairs in rough currents, and Nate balled his fist around it. The zombie turned its one seeing eye up at Nate and tilted its head to one side, as though questioning him, its mouth open and oozing fluid.

Nate slammed the brick down on the top of its head.

The zombie's face bounced off Nate's leg and its stare found him again.

"Fucking die already!" He slammed the brick down again and again, screaming with every blow until the zombie rolled off his legs, its head a caved-in mess.

Nate pulled his legs back. He rose to his feet.

Gabi Hinton was staring at him.

"What?"

She raised her rifle, the business end staring him straight in the eye.

"Whoa!" he said. "Hey, hold on!"

Without lowering the rifle she turned her head and said: "Jimmy, we need to go!"

"I'm working on it."

Nate turned just enough to see Jimmy pulling himself over the flybridge's railing. He grabbed the throttle and eased it forward, the engines responding with a sputtering gurgle that surged the boat forward.

Nate swayed with the sudden movement. When he looked back, down the length of the boat, he saw zombies losing their grip on the railing and falling back into the water. He saw Ben Richardson and Sylvia in the back of the boat, punching at hands with the butts of their rifles. They were moving now, pulling away from the cover of the willow trees and into the wider expanse of the river.

The zombies kept coming, but as they reached deeper water, they sank and drowned.

When Nate turned back to Gabi, he was still staring into the business end of her rifle, the hole at the end of her muzzle looking like an open, toothless mouth.

He blinked at her.

"You saved me, Nate," she said. "But you're infected. I'm sorry."

He shook his head at her, held up his injured hand as though he could turn the bullets to one side.

She backed up, keeping her gun on him. "I'm sorry," she said.

"Stop!" It was Avery Harper. She broke loose from Sylvia's grip and jumped between Nate and Gabi Hinton. "Don't shoot him. You can't. He's immune. He won't turn!"

Gabi stared at her. The rifle didn't move.

"Honey," she said. "Move aside."

"She's right," Richardson said. He was coming forward as he spoke. "She's telling the truth. He really is immune."

Gabi looked from Avery to Richardson, then slowly back to Nate, studying him. "No," she said. "That's . . . impossible."

"They ain't lying to you, Ma'am," Nate said. "Those zombies, they can't hurt me. They can't turn me into one of them, anyway."

"But . . ." Gabi still couldn't believe it. "How . . . why?"

Nate stuck his bleeding hand out between them, almost as though he was offering it to her as a gift.

"I don't know," he said. "But I've been bit plenty over the years. They don't hurt me." He pulled the flash drive from his neck with his uninjured hand and held it up for her to see. "All the answers are here."

"Gabi"—this time it was Sylvia Carnes speaking—"he's telling the truth. I don't know the answers, and neither does he. But he's telling you the truth. Please don't shoot him. I'm begging you, don't. Everything counts on this."

The huge woman shook with indecision, all the while keeping a steady sight picture on Nate.

For a moment, the muzzle of her rifle dipped.

"Impossible," she said.

"Gabi," Sylvia said. She took a step forward. Sylvia held out her hand, but pulled it back when the older woman flinched, half turning the gun toward Sylvia. "Gabi, please, you have to listen to me. Around his neck he carries a flash drive. A military doctor used him to find a cure for this. Don't you see?"

Gabi shook her head slowly, not understanding, or perhaps not wanting to.

"That's what we're doing out here," Sylvia went on. "We're trying to find a friend of ours. The Red Man has her, and we have to get her back."

"You're crazy . . ." Gabi said.

"No," Sylvia said. "Gabi, this is the truth, every word of it. We have to find our friend. She's been in contact with a doctor named Don Fisher. He can use the cure Nate's got with him. He can—"

"Don Fisher?" Gabi nearly spat the name on the deck. "Fisher? He's nothing but a myth. A pipe dream. You might as well be looking for Prester John."

"He's real!" Nate interjected. "I've seen him. I've met him. I've met his family."

Gabi wheeled on him, gun raised high, her gaze narrowed down the length of the barrel.

"Nate, no!" Sylvia shouted.

Nate pushed the barrel of Gabi's gun away with his uninjured hand.

"It's alright," he said. He turned his attention on Gabi. "It's true. I've met him. He helped me when I was sick with the flu."

"Why didn't you give him the cure then?" she said.

She could have pulled the gun away. She could have taken a step back and blasted him, but she was battling more with herself now, her confidence wavering. She didn't want to believe what he was saying. That much was plain from the look on her face. But somehow, and he didn't know how he knew this, only that he did, she needed to believe. Something inside her needed to believe. Against every hard grain of doubt in her being, she needed to believe.

"Because I didn't know who he was," Nate admitted. There was a note of humility in his voice now. "And because I was scared. And stupid. I had the flu when I saw him and he helped me. He gave me medicine and clean water. I should have known he was a doctor."

Just then Richardson stepped between them. He put a hand on the top of Gabi's gun.

Gabi looked at him, and her eyes pleaded for direction.

"I didn't believe it, either," he said gently. "But I've seen the proof. He's telling you the truth."

He put pressure on the gun and she yielded. She lowered the muzzle to the deck. "So what are we supposed to do?" she asked.

"We find this girl, this Niki Booth, and then we find the doctor."

"And then?"

"I don't know," he admitted. "I really don't know."

Without notice, the *Sugar Jane* rocked hard to port, throwing them all off their feet. Nate crashed headlong into the gunwale, hitting his head so hard his legs went numb. He sagged to one knee, looking around, blinking stupidly.

Gabi had lost her gun. She and Richardson were tumbled together in a heap on the opposite side of the deck. Sylvia managed to keep her feet, but only by holding on to the awning above her.

He couldn't see Avery.

Gabi stood, looked around. The fog was thinning, but they still couldn't see much beyond the Red Man's compound rising above the next bend in the river.

"We're turning around."

The engines strained suddenly, causing them all to stagger.

Gabi caught herself on the gunwale and turned toward the pilothouse. "What are you doing?" she said.

But Jimmy was already climbing down. He looked upset, desperate.

"Jimmy? What's going on?"

"We got trouble," he said.

He rushed past her without explaining, unlocked an access panel near the bow, and threw open the hatch. Inside Nate saw what looked like scuba gear: tanks, masks, and hoses.

"Help me with this," he said.

Gabi didn't hesitate. She rushed forward and started pulling metal tanks out of the hold, lining them up against the railing. Jimmy brought out the regulators and together they slid them onto the tanks and screwed them down.

He tested one of the regulators and, satisfied it was working, turned to the others.

"We're abandoning ship," he said. "Everybody up front—fast!"

"What's going on?" Richardson said.

"The Red Man's coming. I caught a glimpse of them through the fog. There's a bunch of boats."

"You can't outrun them?" Sylvia asked.

"Not a chance. Let's go, everybody. We've only got the four tanks, so two of you will have to double up."

Jimmy slipped a tank on his back and pulled the regulator over his shoulder. Then he helped Gabi into hers. Nate looked around. Sylvia and Ben were both putting on tanks, Sylvia pulling Avery over to her side as she did so.

Ben nodded at him. "Looks like you're with me."

Nate opened his mouth to speak, but didn't know what to

say. It was happening again, the confusion seeping into his head like a fog. This was coming at him too fast. He had so many questions buzzing around in his brain he couldn't figure which one to ask first.

In the near distance they could hear the steady thrum of boat engines coming closer.

"Let's get moving, people," Jimmy said. "They'll be on us any second."

He climbed over the railing and looked back.

He caught Nate looking at him.

"What's your problem?" he said.

"I . . ." Nate stammered.

"Spit it out, boy."

"I can't swim," Nate finally said.

Jimmy laughed. It was a deep, phlegmy sound. Then he shook his head. "And here I thought you couldn't get any dumber."

He shook his head again and dropped overboard with a splash.

CHAPTER 17

The Red Man sat in the dark in the middle of the little cabin at the foot of the stairs. The young man who had been given the task to go below and deliver the news stood at the top of the stairs, not wanting to take another step.

He was more than scared. It was coming off him in waves, like heat shimmers rising from the highway pavement in the middle of the desert. The Red Man terrified him in ways he could not even express. He was sweating, unable to swallow the lump in his throat, a chill creeping over his skin with every moment he spent in this devil's company.

"Well?"

The voice startled the soldier and he flinched. The Red Man was stirring, a darker shadow moving through a pool of lighter shadows.

The solder took a few steps down, stopping when the smell assaulted his nostrils.

"Sir," he said, his voice faltering, "we've got the boat. We should be coming up on it any second."

There was movement in the dark, and the next instant the Red Man was standing just below the soldier, staring up at him with eyes that were unblinking and insane. He didn't speak, only stared at the soldier.

The young man wanted to back up, but didn't dare. His name was David Cohen, and he had been a black shirt for a little over a year, ever since the Red Man's army swept over the Las Cruces compound where he'd lived since he was a boy. He'd been working the fields, harvesting squash, when the main attack started. The klaxons had sounded, but David and the three people with him never had a chance to take their stations. Zombies poured through a hole in the fence and overran the main part of the complex. He'd barely cleared the field when the rest of the defenders started running in full retreat toward him.

David was luckier than most. He and a handful of others managed to escape the compound, and he'd wandered, lost and confused, through the surrounding countryside for two days before the black shirts cornered him.

The Red Man had given him a choice: become a black shirt or a zombie.

At the time, the choice had seemed obvious. But the truth was, this was no way to live.

And still the Red Man stared at him, the thoughts behind his eyes and painted face completely unknowable.

Finally the young man could take no more and blurted out: "They asked me to come get you."

The Red Man nodded. It was a subtle gesture, and the young man wasn't even certain that he'd seen it, but he scrambled back up on deck just the same.

Back in the fog, the soldier quickly made his way aft.

This, he thought, was no way to live. No way at all.

But he had seen his compound razed to the ground by the

black shirts, and those who refused to serve the Red Man either eaten alive by his zombie army or impaled through the ass on a forest of stakes outside the Red Man's compound.

This was no way to live, to be sure. But he was living.

That much he would hold on to as long as he could.

The old trawler emerged out of the fog, its stern toward the Red Man's approaching fleet. From the bow of his boat the Red Man studied the trawler. He could see at a glance that it was deserted, save for a few dead bodies draped over the deck fixtures. Its hull was dark with smeared blood and mud, but he could still see the name of the boat, the *Sugar Jane*, painted in solid block letters over the propellers.

"Doesn't look like anyone survived," one of the soldiers said.

The Red Man didn't look at him. He studied the boat for a moment longer, then said: "Bring us alongside. I'm going aboard."

"You don't want us to clear it first? Just to be sure?"

"Just bring us alongside."

"Yes, sir."

They glided up to the other boat, nudging it gently. The crew tied it off and the Red Man stepped aboard. The deck was slick with gore and mud. Spent shell casings glinted wetly from the deck. Quite a few of them.

The Red Man walked forward the length of the boat, noticing the busted window, smeared with blood, the fresh bullet holes in the fiberglass, and older damage, clumsily repaired.

He circled back and went down to the main cabin. He saw beds for five or six, two of them hastily made up. There was a backpack on one and he opened it. A few yellow blister packs of pills and some tattered clothes fell out.

And something else.

An iPad, wrapped in a Ziploc bag.

He opened the bag and slid the instrument out, running the stub of his missing finger down the side. He remembered these things and was surprised that it still worked. The owner must have found a way to recharge it. In a world without electricity, such an instrument was a strange find indeed.

On the screen was a file called "Interviews." He opened it and double tapped on the most recent file. A moment later, the face of a young fat girl appeared on the screen. She looked dimly familiar in a way that so many of his memories did from the time before what he had come to think of as his conversion. This girl, awkward, shy, nervous, hesitant . . . he did know her. But from where?

And then she started talking about Houston during Hurricane Mardell. And having to evacuate. And moving to Gooding, Illinois, to be with . . . her cousin Niki Booth.

Of course, he thought, a smile forming at the corner of his mouth.

One of his guards appeared in the doorway behind him.

"Sir, we've searched all the holds. There's nothing. My guess is they got pulled overboard during the attack."

"I doubt that."

The Red Man shut off the iPad without closing the file. He tossed the iPad on the bed, took one last look around, and turned to face his soldier.

"They're still alive," the Red Man said. "They're somewhere."

"I have boats searching the water now, just in case."

The Red Man nodded, but he knew they wouldn't find anything. These are Niki Booth's friends, he thought. They're coming for her.

Well, that was fine.

Let them come. He reached out to the zombies in his

compound, his mind focusing on them, moving them into place.

"Your orders, sir?"

"Tow the boat back with us. And find the people who escaped from here."

The Red Man drew close to the soldier.

The man stiffened. His mouth twitched, the beginnings of a grimace, partly from fear, partly from the rotten smell.

"There should be a young, fat girl with them. Take her alive. I want her brought to me."

The man swallowed uncomfortably, then nodded, and got out of there as fast as he could.

CHAPTER 18

Nate surfaced, sputtering and coughing. They were underneath a large wooden pier that stretched some hundred feet or so out over the water, and there wasn't enough headroom for him to stand up. But even if there had been headroom enough, he wouldn't have had the strength. He was just lucky to be alive.

He pulled away from Richardson and crawled on his hands and knees onto a stinking, slimy mud bank, the foul taste of the river still in his mouth.

Richardson was beside him, also on his hands and knees. "You okay?" he said. He was speaking in a whisper.

Nate nodded, then coughed again. He glanced toward the river, his eyes following the line of the pier. A thick, drowsy fog hung over the dark water. Waves lapped quietly against the muddy bank, stirring up a smell that reminded him of compost. He found it difficult to process the sleepy ease of the scene, especially after what he'd just gone through. It had been a rough swim. They'd been going with the current, downriver, and Nate was able to let it carry him most of the way. But then the group had reached the pier and turned toward shore. That had been the hard part. He had kicked and beat ineffectively at the water, but couldn't make himself go. The regulator had popped out of his mouth and he'd started to sink. He'd panicked. River water had got into his mouth and he'd swallowed some of it. But then Richardson grabbed his arm and pushed the regulator back in his mouth and carried him the rest of the way.

I almost drowned, he thought. Jesus Christ.

That would have been something. He'd lived through the apocalypse. Four thousand Air Force soldiers died at Minot, but he'd escaped. He escaped the mass suicides at Jasper Sewell's Grasslands compound. He'd even escaped certain death at the hands of the Red Man, the zombie king. It would have been something to live through all that just to drown in the river.

Nate laughed, a gravelly, choking sound that brought with it another round of coughing. His chest and his throat were burning and tight, but it didn't hurt as badly as it had just a few moments earlier.

Nate Royal dodges another bullet, he thought. Yay me.

After another round of coughing, he glanced up at the others.

Jimmy and Gabi were stowing their gear in the joint where the pier met the bank, the two of them all business, as usual.

Sylvia was fussing over Avery. She checked her injuries, then brushed the girl's wet hair back from her eyes with her fingertips.

They made eye contact.

Sylvia whispered something to her and Avery nodded in reply.

Beside him, Richardson was sliding out of the harness that held the air tank on his back. Nate wondered if he too was thinking how close they'd come to drowning. With all his panicked kicking and thrashing, Nate knew he'd been a handful down there, and Richardson was certainly no spring chicken anymore.

"Where are we anyway?" Nate said.

Jimmy wheeled around fiercely, his eyes narrowed, his lips pulled back from his teeth in a snarl. "Keep quiet, you idiot. You trying to get us killed?"

Nate frowned at him.

Jimmy stared back at him, almost daring him to say something else. Growing up, there had been a few years, mostly during middle school, when nearly every word he spoke to his father earned him a slap across the mouth. Kneeling there in the mud, the quiet sound of water lapping against the pier beams all around him, Nate felt the sting of old wounds rising in his cheeks.

He lowered his eyes. "I was just asking," he said.

Jimmy turned away, muttering something about how a man so dumb had no reason to go on living.

When their gear was stowed they crawled over to the pier's shadow line and looked out across the grounds of the Kirkman Hyatt Hotel. A few guards stood by the entrance closest to the pier, but otherwise the field between the water and the buildings was deserted.

Nate's gaze drifted from the water, across the open field, and finally over the buildings. Or building, rather. From the glimpses he'd gotten while they were still on the *Sugar Jane*, it had looked like the hotel was made up of three separate buildings. But it was just the one building, he could see that now. One really huge building. There were three towers, each about nine or ten stories high and made of dingy gray brick. They were arranged in a V shape, each one connected to the others by flat-roofed common areas.

Avery was looking at him. He met her gaze and she smiled.

"It used to be the Kirkman Hyatt Hotel and Convention Center," she said, almost as though she could read his mind. "It was the biggest hotel in the Midwest before the outbreak."

Sylvia looked back toward the water. "The fog's starting to clear," she said. They could hear the Red Man's boats powering slowly back and forth across the river. "They're still looking for us, but once that fog's gone, they'll know we're not out there. That doesn't give us much time."

"To do what, exactly?" Gabi asked.

"We're going in there," Sylvia said. "We have to find Niki. Without her, all this is for nothing."

"I only see the two guards," Richardson said. "We can get past them."

"Listen to you two," Gabi said. There was a smile forming at the corners of her mouth, but it was an expression of disbelief. "You're both absolutely insane."

Gabi looked from Sylvia to Richardson and back to Sylvia again, as though one of them might miraculously come to their senses and tell her they were just kidding. But when that didn't happen she huffed and shook her head.

"What would you have us do?" Sylvia asked. "You know why we're doing this. You know how important this is. Not just to us, but for all of us. People everywhere."

"Save your speeches," Jimmy said. "Just tell me how you're going to get in there."

"We'll have to get around those two guards," she said. She hesitated for a moment, then pointed to the north side of the tower to their left. "Maybe through a window on that side there. That line of shrubs should give us some cover from those guards."

"It'll get us out of their line of sight," Richardson agreed.

"And when you're inside?" Jimmy said. "How are you gonna find your friend?"

Sylvia shrugged. "I don't know. I hadn't thought that far ahead."

Jimmy huffed. "Well, it's your ass."

"Hopefully not." She turned to Gabi. "You two don't have to come with us. It'd help if you could find us a way out of here, though. Maybe have a boat waiting for us?"

Gabi looked at her husband. A silent conversation seemed to play out between them.

Finally, she turned back to Sylvia, nodding. "Yeah, we can do that."

"Good. Ready everybody?"

"Wait," Richardson said. He glanced at Avery. To Nate, it looked as though he was about to suggest she should stay put, or perhaps go with Jimmy and Gabi.

"What is it?" Sylvia said. If she had picked up on Richardson's questioning glance toward Avery, she made no sign of it.

"I . . . nothing," he said. "I'm ready."

A ragged line of red-tip photinias ran along what had once been the hotel's northern property line. It wasn't much for cover or concealment, and looking up at the black, vacant windows on the tower face above them, Nate figured that anybody watching the grounds from up there would spot them easily. But Sylvia guided them to the tower without incident. They ran from the last of the bushes to the side of the tower in a crouch. Like kids playing at being soldiers, Nate thought. The thought might have been funny in some other place, some other time. As it was, he was beginning to feel sick again, as though something long and massive was slowly uncoiling in his gut.

Nate crossed the last few feet of rangy lawn and put his back against the wall next to Richardson. On the other side of Richardson was an empty window, and on the other side of that stood Sylvia and Avery. Sylvia glanced into the opening and seemed satisfied.

"At least we won't have to break out the window," she said.

"Let's just get out of the open," Richardson said.

"Agreed."

Sylvia climbed through the window. Richardson helped Avery through and then went himself. A breeze touched Nate's face, bringing with it the dank, earthy smell of the river. But there was another smell behind it, underneath it, something evil. It sent a chill through him, raising the gooseflesh on his arms.

Maybe this was a bad idea, Nate thought.

But he did it anyway.

He climbed through the window and dropped into what must have been some kind of office back before the outbreak. In the dark he could make out a lot of desks, most of them pushed off at odd angles from their once orderly rows. He could picture people working at those desks, discontented drones engaged in the soul-sucking task of moving paper from one stack to the next. There was dried blood on the walls, a ragged outline of a hand dragged across a grimy wall. How old the blood was he couldn't tell, and he supposed it didn't really matter. Trash was scattered all over the floor. Countless rainstorms had found their way through the windows over the years, and the room had a water-damaged grunginess about it. There was a smell in here, too, that of sodden paper and spoiled food. Rats scurried into the shadows. Nate heard, or at least thought he heard, the sound of their little claws tapping on the hardwood floor.

"Where do we go from here?" Richardson asked.

Sylvia shrugged. "I don't know, Ben. I guess we just start looking around."

"Should we split up or something?" Nate asked.

"No," Sylvia said. "If we get separated we may never find our way back together again."

They found the exit, and on the other side of that a long, narrow hallway. There were rooms all down the length of the hall, darkened doorways leading God knows where.

"I don't like this," Avery said.

Sylvia grabbed her hand and squeezed. "You're worried about zombies in here?"

Avery nodded.

"I don't think we're gonna have to worry about that."

"Why?"

"This is the Red Man's home base. If he can control zombies from miles away, he should be able to keep them under control when they're right here under his thumb."

"How is that supposed to make me feel any better?" Avery asked.

"He uses uninfected troops, too. He can't very well house them here if he has zombies running around everywhere. None of them would stay. My guess is the zombies he does have here are kept out of the way and under tight control."

Richardson scoffed. "Sylvia, that's bullshit."

"Excuse me?"

"You know better than that. They let us get in here. They practically opened the front door for us. This is a trap."

"A trap?" The muscles in her neck twitched. She put her hands on her hips and stared at Ben like he was the dumbest man alive. Nate knew the look well. He was just glad it was pointed at someone else this time.

Sylvia shook her head.

"Ben, you need to make up your mind."

"What's that supposed to mean?"

"You tell me. First you don't believe these zombies are capable of being cured, that their minds are permanently gone, and then you go and suggest they're capable of setting a trap. Which is it, Ben? Make up your mind."

"A Venus flytrap is capable of setting a trap for a fly."

"What does that have to do with anything?"

"Nearly every predator on the planet is capable of setting a trap. That doesn't make them human. And it doesn't prove they can be cured. You're living in La La Land if you believe that."

"And you're being obtuse."

"I am not."

"Fatuous then."

"Hey, I'm not calling you names."

"You said I was full of shit."

"No, I said what you said was bullshit. There's a difference."

"Not from where I'm standing."

These two, Nate realized, were like racehorses going around the track. Their arguments had a sort of useless circularity to them, a constant effort to outdistance one another on a course that went nowhere and proved nothing.

Nate looked at Avery. She met his gaze and he saw exhaustion in her eyes, the same kind of exhaustion he'd seen in the soldiers back at Minot, right after they'd come back from working double shifts at the fence line, where the zombies gathered in crowds hundreds deep, moaning with the voice of hell.

And yet it wasn't exactly the same. Not really. Now that he was studying her, really looking at her, he could see it was actually the exhaustion in him projected onto her. The clarity of the insight startled him. For so long people had told him he was dumb, a moron, and he had believed it. He'd never seen or felt anything to contradict it. And yet, when he was with her, when he was with Ben and Sylvia and Avery, he couldn't help but feel . . . good . . . like he was complete. When the four of them were together, he felt like matching gears had suddenly been pieced together for the first time. This constant arguing between Ben and Sylvia, perhaps it was some kind of courtship between them, something the two of them needed, but it was throwing a wrench in the gears.

"Both of you, stop it," he said. "Just shut it."

They both looked at him, frankly shocked at the tone of his voice.

"Both of you, please. We have work to do."

Sylvia started to speak, then stopped. She huffed in frustration.

"I don't get you, Ben."

"What's to get?"

"Seriously," Nate said. "I mean, really? We've just come all this way, we nearly fucking died out there, and the two of you can't drop whatever the hell it is that's got you both so pissed off?"

Ben pointed a finger at Nate's chest, but Sylvia stopped him.

"It's okay, Ben. Nate, you're right. You're absolutely right. But this is important. This isn't just another stupid argument. Look: I'll come to the point." She turned to Ben. "Why are you here? If this is a trap, like you said, why are you here?"

"I'm a dumbass, I guess."

"You're an ass, Ben, but you're not a dumbass. I'm trying to be serious."

He shrugged.

"Think about it, Ben. Why?"

"I don't know."

"Answer my question, Ben. Why are you here? I know why I'm here. I know why Avery's here. Even Nate has a reason to be here. But what about you? What purpose do you serve?"

Richardson didn't speak. To Nate, it looked like he couldn't, or wouldn't, find the words to say what was going through his head.

"Answer me, Ben. What are you thinking?"

Ben stared at each of them in turn. There was a fierce resistance in his eyes. At least at first. That faded.

Then he spoke.

"You remember when I saw you for the first time?" He was looking right at Sylvia. "I don't mean in Austin. I mean in St. Louis."

She nodded. "I remember. Outside of that pizzeria."

"Yeah."

"I was collecting stories then. That was what sustained me, you know? The thing that kind of kept me moving."

She nodded.

"I had come to think of myself as this sort of roving camera. I used to tell myself that when I saw fucked-up shit. Roving camera, I'd say. Don't get involved. Just watch. Process it. Save it."

"Burn out," she said. "The feeling like you're going round in circles."

"That's right," he said, pointing at her. "Picture this: I'm working on this book, right? It's supposed to be the definitive history of this crisis we're all living through. I've been from one corner of the country to the other. I've broken laws, lived through mass suicides, talked to crazies and politicians and crazy politicians . . . I've seen it all. I've collected thousands of interviews. I've heard every single possible point of view and I've dutifully put them all down. And you know what?"

He looked to Sylvia.

She shook her head.

He looked to Avery, who simply stared back at him, eyes shrink-wrapped as though from incipient tears.

"Tell me," Nate said. "You began to wonder who the fuck would ever care."

Richardson seemed on the verge of tears. "Yes," he admitted. "Yes, goddamn it. That's it exactly."

He looked around the empty hallway, and there was no dread, no fear, no sense of being in way over his head. This place was just empty. Doorways leading onto quiet dead ends . . . though, strangely, Nate didn't see the same pointlessness that Ben seemed to be feeling.

Ben said, "Everything was still there. All my old writing skills. I could still type. I could still get someone to tell me their story, trust me. I could still find the right words. I could keep an interview lively. I could transition from one thought to the next like nobody's business."

"But . . . ?" Sylvia said.

Ben didn't say anything.

"What was missing, Ben?" Nate asked.

He had been looking at the floor. When he met their gaze, his eyes were bloodshot and wet.

"Curiosity," he said.

Sylvia didn't get it. Nate could see that from her frown. But Nate was pretty sure he understood.

"You sold out, didn't you?"

Richardson flinched. He turned on Nate and balled his fists. But there was nothing beyond his posturing, and they both knew it.

He bowed his head.

"Yeah. Okay. That's fair. I was speaking the words, but there was no real content."

"Has something changed?" Sylvia asked.

"We have, I guess."

Nate frowned. At first, he didn't understand. But then he

looked at the others, at Sylvia and Avery, and he saw understanding in their nods. And he too understood. They had come together for a reason. The whole world was butchered and damned. Gone, in the wink of an eye. Yet, despite the seeming futility, the emptiness, the pointlessness of it all, the four of them were together, and they were on the verge of something important. Something that actually had some content to it. This was humanity doing what it did best. What it had always done.

They were fighting back.

After a long time, they had finally found something worth fighting for.

They stood there, processing this new understanding of each other, and themselves. Nate felt good. He hadn't felt this kind of energy going through him in a very long time.

"I guess we go that way?" he said.

"I guess so," said Avery.

Sylvia and Richardson both nodded.

"You want to lead?" Nate asked Sylvia.

She shook her head. "You go, Nate. You're doing fine."

They made it to the end of the hall without incident.

And the next one.

And the one after that.

The place was deserted, it seemed, the only sound the sighing breeze working its way through busted windows and down empty hallways. Nate was up front, Avery and Richardson behind him. Sylvia was bringing up the rear. Everywhere they went they had to step over ceiling tiles that had crumbled and fallen to the floor, making it nearly impossible to walk quietly.

Still, Nate tried. He was, frankly, tired of feeling dumb.

But by the fourth or fifth empty hallway, and entering yet

another empty landing, Nate started to get bored. The miserable, torpid heat that had settled inside the building was getting more of his attention than his tactics.

He stopped and wiped his face with the belly of his shirt.

They were standing in the middle of another large meeting room, much like the one they'd first stepped into when they entered the building, though this one seemed to have been cleared of most of the furniture. A few busted chairs stood out amongst all the fallen ceiling tiles, and one big wooden desk was covered with a thick layer of white dust, but aside from that, it was just another empty room with no air circulation.

Nate walked to the center of the room and stopped. The side of the room from which they'd entered had only one door. But the opposite side of the room had six. Two of those were bathrooms. He could see the dust-covered MEN'S ROOM sign hanging from a single screw next to one of the rooms. But the other four doors could lead, well, anywhere. He looked from one to the other to the other and had no idea which one to take.

He was about to ask Sylvia which way when one of the doors fell open with the groan of seldom used hinges.

They all flinched.

A girl child stepped through the door, leaving it open behind her. She looked to be nine, or maybe ten. She was shabbily dressed in a tattered yellow dress, no shoes, her hair a wild tangle on her head. Her arms hung limply at her side, and from one hooked finger depended a plastic bag filled with half a loaf of bread and some oranges.

She shuffled across the floor, one leg obviously injured.

"Stand back," Richardson said, pushing his way past Nate.

He drew his pistol and leveled it at the little girl.

"No!" said Sylvia. She stepped forward, put a hand on

Richardson's arm, and eased his weapon down. "Look at her," she said.

Nate did.

The left side of the girl's face was all chewed up, but it had been cleaned and had already started to heal. The eye on that side of her face was ruined. The other eye was webbed with white lines, like incipient cataracts. She made her slow, shuffling way across the trash-covered floor and for just a moment turned her one good eye toward Nate. There was a haunted, uneasy vacancy in the back of her stare.

But the girl didn't stop. She kept going across the room, fumbled at a doorknob with a hand that didn't seem to work just right, and finally got it open.

The next instant, she was gone.

Richardson had taken a few cautious steps after her, but now he turned and looked at the rest of them.

"What was that? Why didn't she attack? Why didn't she start moaning?"

Nate shrugged.

Avery grabbed Nate's hand. "I don't like that," she said. "That's not right."

"No," Sylvia said. "No, it's not."

"Anybody want to take a crack at what the hell we just saw?" Richardson said.

Sylvia said, "I think we should go after her."

"What?"

"It looked like she was being led, didn't it?"

Richardson shook his head, scowling like her suggestion was utter lunacy.

But it made sense to Nate. Once again he sensed his thoughts coming together. Something had clicked for him. "It did look like that," he said. He nodded to himself. "Yes." Then, to Avery: "She was carrying food. That was what was in that bag, right? Food?"

"Yeah," Avery said.

"So who was it for?" Nate said.

Richardson shook his head.

Nate frowned at him. It wasn't like Richardson to miss something that seemed so obvious, but he either couldn't, or wouldn't, understand.

"We need to follow her," Sylvia said. "I bet she'll lead us to Niki."

"Exactly," Nate said.

"That's crazy," Richardson said.

"Ben," Sylvia said, "she was being led, directed. The Red Man is controlling her. You have to see that, don't you?"

"No, I don't."

"Why do you find it so hard believe? You yourself told me you've seen Stage III zombies using Stage I zombies like hunting dogs to flush out prey. How is this any different?"

"Because there's a physical agency involved in the way Stage III zombies control the lesser ones. They're exactly like hunters with their dogs. They point them where they want them to go and they let native instincts take over. What you're suggesting would take some kind of psychic power. I refuse to believe that."

"But why?"

"Because it's not rationally consistent."

"I don't even know what that's supposed to mean."

"It doesn't make sense. These are zombies, Sylvia. Zombies. Their minds have been cooked to mush by the necrosis filovirus until there's nothing left. They have no intellect, no consciousness. They don't make plans. They don't play puppeteer with other zombies. And you know why? Because there's nothing for a puppeteer to hook his strings to. You can't control a mind that isn't there."

Sylvia just stared at him.

He huffed back.

"These are zombies, Sylvia," he said again. "When you start giving them psychic powers or whatever the hell you claim this is, they stop being zombies. They become something else, and that's just not consistent with this world."

"I don't see how that makes any of this any less real," she said.

"Enough," Nate said.

He went over to the door and looked down the hallway. The little girl was slipping around the corner at the far end.

"We're gonna lose her if we stick around here arguing."

"He's right," Sylvia said to Richardson. She took Avery by the hand. "Come on, sweetie. Let's go get Niki."

They slipped past Nate at the doorway.

He pointed them down the hall.

"She went around that corner," he said.

Nate turned to Richardson, who was standing in the middle of the empty room, looking frustrated and dour.

"You coming?" Nate said.

CHAPTER 19

They followed the little girl, but stayed well back in the shadows, far enough away—Nate hoped, anyway—that they could turn tail and run if it came to that.

But the girl seemed to be the only thing moving through the hotel. She went from one hallway to the next, winding her slow and steady way through a maze of passageways, never once getting lost, like she was following an old familiar path.

Nate got bored again. His head felt soupy from the heat, which was becoming oppressive the deeper they went. He smelled bad, too. Several times he tried to drive the cloying mustiness of the river out of his nostrils by shaking his head, but the smell enveloped him like a living thing.

He couldn't tell if the others smelled as bad as he did. Probably they did. But they were definitely feeling the heat. He could tell from the labored sound of Richardson's breathing and from the way Sylvia had given up trying to push the hair from her face. It was an unaccustomed look for her. In the week or so he'd been running around with this group, he'd come to expect a certain unflagging resiliency from her.

But now her shoulders were drooping, like the weight of this place and the job they'd set for themselves was weighing down upon her.

Poor Avery, though. She was a different matter altogether. She was soaked with sweat. He could tell it was sweat and not river water because it was popping out all over her skin and running down her cheeks like tears, cutting clean scars through the dirt that covered her pink face. Every step she took looked like it was bought with pain. He wanted to reach out and touch her hand, tell her that—

"Nate, stop!" Sylvia said.

He froze, shook the thoughts from his head. He turned around. The others were three or four steps behind him.

Richardson nodded down the hallway.

The little girl in the yellow dress was about to round a brightly lit corner. Nate could see a flickering orange light spilling across the floor there, setting the girl into relief.

"Go quietly," Sylvia said. "No surprises."

Nate nodded.

They got to the corner in time to see two black shirts opening a large wooden door for the little girl. She walked through, still carrying the plastic bag full of bread and oranges, and never even looked at the two uninfected men. To Nate it was unbelievable, zombies and humans working together like that. It seemed unreal.

A few moments later, the little girl came back through the same door, turned to her left, and walked away down a side corridor.

"That's pretty weird," Nate said.

"I bet she's in there," said Avery. She was trying to be quiet, but the excitement in her voice was unmistakable.

"I bet you're right," said Sylvia. She smiled and patted the younger woman on the shoulder. Sylvia was more restrained than Avery, but she too was giddy. These two, they'd been through hell to find Niki. Now they were like kids at Christmas, the anticipation almost too much to bear.

But then Sylvia's smile wavered.

"What?" Avery said.

"We need to get in there somehow."

Nate didn't like the sound of that. The two black shirts had machine guns.

He pointed at the pistol at Richardson's hip. "Could you shoot them?"

"I'd never get them both," Richardson said. "One of them probably. I might even be able to get the second one, with a lucky shot. But even if I killed them both, the noise would just bring more."

Nate nodded.

Sylvia said, "Well, there may be another way."

"What are you thinking?" Richardson asked.

She glanced down at the baton in her hand and seemed to be turning options over in her mind. "A diversion, I guess," she said at last.

She looked at Nate.

"Do you think you could fool those guys long enough to turn their backs to me?"

"Fool them?"

Richardson chuckled softly, shaking his head.

"What?" Nate said. He was starting to get angry.

"You sure look the part," Richardson said. "I think it could work."

"The part? What the hell are you guys talking about?"

"It's okay," Richardson said. He pulled his blackjack from the waistband of his jeans. "Here," he said, handing it to Nate. "Take this. Palm it as long as you can, tucked up into your sleeve."

He showed Nate how to hold it out of sight.

"There, like that."

Nate was utterly perplexed.

"Don't worry," Richardson said. "I know what she has in mind."

Nate stepped into the open, certain he was about to get shot. This was stupid. He struggled to put some label on how he felt, but the only word that came to mind was *transparent*. Nate didn't know if that was right or not, but it felt right. He did know that these black shirts would have to be idiots to mistake him for one of the zombies. Shuffling toward them, dragging his feet, arms at his side, Nate watched the men without trying to make it look like he was watching them. He turned what he hoped was a dead stare on a spot somewhere near the middle of the door between them, letting his head loll and jerk, his mouth hanging open just a little.

The black shirts weren't expecting anything. That much was obvious from the way they tensed, hands flexing on their weapons, the nervous glances that passed between them. But Nate ignored them. He got to the middle of the hallway and turned slowly to his right.

He started walking.

He made it a few steps into the new hallway when one of the guards said, "What the hell is that all about?"

Nate stopped.

He let a moan escape his throat.

One of the guards had been about to speak, but quickly smothered the sound. Nate slowly turned his head, just as he'd seen countless zombies do during his wanderings. A runner of drool gathered at the corner of his mouth and fell down his chin. Nate fought back the instinct to wipe it away. He took a lurching step toward the guard, and he hoped the vacant look in his eyes was believable.

He would find out any second now, he supposed.

"Ah, shit," the guard said. He slid the machine gun off his shoulder as his partner came around to stand next to him.

But before either man could raise his weapon, Nate let the blackjack drop, his fingers settling into the leather strap. What happened next seemed to happen all at once. His arm came up, the blackjack raised high. The first guard's eyes widened, almost comically. The blackjack came down on the man's chin, accompanied by the sickening crack of lead on bone. The man sagged to the floor.

Sylvia erupted from the shadows, swinging her baton at the back of the second guard's head.

Nate looked down at the first guard, who was writhing lamely on the carpeted floor, groaning in pain. Nate knelt down, his knees either side of the first guard's chest. He brought the blackjack down again and again on the man's face, smashing it to a bloody pulp.

When Nate rose from the man's corpse, he had blood on his hands and in his eyes.

He coughed, not quite believing what he'd just done, and then laughed. "We did it," he said. "Did you see that? They actually fell for it."

Sylvia pushed him out of the way.

"Come on, there isn't much time."

She opened the door the guards had been covering and went inside. Avery and Richardson followed.

And after a pause, so did Nate.

Just enough light spilled in from the doorway for Nate to see the outlines of a bell-shaped cage hanging from the ceiling. It was empty, and the floor below looked wet. He couldn't tell for sure, though.

And he didn't want to find out.

The others were just ahead of him, moving around the cage, giving it a wide berth.

"I have a penlight," Richardson said. "Should we chance it?"

Sylvia stopped and looked back. Her eyes caught the light, flashing like a cat's in the dark.

"Yeah," she said. "Go ahead."

Nate was standing right behind Richardson when he turned his tiny blue LED light into the darkness. He saw a flash of movement, a woman, battered and snarling, moving fast. She lashed out at Richardson, the heel of her hand smashing into Richardson's nose, sending him flying backward.

The penlight hit the floor and rolled away.

Nate was watching it when an iron grip locked onto his throat, fingernails digging deep into his skin.

He couldn't breathe.

Whoever had him was holding him from behind. He started to thrash. His resistance earned him a kick to the back of his knees. He collapsed, but not all the way to the floor, for his captor had grabbed his left arm and twisted it up behind his back.

The grip on his throat slackened for just a moment.

"Stop it!" Nate said.

The grip tightened.

Then a woman leaned in close to his ear and whispered, "Stop fighting me or I'll tear the windpipe from your throat."

He tried to speak and couldn't. He nodded instead.

A little pressure came off his throat, but at the same time his captor bent his arm farther up his back. Nate arched his back against the pain, a little whimper escaping his lips.

"Please stop," he said.

"Who are you?"

"I'm Nate Royal."

She wrenched his arm even farther up his back. "I want to know why you're here. Answer me."

But before Nate could speak Sylvia grabbed the penlight and turned it up at her own face.

"Niki, it's me."

Nate was thrown roughly to the floor. He landed on his chin with an audible *umph* and stayed there. It felt like his arm had been pulled out of its socket and his throat crushed.

It took him a long while before he could sit up. When he did, he saw Sylvia and Avery and the woman they called Niki hugging. Avery was crying. Sylvia looked like a worried mother. She couldn't take her hands off Niki's wounded face.

She kept saying, "Oh, sweetie. Oh no. Don't you worry. We'll get you out of here."

Nate finally rose to his feet. His eyes had adjusted to the dark now, and he could see the three women in shadowed relief. He saw Niki turn his way and there was just enough light to see the distrust on her face.

"Who's that?" she said.

"His name is Nate," Avery said.

Even Nate could recognize the hopeful timbre in her voice, as though she hoped Niki might offer some encouraging words about him. Nate couldn't help but feel a touch of pride. He was thirty years old, but he couldn't ever remember being the cause of making a woman sound like that.

Niki too, it seemed, picked up on it. She regarded Nate with a look he couldn't quite articulate, but it felt like he was being summed up, evaluated in some way. It made him feel all of about two feet high.

"I think your friend is hurt," Niki said.

Nate nodded. "Uh huh."

"You might want to help him," Niki prodded.

"Oh, yeah."

Nate went over to Richardson and knelt by his side. He examined Richardson's face, the smashed nose and upper lip, the blood, the missing front tooth.

"Wow, she fucked you up good."

Richardson groaned. He tried to sit up, but his eyes crossed and he sagged back to the ground.

"Can you stand?"

After a moment, Richardson nodded.

Nate helped him to his feet. The women were standing in a huddle a short distance away, Sylvia and Avery both trying to talk at once.

Niki noticed him and her bruised smile receded.

"Is your friend okay?"

"My friend?"

Nate didn't catch her meaning. He was too busy looking at her face. In the low light it was difficult to make her out clearly, but Nate thought she might have been pretty before she got beat up. Her eyes were blackened and puffy, her lips crusty with dried blood. Her left shoulder drooped, like she was too tired, or too badly hurt, to stand up straight.

"What happened to you?" he said.

Niki huffed. "Your boyfriend's not the brightest bulb in the box, is he?"

"He's not my boyfriend," Avery said, though she wouldn't look any of them in the eye.

Though he couldn't be sure, Nate was certain he saw a high blush rise in her cheeks.

"I'm alright," Richardson said.

"Well, okay then," Niki said. She extended her right foot and shook it so they could all hear the chain cuffed to her ankle rattling. "Somebody got a flat piece of metal? A screwdriver, maybe?"

A pause.

"I do," said Richardson.

He urged Nate to one side, hesitantly standing on his own. "I got it," he said. He reached into the back pocket of his jeans and pulled out a flat strip of metal about the size of a well-chewed pencil. It had a little squiggly hook at the end.

Nate squinted at it, then looked questioningly at Richardson.

"It's a lock pick. On my way to the Grasslands, I traveled with this ex-cop named Michael Barnes. He said he used to carry one of these in his back pocket all the time, just in case somebody handcuffed him."

"That'll work," Niki said. "Here—give it to me."

Richardson handed the lock pick over. Nate stepped forward, instantly fascinated. He'd always found it mystifying that people could manipulate things the way they did. Even back before the world got all messed up, the sight of somebody working on an engine, or installing cable on a new entertainment center, or turning some old appliance into something completely new and clever, was a mystery to him. Machines and electronics were like some puzzle too strange and too big for him to fathom. He was completely incapable of doing it himself, but it still fascinated him.

Like Niki Booth was fascinating him now.

She was digging the pick into the gap between the cuff's ratchet arm and base, her bruised lips pursed in concentration.

The cuff clicked open.

Niki kicked the metal away, then went down on one knee to rub her ankle where the cuff had chafed her.

She got back up quickly.

In the faint blue glow of the penlight Nate could see the dark bruises on her cheeks, the dried blood at her ears and down the sides of her neck, the missing tooth. She swayed uncertainly on her feet. Her captors had really hurt her. But despite the damage, there was an unmistakable aura of certainty and control about her. This one, Nate sensed, was tough. The Red Man had battered her, bruised her, but he hadn't gotten to her core. He hadn't been able to get that deep. There was still a hard grain inside her that was as of yet undaunted and true.

"What day is it?" she said.

"Um, it's Wednesday," said Avery.

Niki grunted. "We don't have much time. I'm supposed to meet Fisher at sunset."

She touched Avery's hand lightly, and the younger woman looked up expectantly.

"How you doin', baby? You okay?"

Avery nodded. "It's good to see you again."

"You too. Listen. I need you to help me. Do you know where we are, on the river I mean?"

Avery nodded again.

"Do you know how to get to a little town called Chester from here?"

"Sure. It's only fourteen miles south of here. We could just follow the east bank of the river."

"That close, really?" Niki looked impressed. The faint glimmer of a smile appeared at the corner of her damaged mouth. "I'm supposed to meet Fisher there, at St. Mary's Cemetery. You know it?"

"You bet I do."

Niki looked at Sylvia and the two women traded real smiles now.

Nate heard something. Behind them, in the dark.

Richardson was a few feet away, still bleeding, his breath coming in wet, nasally pulls through his busted lips. At first that was the noise Nate thought he'd heard, and he was about to turn back to the women when he saw a dark shape moving slowly across the ground just behind Richardson.

Nate turned the penlight on it and let out a gasp. It was a man, definitely a man, completely nude and covered in blood. Deep oozing cuts ran down the length of his body and some looked deep enough to show the yellow layers of fat beneath the skin. A wide smear of blood marked his relentless path through the darkness to this spot.

But as injured as he was, the zombie moved with surprising speed. It extended a gnarled hand and locked it around Richardson's ankle. At the same time he pulled his open mouth toward Richardson's calf and bit off a huge chunk of denim and flesh.

Richardson screamed as he collapsed to the ground.

Nate took a step in that direction, meaning to kick the zombie in the face to get him away from Richardson, but he had barely begun to move when he felt an iron grip on the back of his shirt.

It was Niki.

She pulled him back, nearly throwing him to the ground in the process. "Get out of the way," she said.

The zombie reached for her. She knocked his hand away, got behind him, and pushed the man facedown on the pavement with the sole of her boot. He tried to clutch at her, but his movements were awkward and he couldn't figure out how to turn his arms over to get a grip on her. Niki gave him a solid kick in the ribs for good measure, then stood over top of him and brought her boot down hard on the back of his neck.

There was a loud crack and the man went still.

But Richardson was still screaming.

"We need to keep him quiet," Niki said.

She took the penlight from Nate and turned it on Richardson. His face had gone pale and his mouth was quivering. His eyes were wild with fright. The blue glow of the penlight made his skin look unnatural, like fine marble.

He watched Niki drawing closer, and he started shaking his head. "No," he said. "No, stay back."

"It's alright," she said. "Don't make any noise. I just want to look at you."

"The crows," Richardson said. "No, please. Stay back."

"The crows?" Niki said. She looked back at Nate, but he had no idea what Richardson was talking about. He shrugged.

Somewhere in the darkness, they heard wet, gurgling moans. Lots of them.

They all froze. Even Richardson stopped whimpering.

"What was that?" Nate said.

"Shhh," Niki hissed.

She turned the penlight into the darkness.

Nate strained his eyes to see into the shadows. There were figures moving around in little side rooms along the walls, some just rising to their feet, others already awake and surging against the chain-link fence that had been placed over the entrances to the rooms, turning them into cells. Out of habit Nate tried to count them, but there were way too many for that. All he could see was a blur of ruined faces and shredded fingers trying to squeeze through the diamond-shaped holes of the fence.

One of the zombies tried to climb the fence, and the weight peeled a corner of it away from the wall. He fell, and was trampled by the others surging forward, reaching for the opening that was getting wider with every second.

A moment later the fence tore loose from the wall, and soon dozens of zombies were stumbling across the floor, crunching the pile of trash beneath their feet.

"Time to go," Niki said.

Nate knelt down next to Richardson and tried to lift him, but even he knew the older man was as good as dead. Richardson was already starting to convulse, a sure sign that the necrosis filovirus was waging war in his bloodstream, and winning. His eyes were rolling up into his head and little specks of blood were already starting to appear on his lips.

Niki grabbed Nate by the shirt again and pulled.

"Let's go," she said. "You can't help him now."

Her grip was surprisingly strong. Even if he had tried to resist he probably wouldn't have been able. And she's injured too, he thought. Such strength.

"But Ben . . ." Nate said.

Niki shoved him toward the door again. "Move," she said. "There's no time."

Nate let himself be led out the door and into the hallway, where torches cast a flickering orange light on the black floor and the wood-paneled walls. He was still in shock, unable to resist.

He looked into the darkness of the room they'd just left. The moaning was growing louder, and he could see the shambling forms of men and women moving toward the lighted doorway in which he stood. He knew he had to run. Behind him the others were already heading down the hallway. But something inside him was telling him this was huge, too huge to just walk away from. That was Ben Richardson in there. That was the man who had entrusted him with his life's work. A man was dying in there, and somebody had to pay attention.

Ben Richardson, he thought, trying to wrap his mind around all that the man had come to represent for him. A new beginning. A purpose redefined.

Not since Doc Kellogg had anyone ever bothered to talk to him, really talk to him, about the way the world worked. But Richardson had. They had shared some conversations about this blighted world and how Nate might fit in with it. They had had such huge conversations. They had talked for hours on end. The man's words had been a gift to Nate, the kind of gift that saved lives. And now, Nate was left wondering why Richardson died muttering something crazy about crows.

It didn't make any sense.

He couldn't quite come to terms with that.

CHAPTER 20

"You okay?" Jimmy Hinton whispered.

Gabi had slipped on the muddy bank and landed on her hands and knees. For a long moment she didn't move, so long that Jimmy almost asked her again if she was okay.

But she finally looked up at him. "The ground here smells bad."

"Yeah," he agreed. "It's an evil place."

She stood up and shook the mud from her hands. It was a frustrated gesture, like she was trying to restore her pride. But it was a moot effort at this point. There was more mud on the front of her dress than there was on the ground. The shape of the stain, the way it spread in a semicircle across her lap, reminded Jimmy of an apron. That was funny, he thought, his Gabi wearing an apron. Their marriage, especially these last eight years, had been as much about guns and keeping the *Sugar Jane* afloat as it was about love. This woman, who had meant so much to him, was anything but a domestic goddess. She didn't mouse about the boat, begging him to make their decisions for their survival. She didn't make the bed and cook his meals and cluck over him like an old mother hen. Instead, she killed zombies and river pirates alike, and she did it standing right by his side. There wasn't a trace of squeamishness in her. She didn't fear guns or engine grease or even the zombies that roamed this blighted land. Gabi Hinton was a battle-axe, and he loved her for it. He stifled a laugh.

"What's so funny?"

She was still trying to shake the mud from her hands.

"Nothing," he said.

She gave him a look like she didn't believe him, but let it pass. "Well, let's get moving. We aren't gonna find a ride standing here."

"Nope, I guess you're right about that."

They were following a path of loose gravel that ran between the tall weeds that grew along the verge of the river and the muddy bank upon which Gabi had just fallen. It wasn't a true path. It was overgrown in spots, the gravel not even visible, but it offered the only cover they had this close to the river. The land that stretched out between the top of the muddy bank and the hotel was flat and empty of trees. There were a few rusted pickups and a boat trailer on the drive that led down to the pier, but nothing that could conceal them from the patrols wandering the grounds. They were stuck down here next to the river.

Jimmy's goal was a small wooden shed about thirty yards ahead of them. He envisioned this hotel in its prime, with little boats rented out to guests puttering up and down the slow-moving majesty of the mighty Mississippi and a dull-headed boy on his summer vacation working the shack, taking room keys and handing out pamphlets on the sights. Beyond the shack were a few of those small motorboats, and one or two looked like they might actually be sturdy enough to get them away from this place. Probably not very far, but far enough.

"Can you make it to that shed?" he asked.

She narrowed her eyes at him.

"Okay, then," he said. He held up his palms in mock surrender as though to say he was sorry he asked. "Onward we go."

When they reached it Jimmy saw something he hadn't expected. On the other side of the shed was a concrete drive that sank into the river. Debris floating on the water seemed to be moving slowly, and it occurred to him that the combination of deep water and slow moving currents made this a logical ferry crossing point. He looked across the river for a matching point on the other side, but the fog was still thick enough in places to obscure his view. He had a strong feeling it was there, though, and he kicked himself for his stupidity. The shack wasn't some kind of checkout line for hotel guests. It was the weather shack for the ferry boat drivers. That meant the Red Man would be bringing his boats in here. Especially if he was going to be offloading zombies, which he almost certainly would be.

"This is no good," Jimmy said. "We need to get back to the pier."

"The pier? What for?"

"As soon as that fog clears, I think we're gonna—"

Jimmy stopped mid-sentence. Gabi didn't speak. The two of them had been partners long enough to recognize each other's cues, and she hunkered down, looking at him and waiting.

He motioned to her that he heard something coming from the direction of the hotel. She fell back against the bank and pressed herself into the mud. Jimmy nodded in approval and crawled forward, peering over the lip of the bank.

A guard was standing less than ten feet away, his back to them.

Jimmy gasped silently. If the man had been looking at them just then . . .

"Give me a fuckin' break," the guard said. "I gotta piss."

Jimmy quickly ducked down again, his eyes wide with panic. He motioned to Gabi in the sign language they'd developed over the years.

One guy, machine gun. We need to make that shack.

Gabi nodded back in understanding.

Together they crawled through the weeds and over to the part of the shack that lipped over the river. Jimmy helped Gabi onto the deck and the two of them hid inside an alcove facing the water. The inside of the shack was dingy and had the lingering smell of fish offal, as though it had so long been used to clean fish that the smell had settled into the wood like rot.

They waited there, listening.

Gabi was standing at one corner, her hands up and the fingers curled over like claws. If that black shirt Jimmy had seen happened around that corner, he'd no doubt get his neck wrung like an old rooster in a farmyard. An apron indeed, he thought.

He heard footsteps on the planks of the dock and tensed. The guard—he was no more than a kid, Jimmy could see that now—stepped to the edge of the dock, his rifle slung casually over one shoulder, and unzipped his pants.

A moment later he was jetting a steady stream of urine into the water.

Jimmy put a hand on Gabi's shoulder, urging her back.

She eased back into the alcove, but he could still feel the tension in her. She was ready to kill the guard.

The next instant the young man shook, zipped up his fly, and went back to his patrol. Jimmy could hear his footsteps on the dock, and then in the mud as he slogged his way back up the bank.

He let out a long breath.

"You should have let me kill him," Gabi whispered. "I could have broken his neck before he had a chance to make a sound."

"And then what? His buddies would come down and check on him."

She didn't have an answer for that.

"We can't stay here," he said.

"You said that before."

He nodded. "This is their landing spot. My guess is this is where they're going to come ashore."

That stopped her. She studied the concrete drive, the slow-moving river, and he knew from the look on her face that she was coming to the same conclusion he had just a moment earlier.

"What are we gonna do?" she asked.

"Is it clear?"

She turned so that she was facing the shack, then slowly peered around the corner, up toward the hotel. Jimmy studied her lips, trying to read the words she was muttering. It looked like she was counting.

"Not yet," she said. "I see two patrols. Eight men total. They're coming from opposite sides of the hotel. Both have a clear view of the bank."

"Okay, then. We wait it out here."

She looked sharply at him.

"You said we couldn't stay here."

"We're probably safe as long as there's fog on the water. The Red Man will be out there searching as long as he can."

"You're sure of that?"

He wrinkled his brow. "Why wouldn't I be?"

"I was thinking about what Sylvia said."

"What about it?"

"Do you think it's true? Can he really control zombies like they say?"

"I don't see why not. If he really is what they say he is, controlling zombies should be a piece of cake."

She didn't answer. Instead, she got a faraway look in her eyes, like she was going deep into her own head.

"What's going on with you?" he said. "What are you thinking?"

She smiled. "You know me pretty well, don't you?"

"I hope so," he said. "After all we've been through, if I don't know you like I know my own soul then I haven't been lovin' you like you deserve."

She blushed. He couldn't believe it. The battle-axe blushed. There was a girl in there, delicate and true and needing something just as honest from him.

"You're wondering about our future," he said. It wasn't a question.

She nodded.

"Beyond gettin' out of this?"

She nodded again. "I was thinking about that moron, Nate Royal."

"The redemption of mankind in the hands of a complete and utter dumbass."

She stifled the laugh in her throat.

"Makes you wonder, doesn't it, about God working in mysterious ways."

Her smile faded. "God hasn't lived here in a while."

"No," he said. "I suppose you're right about that."

"So what does that leave us with? We've got no God. The world is a blighted ruin inhabited by abominations. Our future is a huge question mark. And the only answer in sight is a man who probably doesn't deserve the air he breathes. Where does that leave us? What does it mean that we've hooked our anchor to him?"

Jimmy looked out across the water. The fog was patchy, like the way smoke used to cling to the ceilings of bars back in the day. In the distance he could hear birds squawking, fighting with one another, no doubt over carrion. This world had become that, after all, a carrion country. A land feeding upon itself, much as a cancer spread through the body. It was the kind of land a good man wept for. Jimmy had seen as much, time and time again. Men and women breaking down, unable to advance another step, even when that step was as meaningless as the one before it. They were in a land of sand and fog. They were pillars of stone on a windswept plain. But it remained to be seen how much erosion they could withstand.

"We are survivors," he said. "We've lost a lot, but as long as we're alive, the ones we loved will go on living. As far as I'm concerned, that's all that matters."

She looked at him then, and he had no doubt that she loved him. It was written in her eyes. It was on her lips.

"Where do we go from here?"

"I don't know," he said.

"That doesn't worry you?"

"It makes me wonder about our place in this world. I don't know if that's the same thing. I look at the world and I see desolation. I see a world that has turned into something I didn't expect and that I don't especially like. But that doesn't necessarily make it wrong. Maybe this Nate Royal character really is the answer. Maybe he's the kind of man who's gonna carry humanity forward into the world that's yet to be. He seems like a poor choice, if you ask me. Of course, I don't see anybody else standing in line to do that."

She paused, then asked: "Do you care?"

"About the world? About what happens from here?"

She nodded.

"I'm scared," he said. "I want this Nate Royal guy to succeed. So, yeah, I guess I do care. If he's the cure, then I definitely want him to succeed. I prefer a world of possibilities, even bad ones, to a world of madness."

Gabi reached forward and took his hand in hers.

"I'm glad," she said.

The sound of a motor pulled his attention away.

He looked back toward the river, where the fog was still patchy, but not nearly as thick as it had been just a few minutes before.

The prow of a boat emerged from the fog. On the deck were a dozen zombies, all of them standing still and mute, like ghastly parodies of terra-cotta soldiers.

The next instant, three more boats came into view.

"Shit," Jimmy muttered. "The Red Man's come back."

"What do we do?"

Jimmy looked around. They couldn't run to the hotel, too many black shirts. They couldn't go into the water. He had counted at least forty boats while they were fighting out on the river, and they'd have no chance of staying hidden in the water with that kind of fleet coming ashore.

"Jimmy, they're getting close."

She was right. Even as he stood there considering their next move, the Red Man's fleet was nearing the boat ramp.

Then he spotted a wooden bridge leading from the water up to the top of the bank. There was, maybe, two feet of clearance underneath. He pointed her toward it.

"What about snakes?" she said.

"What?"

"I'm not going under there. There might be snakes."

He remembered a time up around Herculaneum. A water moccasin had slithered aboard and she had cornered it between a lawn chair and the *Sugar Jane*'s gunwale. He remembered her screaming at the top of her lungs, all the while blasting holes in the deck with a twelve-gauge as she tried to kill the snake.

He didn't argue. He got down on his back and wriggled his way underneath the wooden bridge.

When he was completely under he gestured for her to follow.

She wedged herself under the bridge and got close to him.

"You have enough room?"

"Yeah."

"Good," he said, like they were divvying up bedsheets.

They waited. They heard men yelling orders and boats dragging bottom as they came ashore.

Then everything went silent.

Jimmy got scared for a second. Something was wrong. The only thing visible from where he and Gabi lay were a few bands of overcast summer sky through the slits between the boards, but he couldn't shake the image of a handful of troops rounding the edges of the bridge with their weapons raised, a look of smug satisfaction on their faces.

But then the first zombies came ashore. He could tell who they were by the slow, shuffling slide their feet made as they climbed the bridge.

And they kept coming. Dozens. Hundreds. Their combined weight shook the bridge and rained bits of dirt down on their faces.

It went on and on.

He felt Gabi grab his hand and squeeze.

He looked at her, saw the fear and worry there.

"We're okay," he whispered.

A thin band of light illuminated her face. A shifting patchwork of shadows from the zombies passing overhead moved across her features, but they couldn't disguise the worry he saw there.

Jimmy was uncertain how long it took the zombies to offload, but he guessed it was the better part of an hour. His back was aching and his mouth hurt from clenching his teeth for so long.

But at last it ended.

The final zombie passed overhead, and then the sky was clear again.

Gabi let out a sigh that sounded like a mountain of fear collapsing in on itself. Even Jimmy allowed himself a moment of thanks.

But all that went away when he heard footsteps on the bridge. It was a man this time. Jimmy could tell from the deliberate step, the control. The man was coming down from the hotel side of the compound, and he stopped directly above Jimmy, so that they had a clear view of the bare chested Red Man coming up from the river.

"I got your transmission, sir, but we haven't found any signs they've been here."

"They're here."

There was a pause. The guard sounded like a man unwilling to point out the obvious to his superior.

Finally, he said, "I ordered my men to search the hotel."

"Have they searched the holding cell?"

"I have guards standing by in front of her cell, sir."

"Have you talked with them?"

"Me? No. But they're two of my best men."

"Call them. Right now."

The guard paused, then pulled a radio from his belt and keyed up. "Parker," he said. "You monitoring?"

A pause.

"Parker?"

Nothing but silence.

"McCullers, you listening?"

Again, nothing.

"Shit," the man said. He keyed up his radio again. "Stevenson, Lardner, Wharton, you guys head inside and check on Parker and McCullers. I want a report as soon as possible."

"That won't be necessary," the Red Man said. "They've already made their way ashore and found their way to Niki Booth."

"Sir, with all due respect . . ."

"What?" the Red Man asked.

Jimmy had missed something, some exchange between the two, but he recognized the threatening tone in the Red Man's voice. The tone of menace and implied contempt in the Red Man's voice was unmistakable.

"Sir," the guard said, "I'm sure we'll get them to answer up."

"Me too," the Red Man said.

He had been drawing near the guard as he spoke, and he suddenly lashed out and bit the man's ear. There was a momentary struggle, two bodies shifting on the bridge's wooden planks, and then the Red Man came away with a piece of the guard's ear in his teeth.

Blood dripped onto the bridge and through the gaps in the boards, landing on Jimmy's chest.

He did his best to ignore the hot wetness that spread across his shirt.

And also the pathetic screams of the wounded guard as he writhed in pain, his face soaked in blood.

The Red Man wiped the blood from his lips and licked his fingers clean. "I want Niki Booth," he said. "And as many of the others as you can find. They're here somewhere. Find them."

From somewhere close by, Jimmy heard a man say, "Yes, sir. We'll find them."

But his eyes were glued to the black shirt facedown on the bridge. Jimmy shifted his gaze until he too was looking right at the injured man, right in his eyes, and he could see everything that ever mattered about the man ebbing away into nothingness.

CHAPTER 21

Three zombies stumbled out of the darkened doorway. The first two were women who had been reduced to walking wrecks—bloody, open sores on their faces and arms, dried blood caked in their hair, hands trembling as they clutched the empty air in front of them. It was their hands that Nate noticed. The fingernails were too long, three inches at least. They were cracked and filthy, the knuckles swollen. He had seen a group of people in New Mexico years earlier, dying of starvation in the desert. Their hands had looked like that, trembling and fragile and horrible.

But without the long fingernails.

Behind the women was a young black man pulling himself along on half a leg. He hobbled badly. It slowed him down, but he looked far stronger than the two women, like maybe he had fed recently.

He would be trouble if Nate let him get too close.

One of the women reached for him, slashing her nails across his face with surprising force for someone so rickety looking. Nate flinched from the pain. He touched his face and his hand came away bloody.

"Bitch," he said.

He made a fist and was about to lay her out with a haymaker when a hand grabbed the back of his shirt and pulled him out of the way.

"What the hell are you doing?" Niki said. "We don't have time for this."

She had put herself between him and the approaching zombies, and stood coiled, perfectly balanced, like a professional fighter. The same woman who had scratched Nate's face tried it on Niki, but this time she didn't connect. Instead, Niki grabbed the woman's wrist with her left hand, pulled the zombie's arm straight, and with the heel of her right hand struck hard on the back of the zombie's elbow.

The arm broke with a sickening crunch, but the zombie didn't cry out. She didn't even grunt. Her expression didn't even change. The lips were still pulled back, exposing cracked and broken teeth. The eyes never blinked. Niki spun her around and planted her boot into the back of the woman's leg, driving her to her knees. Then she kicked her into the other two zombies, knocking them all to the floor.

Niki turned on Nate. "Get moving! I've got this."

Nate backed away, amazed at how Niki moved. She had the grace of a featherweight boxer.

The young black man had gone down with the two women, but he didn't stay down. He threw them to the side, rose up on his one good leg, and reached for Niki. He looked strong enough that he might have been able to snap her neck if he'd been able to get close enough, but Niki was faster. She grabbed his wrist, much as she'd done with the other zombie, but rather than pull his arm straight, she twisted the wrist over backward, doubling the man's arm up on top of his shoulder.

At the same time she spun him around so that he was facing away from her. She didn't give him a chance to readjust. She grabbed his chin in one hand and his hair in the other and gave his head a brutal twist. There was an audible crack, and then his body sagged to the floor.

Nate's mind was still trying to catch up with what she'd done when she started shoving him down the hallway.

"Come on," she said. "Move it."

Niki and Sylvia took the lead. Nate and Avery fell back a few steps, following them down one darkened hallway after another. He could hear the zombies behind them, moaning in the dark.

"I thought we would have lost them by now," Avery said in a low whisper.

Nate nodded. "Ben's back there."

It was finally catching up with him, the fact that they'd left Ben back there to die. Nate felt sick to his stomach.

"Oh, Nate, I'm so sorry."

She took his hand in hers and gave it a light squeeze. Nate looked down at her hand in surprise. He didn't know what to say so he just gritted his teeth and nodded again. He had never been any good at things like this. He had no skill at describing how badly he was hurting inside. Nate wished he could tell her that having her here, next to him, even in this place, somehow made the pain a little easier to bear, but he didn't have the words for that either.

They rounded another corner and the hallway opened up onto a landing. Beyond the landing was a railing that looked down over the hotel's main lobby.

Outside, lightning flashed, brightening the windows. Already they could see drops of water speckling the glass.

But they could hear something else moving down below.

They went over to the railing to investigate. Light was filtering in through the front door and long shadows stretched across the parquet floor and the marble fountain in the middle of the room. And then zombies poured in through the front door.

They kept coming and coming, tracking vast quantities of mud across the floor.

"There are hundreds of them," Nate said.

Niki tried to shush him by grabbing his arm, but the damage was already done. A few of the zombies had heard him, and one by one the zombies all looked up.

The next instant, the moans started.

"Nice move, jackass," Niki said.

Niki stared over the railing toward the landing on the opposite side of the lobby. There was a staircase there, and a few of the zombies were already mounting it.

"Well, we're not going out the front door," she said. "Avery, got any ideas?"

"Where do you want to go?"

"Can you get us to the convention center part of the hotel? When they brought me in I remember seeing a loading bay over there. They have trucks. Maybe they have one there we could take. Might be an easy way to get us out of here."

A stuttering moan behind them caused Niki to turn toward the stairs. A man was staggering toward them on a broken leg, his bare feet leaving a smear of blood on the wood floors.

A large crowd was massing behind him, their eyes glinting in the dark.

"Which way, Avery?" Niki said.

Avery pointed to the far side of the balcony, opposite the stairs. "Through that hallway over there."

"Is there a stairwell that way?"

"I think so. There are elevators over there. The stairs are probably next to those."

"Good."

"I don't understand," Nate said. "I thought you were looking for the convention center."

"Don't you ever shut up?" Niki said.

"I'm just asking."

"Look, we've got zombies behind us, and zombies in front of us, but none above us." She waited for him to say something, one eyebrow arched. "You understand? Any of this sinking in?" She paused. "Oh, forget it."

She turned to Sylvia.

"This is turning into a hell of a rescue."

They got to the stairs and went up to the third floor.

A few zombies managed to climb the stairs behind them, but they weren't able to keep up, and soon Niki was leading them through darkened hallways, past rooms that hadn't been occupied in at least eight years, probably longer.

They reached the convention center part of the hotel a few minutes later. Though the walls were grimy with years of river rot and humidity, most of the signage was still in place, and it didn't take long to find the loading dock, which was a large cement bay, like a subterranean parking garage, only crowded with stacks of moldering wooden pallets and fifty-five-gallon drums.

"Look at that," Niki said. "See that truck?"

They were standing at the mouth of a hallway that gave on to the back of the bay. From their position, they could see a big black pickup truck near the overhead doors of one of the docks.

"That looks like one of the same trucks they were driving when they surprised us in St. Louis," Sylvia said.

"Yeah," agreed Niki. "At least we know they work."

Sylvia asked, "So how do we do this?"

"We've got to get that overhead door open. After that, we'll see what's what. I think most of the activity's probably gonna be down by the river, and if that's the case, then we should be able to get a good head start in that truck. Enough that we might be able to lose whoever they send after us."

"If that thing's got gas, you mean."

Niki gave Sylvia a broad smile. "Come on, Sylvia, a little confidence. We got this."

Niki trotted across the bay. The others followed along behind her, but at a cautious distance. Nate's head was on a swivel, looking around for signs of movement and a place to take cover if anything happened. He had never liked playing soldier like this.

"Take that side," Niki told Sylvia. She turned to Avery. "You two are gonna have to ride in the back. That okay?"

But before either of them had a chance to answer, Sylvia let out a curse.

"What is it?" Niki asked.

She moved around to the passenger side of the truck, where Sylvia was standing, and her shoulders sagged.

"Damn it," she said.

"What's wrong?" Avery asked.

"No front wheel on this side. They've got it up on a jack."

"Oh," said Avery.

Nate looked from one woman to the next. "So what do we do?"

"I guess we're back to the original plan," Niki said. She turned to Sylvia. "You said you had a boat?"

"It was boarded out on the river. But the two people who brought us here are trying to get us a boat."

"You brought somebody with you? Who?"

"Jimmy and Gabi Hinton. Their boat's the *Sugar Jane*."

"The Hintons? The same ones who dumped all that beef they were transporting for our compound?"

"Yeah," said Sylvia.

Niki shook her head. "Unbelievable. This just keeps getting better and better."

"Right now they're the only hope we've got," Avery said.

"I know, Avery," Niki said. She put a hand on her cousin's shoulder. "I know. We have to get out of here first, though."

Niki scanned the wall where the overhead doors were.

"No smaller doors," she said. "We're gonna have to risk cracking open one of these bigger ones. I don't want to risk opening it up all the way, though. Everybody okay with crawling under?"

They all nodded.

"Okay."

She went over to the nearest door and had her hand out to turn the handle when the door lurched and slowly started to rise.

Niki froze.

One by one all the doors down the line started to rise as well. Sunlight and rain poured in through the openings. Nate could see legs, and then torsos, and finally the shadowed faces of hundreds of zombies, waiting to pour through the doors. Behind them, far behind them, were the Red Man's soldiers, riding in black pickups like the one they'd just tried to steal. Even through the rain Nate could see the startled looks on the black shirts' faces.

"Run!" Niki screamed. She was pointing wildly toward a rusting metal staircase along a side wall. "Up there. Hurry, go!"

They ran for it, mounting the stairs just ahead of the first of the zombies. Avery was just ahead of Nate. She was taking the stairs one at a time, her legs pumping hard, her breath coming in short, shallow gasps. One of the zombies hit him hard from behind and he tumbled forward, falling into Avery, knocking her face-first into the stairs.

The zombie was on Nate's back, clawing at him, ripping his shirt, tearing at the skin of his back. The pain was intense, like being scratched with burning wire, and he screamed.

When he opened his eyes again he could see Avery beneath him. Mangled hands were trying to reach around him to grab her, but he raised himself up to a push-up position and shielded her with his body.

"Run!" he screamed.

The staircase was shaking badly and more bodies were piling on top of him. He could feel his arms getting weak. He couldn't hold it.

Avery was trying to crawl out from under him, but between the shaking of the stairs and Nate on top of her, she could barely move.

"Niki, help her!"

Nate saw a flash of black in front of him, then two hands locking onto Avery and pulling her clear.

He collapsed beneath the weight of the zombies on his back. One of them clamped onto his arm and bit down. He screamed and yanked it back, pulling the zombie's bloody face toward him. One look in the thing's eyes and he knew this was a Stage II or Stage III zombie, smarter, faster, more aggressive.

The zombie snarled at him. Its mouth was open, snapping at him like a pit bull, teeth freshly stained with Nate's own blood.

That was enough to get Nate moving. He rolled sideways, shifting the zombie still clawing his back to one side. When he turned over Nate's boots were almost touching the railing. He planted both feet firmly on the metal rail and pushed with everything he had.

The zombies fell down the stairs, even as more scrambled over top of them.

Nate pulled himself to his feet, only to feel the stairs start to sway beneath him. He turned and caught sight of Niki and Avery and Sylvia just a few steps above him. Avery's mouth was open in an O shape, her hands outstretched like she was trying to keep her balance. He had just enough time to register the strangeness of her expression when a painful groan of twisting metal drowned out the moaning crowd and the staircase folded beneath them, knocking them all off their feet.

When Nate looked around, he and Niki were on a short platform at the bottom of the dangling remnant of the staircase. Avery and Sylvia were on top of the other half of the platform about fifteen feet away. The space between them was crowded with zombies.

Within seconds the zombies surrounded the platform. They stuck their bloody hands up through the railing and tried to squeeze their fingers up through the little square holes in the metal grid that formed the platform, but Avery and Sylvia were just out of reach. One of the zombies tried to climb over the edge, pulling itself up the railing, but Sylvia kicked it in the chin and sent it tumbling over backward into the swarming crowd that had gathered there.

"Niki!" Avery shouted. "Niki!"

Nate felt strangely suspended in time. There was so much activity swirling around him. Bodies were surging forward, ripped and ghastly faces, snarling at him, hands reaching for him, and Avery over there, her face contorted with fear, reaching for Niki.

A hand grabbed the toe of his boot and Nate kicked it away, a crazy thought racing through his head as he backed away: This is what a rock star must feel like, all those screaming fans reaching over the lip of the stage, hoping for just a touch.

Beside him, Niki was tugging on part of the railing, every muscle in her arms and neck straining. The next instant the bar came loose and Niki pushed past him, the bar raised over her head like a club.

"Hang on, Avery!" she shouted.

She swung the bar down on top of the nearest zombie's head, smashing it in on one side. Zombies reached for her, groping at the cuffs of her BDU pants. She let them have it, attacking with a ferocity Nate had never seen before. Again and again she swung her metal bar at the crowd, and soon blood and bits of scalp and bone and little kernels of teeth were flying in the air around her.

"Don't you touch her!" she screamed.

Her metal bar was streaked with gore now and every time she swung it clumps of wet tissue went flying. But still the crowd around them grew larger. For every one that she knocked down, more surged forward to take its place. Their hands were slapping at her knees, her thighs, and to Nate it looked like they might pull her down at any second. And they probably would have, too, if at that moment one of the black pickup trucks hadn't roared into the bay and plowed its way through the crowd, stopping in line with the platform where Sylvia and Avery were stranded.

Guards jumped over the side, their weapons pointed at the women.

"No!" Niki shouted. "You leave her alone!"

An amplified voice boomed from the truck. "Drop the bar! Put your hands where we can see them."

Nate caught a glimpse of the driver through the blood streaks covering the windshield. He held a PA microphone in one hand. His eyes were fixed on Niki.

"Niki Booth," he said. "Put it down. You're coming with us."

Beyond the truck, Nate could see Avery struggling with a man who held her arms twisted up behind her back.

"Niki, run!" Avery shouted. "Go, you have to!"

The man twisted Avery violently away from Niki and Nate, bending her over the railing so that her face was just inches out of reach of the zombies clambering to get on the platform.

"Go!" Avery screamed again. "Go!"

Nate saw the fight suddenly drain out of Niki. He was looking at her back, but he could tell the fight was gone. The metal bar she held dipped to the platform.

"I will find you," Niki said. "You hear me, Avery? I will find you."

"Niki Booth, drop your weapon. Now!"

She turned away from the zombies and the men holding Avery and Sylvia prisoner, and when she caught Nate's eye, he could see her heart breaking.

"Come on," she muttered as she passed him. "We need to go."

"Stop!" said the amplified voice.

Niki jammed her middle finger into the air, not bothering to turn around.

Nate lumbered up the stairs after her.

CHAPTER 22

Jimmy and Gabi hadn't been able to move from under the little wooden bridge where they hid when the Red Man's zombies came ashore. They were both flat on their backs in a channel of muddy brown water that was rising steadily with the rain. The bridge's wooden slats were inches above their faces. The rain was falling steadily now, water dripping through the gaps in the planks, churning the runoff water in which they lay into a foam. The steady motion of the rain almost allowed him the illusion of a quiet calm. Except of course the Red Man was still out there, on the lawn. Jimmy had hoped the rain would cause him to move his zombies into the hotel, but instead they seemed to be lining up for review in the lawn not fifty feet away. They weren't going anywhere, and neither were Jimmy and Gabi.

Gabi said, "Jimmy, tell me again about Mexico. I want to hear you tell it, about the fish so stupid they jump into the boat and the lime trees and the way the ocean smells at night. Tell me about that again."

But he wasn't listening. He'd noticed something going on

out on the water and he was trying to see through the tall ditch weeds that grew up around it.

"Jimmy?"

He gave her hand a gentle pat, a warning that instantly silenced her. He glanced at her out of the corner of his eye and she nodded back. She was frowning, but made no attempt to question him about what was going on.

It was amazing to him how fast the dreamer could leave her. In an instant she could revert to the hard, practical woman who had pulled him back from the edge of death so many times. The transformation was so complete, and so instantaneous, it made him wonder if the dreamer wasn't some kind of act put on only for his benefit. Indeed, she never acted that way except when they were alone. Perhaps the dreamer was just a calculated manifestation of the hard, practical woman who did so much for the man she loved. Did she sense that he needed that illusion of being her security, her provider, much as their daughter had needed a nightlight for so many years? Was the fantasy as much for his benefit as hers?

It was certainly possible. For as tough as she was, for as hard as she could be, she was also a woman. And a woman, especially a woman like Gabi, was always so much more complex than men gave her credit for being. He suspected that complexity was the origin of her beauty, the way that even now, overweight and graying, she could shine in his eyes.

He let out a long breath. It had been a month and a few days since he'd run out of his blood pressure pills, and he could feel the closeness in his chest, his pulse uncomfortably fast. Jimmy focused on his breathing, trying to ease down the pounding in his temples.

He turned back to the river.

"Can you see anything?" she whispered.

"A little. There are some boats pulling away from the pier."

"How many?"

"Looks like nearly all of them."

Jimmy was looking through a narrow part in the weeds, and as more boats came into view, he could see men in black uniforms, most of them looking vacant and bored, weapons slung casually over their shoulders, waterproof ponchos pulled down over their faces, watching the zombies on the hotel's lawn.

"What are they doing?" Gabi asked.

He shook his head. "I don't know. They're just sitting there, right offshore. It's like they're waiting on something."

Jimmy thought back to the early days, right after the outbreak. The cops in Gulfport had looked like that when the military was setting up the quarantine wall. At the time, before everybody really understood what the quarantine wall was going to mean to all those refugee families who couldn't get through fast enough, he had pitied those cops. Eighteen hours of manning a barricade, telling every desperate family that came through the same damn thing would change a man.

But when he looked closer he realized these men were something different. They weren't like the cops he remembered. These men were disgusted by the army of zombies up on the lawn, but they had also grown numb to it. They weren't unlike the occasional fakers he'd seen walking among the zombies. Yes, he thought, that was it. That was it exactly. They were another kind of faker. They had lost not only the desire but the ability, to care about what they saw. Disgust passed for compassion. Malaise for empathy. Rather than hating them, Jimmy was disgusted by them. Men like that didn't deserve their lives. Not when so many good people were dead.

He shook the sudden memory of his daughter and granddaughter away and refocused on the problem at hand.

Through the rain and the gray haze sitting over the water it was difficult to be sure, but he counted at least twenty boats out there, most of them medium-size fishing boats like the kind that had cornered them out on the river just after daybreak. When they were hiding with the others under the main pier, he'd counted a number of smaller boats, too, ski boats and Boston Whalers. He didn't see them now.

"Did they take the *Sugar Jane*?" Gabi asked.

"No, that's still at the pier."

Something about Gabi's silence made him stop his line of thought. He turned his attention back to her. She was staring at him, her eyes shining in the shadows under the bridge.

"What are you thinking?" he asked.

"I want to take our boat back," she said.

"What?"

The idea seemed crazy to him. The black shirts, for all their apathy and apparent boredom, were still armed. And as much as it rankled him that they had boarded his boat, he was also a realist. They were the lowest scum he'd ever encountered, but they weren't blind. Unless he and Gabi were willing to go back underwater, the only way they could get back aboard the *Sugar Jane* was to cross sixty yards of wide-open riverbank. They'd be lucky to make it ten feet before the shooting started.

But then it occurred to him that she meant to take the river. God bless her, she wanted to go underwater.

"We'll have to swim for it," he said.

"I don't want to be stuck down here in this ditch anymore. Staying here, we're just asking to get munched."

"Or shot," he said.

"Yeah, that too."

"How's your leg? You gonna be able to crawl?"

"My leg's fine," she said. "Quit stalling."

"Alright," he agreed. He flashed a smile. "You're a crazy, beautiful woman, you know that?"

"And you're a dirty old man." She gave him a shove. "Now go on, move it."

He took one last look through the gap in the weeds and pulled himself out from under the bridge. This was suicide, he thought. All it took was one zombie to spot him and the moaning would start. Within seconds they'd have an army of the things hunting them. But Gabi had a point. They were dead if they stayed under that bridge. Better to go down swinging.

So he crawled through the tall weeds toward the humid reek of the river. He glanced over his shoulder and saw Gabi crawling up behind him. There was pain in her eyes, and he knew her hip and knee were bothering her again. At night, she'd frequently get out of their bed to stretch it, unable to sleep because of the pain. Too long in any one position and it happened, and they'd been under that bridge a good long while.

She nodded for him to move. *Don't wait for me, I'm alright*, the gesture seemed to say.

He nodded back and continued to pull himself toward the verge. A moment later, they reached the edge of the tall weeds, where the water lapped against the muddy, algae-covered bank.

He spotted a pile of ruined lumber that had broken loose from the main part of the pier and that could probably provide some cover as they worked their way into the water.

He motioned at it: *That way*.

She nodded.

The salty dank stench of the algae hit him a moment before he put his hands in it, and his face wrinkled in a grimace. The water here was sluggish and the algae had grown thick. It grew all along the banks of the slower moving parts of the river, but it was usually a vibrant, healthy green. Not gray, like this stuff. Nor did it produce the soap-scummy foam that this stuff did. He could only assume that the Red Man's compound was responsible for this. Poor sewage management; wasted food; garbage indiscriminately dumped; they all did their part to turn the water into this. It was disgusting.

He tried not to breathe in through his nose as he slipped under the water. He swam around the ruined pile of lumber and over to the little wooden boats that were tied up along the shore on the downriver side of the pier. Here Jimmy popped his head up and waited for Gabi to surface behind him.

"You okay?" he asked.

"Yeah, you?"

He nodded.

They still had another thirty feet or so to cover, but most of that was through wrecked and partially submerged boats, leftovers from back before the outbreak, when the hotel was a functioning tourist spot. Most of them were sun-bleached and rusted, squatting deep in the water, hulls turned up to the rain. Jimmy figured they could pick their way through the ruined hulls without having to go back under the water, and that, with luck, they could get all the way to the pier that way.

Getting aboard the *Sugar Jane* would be more difficult, though. There didn't seem to be any way to do it that didn't put them in plain sight of the Red Man's soldiers. Maybe the rain would offer them some cover.

He glanced back to check on Gabi.

She was staring straight ahead at the *Sugar Jane*, and if she was scared, her face didn't give her away.

But she wouldn't be, he thought. Not his Gabi. No way.

They moved slowly through the wrecks, and eventually reached the shelter of the pier. The rain was picking up now, making a sizzling roar on the water. That was good, he thought. It'd cover a lot of careless footwork climbing aboard.

"How's it look?" Gabi asked, gesturing toward the *Sugar Jane*.

Jimmy checked the starboard side first, then the port. It was only tied off in one spot, and she'd been rubbing up against the pier on her port side, but there were no bullet holes down her length. No new ones anyway.

"It looks okay," he said.

She nodded.

"Any idea on how we're going to handle this?" he asked.

"You mean getting Sylvia and the others out of there?"

"Looks to me like we're locked down."

"Yeah," she said, and looked back toward the hotel. "I wish we had some way to contact them."

He could just barely see the first few rows of zombies up on the hotel's lawn. The rain was getting heavy out there and didn't show any signs of letting up. Zombies didn't care about the rain, of course, but the Red Man was no ordinary zombie. Surely he had a plan. Why else would he have ordered his soldiers offshore?

"We ought to get aboard," he said. "I don't think we'll have long to wait. Whatever's gonna happen is probably gonna happen soon."

"You think the soldiers will go back ashore?"

"Either that or they're about to go out on some other mission. But if they dock again there'll be too many of them crawling around this pier. We'll never get away at that point."

"Okay." She gestured toward the boat. "After you."

A few rough planks had been nailed across one of the beams holding up the pier, forming a crude ladder. He climbed up it, then threw his legs over the *Sugar Jane*'s gunwale and slid onto the deck. Jimmy leaned back over the railing, extending his hand for Gabi.

"I got it," she said.

She was at the top of the ladder when they heard one of the soldiers yelling.

Jimmy looked over his shoulder. A young man was leaning over the railing of a nearby boat, pointing at them through the rain.

"Over here!" he yelled. "I got two of them over here."

Through the blearing rain Jimmy could see soldiers gathering around the younger soldier, squinting into the rain.

"Oh shit," Jimmy said. "There goes stealth mode."

Gabi looked up at him. "Okay, I'll take that hand now."

"Right."

He grabbed her hand and pulled her over. Once aboard she quickly unwound the rope that held them fast to the pier, while he slipped into the cabin, pulled the mattress off the bed, and removed two rifles and their last box of the M67 fragmentation grenades.

She took the box and one of the rifles from him.

"Only eight left," she said, looking into the box.

He forced a smile and shook his head. "I guess we better make 'em count."

CHAPTER 23

The black shirts handed Sylvia and Avery off to a third man already in the bed of the pickup. He was carrying a pistol and made them sit with their backs against the cab. The third guard looked exhausted, but right away Sylvia sensed a nervous tension coming off him, like an animal waiting for a hunter to pass it by. He went down on one knee, the pistol resting across his thigh. Sylvia noticed he tried to stay as close as possible to the middle of the bed. Though there were wooden railings extending upward from the sides of the pickup's bed, and a protective layer of chicken wire strung over the wooden rails, this man didn't seem to trust it. He watched the zombie crowd pressing up against the truck out of his peripheral vision, and it occurred to Sylvia that he was probably as scared as she was.

The other two black shirts, the ones who had taken them prisoner on the platform, climbed over the cab and dropped down into the bed. They slapped the roof of the cab and the vehicle slowly reversed, knocking down zombies as it cleared the bay and emerged into a steady rain that had turned the landscape a watercolor smear of gray and green and ochre.

Sylvia looked up at the sky, blinking the rain from her eyes even as she savored the taste of it on her lips. It was cool, and her lips were cracked and dry. It felt good.

The soothing coolness of it gave her an idea. She looked at the guard directly in front of her, the one with the pistol. "Why do you serve him?" she said.

He looked at her dully, not answering.

She looked at the other two. "Why do any of you serve him?"

"Shut up, lady," said one of the guards, an older, battle-scarred man leaning against the railing. He refused to look at her.

"Sylvia, what are you doing?" said Avery.

Sylvia flashed an *It's okay; I've got this under control* smile.

She turned to the first guard, the scared one with the handgun. He was staring at her from under the brim of a cowboy hat. She could hear the rain striking the brim, like finger taps on a sheet of cardboard. His mouth was set in a deep frown. But there was something sad in those heavily lidded brown eyes of his, something tragic, and she thought: *His spirit's broken. That man is soul-sick and rotting inside, and he doesn't have the guts to admit it to himself.*

"I don't see how any of you can do it."

"Lady," the older guard said, "I'm warning you: You know what's good for you you'll shut your mouth."

"Sylvia, please . . ." Avery said.

But Sylvia pressed on. "Is it so horrible in your world, so empty, that this is what you're willing to call your life? I've seen the fakers trying to pass for zombies, and you're just like them, except that the fakers don't pretend they're still human."

"That does it," the guard said.

He grabbed her by her hair and threw her facedown in a pile of old oily rags.

"Sylvia!" Avery shouted.

"No!" Sylvia answered, turning her head enough to see Avery trembling against the far side of the truck, a guard holding her down. "No, baby, it's okay."

"Like hell it is," the guard on top of her said. Rainwater channeled off the brim of his hat and fell into the pile of rags next to her face. "You want to know why we work for him? Do you? Well, you're about to find out."

A few moments later the truck trundled to a stop. The women were pulled to their feet and pushed out the back of the truck. Sylvia took a look around and gasped. There were zombies everywhere, hundreds of them standing absolutely still in the falling rain. The smell of rot and mud caused her to gag, but despite the retching noises she made, not a one of them moved. They stared out toward the verge of the river, where a metal platform two stories high stood facing the hotel. Beyond the platform, floating just offshore, were dozens of boats. Black shirts stood on the decks, watching in silence.

I'm going to die here, she thought. Right here. This is the end. But with the same mental breath she thought: No! I can't let the fear show. Not in front of Avery.

But it was hard. She was so scared.

She looked at Avery to see how she was holding up. Avery's behavior since losing Niki in St. Louis had been troubling her—troubling her a lot. She'd become so quiet, a lot like she'd been all those years ago, when a much younger Niki Booth had led her into the compound and stood watch over her like a mama bear does her cub, nearly ripping the hands off anyone who tried to touch her, even though it had been obvious they needed help. The two girls had been nearly feral, though Niki had come around soon enough.

Even thrived. But Avery had taken a lot longer. Reaching her had been hard. Even as a kid she'd been scary-smart when it came to maps and knowing the lay of the land. So much so that for a while Sylvia thought she might be autistic. Eventually, though, she came out of her shell, and Sylvia was able to see the bright, kind, fragile young girl that a blighted world had nearly destroyed. She blossomed.

But then, when they lost Niki back at St. Louis, it had done something to her. It caused her to rewrap herself in the same protective shroud of silence and despair she'd worn after her father died, and throughout those early years at Union Field. Thinking of the child Avery had been nearly overwhelmed Sylvia's resolve and she could feel a sob rising in her chest. She forced it down as best she could, for Avery's sake.

Those were her thoughts as the old guard stepped around the side of the truck and out of sight and the rain continued to fall in her face.

His radio crackled.

"He's coming," said a man's voice. "Bring them up."

"You want us to bring the truck?" said the old guard at Sylvia's right, the one with the scarred face.

A pause, and then the radio crackled to life again.

"He says no. Walk 'em up."

Sylvia heard the man mutter a curse under his breath, but when he looked back toward her and Avery he was all business again.

"Alright, we're walking 'em up. Let's move it."

Rough hands grabbed Sylvia. Next to her, she heard Avery let out a yelp. The mother instinct rose up in Sylvia then and she started to thrash.

"Damn it," the old guard said, grunting as he struggled to regain control.

A ripple of interest spread outward through the zombies standing around them, but they held their positions. Sylvia could see their dead eyes following her as she struggled with the man. She could see their hands wanting to come up, their mouths working slowly in involuntary chewing motions.

"Let her go," Sylvia demanded.

The man threw her against the truck and she hit the back of her head against the wooden extension on top of the bed. For a moment her vision turned purple and her legs buckled, but the man grabbed her arms again and wouldn't let her sink to the ground.

He put his face close to hers, his breath hot and smelling of stale tobacco and meat. The urge to gag nearly overwhelmed her again, but she fought it down.

"Please don't hurt the girl," Sylvia said.

Her voice was a whisper, spoken through sobs.

The man locked eyes on hers, his stare narrowing in menace.

"Please, she's just a child. You know what they'll do to her. She's too young to suffer like that, to become one of those things."

He didn't say anything for a long moment. The silence went on and on, so long that she actually let the thought enter her mind that she had reached him and that the shred of humanity that must surely remain within him had been stirred to pity.

But instead he said, "Too young don't make any difference anymore, lady. The world's too far gone for that."

He peeled her off the truck and shoved her toward the river.

She staggered through the motionless crowd of zombies in a haze. This close, she could hear the faint, rhythmic moaning the zombies made under their breath, almost like religious zealots murmuring their prayers. It raised gooseflesh on her arms, despite the oppressive heat.

She slipped trying to step up the curb from the parking lot to the grass, sending another restless wave through the nearby zombies. The old guard stepped up behind her then and his grip on her arm was surprisingly gentle as he helped her back up.

"I'm sorry for this," he said. "I had a kid about her age, long time ago."

She looked back at him in surprise. His face was a hard mask without a trace of pity or compassion. Sylvia opened her mouth to speak, but he nodded for her to turn and face the platform.

She did.

Something was happening up there. She couldn't see what, not at first, but there was an agitation spreading through the zombie crowd. They remained standing in their spots, though now they were shifting from one foot to the other, low moans rising here and there throughout the crowd.

And then she saw him, the Red Man. He limped up the grass toward the raised metal platform and slowly climbed the switchback staircase to the top level. The red paint all over his body looked dark as rust in the morning light. The river behind him seemed to boil. The smell of heated vegetation and mud mixed with the rotting bodies, and everywhere she looked she saw water running down ruined, blistered faces. Uneven moans rose from the crowd, and it occurred to her then that this was some kind of hell. It had to be. Nothing like this could exist in a sane world.

One of the Red Man's guards slogged his way through the mud over to her captor, rainwater dripping off the bill of his cap as he met the older man's gaze.

"He wants 'em up there, with him."

"I'm not walking 'em up there," Sylvia's guard said.

The other guard, a much younger man, but nonetheless the one in charge, said, "Yeah, I don't want to, either." He looked up at the platform, then back at the guard and shrugged. "Fuck 'em, they can walk up on their own. He wants all of us on the boats."

"Right now?"

"He ever give you an order you could wait on if you want to?"

"No."

"Then get 'em up there."

The older man nodded, then turned to Sylvia. "Alright, you and the girl get up there."

"No way," Sylvia answered.

"You need to move it."

"We're not moving. I heard you. You're scared to death of him, aren't you? Admit it. You're so terrified you're willing to do things that make no sense. Don't you understand there's a better way? You can fight. Isn't that better? Isn't that what you would want your kid to see? It can't be this."

He leaned in close, and once again she could smell the stale tobacco on his breath. "Lady, you and the girl need to get your ass up there. Right now."

"We won't," she said. She raised her chin high. "You'll have to carry me up."

"Lady, you'll go."

"I tell you I won't."

"That little girl behind you, the fat one? If you don't go, I'll cut her."

He looked down. She followed his gaze to where his hand was fingering the hilt of a small utility knife.

"Climb those stairs," he said.

"You bastard."

He didn't respond.

Sylvia turned around and took Avery's hand. The fear in Avery's eyes broke her heart all over again. "Come on, baby. Let's go up. We'll be together the whole time. I promise you that."

Together, they climbed the stairs.

The Red Man watched them climb the last few steps, his eyes never leaving Sylvia's, his lips parting slightly, exposing teeth the color of dingy bathroom tile. Rainwater ran down his bald head and dripped from his nose, his chin, his ears. The water looked red next to his skin, like blood.

"Where do you want us to stand?" Sylvia said with a forced calm she most certainly did not feel.

The Red Man's parted lips melted into a frown.

He motioned with a nod toward the space behind him.

Sylvia took Avery's hand and together they walked to the back of the platform, nearest the river. She could hear the rain beating down on the water out there, an ominous sound.

When she finally found the courage to turn around she couldn't stop the gasp that came out of her. So many zombies. Not hundreds, but thousands. The rain fell on them and they didn't move. They stood absorbed, staring in complete devotion to the crazy man painted all in red above them. Something Ben Richardson had said came back to her then, his description of Jasper Sewell, the deranged preacher of the Grasslands Death Cult, the way he had held sway over his church.

This is a cult, she thought. A death cult in its purest, most vile form.

And that man, that Red Man, is their god.

Almost in answer to her thought, he whirled toward her.

"Where is Niki Booth?" he said.

She shook her head.

"My patience is at an end," he said. "You're going to tell me."

"Go to hell."

He nodded slowly. "Perhaps." He glanced over at Avery, who had pressed as far as possible into the corner of the platform. The Red Man smiled, then glanced back at Sylvia. "You're going to tell me what I want to know," he said.

His hand moved to his chest, and for the first time Sylvia noticed—really noticed—the necklace of shriveled, mummified human ears that ringed his throat.

"You will tell me," he said again.

"Or what?"

He smiled. He leaned close to her, so that she could smell the rot on his breath. He said, "Or I will eat you, and make her watch."

CHAPTER 24

Niki walked confidently out of the shadowed protection of the hallway, the metal bar down by her side, her shoulders loose and ready. Nate followed along behind her, his nerves humming with adrenaline. At this point, after seeing her fight, he was prepared for just about anything.

Five zombies were staggering around the landing, unable to find their way downstairs. But when Niki stepped into their midst they all turned as one, their bodies twitching with the excitement that came from an imminent meal.

"Ruh," one of them grunted as he stumbled forward. His mouth was hanging open, his dead gaze locked on Niki's neck.

He never saw the blow that killed him.

She dodged to one side and came up behind him and before he could react swung the bar at the back of his head. It connected with a sharp crack and the zombie pitched over forward, hitting the wall head-first. He slumped to the ground, landing on his hands and knees. Niki was beside him before he could stagger back to his feet, bringing the weapon down at the point where his skull met his spine. He fell to the floor and didn't move.

Niki's face was twisted with rage and anger, and another emotion that Nate didn't quite recognize. But it almost looked like she was enjoying the fight. Really, really enjoying it. Like the girls in the porno movies he used to watch.

But the next instant the look was gone, lost in the shadows and her twisting and turning. He watched her. He was no longer frightened. Not like he had been. Connecting the look on her face to the girls in porn was something of a breakthrough for him. Niki Booth was in love with killing zombies. Maybe love wasn't the right word, but she certainly liked it.

Another zombie went down. Niki turned from it just as a woman with dark stains all over her dress reached for her. Niki sidestepped the woman's hands and crushed her knee with the bar. The zombie sagged to the floor without so much as a grunt of pain. Niki leapt over her and kicked another zombie in the groin.

Its legs went out from under it and it landed facedown on the floor.

It was dead with the first blow, Nate was sure, but Niki hit at least a dozen more times, turning its head to a bloody soup, spattering the walls with clumps of its brains and scalp.

Niki stood up from her kill, chest heaving, and turned back to the woman in the dress. She was trying to rise on her broken knee, but her legs wouldn't work right. Niki kicked her over onto her back and jammed the jagged end of the metal bar down into the woman's right eye.

The zombie went still instantly, her arms falling to her side.

The final zombie was still leaning against the far wall. He hadn't moved throughout the entire fight, just stood there bobbing his head, his mouth miming an eating motion.

Nate had seen this kind before. Too addled by the necrosis filovirus to do anything but follow a larger crowd. Most were on a short countdown to starvation, because on their own they were helpless. They couldn't hunt, couldn't even fall on food that wasn't already dead or dying.

They weren't completely harmless, though. No zombie was harmless. They were all walking virus bombs. But Nate had learned to just keep an eye on them as he moved on past. No need to fight when he didn't have to.

Niki was trying to pull her metal bar from the dead woman's eye socket. She put her boot on the dead woman's neck and gave it a hard yank, but the bar didn't budge.

"Suction," she said, and kicked the body away.

She looked at Nate, then back at the zombie still making chewing motions over at the wall.

"Goddamned wallflower," she said. "I'll get it."

Before Nate could say anything she walked over to the—what had she called it, the wallflower zombie?—man and grabbed him by his hair. She twisted him around so that he was facing Nate and their eyes locked. His dead stare never wavered as she twisted his head sharply to one side, cracking his neck with the soft, muffled crunch of deep-down bone going where it wasn't meant to go.

He fell to the floor with the same dead look locked in his eyes.

Nate's gaze rose to Niki Booth, who was staring at him, bloodlust in her eyes, even while her mouth twisted with the pain in her ribs and lower back. Her chest was heaving, her tongue dancing at her lips.

"We need to find Avery," Nate said.

The sexual intensity in her eyes melted away at the mention of Avery's name, and a different sort of intense stare took its place.

This look, Nate couldn't put a name to. But he recognized its directed ferocity just the same.

She nodded. "You're right. We need to go."

* * *

Niki walked away from the kill without looking back, and Nate fell in behind her. She was at the stairs that would take them down to the hotel's main lobby when a middle-aged man in a blue sport coat and khaki slacks, now grotesquely emaciated, his suit hanging off him in filthy rags, hair matted with mud and blood, one eye ruptured and the remaining jelly congealed in the socket, grabbed Nate from behind and pressed him against the wall. Niki took a few steps back and scanned left and right, looking for more zombies; there were none. Nate struggled to get away, jamming the heel of his hand into the zombie's mouth as he tried to get enough of a grip to throw the man aside. The man let out a rusty moan and shuffled his feet, a movement that put him off balance just enough to give Nate the leverage to push him away. As they broke contact Niki stepped in and killed the zombie with three sharp punches to his Adam's apple.

When she looked up from the corpse, Nate was holding his wrist, the heel of his hand leaking blood from a fresh cut.

"How is it you're still alive?" Niki said.

He shrugged. "I'm immune. The disease can't hurt me."

"I know that. I mean how come you haven't gotten munched yet?"

"Um," he said, then trailed off. He evidently didn't have anything else to say, because he shrugged again.

Outstanding, she thought. *He's too stupid to realize I'm making fun of him. Just great.*

She didn't bother to pursue the point. There was no point, and no time. But Nate was still standing there, his mouth open showing a fairly pronounced set of horse teeth. It was still unbelievable to her that anyone could actually be immune to the necrosis filovirus. After all the death that she had seen, all the heartache that disease had caused, the idea that someone was naturally immune to it simply boggled her mind. Too bad that immunity had to come in such a pathetic package. She'd known a lot of great zombie fighters over the last eight years. If any of them had been blessed with Nate's immunity . . .

It was a shame.

"Are you okay?" he said.

Her eyes narrowed. "I'm fine."

"What are you thinking about?"

"What?"

"Well," he said, and then paused. "It just looked like you were, I don't know, thinking about stuff."

Her first instinct was to turn away. They didn't have time to stand here gabbing about things that didn't matter, but there was something about him, an open, questioning look in his eyes. She wondered if that was what Avery saw in him.

"Just about how everyone I've ever loved is dead," she said, and the honesty and vulnerability in her tone surprised her. "Everyone except Sylvia and Avery."

He frowned, whether out of pity or understanding or confusion, she couldn't tell.

"Your immunity, it could wipe out the necrosis filovirus?"

"That's what they tell me."

"Will it cure those already infected?"

"I don't think so. The doctor who was working on me said that he could make others immune, like me. He never said anything about curing zombies. But then I don't really understand it all that good. He was always talking about gene ripping and stuff like that."

She let out a long breath. "I've known a lot of great men and women who could have benefited from your immunity."

He looked down at his feet, and this time she was pretty sure he was ashamed. "I know," he said. "Ben Richardson used to tell me the same thing. He said he knew this guy when he was living in the Grasslands compound that was some kind of super zombie fighter, like you. He used to talk to me about how things might have been different if that guy had been immune instead of me."

"Well, we all play the hand we're dealt, I guess."

She paused for a moment and listened to the rain outside. It didn't sound like it was going to stop for a good long while, and she figured that was good. They could use the weather for cover, maybe.

She said, "You cared a lot about that old guy back there, didn't you?"

He shrugged, then lowered his head and nodded.

"I'm sorry."

He nodded again.

"You like Avery too, don't you?"

He looked up, meeting her eyes for the first time. "How did you know that? I didn't tell you that."

She laughed. "You didn't have to. I can see it in the way you look at her. She likes you, too. You know that, right?"

He smiled.

"I was impressed by what you did back at the loading dock to protect her, when the stairs collapsed. You shielded her. That had to hurt a lot."

"It did. But I wasn't thinking about it at the time."

"I know," she said. "You never do, when it's someone you love. Listen, we're gonna get out of here, and we're gonna get Avery and Sylvia back, too."

"I know."

"Good."

She looked around the landing, and then her eyes narrowed on a shadow in the corner.

"What is it?" he asked.

But she was already crossing to the corner. She pulled a rusted metal chair from underneath a curling section of wallpaper and brought it over to him. Before he had a chance to speak she kicked it, breaking it to pieces. And after it was completely smashed she reached into the wreckage and came up with two nasty-looking pieces of metal tubing.

"Not bad," she said, testing the heft of one of them. She handed the other to him. "You think you could do some damage with that?"

"Oh," he said. He reached into the waistband of his jeans and came up with the blackjack. "I don't need that. I've got this."

She stared at him.

"What?" he said.

"Seriously? We've been fighting our way all through this freaking hotel barehanded and you had that thing all along?"

"I—"

"Look," she said, heat spreading across her face, "you need to get your act together. Got it? This is our survival here. This is everything. Everything. It all hinges on what we do here. Avery and Sylvia and everybody else we care about are counting on us to do this right. We cannot afford for you to be careless like this."

"I'm sorry," he said.

She wanted to slap him. The idiot. How in the hell had he managed to stay alive for so long?

"Just take this," she said, handing him the metal chair leg. "And stay close."

They started down the stairs to the main lobby.

Rain was coming in through the open front doors, splashing a dark and rank-smelling mud all over the marbled lobby floor. Niki motioned for him to follow her into a sitting area to one side of the doors. They picked their way through busted tables and moldy leather chairs and climbed up on the ledge so they could see through the windows there.

Niki whistled softly. "That's a lot of zombies."

"Yeah," Nate agreed. "Do you see Avery?"

Niki scanned the open area down to the river. There had to be over a thousand zombies out there, standing as still as flagpoles in the rain, all of them facing the river. The soldiers had taken most of the boats out on the river. Something was going on, or was about to happen, but she couldn't—

"Wait a second."

"What?" Nate asked.

"There, up on that platform." She pointed across the field to a raised metal stand, like something from which a marching band director would watch his band practice, except larger, and equipped with a switchback staircase leading down to the field. She had seen a flash of red up there through the gray sheets of rain. Loren Skaggs, that insane son of a bitch. "You see it?"

"Is that the Red Man?"

"Yeah. You see behind him? I think that's Avery and Sylvia."

He looked from the field to Niki. "Why would he have them up there with him?"

"Because he wants me."

"You? Why, because you know where Dr. Fisher is?"

She stared through the rain at the Red Man, thinking back to the streets of St. Louis. He had her facedown on the pavement, his face inches from hers, his breath hot and foul, the stench of rot strong enough to make her gag. She remembered his hands moving over her butt, cupping the tops of her hips, gripping them like handlebars. The thoughts going through his addled mind had been obvious from the way his fingers trembled, the way his breath hitched in his throat. The virus had chewed his brain to a honeycomb, it had cracked his skin and swollen his joints, but it hadn't killed the desires that lurked within him. Or perhaps his loneliness.

"Is that why he wants you?" Nate said. "Because of Dr. Fisher?"

She stared through the rain at Loren Skaggs, the Red Man, and hate swelled up inside her.

"Yeah," she said. "That, too."

Nate didn't respond. He didn't understand. That much was obvious from the vacant look in his eyes, but that didn't matter.

"Nate," she said, "he has to die. We have to kill him. Even if we get away, even if we manage to get to Dr. Fisher and deliver the cure and move halfway across the country, it wouldn't matter. He'd come for us. He means to turn us all to be like him, to serve him. As long as he walks this earth, he's going to continue to be a threat. He has to die."

Nate nodded.

"I'll go," he said.

She laughed. "Don't be stupid. I've seen you fight. You'd make it about thirty feet before they munched you."

"Yeah, and how far will you make it?"

That stopped her, the way he said it, like he was mocking her.

"Excuse me?"

"You heard me. How far would you make it? Look at all those zombies out there. There must be a thousand or more. What are you going to do? You would need a hunting rifle to kill him. Or you could wade in there like you always do. You could probably kill a bunch of them, too. You're good enough. But all it would take would be a bite, or a scratch. Even a spatter of blood in your eye would do it. Before you know it, you'd be one of his slaves, groveling at his feet all day. But not me. I can wallow around with 'em all day long and it won't hurt me. I've been bit and scratched by them so many times I'm practically one of them."

He took a deep breath and climbed down from the ledge.

"It has to be me."

He was right. She hated to admit it, but he was right. Like it or not, he was their best hope. He was their only hope.

"We have to get Avery and Sylvia away from him. Promise me, Nate, you'll do that?"

"I'll try," he said.

"No. Don't try. Promise me."

He paused for a long time, but then he nodded.

"I need you to do something for me," he said.

"What?"

He reached into his pocket and took out a Ziploc baggie and held it up for her to see. Inside was a flash drive attached to a lanyard.

"Is that . . ." she asked, eyes wide.

He nodded. "Can you get this to Dr. Fisher? The doctor who worked on me said this contained everything someone who knew what they were doing would need to work up a cure."

She took it from him. She tried to speak, but her throat wouldn't work.

"I've seen what's on it," he said. "It's a bunch of chemistry drawings and stuff like that. Looks like a bunch of math."

"I can't believe it's real," she said. "I've wanted something like this for so long."

"You can get it to Dr. Fisher?"

"I will," she said, nodding slowly. "I'll get it to him."

"Wish me luck."

She nodded. "Good luck," she said. "I'm gonna work my way down to the river. I'll look for your friends, but if I can't find them I'll steal us a boat of our own."

"I'll look for you in the river."

"Count on it."

Chapter 25

Gabi started shooting before Jimmy made it up to the flybridge. He glanced down through the rain and saw her directing concentrated fire on the men who had spotted them.

She moved aft, stepping through wet puddles of blood and mud and ropes of guts left behind from the zombie attack early that morning, right out onto the open part of the deck.

"Gabi, get behind cover!" he shouted.

She didn't bother looking back at him. "Get us out of here!"

He hit the ignition and the Cummins diesel fired up with a cough, sending a tremor through the boat. "Thank you, baby," he muttered to the boat, stroking the navigation console. God, he loved this boat.

He fed the throttle and a thick cloud of black smoke rose up from the engine. For a moment, it obscured Gabi from his view. When the smoke cleared, she had sighted her rifle on another of the Red Man's boats, this one less than fifty yards to starboard. The men who had first spotted them were dead, one of them bent over the railing, his fingertips dragging the glassy surface of the river.

"Let's go," Gabi shouted. "Come on, Jimmy, get us moving!"

The *Sugar Jane* gained speed slowly. The first boat was dead in the water, but to back away from the dock they'd have to go right between two larger trawlers. Jimmy could see black shirts aboard, but couldn't count them. Not through the smoke and rain.

He glanced down again at Gabi. It scared him that she was so out in the open, so exposed, but there was nothing he could do about it. This first maneuver was going to put her even more in harm's way.

"Okay, coming about," he called down to her.

She didn't acknowledge him. She went down to one knee and resumed firing, her bullets tearing up the trawler just off the starboard bow.

Jimmy cut the wheel hard to starboard and the *Sugar Jane* began to rotate, the bow swinging around toward the shore.

He saw the little speedboat just as they started firing. A bullet hit the navigation console in front of him and peppered his face with bits of burning fiberglass and wood splinters. Jimmy flinched away from it, shielding his eyes.

There were three men in the little boat.

"Piece of cake," he muttered.

He grabbed his AR-15 and sighted it over the railing. Despite the rolling of the boat and the driving rain he managed to fire off three quick rounds, one of which struck a black shirt with a handgun and dropped him. The remaining two black shirts ducked down behind the gunwale, but their boat offered little in the way of cover, and as the *Sugar Jane* continued to swing around, bringing the flybridge directly over their position, Jimmy had a clear shot. Six shots later all three men were dead.

But the *Sugar Jane* was still coming around and Jimmy had to drop his weapon to correct the steerage back on course. He reversed the engine and started feeding throttle as fast as he dared. She was a temperamental boat these days, and too much throttle would almost certainly cause the engine to sputter and die, dooming them both.

Ahead, two of the Red Man's larger boats were barreling down on them, hoping to box the *Sugar Jane* in before she had a chance to pull away from the angle created by the pier and the shore.

Jimmy saw only one way out.

He said a silent prayer and pushed the throttle as hard as it would go, grimacing at the straining groan of the Cummins behind him. The first boat, with its dead crew, was still a good seventy feet from them. Jimmy turned the *Sugar Jane* to pass across its bow, a maneuver, he hoped, that would force the second of the two approaching trawlers to pass across its stern. It would give them some cover and take the boat out of the fight. At least for a moment.

That would just leave the other trawler, and Gabi was already laying fire down on them.

He held his breath as the dead boat loomed closer, ignoring the rain driving into his eyes and the occasional bullet that smacked into the walls of the flybridge. Jimmy was intent on gauging the pass, aiming to put the tip of the dead boat's bow just inches off the *Sugar Jane*'s starboard side, and he didn't hear Gabi's screams until they'd reached a desperate pitch.

When he whirled around she was curled into a fetal ball against the port side gunwale, her rifle tucked under her. Six or seven black shirts were pouring down fire on the *Sugar Jane*'s stern, chewing up the hull and filling the air with splinters.

He grabbed for his rifle to return fire, but stopped short. Not far from Gabi's head was the upturned box of M67 grenades, the contents now spilled out like billiard balls across the deck.

"Gabi," he yelled, "throw me a grenade."

He couldn't tell if she could hear over the rain and the rattling cough of the rifles.

"Gabi!"

But she was already moving. Without getting up she lunged across the deck and caught one of the rolling grenades before the motion of the boat carried it away from her. Then she rolled over on her back and threw it up at Jimmy.

He caught it like an egg. These things had saved their ass more than once and he had a great respect for their power.

"Stay down!" he yelled to Gabi.

Then he turned the *Sugar Jane* hard toward the trawler and pulled the pin on the grenade.

The sudden move surprised the black shirts and for a moment they stopped firing, a few of them backing away from what looked like an imminent collision between the two boats.

Jimmy waited until they were almost even and hurled the grenade. It smashed through a window and exploded inside the cabin with a muffled roar, throwing the black shirts into the water, their bodies trailing smoke. An instant later the trawler was a churning ball of black smoke laced through with orange tongues of flame.

"Got him!" Jimmy shouted. "Damn straight!"

"Jimmy!" Gabi said. "Starboard side, we got trouble!"

He glanced that way. Its captain wasn't as foolish as Jimmy had hoped. He hadn't been fooled by Jimmy's attempt to put the dead vessel between them. Instead, he'd come to a full stop and rotated back to starboard, so that now, as the *Sugar Jane* picked up speed to flank the trawler, she was presenting her bow full-on to the black shirts' vessel.

Gunmen were already moving into position, low-crawling toward the point of the bow with rifles up and pointed downrange.

Jimmy realized he was stuck. His only hope now was to outrun them, but the *Sugar Jane* was already at full throttle and her diesel engine starting to sputter and smoke. They were making maybe eight knots, but the Red Man's trawler was almost certainly capable of more.

"Jimmy?" Gabi called up to him.

He locked eyes on her. Her mouth was set in a tight line, her stare unblinking. He returned her gaze, unwilling to look away.

"You be ready with one of those grenades," he said.

"What are you going to do?"

"They're gonna catch us," he said, "so I'm gonna let them."

"What?"

"Just be ready."

Bullets smacked into the flybridge and Jimmy ducked down out of sight. He just needed a few more seconds. A few more . . .

He rose up just enough see over the railing. As he suspected, the trawler was gaining on them. Its captain had her at full throttle, aiming to close the gap enough for his shooters on the bow to fire down into the *Sugar Jane*'s stern the same way Jimmy had done against the little speedboat closer to shore.

"That's it," he muttered. "Closer, closer . . ."

He reached up and pulled back on the throttle, bringing the *Sugar Jane* to half speed. The diesel coughed and sputtered, but kept working.

The *Sugar Jane* eased down slightly in the water.

At the same time, Jimmy shouted, "Now, Gabi! Give it to 'em!"

She rose up on her knees and tossed her grenade at the surprised black shirts on the trawler. They were gaining too fast now to turn away. The grenade hit the pilothouse, bounced forward, and rolled down into an open hatch leading to the forward hold.

The explosion blew a massive hole in the port bow, killing two of the black shirts directly above it and flooding the hold with river water.

And still the trawler sped forward, unable to check its forward momentum. The bow ducked toward the water and continued to drive down, going lower and lower until the boat slowed to a stop and gradually began to sink. Within seconds, most of its bow and pilothouse were underwater, only its stern jutting up at a sharp angle from the plane of the water.

Jimmy watched it as they pulled away, his chest heaving, and he almost allowed the warm glow of victory to overtake him. But Gabi was rolling around the deck, holding her arm.

"Gabi!"

He rushed down to her side and lifted her up, her head on his thigh. Smoke was seeping up through the seams of the engine compartment and the engine was making a series of consumptive coughs. Through the rain and smoke he peered at her injury. It didn't appear too deep, but it was bleeding a lot.

"I'm okay," she said.

"I know, just let me work."

He took a soaking wet handkerchief from his back pocket and tied it around her upper arm, as close to the shoulder as he could manage.

"Tight?"

She was grimacing from the pain. She nodded, unable to speak.

"We're in trouble, baby," he said.

"No shit," she gasped.

He laughed. He couldn't help himself. "That's my girl."

It was hard to tell if that was rain or tears in her eyes. He suspected tears, even though she too tried to laugh.

The engine's coughing turned to a series of loud knocks, like some little gremlin was inside there banging against the hull with a hammer. Suddenly billowing clouds of black smoke poured up through the engine compartment seams, enveloping them both and causing them to hack.

The next instant, the engine died.

Through the smoke and rain, Jimmy could see the rest of the Red Man's fleet racing toward them. They had been stuck on the opposite side of the pier and he had hoped that that would buy them the time they needed to escape, but it was obvious now that was not to be. A lot of water had passed under this boat of theirs. It had been their home, their refuge, their one solid link to the dream of Mexico they both shared. And now, quite possibly, it was going to be their coffin.

"I'm out," she said.

For a moment, he wasn't sure what she was talking about, whether her rifle or some deeper reserve of her being, but then she held up the rifle and the empty magazine.

He should have known.

"Wait here," he said.

He went forward into the cabin and looked around for the last time. He saw the pictures of their daughter and their granddaughter broken on the floor, crushed by muddy boots, the sheets torn from the bed, the cabinets hanging open. They had searched it, rifled it, but they hadn't changed it. For him, the substance of this boat was always there, even as it filled with smoke and the sounds of the Red Man's fleet and his screaming black shirts bore down upon him. He took Ben Richardson's backpack from the bed and pulled off the cushion and exposed the hidden compartments he and Gabi had secreted there. He pulled out two more of the ARs and a handful of loaded magazines and brought it all aft to take his position next to Gabi.

She looked down at the stuff he'd brought forward and nodded, a pained smile crossing her lips.

"Not gonna give up yet, huh?"

"Never," he said. "Not while I've got you next to me."

She smiled again, and this time it wasn't laced through with pain.

With his help, she pulled herself to her feet. Her left arm was hanging by her side. But she still looked like the mama bear he knew her to be, always ready for the fight.

Thick clouds of acrid-smelling smoke swirled around them as they turned to face the oncoming fleet.

He reached down and took her hand, and together they waited.

Chapter 26

Niki watched Nate slip out the main doors and into the rain with mixed feelings. The man was, she decided, part cockroach. Had to be. There was no other way to explain the fact that he was still alive.

And there was something else, some nagging intuition that told her he was just a little bit off. It was more than his obvious lack of good sense, more even than the veil of contrition he seemed to live behind, as though he were wandering the world looking for somebody to forgive him for some past sin. There was a sin there, somewhere, in his past. She would have to watch that before he got too close to Avery.

Which was another thing.

Assuming they all lived through this, Avery was going to want that man in her life. A relationship like that would go all kinds of places, and most of them were places that Niki knew were bad. Avery, as fragile as she was, would no doubt throw her heart into that man. He was just the sort to draw her out into the open, and then leave her high and dry.

She pushed the thought back down. All of this was pointless. They were neck-deep in a world of crap and here she was worried about Avery's love life.

She took a deep breath and refocused on Nate.

He was walking through the rain, stepping up onto the curb, the metal rod down at his side. Here at the back of the Red Man's zombie army the stragglers were spread apart, and Nate walked between them, not bothering to slow down and not wasting his time engaging them.

That was good, Niki thought. Loren had told her that he could sense the morphic fields that the surrounded the zombies, like they were heat shimmers rising off the desert or something. She didn't know if she believed that or not, but she supposed it didn't really matter. He had brought all these zombies here just the same. And he was continuing to hold them steady even now, in this pouring rain.

The first few zombies Nate passed didn't stir, at least not until it was too late. He was coming up from behind them, and even as he passed them, they remained still, caught between their own atavistic impulses to kill and their obedience to the Red Man's commands that held them in their place.

But once one began to moan, that control wavered, and soon the zombies he passed were stumbling after him.

That was her cue.

She slipped out through the front doors and moved along the walkway next to the building. Red-tipped photinias, now run to riot, lined the walk, giving her a little cover. The rain helped some too. Within minutes she had made it to the edge of the building with nothing but a parking lot and open space beyond that stretching down to the river.

Three zombies were standing out in the middle of the parking lot, all of them swaying in place, staring dumbly toward the Red Man's platform.

She waited.

Back on the main part of the lawn, Nate was causing quite a stir. Even the zombies on the fringe were advancing toward him, and a momentary twinge of excitement went through her to imagine Loren up on that platform, losing control.

But these three zombies weren't moving like all the others.

She looked to her right, but there were no more back that way. Just these three, standing still, looking like emaciated wraiths out there in the otherwise empty parking lot.

She heard a muffled crash and at first thought it was thunder. But it was too close. She scanned the river and saw there was something going on over there. Several of the boats were moving, and black smoke was coming up thick from one of them.

And something else, too.

Muzzle flashes.

"What the . . ."

That was the Hintons. Had to be. The ones who brought Avery and Sylvia and Nate down here, and who were supposed to be waiting to ferry them to safety. They're running off. Niki sucked her teeth in dismay. The cowards. The miserable cowards.

She strained her hearing to pick up the telltale sounds of gunfire, but there was nothing. Watching the little bursts of fire a thought occurred to her. Back at Stoler's compound, back when she was first starting to come into her own as someone who could teach others to kill zombies, she read Bruce Catton's account of the battle of Vicksburg, during the American Civil War. The fighting and killing had been atrocious, and yet observers on the fringes of the battlefield reported an eerie silence coming from the heart of the fighting. They were less than a quarter mile away from the worst of it, and they heard none of it. And yet, twenty miles away, farmers reported the noises were so loud, so deafening, that horses scattered in panic and their windows trembled like eggs that hadn't quite yet set in the pan.

Was that what she was experiencing here? Were the rain and the wind somehow masking the sounds of the fighting out there on the river?

The questions hung unanswered, for at that moment there was another muffled boom, and a third boat started spewing black smoke. It was covering the river now, and the rest of the Red Man's fleet was going that way.

Her anger and dismay disappeared. Maybe this wasn't such a bad thing after all.

She looked back to the parking lot. She had been worried that killing these three would leave her little better than she was back at the hotel, her only choice a sprint toward the river where the black shirts waited on their boats.

But now . . .

Time to move, she told herself.

The three zombies were decrepit-looking wrecks, and though a faint warning bell was sounding somewhere in the back of her mind, she ignored it and charged into the open. She was running at a light jog, her metal bar coming up for the strike, when she realized her mistake.

The zombie, a woman in a blue T-shirt and jeans, now hanging off her emaciated frame like a bag, her face oozing pus from open abscesses and unhealed cuts, turned toward her, and as she closed on it, Niki saw for the first time the sudden sureness of footing, the defensive posture, the look of brutal, feral intensity in the woman's bloodshot eyes.

Stage III zombie, Niki thought. Oh shit.

But it was too late now. She swung for the woman's head and was stunned when the zombie stepped back to avoid the blow.

Niki recovered quickly, but not quickly enough. The woman

was on her before she knew it, the stink of her breath hitting Niki in the face even as her fingernails slashed at the air, trying to catch a piece of Niki.

Niki danced to one side and swept the metal bar across the woman's knees, sending her tumbling to the cement of the parking lot. The zombie lashed out again, but that time Niki was ready for the quickness of her motions and was well out of reach. She moved around behind the woman before she could stand and brought the bar down on the back of her head, slamming her face into the ground so that it bounced off the cement and came up bloody.

The metal bar came down five more times before the woman stopped moving.

Niki was about to turn around when a tight, cold grip clamped down on her wrist. She let out a bark of surprise to see the other two zombies right on top of her.

But they were so far away, she thought. How did they close the gap so quickly?

They're both Stage III zombies, she realized all at once. They can *move*.

Whirling around she saw the man who had her by the wrist. His face had rotted around the nose like a leper's, pulling his upper lip into a clown-like, impossibly huge grin, exposing blackened teeth and a tongue oozing with sores. She couldn't get the bar up—they were too close in for that—and so she dropped it and spun around, throwing the grinning man off balance.

He lunged for her arm, mouth open for a bite, but she slapped him across the forehead hard enough to cause his brain to skip a gear. For a crazy second he stood there, grinning at her, holding her wrist like she was a struggling child.

That was the opportunity she needed.

She whirled around again, pulling him forward, and at the

same time kicking the back of his knees so that his feet disappeared from under him, causing him to land flat on his butt.

The third zombie was a middle-aged woman whose green dress was ripped from the neck to the waist, exposing a pair of heavy dugs laced with the scars of old bite marks. With her hands free, Niki did a skipping side kick that caught the woman in the windpipe, crushing it. The zombie dropped to the ground, gasping, choking on its crushed airway.

Niki turned on the grinning man, who was climbing back to his feet. She picked up the metal bar and advanced on the man. He had his mouth open for another bite, but Niki didn't give him the chance. She swung hard for his face, connecting with his jaw and snapping his head around. Teeth went skittering across the wet pavement.

She hit him three more times just to be sure, then stood there, looking at the two dead zombies and the third who was still choking on her own throat as the rain fell all around her.

"Alright then," she said. "To the river."

Off to her left a crowd of zombies pressed inward, toward the platform. Nate was still moving; that was good. As long as he was moving he stood a chance.

She, on the other hand, had pretty much a straight shot to the river.

No more zombies.

She was almost there when she got a glimpse through the smoke that covered the river. She had only seen Jimmy Hinton once before, and that was at the docks at Herculaneum while she was busy coordinating her squads, but she recognized him at once. And the woman next to him, the one holding his hand, a bloody wound on her arm, had to be Gabi, his wife. The two looked resigned, but content in each other's company, even as the bulk of the Red Man's fleet barreled down on them.

Were they giving up?

From the things she'd heard about the Hintons she found that hard to believe. They were dirty business partners, yes, but certainly not the kind to just give up.

And then the gap through the smoke was gone, and once again the river was covered by a churning black fog.

The explosion came a few moments later, and it nearly knocked Niki off her feet. Instinctively she turned her head away, shielding her eyes. When she looked up again, there was nothing left of the Hintons' boat but a burnt, soap dish–shaped piece of hull floating on the water.

Impressive, she thought.

The black shirts were coming in their boats. Soon, she realized, they would be all over the area. If she was going to find a boat, she needed to do it in a hurry. Otherwise, they could forget about getting away from the Red Man's compound.

And then she saw it, the little speedboat with the dead black shirts in it.

"Hello," she said.

She looked around to see if any of the Red Man's zombies were close by and felt a sharp pain in her right side. Niki touched it gingerly and winced. Up to now she'd convinced herself the ribs there weren't broken, but it was getting harder and harder to lie to herself, and now that she was standing here, with escape so close at hand, the pain was catching up with her.

She closed her eyes and forced it down one more time. Just one more time, she pleaded with herself. Just once more.

Then she opened her eyes and waded into the river.

CHAPTER 27

Amid the wreckage of the Red Man's lunacy, Nate stood, letting the rain hit him full in the face. The zombies, an ocean of them, stretched out before him. They hadn't seen him yet—he was still too far behind the rearmost of the crowd for that—but they would notice him soon enough.

Nate smiled grimly.

Somebody was moving through the standing ranks of zombies, coming toward him. It took a moment for Nate to recognize Doc Kellogg, but when he did, his grim smile turned warm.

"I thought you'd stopped coming around," Nate said.

Kellogg cleared the last of the zombies, then half turned and gestured at the waiting army. "And miss this?"

"You think this is suicide, don't you?"

"What do you call it, Nate?"

"I don't know. That's why I'm asking you."

Kellogg shrugged. "I call it stupidity, but . . ."

"You can do better than that."

"Okay," Kellogg said. "I think life is a struggle to test the fragility of man against the rock of the world."

Kellogg had always talked like that. When they first started having their regular chats at dinner or in the lab, Nate figured the man was making fun of him. But it didn't take him long to figure out that Kellogg simply wasn't capable of talking any other way. He was as dense in his education as Nate was in his ignorance. There was a gulf between them, a gulf far wider than that between brilliant doctor and penitent criminal.

"Now you're starting to sound like the Kellogg I remember, but I still don't understand. I'm sorry. I don't. I want to know what I'm supposed to do. I want somebody to draw me a picture. I need answers, not poetry."

Kellogg nodded. The man was not without pity.

"I'm sorry, Nate, but there are no answers. No pat, easy ones at any rate."

"So I go through life like one of those things out there?"

"No, not that either."

"What then?"

"You have to answer for yourself what your life is worth. It's a journey, Nate. Sometimes it's an easy one. But sometimes it sucks too. Most of the time it sucks. That's the kicker. You can be a coward, and never find out what your life is worth, or you can show some moral courage and come up with an answer."

"And what if I find out my life ain't worth shit?"

Kellogg had laughed. The rain went right through him. "There's always that chance, though I suspect the harder you look for an answer, the less likely that that'll be the case."

"Thanks a lot, Doc."

Nate looked past Kellogg for a moment, toward the field where the zombies stood waiting on the Red Man to tell them what to do.

He wasn't like them at all, Nate realized. They stood and waited. But Nate, he moved.

Kellogg was gone. Nate knew he would be, just like he knew that this was the last time he would probably see the man.

He breathed out slowly, trying to calm the heart pounding in his chest.

"What is my life worth?" he murmured. "Time to find out."

He took a step forward, and another after that. And soon he found himself closing the distance between himself and the rear guard of the zombie crowd.

Any second now.

Before he knew it the zombies were all around him. He could hear rain drops slapping against their clothes, all tatters and dingy gray. He could hear coughing, too, and that surprised him. In all his travels, and despite all the craziness he'd seen, he'd never seen so many of them all together, and so quiet. It hadn't occurred to him that they still coughed, that they could be so like a congregation at church, all with their eyes turned to God. Or, at least, what passed for God in this wasted land. He passed a man with his mouth hanging open, rainwater dripping from his cracked and peeling lips. The woman just beyond him was twitching slightly, as though her body were being hit with a weak electric current. When frozen like this, they could almost seem human. Broken, but human.

Except for the smell.

This close, surrounded by them, not even the rain and the rich pungency of the river could mask the smell of their rotting wounds and the sour stench of excrement on their clothes. He had forgotten how bad so many of them together could smell.

Already the zombies around him were starting to stir,

alerted to his presence. Their moans rose above the driving rain, and more and more were breaking ranks to follow him.

This is it, he thought, and quickened his pace.

In the distance, a muffled boom rolled across the river. The rain-streaked sky above the brown expanse of the water filled with a black, oily smoke. Nate wondered briefly what it might be, but the thought was gone as quickly as it occurred to him. All around him, zombies turned in his direction. He kept moving, threading his way through their ranks like a man trying to work his way up through a concert crowd to the front row. But his fear was mounting with every step. The energy of the crowd was turning inward, pulsing through the assembly like an electric current. It was always the same when they sensed a meal.

A woman, her legs bent and her face a rotting mess of abscesses and open sores, stumbled into Nate's path. He huffed in surprise and only just managed to catch her by the shoulders, holding her snapping teeth at bay.

She groaned, her hands slapping at his elbows.

Grunting, struggling against the suddenness of her attack, he had a hard time tossing her away. He was off balance and falling over backward.

A huge man shambled toward him, his arms outstretched. Nate rotated, hoping that his old ankle injury from his high school track days wouldn't choose this moment to blow out on him, and tossed the snapping woman into the man's waiting grasp. To Nate's surprise, the man fell on her and started feeding, pulling her apart with his teeth even as she kept her eyes on Nate and struggled to get back up.

Nate stumbled backward. Another zombie, this one a teenager in jeans and part of a Lakers basketball jersey, bumped him and shuffled past. The teenager fell on the woman. Several others joined them. She made no sound, even as they began to rip strips of flesh from her arms and back. Her head was thrown back, her neck exposed. Teeth found out the soft spot below the chin and a stuttering gurgle escaped her lips.

She stopped struggling after that, though her corpse continued to jerk and twist as the others pulled her apart.

Nate had never seen anything like that. This was something new, zombie attacking zombie. In eight years of wandering, he'd never seen them do that. The zombies continued to surge past him, falling on the corpse, opening her torso like the belly of a canoe.

Soon the tangle of bodies was the color of mud. He couldn't tell one from the other. Not even the dead woman's blood was visible in that orgiastic mass of writhing flesh. It was just mud and tangled limbs.

He turned away, back toward the platform.

Hundreds of dead, vacant eyes met his. His gaze darted from side to side. He pivoted in a circle, staring all about him. But the dead eyes were everywhere.

"Ah, shit," he said.

Zombies surged toward him from every side. Nate swung the metal bar Niki had given him, but hands were already on him, clawing at his shoulder. The metal pipe was pulled away. He was bleeding, his shirtsleeve ripped away. He turned to run, but there were no open lanes through the mass of bodies. They tackled him, slipping on slimy ground. He tried to kick them away but his feet were mired in the mud, and when he went down they came down on top of him in a mass of limbs.

They pulled on his arms and legs, trying to get their mouths on him, but still he kept fighting. He rolled from one side to the other. He jammed his right knee into a man's chin, knocking him back into the throng. The zombies moaned and surged forward, reaching for him. He pushed his way back to his feet, and for a moment he felt like he was moving with all the speed and confidence he'd possessed as a seventeen-year-old track star racing through the Pennsylvania woods. It was as though he'd never left the thrill of the run or the joy of knowing you still had more reserves deep inside.

A zombie reached for him and he threw it into the mud, stepping on its back as he hurtled through the crowd. The lacerations on his back and arms and face sizzled like splashes of hot grease against his skin, but they didn't slow him down. He kicked and punched and shoved his way through, pushing the zombies into each other with strength he thought he'd lost long ago.

Four zombies grabbed his shirt and pulled him toward the ground. His swung his elbow, trying to knock their hands away, but one of them had its fingers tangled up in his shirt. The hand wouldn't come loose. Nate raised his foot to kick the zombie away, but he lost his balance and stumbled. Another zombie slashed his cheek with its fingernails and blood flew into Nate's eyes. He staggered again. The ground rolled beneath his feet and his arms pinwheeled as he fought to keep moving.

More zombies pulled on his clothes. He could hear them tearing. Nate lashed out with a wild punch, knocking a zombie down, but it wasn't enough. He knew it wasn't enough. The press of bodies was overwhelming now and a violent, claustrophobic panic surged through him. His heart was racing. He lurched to one side, throwing a shoulder into a zombie's chest and bouncing off. Their hands kept reaching for him, pulling on him, turning him around. His foot slipped out from under him and finally his ankle couldn't take any more.

He sagged to the ground.

Fingernails tore at his shirt, ripping it away, ripping into his skin, his ears, his lips. He screamed, but couldn't find his legs. Every time he tried to stand, they pushed him down again.

Nate didn't even feel the last shove, the one that landed him flat on his back.

He looked up, and saw a huddle of torn and snarling faces staring down at him, hands reaching downward.

CHAPTER 28

The rain was cold. Sylvia sat against the back railing of the platform, shivering and miserable, her arms wrapped around her knees. The world seemed to swirl around her in a blur of muddy images. Since being led up to this platform she had managed to hold herself together, but that was becoming harder with every passing second. The thought that she was going to die here couldn't be pushed down anymore, and with it came nausea and a fear that prickled her skin and made her lips tremble.

She glanced over at Avery, and for a moment, the girl was ten years old again, a plump little waif in ruined clothes hiding behind Niki, so fragile it made her heart break for all the good that had been drained from the world.

Avery was staring back at her. *What are we going to do?* she said, silently mouthing the words.

Sylvia wanted to answer, but couldn't.

She didn't know, and the memory of the last time she had tried to scoot over next to Avery rose up in her mind, the way the Red Man had whirled around on them when he saw them together. She remembered the way his filthy hands had felt on her skin, the stink of his breath. And the words he'd whispered into her ear.

"Think about this as you wait for Niki Booth to come for you. Think about life. Did you love it like you should have, while you were holding it in your hands? Did you love it enough to go into this moment with an open and a ready heart?"

The sting of those words was still hot on her cheek, for she knew the answer was no. There were too many regrets and too many broken hearts.

She looked again at Avery and shook her head in resignation.

Avery's gaze sank to the plank boards under them, and when she started to sob, it felt to Sylvia like the worst sort of accusation.

It had been like this after San Antonio all those years ago, her greatest failure. She became a college professor because she loved the glory of a young mind opening to the world. Ben had been wrong, all those years ago, when he condemned her motives. She really did set out to teach, not just to publish her way to tenure, but to teach. She loved the vitality of youth, its blind trust and violent rebellion. She loved its innocence, and its skepticism. She loved all the contradictions that made a college student a child on the cusp of adulthood; and yet, despite that love that had shone so brightly and so intensely, she failed the youth who had trusted her back then, just like she was failing Avery now. But the real tragedy of it all, the thing that really made her angry, was that she didn't even know why she failed. She couldn't fathom it. Love was supposed to find a way.

Feeling like she was groping blindly for an answer that would always elude her, she glanced up at the Red Man. His back, dripping with bloodred rainwater, filled her with dread.

There were no answers there. A part of her wanted to ask what he was waiting for, but in truth she already knew. He was waiting for Niki to come to him. And why shouldn't he? He had his black shirts on their boats watching the riverbanks, and on land he had his army of rotting slaves. There was no way for Niki to get to him. And that meant that time was on his side.

A sudden crackle from over by the river broke her thoughts off clean. It took a moment for her mind to realize that she was hearing gunfire, but that's what it was. It had to be.

And something else, too.

Men yelling. Yells turning into screams of rage and pain. Even over the pounding rain, she could hear the emotion in those screams.

Niki, she thought, and perked up. She looked over her shoulder, toward the river.

Not Niki. It was the Hintons!

And then confusion set in. What were they doing? Were they leaving? Abandoning them? She could see the *Sugar Jane* backing up, Gabi down in the rear deck firing at the black shirts on the nearby boats. Sylvia looked over at Avery to see if she was seeing this. Avery's eyes were wide, staring down through the smoke swirling over the water, absorbing the slow, cumbersome movement of the boats.

The Red Man slowly crossed the platform and put his hands on the railing. But to Sylvia's surprise, he wasn't upset. At first he showed no emotion at all. But then a slow, sly grin tugged at the corners of his mouth, exposing the tips of his brown teeth.

Sylvia looked away, focusing instead on the boats.

The river battle pondered on. From up here, the battle developed with the rigid predictability of flotsam caught in a river of molasses. Sylvia found herself strangely torn. She saw the violence unfold, and she cheered under her breath as the *Sugar Jane* destroyed three opponents in turn. But at the same time another part of her, the skeptic, was burning with the rage of betrayal.

And then the Red Man laughed. Even as the *Sugar Jane* pulled away, he laughed.

Sylvia looked up at him, and was surprised to find him meeting her gaze.

"Looks like your friends have had enough," he said. "That was your ride, wasn't it?"

"They're beating your men," she countered.

He shrugged. "That matters to you, does it? The lives of a few dozen men?"

She almost snapped off an answer, but was horrified by what she realized she was about to say. *Not your men.* As if the loss of a certain class of men was somehow a good thing. She recoiled at the heresy that nearly passed her lips. She had devoted her life, and especially her life after the outbreak, to the belief that all life was precious, even that of the zombies. And now look at her.

But she was more horrified by the look on his face. All the red paint in the world couldn't hide the smug superiority, the knowledge that he had reduced her to his level.

The wind stirred, gusting all around her. It blew a strand of her wet gray hair into her face. She brushed it aside.

He looked amused by her distress.

"You're a bastard," she said.

He shrugged again.

Suddenly bored with her, his attention drifted back to the river battle. The screams had stopped. The river was enveloped by a foul, roiling black smoke, but the *Sugar Jane*'s progress was still easy to see as it tracked its slow course out to the middle of the channel. The Hintons were standing in the stern, watching the black shirt fleet that was rapidly overtaking them, hand in hand.

"Your friends have not only abandoned you," the Red Man said. "Looks like they've given up entirely. This part should be fun."

On the bow of the approaching boats Sylvia could see black shirts on their bellies, their rifles flashing as they fired on the fleeing *Sugar Jane*. It was only a matter of time now, she knew.

She was watching one of the black shirt snipers when the *Sugar Jane* exploded. The power of the explosion caught her off guard, but she did not flinch. Instead, her gaze rolled slowly across the smoky water, across the burning debris still streaking through the air, trailing smoke like little comets, and finally settling on the blackened, rectangular raft of fiberglass that was all that remained of the *Sugar Jane*'s hull.

There was no sign of the Hintons.

The Red Man sighed and turned away. "Well, I don't know about you, but I was hoping for a bit more than that."

Sylvia stared up at him, dumbstruck. There was so much rage coursing through her, so much horror and resentment, that she couldn't put it into words. And for a moment, it almost overcame her.

Perhaps he saw it in her face, for his smile suddenly evaporated, and his bloodshot eyes narrowed.

"I wouldn't," he said.

"Sylvia, look!"

Sylvia looked past the Red Man to Avery. She was crawling forward on her knees, mouth open as a smile started to form there.

"Get back," the Red Man snarled at her, his hand raised like he might backhand her across the cheek.

Avery froze, but the half-formed smile remained.

"It's Nate," she said.

Sylvia followed Avery's gaze out to the muddy field before the platform. Her eyes were immediately drawn to Nate, fighting his way through the center of the zombie crowd. She gawked at him, pushing and shoving and kicking his way through the throng of zombies. They were surging after him as he passed. Ahead of him, a few heads turned to investigate the moaning of their brethren.

"He's coming for you," Sylvia said.

She meant it to sound derisive, baiting; but she couldn't help but wonder where Niki was. Sylvia scanned the field without trying to be obvious—and then she saw her! She was moving along the far side of the field, near the hotel, looking for a way to flank the zombie crowd.

It's perfect, she thought. Nate draws the zombie crowd like a magnet dragged through metal shavings while the Hintons draw the black shirts away, down the river. And meanwhile, Niki creeps silently along the riverbank, coming up behind the Red Man. It was perfect.

"Oh," said the Red Man.

Sylvia heard that startling smugness in his voice and turned her attention back to the field.

"No," Avery said. "Nate, no!"

Nate was faltering down there. He stumbled, went to a knee, and the next instant, four zombies waved over top of him, dragging him down into the mud.

More zombies fell on top of him. The scene, perversely, reminded Sylvia of football games she'd seen in long-gone days. Adults rolling around in the mud like children. But this was no game, and she didn't need the hitching whine in Avery's throat to remind her of that.

Nate was down there.

And he was dying.

He fought to his feet, shucking his elbows from side to side like some huge wounded beast. Nate stood there for four, five, six seconds . . . and then he was down again. The pile of bodies on top of him grew ever larger, and soon all she could see was a heap of writhing figures squirming around in the mud like worms. Even the blood was lost beneath the mud.

"And he's dead," the Red Man said.

Avery climbed to her feet.

"Sit down," the Red Man said.

"You killed him," Avery said. There was a wounded rage in her eyes that Sylvia had never seen before. It both startled and amazed her, like someone had ripped away a mask, revealing some new wonder of creation.

"Sit down," the Red Man said, this time through gritted teeth.

Avery took a clumsy swing at him.

The Red Man sidestepped it easily, then lashed out at Avery with a fierce backhand, his knuckles cracking against the line of her jaw.

"Avery!" Sylvia cried.

She jumped to her feet and rushed the Red Man. He turned just as she made contact and the two of them flew into the metal railing, shaking the whole platform and nearly sending them both over the railing.

Grunting, he threw her back.

She struggled to regain her footing on the slick platform. He loomed above her, red and strange and fierce, but her fear gave her strength. She lunged for him again, this time meaning to throw her shoulder into his gut and send him sailing over the edge, knowing that she had just this one chance to get it right or they were both dead.

She never saw the foot that swept her legs out from under her. One moment she was rushing headlong toward him, and the next she was flat on her back, staring up at him, at his red face and leering black smile.

"You do not get to win," he said. "Not today."

And the next instant he fell on her, his hands turning her face to one side as his teeth pushed their way through her hair and over her ear.

The pain was intense.

She felt as though the whole side of her face were being ripped away. She screamed up into the rain, hands instinctively moving to the torn flesh that only a moment before had been her ear.

Through tears and rain she blinked at her hands. They were bloody and her face felt like someone had pressed a hot iron against her flesh.

Then the Red Man came into focus.

He was holding something white in his bloody fingers. Her left ear.

He took another bite and chewed it while he watched her writhe on the platform. "You don't get to win," he said. "I told you that. Not today."

But all she could think of was her life.

How she didn't love it nearly enough to meet this moment with an open and a ready heart.

Chapter 29

The boat was a white-over-yellow Moomba Mobius with a raked-forward canvas canopy over the steering wheel. The canopy was in tatters now, flaps of it fluttering slightly in the breeze. Niki could see three dead black shirts sprawled out over the seats and a rifle hanging from one of the dead men's hands.

She stopped, knee deep in the water, studying the corpses. Something didn't feel right. She had that familiar prickling feeling along the back of her neck, a sudden alertness that she had come to trust over the years.

Where were the other rifles? Every black shirt she'd ever seen had carried a rifle, yet she saw only one here.

She waited, but none of the men moved. And judging from the amount of blood pooled on the seats and dripping down the sides of the boat, they weren't likely to do so any time soon.

She was getting paranoid, she decided. Of course they're dead. They'd have gone after the *Sugar Jane* if they weren't—

or at least sought some medical attention from the other boats if they were wounded. Of course they were dead.

She took another step into the river, but the sounds of moans behind her made her stop.

She whirled around. Not all the zombies had gone after Nate, it seemed. Twenty, maybe twenty-five, were staggering down the grassy slope toward the river, their vacant stares locked in on her.

"Shit," she said.

She looked back to the boat, and her eyes settled on the rifle hanging from the dead black shirt's hands. Niki glanced out to the river, where smoke from the *Sugar Jane* had lowered a curtain of inky blackness over the water. The Red Man's boats were heading into that veil, disappearing inside it. That meant the Red Man's back was exposed. A thrill went through her. The rifle—it would be an easy shot from the water. But she would have to hurry. The boats would be returning soon.

She ran for the little speedboat.

One of the black shirts was bent facedown over the gunwale. He had a pistol on his hip, as did one of the other soldiers, who was lying facedown in a thick pool of blood. She grabbed the gray hair on the back of the man's head and pulled it up so she could see his face.

Niki sucked in her breath.

It was the older guard from the bed of the pickup, from back in St. Louis. The same one she'd kicked in the jaw when she tried to make a run for safety. The same one who had shot her in the ribs with a rubber slug from his shotgun.

"Not so tough now, huh?" she said.

The man's dead eyes stared at nothing. His mouth hung open uselessly, gathering flies. She let his head drop and his face thunked against the gunwale. Niki grabbed him by the back of his belt and pulled him into the water. The alligators or the zombies could have him, she didn't care which.

She climbed aboard and took a quick inventory of the weapons the dead men had left behind. She saw one pistol and one AR-15. There were two men with hip holsters, but she didn't see the other pistol. It must have gone over the side, she thought ruefully. Too bad. There was no time to look for it, either. The first few zombies were almost to the waterline now. Niki turned the black shirt with the rifle over and was surprised at how young he was. Avery's age, maybe even younger. Such a shame. So young and already things were bad enough he felt the need to join up with this lot. She thought of the men impaled on spikes on the opposite riverbank, and what the black shirt there had said. Those were all the ones who wouldn't serve the Red Man. She wondered if this boy here had been presented with the same choice, and she found it hard to hate him.

She searched his corpse and came up with two fully loaded, thirty-round magazines for the AR-15. A good haul.

She put her boot to his chest and shoved him overboard.

"Okay," she said, turning to the third black shirt. "Your turn."

She flipped him over, wincing from the pain in her side, and froze. As soon as she saw his eyes open and his pistol coming up, she cursed herself for her stupidity. A rookie mistake if there ever was one.

He motioned for her to put up her hands. "Real slow," he said.

She raised them halfway, at the same time gauging the distance to the AR-15 leaning up against the captain's chair.

"I wouldn't," he said. He slowly climbed to his feet, careful to keep the pistol trained on her chest.

She stared into his eyes, taking the measure of the man. He had a round face with a thick black beard. There was blood in his beard and in his hair, but that didn't bother Niki. She had seen blood before.

Instead, she kept coming back to his eyes.

Niki had never seen the man before, she knew that, for she would have remembered eyes like his. They were cold and brutal. He didn't serve the Red Man out of fear. He was too emotionally dead for that. Too hollow inside even for something as instinctive as fear. No, he served the Red Man because he liked the killing. She had been wondering about the bodies on spikes on the opposite riverbank since she first saw them, not only at the courage and pain of the dead and dying there, but also at the men who put them there. How fucked up and depraved did you have to be to impale another man through his ass on an eight-foot spike?

Well, here was her answer, staring her right in the eye.

Niki's lip curled in disgust, but not because he offended her sensibilities. He disgusted her because she had had dreams of looking in the mirror and seeing eyes very much like his staring back at her.

That recognition scared her the most.

"You ought to shoot me if you're gonna do it," she said. "I'll kill you if you don't."

"Not the way you're favoring your ribs there. You'd never make it."

She forced a smile. "No," she said, "I guess not."

CHAPTER 30

Shivering all over, Sylvia touched the searing wound where her ear had been. It was hot to the touch and sticky. Her hand came away bloody. She didn't believe that she was going to die like this. She didn't *want* to believe it. Not after all these years, and all that she'd been through. But here it was, her life dripping from her fingertips, turning pink in the rain and fading away to nothing as it splashed to the floor.

She looked over at Avery. Sylvia had hoped to find some strength there, some hope, some desperate child need for her mother, but the girl looked beaten and resigned, dark circles of exhaustion under her eyes. And somehow, that look of defeat on Avery's face was harder to bear than the wound itself.

To the Red Man she said, "You had no right to do this. I don't want this. I don't want it."

She expected to be ignored; or, if he paid her any mind at all, to be backhanded across the cheek for her insolence. Either of those actions she was prepared for. But she wasn't prepared for him to kneel next to her and speak so kindly, so gently.

"But it will happen. Whether you want it or not, the course is set. There is no free will, no decisions, no choices."

She sniffled.

His face was next to hers, his breath on her cheek. She wouldn't look at him, though. She couldn't.

"You've been through this before," she said. "You know how bad I hurt. Why would you do this to me, knowing that?"

"It does hurt. I remember. You feel like your lungs are filling up with blood. It's hard to focus. Your mind is racing with all the things you wished you'd done. The regrets are piling up in your mind like unpaid bills."

"Yes."

"All of that goes away," he said. "You hate me right now because you don't understand. But I've set you free. Here in just a moment there will be no guilt, no shame, no regrets. Nothing bad lives here. You are about to be reborn, and when you come out on the other side, I'll be waiting for you. And I won't be a monster then. I'll be your god. I'll be the voice that tells you where to walk, when to eat. For the first time in your life, you will rest easy. I guarantee it. You haven't felt this way since you were a baby."

"But my mind will be gone. All that I am will go away."

"Evolution is painful, and it doesn't always take us in the direction we want to go. Don't you see? That's what's happening here. This is evolution. What you're feeling, this is the future of humanity. This is more than what you're feeling. This is more than you changing. The world is changing. And those who don't change with it will become casualties of it."

Her eyes kept wanting to roll back into her head. She was sweating, but the rain was cold on her skin. Her mind was drifting, unable to lock onto a clear sense of where she was or what she was feeling or what she should do. There was a lump in her throat but she couldn't swallow it. Her heart was pounding furiously, but no matter how hard she tried to fight it she couldn't stop her mind from floating away. Thinking used to be so easy, she told herself, such a necessary part of who she was. But now it seemed unimportant, like a daydream.

"This is a good thing," he said.

No, her mind screamed. *Fight, damn it!*

She reached down to his crotch and squeezed his balls as hard as she could. Zombies felt no pain because they lacked a sense of self, but she figured he'd be different. His howling in pain was enough to convince her she was right as she tried to roll over onto her hands and knees.

Why was it so difficult? she thought, willing herself to do it. Something so easy.

She heard him raging behind her. Her body rebelled against the sudden exertion and she began to cough and hack, but she no longer felt like she was drifting. She felt solid, like she had purpose.

His hands were pawing at her back, but that was okay. Lead him away from Avery, she thought. Give her the opportunity to escape.

She didn't make it far.

The Red Man was on her like a cat on a bug. He grabbed her shirt, her hair, her shoulders. He threw her back onto the platform and she landed in a heap against the metal railing.

The Red Man was standing over her, breathing hard, but the significance of it didn't make sense.

At least at first.

His gentle demeanor was gone. His eyes were bloodshot again, and he was looking at her like she was food.

"No," he said, and shook his head violently from side to side. "No."

She had no idea what he was talking about, what he was objecting to, until the sense of calm overtook her once again. And that's what it was too, a sense of calm. She had feared it earlier, but now she was better. Suddenly the calm seemed welcoming, not something to be feared.

No, she thought. No, something's wrong.

But it was the kind of wrong that she couldn't put her finger on. Every part of her was screaming that something was seriously *off*, but her mind wouldn't be bothered by it. All she wanted to do was drift away, like she did when she heard some old song she'd loved so long ago.

And that's what it is, she realized. It wasn't fear; it was movement. Her mind was drifting into forever, while her body waited patiently somewhere far behind. A comforting stillness fell over her, and the urge to let go became overpowering. There was no need to be afraid. All this was going to be okay. Avery would be okay. Even Niki, so angry and so violent all the time, would be okay.

All she had to do was let go.

For a moment, she fought it. She rallied. She willed the fog from her mind. But there was never really any chance of clearing her brain. She was slipping beneath the waves, and it only hurt when she fought.

Stop fighting. Make the pain go away.

Stop . . .

For a moment, there was nothing. Not even any pain. There was only a need to stand and wait.

The Red Man would move her when he wished.

There were mangled faces huddled above him. Hands reached down. They scratched and tore at Nate's face and what remained of his clothes. He twisted left then right in the mud and swatted at their hands, kicked them when he could. And then, between their legs, he saw a flash of daylight.

It had been like this once before, years ago, when he was still running track in high school. He'd been racing a senior from the nearby town of Gatlin on a cross-country course through the forest out behind the high school. They rounded the last bend, neck and neck, the opening out of the forest just two hundred yards ahead. Nate saw the patch of daylight at the edge of the trees and a thrill went through him. He'd heard the note of exhaustion in the other boy's breathing, but Nate knew he had more. He had this. Run to daylight, he'd told himself. Run into the daylight.

Now, with a mountain of sin and shame behind him, he was seeing that daylight again.

Run, he told himself. Run into the daylight.

He flipped over onto his hands and knees and scrambled through mud, clawing his way through the forest of legs, until he came up on the other side. Nate was covered head to foot in brown mud. He stood on shaky legs and pivoted in a circle until he found the Red Man's platform again.

A man with long wild hair lunged at him. Nate stepped to one side and pushed him down into the mud.

Nate's hand slid across his waist and touched the blackjack's hilt. He had forgotten about it again. Another zombie, this one a woman with deep black gashes down her cheeks, like deep fingernail scratches, tried to take a bite out of him.

Nate swung the blackjack, intending to catch her right above the ear, but caught her in the mouth instead. Her teeth shattered with a nasty crunch he could hear even over the collective moaning of the crowd and she staggered back. Nate advanced on her again and this time got her right above the ear, dropping her to the mud.

They were all around him, a blur of faces.

Nate didn't stop moving. He knew stopping would get him killed and he had no intention of dying just yet. He twisted away from another zombie, put his hand in a woman's face to block her snapping teeth from his neck, and pushed on.

One of them got its fingers caught up in the tattered clothes hanging around Nate's waist and he had to spin around in circles to try to throw the zombie off balance. "Let go," he said, and slapped at the zombie's arm with his weapon. But the zombie's grip was strong and when Nate finally shook it loose it came away with a muddy clump of his shirt in its fingers.

"Fucking bastard," Nate screamed, and swung his blackjack overhand, coming down on the zombie's head. It hit with a crack as the scalp split in two and fell away from the skull.

At the same time, more hands were reaching for him. Nate hit one of his attackers in the face with the club. It was an awkward swing, and he lost his footing in the slick mud. He landed on his side and felt the air rush out of lungs.

He gasped for breath, and was still fighting to pull air into his lungs as he scrambled away on his hands and knees. A moment later he was on his feet again. There was a gap between the two zombies directly in front of him and he ran for it. They clawed at his face but he didn't let them slow him down. The Red Man's platform was less than a hundred feet away now. He was close.

A man tried to wrap his arms around Nate's neck, but he ducked and twisted around, coming under the tackle. Nate swatted the man in the groin with the blackjack and almost laughed at the grunt that came from him. The zombie pitched over forward, but didn't stop. He kept kicking its knees at the earth, swaying from the blow, trying to climb back to his feet.

But if he ever made it, Nate didn't know and didn't care. He was already pushing his way toward the platform again, pushing bodies aside, swimming over those he couldn't move and crawling like a worm under them.

Then—there was daylight again!

He was through the crowd and standing at the foot of the metal stairs that led up the front of the platform.

Nate stumbled up the first few steps and stopped.

He looked back.

The zombie crowd was a riot slowly pushing itself toward his position.

He stood there, his chest heaving, watching them surge forward, not quite believing that he'd come this far. It didn't seem possible, even though his body was screaming from a thousand cuts and bites and scratches.

"Nate!"

He looked up. That was Avery's voice! He turned away from the crowd and started up, crashing into the railing like a pinball as he tried to clear his head. The zombies hadn't killed him, but they had torn into him, and his mind felt like a soupy mess from the pain.

He was still four or five steps from the platform when he saw the Red Man staring down at him, his bloodshot eyes seeming to blend in with the paint on his skin. But Nate could still recognize the look of shock on the Red Man's face. The Red Man looked at the stub of his finger and then at Nate.

"You," he said. "That's not possible."

"I guess this ain't your day," Nate said, and raised his blackjack.

He was about to swing when a woman stepped in front of the Red Man and fell forward into Nate's arms. Nate stumbled backward a few steps while struggling to keep the zombie at arm's length. Only then did he recognize Sylvia. The side of her face was a mixture of fresh and dried blood, the frizzled gray hair there matted and sticky. Her mouth curled down at one side where the lip was busted. Her teeth were red with blood.

"Sylvia," Nate said. "No."

She snarled and lunged for him, teeth snapping. He was caught off guard, and she nearly got his upper lip. But Nate recovered in time to throw her to one side. She staggered, caught herself on the railing. Nate punched her in the nose with his free hand and knocked her off balance enough for him to get his foot up to her chest and kick.

She tumbled down the stairs and into the arms of the zombies coming up from the field.

Nate headed back up the stairs, the blackjack raised high.

He swung with everything he had, but the Red Man had the advantage of height and he blocked it by throwing his left forearm across Nate's wrist.

Nate teetered on the stairs, off balance.

The Red Man lowered his arm and then hit Nate in the mouth with a fierce left jab. Nate's vision turned purple for a second and he felt his legs turn to water. He couldn't remember ever being hit so hard, and as he started to fall backward he pleaded with himself to keep his feet, keep his feet.

But it was no use.

His body wouldn't cooperate, and he fell over.

A pair of arms fell on his shoulder and Nate blinked up at the torn and bleeding man who held him fast.

"Ben!" Nate said. "Oh Ben."

But this wasn't Ben anymore. The body was the same, but the eyes were vacant and dead. His face was a crisscross pattern of dried cuts and there were deep bite marks all over his arms and legs.

He staggered toward Nate, a gurgle in his throat as he pawed at the space between them.

Nate tripped on the stairs and landed on his butt.

Then his eyes caught a flash of something protruding from the holster on Ben's hip.

His pistol!

The next few moments were a blur.

Nate reached for the gun and pulled it.

His gaze fell on Ben's dead eyes and he said, "I'm so sorry, Ben. You deserved so much better than me."

The shot.

Ben's head snapping back.

A spray of blood and bone and bits of hair flying out behind Ben's head, covering the zombies behind him.

Ben's body flying backward, knocking the zombies there down like bowling pins.

The echo of the shot rolling over the open field, drowning out the moans.

Then Nate looked down at the gun in his hand and for the first time in his life he knew without a doubt what he had to do. He turned and headed up the stairs. Avery was huddled against the railing in the far corner. The Red Man was standing in the middle of the platform, staring at him.

"Put the weapon down or they will kill you," the Red Man said.

Nate didn't answer. He stepped forward and raised the pistol.

"Stop. You're a dead man if you do this."

Nate smiled.

"You're wrong. I just started living."

He fired twice, hitting the Red Man in the chest and sending him backward, his arms pinwheeling madly.

The Red Man landed with his back on the railing, his bloodshot eyes staring up into the rain, his mouth opening and closing, opening and closing, as though he were trying to speak but couldn't get the air in his lungs to do it.

Nate closed the gap between them and fired again, this time hitting the Red Man in the crease between his nose and upper lip.

The Red Man's head snapped back just as Ben's had and he died, curled backward over the top railing, body slack, his arms spread wide and hanging into the open air, rainwater dripping from his fingertips.

Nate stared at him, fascinated.

The whole world seemed frozen around this moment, and for a long time Nate had the feeling he was floating through a forest in Pennsylvania, a patch of daylight at the edge of the trees looming ever closer, his lungs bellowing in his ears, the feel of daylight on his skin and its warmth welcoming, like it would pull out of all this death and propel into a world that finally made sense.

A moaning from behind him shook him from the reverie.

"Nate!" Avery said.

He looked at her, and then followed her gaze toward the stairs.

Sylvia, bloody and vacant-eyed, was standing there.

"Back away," the man said. He waved Niki toward the port side with the barrel of his pistol. "Over there."

Niki glanced over her shoulder, where the zombies were wading into the river. There wasn't going to be much time, and she was only going to get one chance to do this right. But his gun hand was just out of reach. Maybe a kick, she thought, then dismissed that idea. The man's eyes were hard and calculating. He looked ready for something like that, almost like he was hoping she'd do it. He had orders to get her to the Red Man, she was certain of that, but a part of her couldn't help but wonder if he really cared about orders. Was he just looking for a reason to put a bullet in her?

She thought so.

And she was not going to die that way.

"Move it!" he said.

"Okay, okay," she said, and stepped where he wanted her to go.

He got the AR-15 from the captain's chair and laid it down in the puddle of blood on the deck.

He was smart about that, at any rate. Only an amateur would try to use a rifle in the close confines of the boat.

But then she looked at his face again, at the blood crusting in his beard. At the pink rivulets of bloodstained rainwater dripping from his chin.

"You don't care about the Red Man," she said.

She could hear the moaning over her shoulder. The zombies were getting close now. The man didn't look at them, though. Instead, he smiled at Niki, playing the game with her. He wasn't going to betray his fear by looking at the zombies, gauging the distance. He went on smiling, and the look seemed to say, *Fine, you want to play chicken. Let's play.*

"You don't serve him because you care about what happens here," Niki said. "You do it because you're scared. That's it, isn't it? You're scared."

The smile slid away from his face.

She took a quick glance to her right. The first three zombies were less than ten feet away now.

"That is it. You're scared. That's why you played dead, isn't it? You weren't trying to trick me. You were hoping to slink away like a coward. I thought I saw the killer in your eyes, but that isn't you, is it? You're just a coward."

"Bitch, you're gonna get a bullet in your head."

"Then do it!" she snapped. "Come on, coward. Do it!"

The rain fell.

They stared at one another, and for a moment, she thought she had him. But then the smile came back, sinister and cruel.

"No," he said. "Not yet." He flicked the barrel toward the captain's chair. "Over there. You're gonna drive us over to the platform."

"Just like that? You don't want to play anymore?"

"Nobody's playing any games here." He motioned to the chair again. "Move."

She shrugged, then walked over to the chair, but didn't sit down. She focused on the sound of the rain pattering against his coat, gauging his location. He was behind her, just a little to her left.

Just about perfect.

Suddenly she rocked forward, simultaneously throwing a mule kick in his direction.

But something was wrong. Her aim was true. She had gauged the distance right. She should have connected. Only the man wasn't there. He had side-stepped her at the last second and now he was right up on her, one hand balled in her hair, the other jamming the barrel of the gun into her broken ribs.

She screamed from the pain, unable to control it.

Her pulled her away from the captain's chair and threw her onto the gunwale so that she was bent over the side, her face right above the weeds poking out of the water.

"You want to play games with me, bitch? Huh? That what you want?" He pulled back on her hair so she could watch the zombies closing on the boat. "How's this? Let's see how you like this."

She tried to kick and buck him off her, but he jabbed the barrel into her ribs again and her legs turned to water.

But she had to act.

The zombies were almost on them, closing in.

She bent her knees slightly, just enough to get some leverage against the floor. He was leaning over her, using his weight to pin her over the gunwale. As soon as she felt the gun pull away from her ribs, she jumped up and forward, carrying him on her back over the side of the boat.

He let out a grunt of confused panic as he splashed into the water and weeds.

He came up spluttering.

But Niki didn't give him a chance to react. She swatted the gun from his hand and then grabbed the sides of his head and jammed her thumbs into his eyes, digging into the oozing jelly with everything she had.

He screamed and grabbed her wrists, but there was no strength in his hands. His whole body seemed to tense, and then sag into itself.

Niki shook his hands loose from her wrists and pushed him into the approaching zombies. His screams started anew as she backed away. He was still screaming when they pulled him down into the weeds, a dark red shadow spreading out from the huddle.

She stood there, trying to catch her breath, eyes tearing up from the pain in her side.

A shot echoed across the river, and Niki turned sharply toward the platform.

It was followed by two more, and then a fourth.

"Avery," she said, and jumped into the captain's chair.

Sylvia pulled herself up the stairs. She could barely stand and had to lean on the railing for support, but she kept coming, wobbly legs shaking beneath her. Her moaning was a choppy, breathy gurgling, like there was fluid in her throat. There was unmistakable hunger in her eyes, though.

Behind her, the stairs were crowded with zombies. The entire field was closing on the platform now.

Nate raised the pistol and sighted it on Sylvia's forehead.

"Nate, no!" Avery shouted.

"That's not Sylvia," he said.

"Don't."

She shook her head, pleading with him.

He lowered his pistol and pulled her to the back of the platform, next to the Red Man's corpse, his eyes still open and staring up into the rain. Far out on the river Nate could see the Red Man's fleet coming back to the hotel docks. He looked down at the water two stories below and shook his head. With the way his head was swimming, he doubted he could clear the short stretch of grass between the platform and the water.

"Avery, we're gonna have to jump."

She looked over the railing, her face stricken.

"I can't."

"You're gonna have to. We can't go anywhere else."

Sylvia tripped on the last step and fell to her hands and knees on the platform. She looked up at them and groaned, then slowly climbed to her feet.

Nate turned to Avery. He gestured with the gun.

"She wouldn't want to be left like that."

"Don't," Avery said again. "Please, don't. I couldn't bear that."

"Alright then. Climb over the railing. I'll cover you."

Avery was climbing the railing when Sylvia let out a long, stuttering moan. Both Nate and Avery turned toward her just as a shot rang out and Sylvia's head snapped back.

She folded to the ground.

"Sylvia!" Avery screamed.

Avery tried to reach out for the dead woman but Nate grabbed her by the hips and pulled her back. More zombies were already mounting to the top of the stairs.

They were running out of time.

He turned toward the river. Niki was down there, looking up at them over the sights of a rifle. Her face looked twisted, and he could read the pain there, even through the rain.

"Jump!" she yelled. "Avery, you have to jump right now."

Nate put a hand on her butt to help her over. "Come on, Avery, you got it."

To his surprise, she didn't need much coaxing. She went over, hung on the railing for just a moment, and then jumped for the water.

She landed hard, but the next instant she was up.

Two more shots rang out, and Nate turned to see two more dead zombies at the top of the stairs.

He looked back to the water where Niki was lowering her rifle.

"Come on," she hollered. "Your turn."

Niki rushed into the water and grabbed Avery's hand.

"Baby, you okay?"

The girl's eyes were red from tears. "Sylvia's dead," she said.

"I know, baby. Come with me, please. We don't have much time."

Slowly, too slowly, Avery took her hand. Niki pulled her into the river, the water rapidly climbing up to their waists. Out on the river, the Red Man's fleet was coming closer. The boats were big, and the crews well armed, but they were slow. There was no way they'd catch the little speedboat. All they had to do was get a small head start.

They reached the boat and Niki helped Avery climb in.

"You got it?"

"Yeah," Avery said. Her voice was a strained grunt as she tumbled over the gunwale.

Niki turned back to the platform. She could see the Red Man dead on the railing, and she thought she should be glad for that, but the cost had been so damn high.

She choked back her tears for Sylvia and climbed into the boat. With a little extra height she could see over the platform's railing. Nate was backing away from a growing crowd of zombies. Even from the water she could see the cuts and bites all over him and she marveled that he was still on his feet. Clearly he was made of stronger stuff than she'd given him credit for.

"Nate," she yelled, "you have to jump!"

He fired the pistol, but the shot went wide of the mark, hitting one of the zombies in the shoulder and spinning it around, but not dropping it.

Zombies closed in around him.

Niki looked back toward the river and saw the black shirt fleet closing in. The head start she'd been hoping for was rapidly disappearing. Another thirty seconds and they'd have the little speedboat surrounded.

"Nate! Goddamn it, you have to jump. Now!"

A woman climbed over the bodies at the top of the stairs and staggered toward Nate. There were lesions around her eyes, the pupils like black glassy disks in a sea of bloodshot infection. She snapped at him, drawing his attention toward the ulcerated skin around her mouth, the skin there green and crusty around the holes in her cheeks. He raised his weapon to fire at her, but she was too fast. She was on him before he could pull the trigger, raking her fingernails across his face and his hands, and the pistol went flying. He grabbed her wrists and twisted one way and then the other, trying to throw her off balance, but she wouldn't budge.

Two more zombies hit him from the right and their combined weight was enough to throw all of them to the floor.

Nate twisted away, but he was off balance and his head slammed into the railing. He fell to his knees, bright lights going off behind his eyes as he struggled to regain his feet.

"Nate!" Niki yelled. "You have to jump. Now!"

The woman with the diseased mouth piled onto Nate's back, biting at his bare flesh. He shook under her, staggered to his feet, and poured himself over the top of the railing.

He tried to hold on, to control his fall, but his head was spinning. His fingers wouldn't grab at the rail.

And then he was falling, tumbling in space.

He hit the ground on his bad ankle and heard something crack. The pain shot through him like a lightning bolt, and for a moment, that was all there was. Blinding, mind-crippling pain.

Niki's voice broke through the pain first.

He rolled over, disoriented, trying to spot her. The whole world seemed to be moving like the horizon as seen from a ship at sea.

Images flashed in front of him. The back of the platform, a lacework pattern of crisscrossing metal beams, shaking beneath the weight of so many zombies. Figures lumbering toward him, splashing clumsily through the water. Others falling from the top of the platform, dropping like lemmings from a cliff all around him.

He could feel the water at his back and he pulled himself that way, but it was so hard to keep his head above the pain. It was like a wave threatening to overtake him and pull him down.

Faces were all around him. He heard coughing, and felt hands on his back, gripping at his arms.

Then he blacked out.

CHAPTER 31

Niki lowered her rifle.

"Help him!" Avery shouted. She was hysterical, screaming in Niki's ear. "Do something."

"I can't get a shot," Niki said.

She raised her rifle again, squinting through the sights, but there was no way she could squeeze off a shot like this. Not while the little boat was rocking in the current and Nate was up there getting mobbed. She was good, but she wasn't that good. She knew that.

And she already had one friend's blood on her hands.

"Nate," she yelled, "you have to jump. Now!"

Up on the platform Nate was struggling to get back on his feet. The man was a fighter, that was plain. He managed to get his feet under him and pushed up to a crouch. Then he buckled again and pitched forward, hitting his head squarely on one of the railing's post bars.

But he didn't go down. He kept pushing, and somehow managed to spill over the top of the railing.

She watched him fumble for a handhold, miss, and tumble to the ground below.

He landed badly. Niki knew he was hurt from the way his leg folded under him. The ankle, she thought, with a strange clinical detachment. Broken, has to be.

Avery had both hands on the gunwale and she was screaming Nate's name over and over again. Niki stepped forward, raising her rifle as she came. Zombies were coming around both sides of the platform, and more were falling from the top. Too many. Niki fired again and again, dropping at least eight, but it was a losing battle. There were just too many.

"We have to help him!" Avery said.

Niki met her gaze, shocked at the look on Avery's face. Niki knew well the panicked animal flicker that sometimes darkened Avery's expression. She had seen it often enough during those terrifying early days when they first found themselves all alone. But this was something new. The look in her eyes wasn't panic, or fear, but fierce determination; and banked beneath it, defiance. She was daring Niki to stop her.

Niki looked away. Behind them, the black shirts were drawing ever closer. Already the first few boats were rounding the tip of the pier.

"We have to go," Niki said. "We only have—"

"I am not leaving him," Avery shouted.

Niki put a hand on her arm but Avery slapped it away. Niki drew her hand back, stunned. "Avery—"

But it was too late. Avery turned away and bounded over the gunwale, landing with a splash in the weed-choked water. The next instant she was rushing toward Nate and the zombies gathering around him, her knees churning, water splashing all around her.

"Avery, no!"

One last glance at the river. The black shirts were coming. The window was closing. A sudden calm dropped over Niki, and her options appeared before her as though laid out on a chart. This was her gift, she knew, the ability to focus when everyone else around her was losing their minds. And in that moment, the pain in her ribs was gone, the pain of Sylvia dead by her hand was gone. There was only the choice: save Avery, or save herself and the cure. She couldn't do both.

But it really wasn't a choice at all. It never had been.

She slung the rifle over her shoulder and went over the side. Avery had already reached Nate and she was trying to pull him into the water, but she could barely lift him. Niki stepped in beside her, her hands under Nate's arms, and quickly pulled him back.

His body was slick with mud and blood but once they got him to deeper water it was easier to hold him up.

"Get in the boat," she said to Avery. "I'll hand him up to you."

Avery grabbed the top of the gunwale and pulled herself up as far as she could.

The zombies were entering the water behind them.

"Come on, Avery."

"I'm trying."

Niki eased Nate down onto her knee to keep his head above water. Then she hugged Avery's legs and pushed her over the edge of the boat. Nate was unconscious now, dead weight, and he was harder to lift. But Niki managed to get her arms around his thighs and hoisted him up.

A woman splashed her way toward them, out ahead of the rest of the zombies. Niki still had her arms around Nate while Avery fumbled with him up above. "You're gonna have to lift him, Avery. I got company down here."

"I'm trying. Lift him higher."

"I can't."

Grunting with the effort, fighting against the pain in her ribs, she shoved Nate upward. It was enough. Avery got him by the arms and pulled him over the side, both of them falling to the deck in a heap.

Just in time, too.

The woman was only a few feet away now. Niki shrugged the rifle off her shoulder and swung it butt-first into the woman's face, her teeth shattering with a sickening crunch. Then she sagged into the water, coughing while she sank beneath the surface.

Niki watched her fall, feeling numb inside. More zombies were coming, but suddenly all the hatred was gone. She didn't feel fear or rage. The hunger to kill those slavering things was gone. She just felt tired.

Wincing, she clamored into the boat.

Avery had pulled Nate onto one of the forward bench seats, a smear of blood and mud across the white deck marking his path. Niki scrambled past her and got behind the wheel. She fed the throttle and turned the boat into deeper water, but almost immediately came to a stop. The black shirts were in formation all around them, riflemen leaning over the bows of their boats.

They were surrounded.

Niki stared from one man to the next. She watched them adjust their grips on their rifles and sighed.

So close, only to end like this.

She coughed blood again.

The black shirts stared back at her, their faces impassive, unreadable. Niki emerged from behind the wheel and walked forward, into the little open area where Avery was still tending to a groaning, unconscious Nate.

"Niki," Avery said.

Niki gestured for her to be still. She stared back at the black shirts, aware of every twitch, every nervous cough. Aware too of the moaning and splashing behind her. What were the black shirts waiting for?

Finish it, she thought. I would if I were you.

The rain, she noticed then, had slackened off to a fine mist. When had that happened? Strange that she could be so alive to the minute movements of the black shirts, but fail to notice something like that.

Strange.

"They're not going to shoot us, are they?" Avery asked.

Niki startled at having the answer supplied for her so unexpectedly. She had been fighting for so long, and so hard, that something vital had ossified inside her. She was blind, she realized, to anything else but the fight. But once Avery put the truth of it into words, she could see the black shirts glancing nervously up at the Red Man's body, still hanging over the platform's railing. She could see the questioning glances back and forth between the men. She could see their resolve wavering.

"Tell them to let us go," Avery said.

Niki opened her mouth to speak, but the words died in her throat.

"Let us go," Avery shouted. "What are you doing this for? There's no reason for it. He's dead."

Niki flinched, wanting to tell her to be quiet. But she held her tongue. She was too proud. That was always her problem. It was pride that kept her from letting Stoler's people bring them in all those years ago, and it was pride that made her turn her back on him years later. It was pride too that kept her from admitting that the shivering, bleeding, shell of a man curled up on the boat's bench seat beside her was the answer to humanity's greatest blight. And it was pride that kept her from pleading for her life now, even when so much beyond their lives was at stake.

But Avery's words worked where her pride did not.

The black shirts lowered their weapons. It started slowly at first, one or two here and there, but soon they were all lowering their weapons.

They said nothing. They didn't have to.

A path between the boats zippered open.

Beyond, the river, shrouded in mist, waited.

Without speaking—she was too afraid to speak, as though her voice might crack and expose the brittle weakness she felt within her—Niki went back to the controls and fed the throttle.

They glided through the black shirt flotilla, and the black shirts all lowered their eyes as they went by.

"It's another few miles downriver," Avery said. She was sitting next to Nate—who had finally, and mercifully, passed out—damping a wet rag against his forehead. "It'll be on the east bank."

"You'll recognize the right spot when we come to it?"

Avery just nodded. She went on mopping Nate's forehead and brushing the sweat from his eyes. Immune or not, Niki thought, he wasn't doing well. Despite the rain and dragging him through the river, he was filthy with mud, and the parts of him that weren't muddy were running with blood. There were slashes on his face and deep bruises and bite marks on his chest and arms. The zombies had literally torn him to shreds.

He was shivering, too. Even unconscious he was groaning in pain.

"Shhh," Avery said.

She was cradling his head against her stomach, and watching her, Niki thought of something that happened a long time before, before the compound, while the two of them were still wandering the ruins of their little town and living off scraps left behind by the rape gangs and the hunters. They had taken shelter for the night in the map room of a library because, even then, Avery loved her maps.

"You need anything?" Niki had said, and waited.

Nothing.

The girl had a map of St. Louis spread out across the floor, and she was rocking back and forth while she quietly chanted the names of streets and parks and railroad lines, burying them deep in the labyrinthine mines of her brain.

"I'll be back in a sec, okay? I'm just going to scout around a bit."

Niki waited again, but there was no reply. She turned away, frustrated, angry that she'd been stuck in this world, everything she loved taken from her, and that she'd been left with the custody of this kid who rarely talked and had no interest in anything outside of reading maps. She went out, intending only to look around a bit and come right back. And so she'd wandered the stacks looking for books on killing. As it turned out, there was a bunch. People liked to kill, and people liked to write about it. She opened a book on the tunnel rats of Vietnam and became engrossed, mesmerized by the killing power of men pushed to the limits.

Only then did she hear Avery's screams.

She drew the pistol and ran for the map room. Crashing through the door she saw Avery on the ground, on her back, struggling weakly against a man kneeling between her legs, trying to pull her pants down. Two more were standing over her, eyes wide with lust and something akin to hunger, mouths open in anticipation of their turn.

They looked up in time to catch a bullet between their eyes.

The man between Avery's legs lunged to one side for his shotgun, but Niki was faster. Her first kick caught the man in the solar plexus, knocking him onto his back where he gasped for breath like a fish tossed on the shore.

She stomped on his throat.

She rammed her heel into his nose, breaking it.

She threw him on his back and mounted his chest and slammed the pistol butt down on his mouth, sending kernels of teeth skittering across the wooden floor.

Again she hit him. Again and again and again.

The skin of his face split open. Blood flew everywhere. The man's hands had groped bootlessly against her shoulders, but now, even those efforts ceased.

He was nothing but a meat puppet, jerking and twittering beneath her blows.

There was a thrill, a giddy joy in it. Release. The more she beat on him the more the rage seemed to change into something that was beyond sexual. She snarled and screamed and howled, as though in the act of killing she might actually negate herself and make this horrible world that wasn't worth a damn go away.

And then it was over.

She stopped hitting, the rage ebbing away from her so slowly its leaving was almost painful, and the only sound was Avery's sobbing.

The red cloud that had dropped down over her eyes was gone and in its place was responsibility and obligation and a thousand other things that seemed like grown-up jobs. She was twenty years old, for Christ's sake. It wasn't fair.

It wasn't.

But the job was hers and she couldn't—

"—he'll be okay?"

Niki shook her head, sending the memory into the recesses of her mind.

Avery was looking at her expectantly.

"Will he be okay?"

Niki's eyes flicked to Nate, taking in his shivers, his foot that was obviously limp, and probably broken.

"We need to get him to Dr. Fisher," she said. "He's hurt pretty bad."

Avery started to speak, then suddenly stood up and pointed toward the shore. "Look!" she said. "You see that?"

Niki squinted through the mist covering the river. Up ahead she saw a piece of river trash, white fiberglass maybe, caught up in the weeds. The humps of what looked like two human bodies were curled up behind it, not moving.

"What is that?" Avery asked.

Niki went back to the captain's chair and turned the boat toward it.

"What do you see?" she asked Avery.

"Keep going," Avery said. She was leaning over the edge of the boat, frowning at the bodies. "We're almost there."

"What is it?"

"I don't know." She turned back to Niki. "We're almost there. Just a little closer."

Niki stood up, trying to see over the windscreen.

"Tell me what you—"

Suddenly, Avery screamed. Niki was beside her in a second, her rifle pointed over the gunwale.

Jimmy Hinton was staring back at her over the sights of his own AR-15.

Niki let out the breath she'd been holding and lowered her weapon.

Jimmy did the same.

That was when she noticed that Gabi was holding what looked like an iPad inside a Ziploc baggie.

Niki nodded toward it. "What do you have there?"

They motored downriver.

Around dusk Avery spotted an access bridge spanning the river and told Niki to pull over. "That's the main road into town," she said. "If we climb up here it should take us almost all the way to the cemetery."

"Okay."

"Why did Fisher want you to meet him in Chester?" Jimmy asked from the back of the boat. He and Gabi were shivering when she pulled them from the river and had stayed under a blanket most of the way downriver.

Niki shrugged. "I don't know."

"Seems like a strange choice to me. The place has been a ghost town since the outbreak."

Niki did her best to disguise her irritation. She had come this far south on a few occasions, on scavenging missions before the free market at Herculaneum got going, and she remembered how the river could take on a cathedral-like stillness if you let it. It could be beautiful, the fog pooling in the gaps between the trees, creeping over the water, the whole world glazed orange and red by the sunset—one of nature's miracles. Jimmy Hinton and his wife had been quiet enough after Niki pulled them from the river, but the farther they got from the Red Man's compound, the more he started to chatter. She was tempted to toss him over the side again, let him talk to the alligators.

Instead she guided the boat to the bank and grounded it on the grass. It heaved back and settled and she cut the engine.

"You're sure he meant this place?" he asked again.

"I'm sure," Niki said. "We're in the right place."

"But why? There's nothing down here. And I mean nothing. Just empty buildings and empty houses. Seems to me if you were gonna develop some kind of cure you'd wanna go someplace like Cape Girardeau where they got hospitals and stuff."

"Cape Girardeau is crawling with zombies," Niki said.

"You know what I mean. At least down there they got facilities to work with. Maybe there ain't nobody left to work in those hospitals, but they would have left stuff behind. Stuff you could use to work on a cure."

Niki's temper was starting to rise, but she forced it back down. "He said to meet him here, in Chester, at sunset."

"Okay," he said, and held up his hands in mock surrender. "I'm just sayin', it's not the smartest choice there is."

"Next time perhaps somebody will bother to ask your opinion first."

"Hey," Jimmy protested, but she ignored him.

Two zombies were walking along the rail line that ran parallel to the river. A moment later they saw the little boat and started down the grass. Niki grabbed a wooden club she found on the boat and went up to meet them.

"Why don't you just shoot them?" Jimmy called after her.

Niki kept walking. She reached the zombies and as she bashed their heads in she wondered about what Jimmy had been saying a moment before, about Chester being empty. Why *had* Fisher chosen this place? It really was a ghost town. The people who had lived here had fled as the zombies busted out of the quarantine zone down in Texas years before and no one had bothered to return. It had gone untouched since then, one of the silent towns that stood like haunted memorials of a world long dead and gone.

Though she'd never met Fisher in person she had traded a number of messages with him over the last year. At first their dealings were businesslike, short and to the point. But soon his personality crept in. She realized he had a playful streak, that his brilliant mind had a penchant for metaphor and symbols. Meeting here, in Chester, a place famous for its desolation, would not have been an accidental choice on his part.

Its emptiness would not have gone unnoticed.

Why had she not asked herself that before?

One of the zombies groaned weakly and Niki clubbed it again, this time making sure it was dead, its skull shattered and smashed. She stood over the body, considering the violence that she had carried with her in this world. She had been as empty of mercy as this place was of life. She was—

But she stopped there, coughing, touching her ribs gingerly, and smiled, for she thought she finally understood Fisher's joke. She shook her head and went down to the boat to help Avery carry Nate to the cemetery.

It wasn't far to St. Mary's Cemetery, a few miles, but between carrying Nate and the mounting pain in her sides, it felt like a long walk. Avery was on the other side of Nate, supporting as much of his weight as she could, but Niki was doing most of the work. It was fortunate, Niki thought, that the idiot had nearly starved to death before running into Sylvia and Avery. She couldn't imagine what it would be like to carry a well-fed man in her current condition.

Night had already fallen when they crested a rise in the road and found themselves at the entrance to St. Mary's Cemetery. Silvered moonlight glinted off the tops of white tombstones poking up above a sea of overgrown grass and tangled shrubs. In the distance, toward the back of the cemetery, was a white barn-like building with a green metal roof, the one Fisher had told her about. Getting back there through the tangled brush that had grown up between the tombstones was going to be hard, especially carrying Nate, but she didn't see that she had much choice.

"This is the place?" Jimmy asked.

He and Gabi had fallen in behind them on the walk over from the river, and he had been quiet until now.

Niki nodded.

"I don't see anybody."

"We're late," Niki said. "I was supposed to meet him here at sunset."

"Yeah, well, it's past that now."

Niki fought down the urge to knock the man's teeth down his throat. And if she hadn't had Nate's limp weight resting on her shoulder she might not have been able to resist.

"How do you know he's even still here?" Jimmy asked.

Niki turned her head enough to give him a hard look, then forced herself back under control.

"He has a family with him," she said. "They'll need a place to bed down for the night."

"And you think they'll do it in a graveyard?"

Niki's fingers curled into a fist. She had despised him before, when he dumped all that beef bound for the compound, but now that she'd spent a day in his company, she was ready to punch him in the throat and watch him choke to death on his own broken windpipe. It would be easy to do, the blade of her hand right below his Adam's apple . . .

Her pulse quickened just thinking about it.

"Jimmy," Gabi said, resting a warning hand on his arm.

He caught her eye.

"What'd I say?" he asked her.

But to his credit he kept quiet after that.

Niki turned back to the graveyard, and her laughter caught her unexpectedly. Avery looked at her, but Niki just smiled. Unwittingly, Jimmy Hinton had asked just the right question. Fisher had known what he was doing in choosing this place. Here where life ended he was planning to show her a cure that had a chance of a new beginning.

She laughed again, wondering what he would think of the cure she was bringing him.

They entered the graveyard and followed an overgrown trail between leaning headstones.

Suddenly Nate groaned.

"Easy, Nate," Niki said. "We're almost there."

They'd better be, she thought. His skin was a furnace. No telling what kind of infection he'd caught from all those bites and scratches.

He groaned again.

"Something's wrong with him," Avery said.

Niki shifted her weight to lay him down, but Nate fought her.

"No," he said. His voice was weak, still little more than a groan.

"What is it?" Niki asked.

"Over there. Look."

He could barely lift his hand to point. But Niki could see it now, something moving in the shadows. Something big. At first she couldn't figure out what it was, but then its head came up, and another one behind it.

"Horses," Avery said.

Niki smiled at the delight in Avery's voice. The girl had always loved horses.

The first animal regarded them for a long moment as it chewed its dinner, perhaps pondering if they were zombies or not, and then dipped its head back into the grass between the tombstones.

"They're so pretty," Avery said.

"Yeah, they are," Niki agreed.

She looked around. Nothing but grass waving in the evening breeze.

"Hello," she called out. "Anybody out there?"

"Hey," Jimmy said, his voice a harsh whisper. "What the hell are you doing?"

"Relax," Niki said. "If there were any zombies around here they would have already spooked those horses. And besides, my contacts told me that Fisher is crippled. He uses a horse-drawn cart to get around in. I bet he's around here somewhere."

She looked around again, more hopeful now.

"Hello? Dr. Fisher?"

A dark figure rose up from the grass about twenty feet ahead of them. There was enough moonlight for Niki to see it was a young man in his early twenties. He had a shotgun pointed at them.

"Are you Eddie or Jason?" Niki said.

The man lowered the muzzle of his shotgun just a tad. "I'm Eddie," he said. He nodded off to Niki's right. "That's Jason over there."

A man with a pump-action shotgun rose up from behind a tombstone.

Good tactics, Niki thought. The two men had them in a classic killing funnel, and she hadn't seen it coming. She must really be tired.

"You Niki Booth?" Eddie said.

"Yep, that's me."

"You're late."

"It's been a hell of a trip."

"What's wrong with your friend there?"

"He's sick," Niki said. "It's a long story."

"Wait a minute," Eddie said. "Hey Jason, that's the guy from the river, the one with the flu."

"No kidding?" The one named Jason squinted at him. "Wow, you're right. God, he looks even worse than the last time we saw him. What happened to him?"

"He got hurt," Niki said.

"You sure he's not infected? He looks like he got tore up."

"He's not infected," Niki said. "You mind if I see your dad now? I got a lot to talk to him about."

Eddie lowered his shotgun and motioned for Jason to do the same.

"Sure," he said. "You guys come on. It's this way."

Fisher was lying on the grass, his useless legs stretched out beside him. His children, the two little girls and the youngest boy, were farther off, with their mother. But when Niki and the others entered the circle of light from their campfire they all inched closer.

"Dr. Fisher?" Niki said.

He nodded. "Are you Niki?"

"In the flesh."

"Based on your reputation, I was expecting somebody taller."

Niki laughed, then winced at the pain in her ribs.

"You're hurt," Fisher said.

"Yeah, pretty bad, too. I think I broke my ribs."

"And your friend there, too, it looks like."

"Hey Dad," Eddie said from behind them, "that's the guy from the river. The one that had the flu."

"Really?" He studied Nate anew. "Well, I'll be. Here, Niki, set him down here. I'll look at you both."

Niki put Nate down and sat down next to him. All at once the exhaustion overwhelmed her. All she wanted to do was fall asleep.

Fisher crawled over to Nate and squinted at his injuries. Then his face hardened. "This man's been bitten," he said. "You brought an infected man into our camp."

Eddie and Jason moved in immediately, weapons up.

"No," Niki said.

Quickly she explained. She told them about Nate's immunity, and the flash drive, and about the Red Man's death. Eddie and Jason didn't look like they believed any of it. But Fisher was different. The suspicion was already leaving his expression.

"You say the Red Man's dead?"

"Nate here killed him."

"And you say he's immune to the necrosis filovirus?" His eyes flickered in the firelight. "Fully immune?"

Niki turned to Gabi. "Let him see it," she said.

Gabi took the iPad out of its plastic baggie. She handed it over to Fisher.

"What's this?" he said, taking it.

"That's the cure," Niki said.

Half-smiling, Fisher ran his finger along the edge until he found the device's on switch. "I used to have one of these," he said. "God, I loved mine. Used it all the time. Remember, honey?"

His wife was kneeling next to him. "I remember."

"This one's got a lot of videos on it," Fisher said. "Still works though. A little cracked, but— Hello! Here it is."

His face took on a milky hue in the glow of the iPad's screen. His eyes moved across the text, not blinking.

"Who authored this?"

Niki looked at Avery.

"Nate said the man's name was Dr. Kellogg," Avery answered. "I didn't catch his first name."

Fisher shook his head. "Never heard of him."

He studied the display again, dragging more of the text onto the screen.

"No," he said to himself. "This is . . . I wasn't going this way at all." He shook his head. "Not at all, but . . . this is a vaccine, not a cure. My God, this is brilliant."

Niki felt his pulse pounding. "You think it'll work? You can use that?"

Fisher took a deep breath. He was still smiling, still a little stunned.

"Yes," he said. "I mean, if we were able to produce this in quantity and vaccinate people . . ." His attention went elsewhere for a moment. Then a smile lit the corner of his mouth. "Yes," he said. "Yes—This'll work." He looked at her. "We can do this!"

CHAPTER 32

Hobbling along on crutches, bandages all over his body, Nate propped the iPad up on top of a tombstone and sat down on the marker opposite it. He scratched at a sticky spot on his neck where the bandage had separated, coughed, and cleared his throat. He drew in a ragged breath and started speaking:

"Hi, I'm Nate Royal. This isn't my computer. Or . . . well, I guess it is now. Before me it belonged to this guy named Ben Richardson, who was one of the two smartest men I've ever known.

"Ben used to be a reporter for a magazine. I don't remember which one and I guess at this point it doesn't really matter. Before everything pretty much went down the toilet Ben set out to write the whole history of the zombie outbreak. Things went south on him before he got a chance to finish, but he didn't give up. He went on collecting stories. For eight long years he wandered this used-up garbage dump of a world we live in, collecting stories from everyone he met."

"Nate?" It was Avery, calling to him from the clearing that Nate and the others had been sharing with Fisher and his family for the last week while everyone mended.

He waved to her.

"Over here, Avery."

He turned back to the iPad.

"Where was I? Oh yeah: stories. Ben believed that stories were the glue that held us together. He said they were as much a part of us as the blood in our veins, and that we needed them just as much. For him, getting somebody to tell their story was as natural as breathing. He had this crazy dream that one day, when the zombies were all gone, all the survivors would gather round and the stories they told would reshape the world into something better than it was. He thought humanity was something wonderful. He thought that we naturally went to the good, that we listened to the better angels of our nature. I . . . don't know about that. I haven't done a lot of listening to my better angels during my time on this globe of ours. But, like I said, Ben was a better man than me, and he said that stories were like a magic mirror that showed us what was best about ourselves. Maybe that's true. I don't know. But I do know that his eyes used to shine when he talked about it. He really believed it. It wasn't just words to him. Stories were his religion, and, for him, collecting them was the most holy thing a man could do. It makes me sick to my stomach to think that the world's got to count on me for that now."

He shook his head, coughed. Everything hurt.

Nate straightened and blinked away the pain.

This was for posterity. It had to be good.

He said, "I think about the two great men I've known in my life—Ben Richardson, who I just told you about; and Dr. Mark Kellogg, who used my blood to figure out a vaccine for the zombie virus—and I want to weep for all that we've lost.

So much goodness, so many great minds . . . just gone." He smiled bitterly, and shrugged. "The world is passing on to mediocre men who remember great men. We are only echoes of them, and not very good ones."

"Nate," Avery called to him. She was coming up behind him, breathing hard from the climb up the hill. "You almost ready? Dr. Fisher says we need to get going before the day gets too hot."

"Yep," he said. "Almost."

He focused on the iPad again.

"Time to wrap this up. This is Ben's book that I'm trying to finish here, so I might as well leave you with something Ben said to me a few days before he died. He said we all do the best we can, and that most of the time, that's good enough to get the job done. And if it doesn't do the trick, well, we still own it. We may have lost the old world, but that doesn't mean we can't find a new one. We just stagger on, zombie-like, one foot in front of the other, and trust we'll get there eventually. And you know what? I think we will."

He shrugged, then smiled.

"That's it. That's all the wisdom I got."

He leaned forward and tapped the screen to stop recording.

Avery, wearing a sundress borrowed from Dr. Fisher's wife, stopped a short way off and waited for him.

"What are you doing up here?" she asked.

He turned.

Richardson was standing on a small rise behind her, facing east, watching a golden haze looming in the trees down by the road.

"Ben . . ."

Avery followed his gaze, her brow wrinkled. "You okay?" she asked. "What are you doing up here?"

Nate stood, favoring his broken ankle as he slid the

crutches under his arms. "Can you help me with the iPad?" he asked.

"Sure." She tucked it under her arm and stood next to him. "Can I help you?"

"Yeah, that'd be nice. Thanks."

"You didn't tell me what you were doing up here."

He gestured at the iPad with his chin. "Just finishing up something for Ben. Something I promised I'd do."

She smiled uncertainly, as though she didn't quite know what to say. "Are you ready to go? Dr. Fisher wants to go."

He looked over at the next rise, but Ben was gone.

To Avery, he said, "Yeah, I'm all set." And together, the two of them walked down to the camp in the late morning sun.